Praise For Terry Bisson

"TERRY BISSON can charm your toes off."
  —*Washington Post Book World*

"HIS QUICK JABS to the funny bone and the intellect often are more powerful than many a lesser artist's attempt at a knockout punch."
  —*San Diego Union-Tribune*

"TERRY BISSON has always been unique—in the best sense of the word. He writes stories and novels which simply could not have come from anyone else."
  —Stephen R. Donaldson, author of *The Runes of the Earth* and the Chronicles of Thomas Covenant series

"EVERY WORD HE WRITES is worth reading, even though a lot of them are the same ones."
  —John Crowley, author of *Little, Big* and *Lord Byron's Novel*

"BISSON'S PROSE is a wonder of seemingly effortless control and precision; he is one of science fiction's most promising short story practitioners, proving that in the genre, the short story remains a powerful, viable and evocative form."
  —*Publishers Weekly*

"GENEROUSLY ENDOWED with sharp wit, dead-on dialogue and the storytelling gifts of a born raconteur."
  —*Science Fiction Weekly*

"SPECULATIVE FICTION that transcends its genre . . . one of SF's leading innovators."
  —*Booklist*

"THERE IS in the best of Terry's work a quiet and subtle restraint that nevertheless delivers a more vivid emotional clout than any amount of overheated prose ever could."
  —Michael Swanwick, author of *Bones of the Earth* and *Cigar-Box Faust and Other Miniatures*

GREETINGS

GREETINGS

TERRY BISSON

TACHYON PUBLICATIONS
SAN FRANCISCO, CALIFORNIA

GREETINGS

COVER ILLUSTRATION AND DESIGN © 2005 BY JOHN PICACIO
BOOK DESIGN BY ANN MONN

TACHYON PUBLICATIONS
1459 18th STREET #139
SAN FRANCISCO, CA 94107
(415) 285-5615
www.tachyonpublications.com

SERIES EDITOR: JACOB WEISMAN

ISBN: 1-892391-24-4

PRINTED IN THE UNITED STATES OF AMERICA
BY BANG PRINTING, INC.

FIRST EDITION: 2005

0   9   8   7   6   5   4   3   2   1

SELECTED BOOKS BY TERRY BISSON

FICTION

Wryldmaker (1981)
Talking Man (1986)
Fire on the Mountain (1988)
Voyage to the Red Planet (1993)
Bears Discover Fire and Other Stories (1996)
Pirates of the Universe (1996)
In the Upper Room and Other Likely Stories (2000)
The Pickup Artist (2001)
Greetings (Tachyon 2005)
Numbers Don't Lie (Tachyon 2005, forthcoming)

MEDIA TIE-INS

Johnny Mnemonic (1995)
The Fifth Element (1997)
Alien Resurrection (1997)
Galaxy Quest (1999)
The X Files: Miracle Man (2000)
Boba Fett: Crossfire (2003)

NONFICTION

Nat Turner: Slave Revolt Leader (1988)
On a Move: The Story of Mumia Abu Jamal (2001)
Tradin' Paint: Raceway Rookies and Royalty (2001)

COLLABORATIONS

Car Talk with Click and Clack, the Tappet Brothers
with Tom and Ray Magliozzi (1991)
Saint Leibowitz and the Wild Horse Woman
with Walter Miller, Jr. (1997)

Table of Contents

I Saw the Light

I saw the light. So did you. Everybody did.

Remember where you were the first time you saw it? Of course you do.

I was living in Arizona, Tucson, more or less retired. I was throwing sticks. They say you can't teach an old dog new tricks, but who would want to? There aren't any new tricks, just the old tried and true. "Good boy, Sam," I would say, and he would say "woof," and there we would go again. I used to amuse myself thinking it was Sam who was teaching me to throw, but I don't think that any more.

It was night, and desert nights are bright, even with a quarter moon. Sam stopped, halfway back to me, dropped his stick and began to howl. He was looking up, over my head. I turned and looked up toward the moon, and you know the rest.

There it was, blinking in threes: *dot dot dot*, twice a minute. On the Moon, where no one had been in thirty years. Twenty nine, eight months, and four days, exactly; I knew, because I had been the last to leave, the one who locked the door behind me.

Sam's a big yellow mutt; his first name is Play it Again, so I always call him by his last. He was a parting gift from my third ex, who was himself a parting gift from my second. Lunar subcrust engineers shouldn't marry: our peculiar talents take us to too many faraway places. Or to one, anyway.

"Come on boy," I said, and we headed back into the minimally furnished condo I call home, leaving the stick behind—even though sticks are not all that easy to find in Arizona, or for that matter on the Moon.

The light on the Moon was front page news the next morning—*dot dot dot*—and by the third day it was estimated that all but a tiny fraction of Earth's 6.4 billion had seen it. UNASA confirmed that the light was not from Marco Polo Station (I could have told them that) but from a spot almost a hundred kilometers away, on the broad, dark plain of the Sinus Medii: the exact center of the Moon as seen from Earth.

I figured there would have to be be an investigation, so I made a few calls. I was not really hopeful, but you never knew. I still had a few friends in the Agency. I was hoping that, if nothing else, this light would get us back to the Moon. It wasn't only or even primarily for myself that I was hoping; it was for humanity, all of us, past and future. It seemed a shame to learn to soar off the planet and then quit.

Okay, so it's not soaring: it's more like a push-up, grunting and heaving, but you know what I mean.

First Contact: strange lights on the Moon: may we have your attention, please. The tabs speculated, the pundits punded, and UNASA prepared the first international expedition since the abandonment of Marco Polo in 20—. I had made, as I mentioned, a few calls, but I hadn't really expected anything. A sixty-one-year-old woman does not exactly fit the profile for space flight and lunar exploration. So imagine, as they say, my surprise, when the phone rang. It was Berenson, my Russian-English boss from the old days. I knew him immediately by his accent even though it had been twenty-nine years eight months and seven days.

"Bee!?" (Which is what we called him.)

"I requested you as number two for the tech team. Logistically this is a cakewalk and age is not a problem, if you're still in shape. There will be five altogether, three SETI and two tech."

"How soon?" I asked, trying to hide my excitement.

"Start packing."

I hung up and screamed, or howled, or whatever. Sam came running. "I'm going back to the Moon!" I said.

"Woof!" he said, jowls flopping; as always, happier for me than for himself.

Our trip was put together with a minimum of publicity and fanfare. We were due at Novy Mir in less than a week. I wasn't to tell anyone where I was going. Of course, I had already told Sam.

"I'm leaving you here with Willoughby," I said. "I'll be back soon. Three, four weeks max. Meanwhile, you be good, hear?"

"Where are you going, exactly?" My next door neighbor, Willoughby, is a retired FBI agent, a type that both hates and loves secrets, depending on who is keeping them, and why.

"An old lover," I said, with a wink. It was one of my better moments.

———————

Zero G felt perfectly normal; you don't forget how to fly, just as you don't forget how to walk. I felt ten years younger immediately. It was great to be back in the Big Empty, even if it meant a night or two on Novy Mir, the sprawling, smelly space station in Clarke orbit.

Bee was the first one I saw when I entered the day room we had been assigned. He was with Yoshi, his old number two.

"I thought I was number two!" I complained.

"You are," Bee replied with a laugh. "Yoshi is number one." Turned out he was leading SETI. His partners were a scowling Chinese biologist named Chang, and a smiling Indian linguist named Erin Vishnu whose mother had gotten pregnant during Julia Roberts' Academy Awards acceptance speech. I didn't learn this until later, of course; at first the "sadies" (as Yoshi and I called them) were very reserved.

———————

It was a two-day trip from high Earth orbit to the Moon. Bee and I caught up on old times (he had saved my life twice, which cements a friendship) while Yoshi flew the ship and studied the manuals, which she already knew by heart. So did I. I had helped her and Bee run the pumps, extracting environmentals from buried comet ice, for almost six years at Polo.

The SETI team, the sadies, were the scientific payload. The heart of the matter, as it were. They had been established to deal directly, discreetly, and creatively, with any First Contact situation, answerable to no government—not even UNASA.

"No one really thought it would ever happen," Bee told me. "So we have complete autonomy; for two weeks anyway."

We were just preparing for lunar capture when I got the call from Willoughby—my next door neighbor, remember? It was Sam. He was desolate, disconsolate, wouldn't eat; he just howled—at the moon, of course, as if he knew where I was headed.

"How the hell did you get through to me here?" I asked. I needn't have. Those FBI guys never let go of their connections. I could hear Sam in the background, whining.

Willoughby held the phone, and I said, "Hang in there, boy, I'll be home soon."

"Woof," was his answer; he was nothing if not unconvinced.

The light source was about a hundred kliks from Marco Polo, and we crossed over the old station on our recon orbit. I got all teary-eyed, seeing our domes and tunnels, still intact here where the weather runs in billion year cycles; every scratch and scuff in the lunar dust just as we had left it, twenty-nine years eight months and eighteen days before.

Then we saw the light itself as we passed over Sinus Medii. It was coming from a perfect jet-black pyramid, ten meters on a side, too small to show up in amateur photos but plenty large enough to have been studied from Novy Mir.

"There haven't been any pictures of this!" I said. "Not even on the internet." Bee just smiled and I realized then that his SETI team had powers that belied their modest size and relative obscurity.

The pyramid was pure black, the only pure thing on the Moon, which is all shades of gray.

It was still throwing light, *dot dot dot*, a new sequence every twenty-seven seconds.

We set down next to the pyramid in a cloud of slow-settling dust. If we had hoped to be greeted by the aliens when the dust cleared (and we had; hopes are less restricted than expectations), we were duly disappointed.

The pyramid was silent and still, as black as a rip in the universe. It was still (we confirmed from Novy Mir) transmitting its *dot dot dot* twice a minute, but the light was, for some reason, invisible from our position beside it.

Still teary-eyed, I felt like a dancer; light on my feet, without the creaking that comes with age and miles. I realized that it was not the Moon I had missed all these years, but the one-sixth gravity, and of course my youth.

SETI had arranged for a two week stay, so I immediately sank a probe and hit pay dirt (or ice). The sadies went to work, photographing the pyramid from all sides, while Yoshi and I unfolded the dome and adjusted the environmentals to break down the oxygen and hydrogen (for fuel) extracted from the cometary trash embedded under the lunar crust.

By Day Two (sticklers for tradition, we ran on Houston time) we had the ship for a dorm, and the attached geodesic as a day room and observation dome, complete with fast-plants and a hot tub that also heated the dome and ship.

By Day Three I knew I should have been bored. Shouldn't something have happened by now?

"What would you have us do?" Bee asked, "knock?"

"Why not?" I said, returning his smile. I was in no hurry; I was just glad to have a reason to be here, back home, on the Moon. It felt—right. Even Yoshi, an olympic complainer, was not complaining, though her narrow face was not exactly wreathed in smiles. "What about ground control?" she asked. "Aren't they pushing you?"

"There isn't any ground control," Bee said. "Or haven't you noticed?" The SETI mandate was a blank slate, designed to remove First Contact, if it ever came to pass, from the constraints of diplomacy and politics. The pace of events was their call.

By Day Four Yoshi and I had nothing to do except watch the sadies in their clumsy white suits measure and photograph and analyze the pyramid. I kept my doubts to myself, reluctant to interfere, but Yoshi was never one to recognize such restraints. "Aren't you guys disappointed?" she asked at the end of the day.

"Not yet. It feels right to go slow," Bee replied. He was sitting with us in the hot tub, soaking off the chill that comes with EVAs, even in a suit. "Can't you feel it?"

Feel what? We both looked at him, puzzled.

"The familiarity. I feel it; we all feel it. A feeling that we are in the right place, doing the right thing."

"I thought it was just me," I said. "Being back here."

"We all feel it," said Chang, who was sitting on the floor in his long johns, tapping on a laptop. "We are here to record and evaluate everything. Feelings included. Right, Vish?"

"Right."

"You've got another week," said Yoshi.

"Knock and you shall enter," I said.

"Hmmmm," said Bee.

And knock he did. The next day, at the end of their routine explorations, he reached up with a heavy gloved mitt and rapped three times on the side of the pyramid.

Yoshi and I were watching from the dome.

"I knocked," Bee said to me, as he was unsuiting just inside the airlock (we entered and exited through the ship). Instead of answering, I pulled all three of the sadies into the dome, and pointed across the little plain of dust toward the pyramid.

"Damn," said Chang. He all but smiled. Vishnu looked amazed. Bee, delighted. There it was:

A handprint, in bright yellow, against the darker-than-midnight black, halfway up the pyramid.

The next "morning" the print was still there, and the sadies were suited up early. Yoshi and I watched them jumping clumsily around, stirring up the dust, fitting their stiff gloves against the handprint, waiting for something to happen. Hoping for something to happen.

Nothing did.

Later in the hot tub we were all silent. Outside the dome, we could see the print, bright yellow in the Moon's cruel gray. We felt gloomy and hopeful at the same time. Familiarity had been replaced by a kind of desperate eagerness.

"It wants something," said Bee.

"Maybe it wants a touch," I said.

"A touch?" Chang was scornful.

I ignored him and addressed myself to Bee. "You know, not a glove."

"It's high vac out there," Vishnu reminded me. "We can't exactly take off our gloves."

"But of course we can!" Bee said, slapping the water like a boy. I grinned and gave him five. There were the peels.

Peels are emergency spray-on suits to be used in case of sudden decompression. Coupled with a "paper" helmet, a peel will give you anywhere from two to twenty minutes to find an airlock or an emergency vehicle—or say your prayers.

I was in fact the only one present who had actually used a peel, after a sudden rockslide collapsed Polo's ag dome. Thanks to the peel I had survived the twelve minutes it took Bee to get to me with a Rover. I could still feel the cold of those long twelve minutes in my bones.

The next "day" (Six) they tried it. Yoshi and I watched from the dome as Bee in his peel and the sadies in their white suits approached the pyramid, Bee in the lead. He was hurrying, of course; there's no other way to moonwalk in a peel. I could feel how cold he was.

They all stopped and stood in a line, right in front of the print. With his left hand Bee grabbed Chang's mitt, and Chang grabbed Vishnu's. Then Bee placed his right hand high on the side of the pyramid, directly over the print.

And it happened.

Something—a lens, a door?—opened in the side of the pyramid, and they stepped through: one, two, three: Bee, Chang, Vishnu. It closed behind them and they were gone.

"Holy shit," said Yoshi.

"Knock and it shall be opened to you," I said. It was another of my better moments.

Yoshi and I watched the pyramid, wordlessly. Was there air in there? How could Bee survive? After twenty minutes Yoshi began to suit up for a rescue EVA. I was the only one watching two minutes later (21.4 minutes from entry, timed on the sadies' fixed video camera) when the lens opened and the three emerged, stumbling, Bee in the lead. Yoshi opened the airlock for them and they staggered in, Bee falling into my arms. While Yoshi helped the other sadies un-suit, I ripped off his paper helmet and pulled him into the hot tub, which would dissolve his peel. He was shivering and grinning.

Yoshi joined us, feet only. "Why's he grinning?"

"Ask him," I said. I was rubbing one of his feet while he rubbed the other.

Bee was opening his mouth and closing it without making a sound, like a fish.

"It was big in there," he said, finally; still with the goofy grin. "Bigger on the outside than on the inside."

"What happened?" I asked.

"We went in and the door closed behind us. It was dark but we could see, don't ask me why. We took our helmets off . . ."

"Took your helmets off!?" Yoshi was offended.

"Don't ask me why. We just did, all of us. Then we stepped forward, all together I think, and saw the light."

"Wait a minute," I said.

"It was like a glow."

"But bright," said Chang, who had joined us. "The brightest thing I have ever seen."

"The next thing I knew I was on my knees," said Bee. "I could feel this hand on the top of my head."

"A hand?" Yoshi was offended again.

"It felt like a yellow hand," Vishnu said, peeling off her long johns; it was the first time I had seen her undressed.

"It was definitely a hand," Bee said. "I could tell it was a hand though I couldn't see anything. I don't think I even looked."

"It was all light," said Chang. "And this feeling. It was a hand on the top of my head."

"It felt so good," said Vishnu, lowering herself into the water. She had the body of a girl.

"Sounds like an acid trip," I said. "Or a three-armed alien."

"What was the communication?" Yoshi asked. "What was said?"

"The feeling was the communication," Bee said. "That was all. Nothing was said. We were just there, all three of us, on our knees, looking into the light."

"With a feeling of . . . of . . ." Chang gave up.

"I don't like this," said Vishnu, looking down at herself, as if just realizing she was nude. "Shouldn't we be talking about this among ourselves first?"

"It's OK," said Bee. "We can proceed any way we decide is best, and this feels OK, doesn't it? These are our closest comrades here, after a million years of evolution."

Huh? He looked stoned to me.

"So whatever it is, it came all this way to pat you on the head?" Yoshi grumbled.

Bee and Chang just grinned. Vishnu looked troubled. I wondered if she were wishing she had kept her long johns on.

"Maybe it's God," I said.

"It's a they," Bee said, shaking his head.

"More than one," said Vishnu. "Many."

"And they know us," Chang said.

"Yes! That's the communication," Bee said. "They know us, and we know them. That was the feeling, more than a feeling, really. That's what they wanted to tell us."

"They?" Yoshi rolled her eyes. "They called you up here for a feeling? There's no communication?"

"Feelings are real," said Bee. "Maybe that's all it will be. Who knows. The idea behind SETI is that First Contact will probably be something unexpected."

"This is unexpected," said Vishnu. "But not unfamiliar. Very familiar. We have been here before."

"Here?" I asked.

"In their company," said Chang. "Being with them felt good. Better than good. Great."

"Great," said Yoshi, looking disgusted.

"And now?" I asked. "Next?"

"I don't know," said Bee, looking out toward the black pyramid, with its yellow print halfway up the side. "There's something, something else. I guess we go back."

And so they did. The next "morning" they all went out again, Chang and Vishnu suited and Bee leading, in his peel. They emerged after only twenty minutes this time, with the same lunatic grins.

"It's not like we aren't conscious in there," said Chang, as his helmet came off. "It's more like we're conscious for the first time."

"Right," said Vishnu.

I would have made another acid trip joke, but I didn't want to discourage them. This was, after all, I told myself, the long awaited First Contact, for which humanity had waited a million years or more.

Wasn't it?

"Who are they? What are they? What do they want from us?" asked Yoshi.

"They want to be with us," said Vishnu, dreamily peeling off her long johns. "Just like we want to be with them."

"It's all feelings," said Bee, slipping into the pool beside me. He looked like the Michelin tire man in his foam suit, before it started to dissolve into harmless polymer chains. "But the feelings contain information."

"They sort of precipitate into information," said Chang.

"The feelings *are* information," said Vishnu, nude again. "We are in contact with an entity that we have been in contact with before. And have always wanted to be in contact with again."

"That's the feeling!" said Chang eagerly. "Desire, and the fulfillment of desire."

"Sounds sort of sexy," I said.

"It's a wonderful feeling," said Bee, taking me more seriously than I took myself. "But it's changing, too. There's something else."

"Something dark," said Vishnu.

"Dark how? Dark what?" Yoshi was putting the helmets and suits away, looking annoyed.

"It's too soon to say," said Bee. "First we all need to get some sleep. That's an order."

———

"Wake up."

It was Yoshi.

"It's Berenson, he's gone. He's in there."

"What?" I sat up, almost spilling out of my hammock. I had been dreaming I was home on Earth with Sam, trying to explain something to him, about sticks.

"I thought I saw him, in a peel, going in, about five minutes ago."

"Are you sure?"

"I thought I might be dreaming, so I checked and the other sadies are in their hammocks. But Berenson is gone."

"What do you think we should do?"

Twenty minutes later I was in boots and long johns, spraying on a peel. I shook open a paper helmet, checking to make sure it had two full air cans (twenty minutes). I had thought I remembered the cold and was prepared for it, but I wasn't. It was insulting, crushing, humbling.

I hurried toward the pyramid. The dust cracked under my feet with that weird squeak of molecules that have never—not by wind, not by water, not by weather—been rubbed together. The *squeak* came up through my bones as sound. I had forgotten it.

I saw Yoshi and the sadies, awake now, watching from the dome. I waved as I ran. I could feel the vacuum slicing my fingertips, like steel knives.

I put my hand against the side of the pyramid, covering the print, and *something* happened. I wasn't sure what. It opened, I went in; it was dark, I was alone.

—————

I was inside. I didn't know, still don't know, how I got there. Before I knew what I was doing, I was taking off my helmet.

The air smelled like lemons. It was cold, but not Moon cold. The pyramid was larger inside, just as Bee had said, tapering up to a cone of darkness in the center.

And there was a light. Also in the center. It had a kind of substance that light doesn't always, doesn't often, doesn't ever, have. It was beckoning; I approached. It all seemed natural, as if everything I was doing was what I had always wanted to do. It felt good; very good. It felt great. The light grew brighter and I fell to my knees, but it was more like rising, really. I couldn't stand but I didn't want to stand. I felt a hand on my head: I knew it was a hand, and I knew what hand it was! I had a million questions, I knew, but I couldn't think, even when I tried. I was so very glad to be here, back here, where I belonged. Where I was glad to be.

I felt a hand in mine. Bee. He was pulling me backward, away from the light, into the cold and the darkness. We were putting on our helmets, Bee and I. We were stepping together across the squeaky surface of the moon, toward the lighted dome, which looked like a zoo, full of puzzled friendly faces, pressed against the glass.

"Are you OK?" Yoshi asked.

I saw my breasts floating in front of me and realized I was in the hot tub. I laughed. Bee laughed with me. I knew that the grin on his face was a reflection of my own. We were in the water and someone was handing me a cup of coffee.

Joe, they used to call it. A cup of joe. "I'm OK," I said. "I went in to get you, Bee."

"I know, but you shouldn't have. You should have awakened the others."

I understood. It was a break in the protocol. "We know them and they know us," I said. It was like remembering something; it was easy, and yet impossible if you couldn't do it. "They are glad to see us."

"Not exactly," said Bee. "There's a melancholy, too."

"Something very sad," said Vishnu. She was wearing her nightgown and her tiny feet were in the water next to my shoulder.

She was right. There had been a reproach, a disappointment. "I can feel it, too," said Chang.

"Feel what?" asked Yoshi, tapping me on the head with a long finger, like a teacher admonishing a bad student. "Tell me what happened. Now."

"There are just these feelings," I said. "Then afterward,

they sort of turn into, not ideas exactly, sort of like memories. Is that what you want to know?"

"I want to know what's fucking happening. And I want you to tell me."

"Don't be hard on her," said Bee. "We're all just figuring it out."

"Figuring what out?!"

"What they want," said Chang. "They love us, they wanted to find us. They found us."

"And we love them!" I said. "That's why we can't see them."

"That's right!" said Bee, looking at me as if I were a genius. "We love them so much that all we can see is the light of our love."

"I hope this is all going in your fucking report," said Yoshi, sounding disgusted.

"They found us again," said Chang. "That's why we are so happy."

"But something is wrong," said Bee. "We have to go back in. Once more."

"And do I get to go?" I could still feel the hand on my head. I wanted to feel it there again, more than anything.

"We'll all go this time," Bee said.

But we didn't all go. Yoshi had no desire to go; plus, she explained, she felt that somebody had to stay behind and stay on top of systems.

"Designated driver," said Bee, laughing as we sprayed each other. He and I were the only ones in peels. Chang and Vishnu wore suits. I felt I was one of the sadies now, and they treated me as such. Even Chang. We crossed the squeaky dust and held hands by the pyramid. Looking back I saw Yoshi watching from the dome, looking a little bit abandoned.

Bee hit the print and there we were, inside. I unstuck my helmet and looked for the light. I fell to my knees. "Oh boy," I said when I felt the hand on my head.

Something was wrong. Everything was OK but something was wrong. After a few moments of confusion, we were pushed out the door, holding hands, into the cold. I couldn't remember putting my helmet on, but I was breathing as we hurried toward the lights of the dome.

We were shaking. I was shaking all over. I sat in the hot tub and watched my suit dissolve, like dry ice, leaving no trace.

"Hey, don't cry," said Bee. "I know we're all upset."

"It's OK to cry," said Vishnu.

I was crying.

"What happened?" asked Yoshi. "Goddamn it, tell me."

"They're leaving," said Bee.

"They don't want us," I said. "They don't want us any more."

"What the fuck are you talking about?"

"We should all just be still for a while," said Bee. "Come and get in the water, Chang. Vishnu. Claire."

Claire. My parents gave me that name. I hadn't thought about them in a long time. I started to cry again, really hard this time.

By noon we were warmed and fed—and dejected. "It's over," Bee said finally.

"They're leaving," Chang said. I knew it too. We all knew the same things. The feelings turned into ideas, gradually, like the graphics in a slow Web connection. Sooner or later we all had the same pictures in our minds.

"They're disappointed in us," I said.

"I want them to stay," said Vishnu.

"Of course, we want to be with them," said Bee. "But we can't make them want to be with us."

"What in the hell are you all talking about?" asked Yoshi.

"They're leaving," I said. I pointed outside. The yellow print was gone, and the pyramid looked black and forbidding. Closed.

"Explain, damn it."

"The thing is, we knew them long ago," said Bee. As I listened, my emotions were spinning, like dust in sunlight, settling as he spoke onto the table of my mind, in which his voice, like a fingertip, traced his words: "This is not First Contact, it is Second Contact."

And what he was saying, we all knew.

"They were our gods," said Chang.

"Not exactly," said Vishnu. "We were their companion species, their helper. We lived only to please them. We looked up to them."

"Their favorite," I said. "Their pet."

"And they loved us," said Change. "And they love us still."

"But they wanted more," said Bee. "They set us free so we could develop without them. They put us down on Earth, where we could escape the worship of them that makes our knees go weak and our minds go blank. They wanted a true companion. They though if they left us alone we would develop into a sentient race on our own."

"And we did," I said, surprised at how much I knew; at the depth of the ideas and images that had been implanted in me. "The light was a test, to see if we had developed enough to leave the earth and come to them."

"They knew better than to appear among us," said Chang. "Can you imagine the chaos?"

"It might have been great," said Vishnu.

"It was a test," said Bee. "And we did it, we passed. They were so pleased."

"But then disappointed," I said. "Because nothing had really changed."

"It might have been great," said Vishnu, again.

"We still can't see them; our minds still go blank in their presence. We fall to our knees and worship them, and that's all we can do, even now."

"We can't love them less," said Chang bitterly. "How can they expect us to love them less?"

"There's a message for you," said Yoshi.

"For me?" My mind wrenched itself back to the real world. I stood up, dripping. Water drips in long sheets on the Moon. I looked outside and saw that the pyramid was gone.

———

"How did you find me here?"

"Haven't we been though that before?" It was Willoughby, my next door neighbor, the retired FBI agent. "The light's gone out, what did you guys do?"

"Put Sam on," I said.

"He won't eat. How long before you get back?"

"A week, probably," I said. "We will have to write a report." I heard a noise behind me; it was Chang in tears.

"Is something wrong?"

"No, we're fine," I said. It was over and I was glad. "Put Sam on."

"Hold on"

Yoshi had joined them in the pool, standing there in her orange coveralls, wet to the knees. They were hugging and crying. I heard a sort of gruff whine.

"Sam, is that you?"

"Woof!"

"Sam, listen carefully. Can you hear me?"

I could imagine Sam looking around, sniffing, trying to locate the face and hand and smell that went with the voice.

"I'll be back soon" I said. "Did you miss me?"

"Woof."

"I'm coming home, and I won't leave you alone again, I promise."

DEATH'S DOOR

Her back was broken. Henry knew it as soon as he saw her trying to crawl out of the street, her hind legs useless.

"Daddy daddy daddy!" screamed Carnelia, often called Carny, but not today; not on this awful day in every child's life when, Henry knew, Death is discovered.

"Come here, Carnelia, honey," he said, scooping his seven-year-old daughter into his arms. She was light, and seemed even lighter, as if Death's heavy presence had given wings to Life.

But Marge wasn't dead yet. She was still pulling herself toward the curb, her hind legs twisted in a strange shape that made her look less like a dog than a giant squid that was somehow no longer giant and no longer squid.

"Daddy, Daddy!"

"She's been hit by a car, honey," Henry said. As if Carnelia hadn't seen the whole thing.

"They were going too fast," said Carnelia, and for the first time Henry saw the ambulance, pulled up at the curb, the light still flashing; and the young black man in the long white EMS coat running across the street toward him.

Oddly, he ran right past the dog, Marge. I'm already thinking of her as the dog, thought Henry.

"The dog ran out in front of me," the young man said. "I couldn't stop. We are on our way to . . ."

"It's okay," said Henry. "Go. It wasn't your fault, I'm sure."

He set his daughter down and followed the EMS guy to the middle of the street. Marge was still trying to make her way toward the curb, as if hoping that once there she would be restored somehow.

"Go," Henry said again.

Her eyes were open and her tongue was hanging out. Bubbles of blood appeared on her black lips and nose. One was big and it lasted a long time. Henry kept hoping it would disappear before Carnelia got there, but it didn't.

"She's going to die! She's going to die!"

Henry stood up and put his arms around his daughter's shoulders; she felt enormously, alarmingly frail. "Yes, honey," he said, gathering her to him. "Now do this for me, and for her: run into the house and get that big box out of the garage, the one the lawn thing came in."

"What for?"

"She needs a place. Just do it, okay?"

Carnelia ran off. Marge was lying on the strip of grass between the curb and the sidewalk, eyes closed, waiting for the transformation that was about to come over her: Death, the Redeemer. It would make her whole again.

"Is she going to be all right?" Carnelia asked breathlessly. She was towing the box behind her, and had picked up two more of the neighborhood kids.

"No, honey," Henry said, kneeling down. "She is going to die. Marge was hit by the ambulance and it's all over for her. Help me now."

The ambulance was driving off, light spinning. Henry eased the dog into the box. He carried the box into the garage, and placed it on the floor under his tool bench.

"Now get her some water," he said. "Bring her a blanket, from that box by the door. Not that one.

She's going to die. It's okay; all things die."

Carnelia began to cry again. "This is the blanket she likes."

"OK, then. Now let's leave her alone. Dogs like to die in private."

"How do you know?"

"I just know." Henry knew because he had done the same thing with his dog, Dallie, thirty-one years before.

"If I leave her she'll die."

"She's going to die, honey. All things die, It's the way things are."

"I don't like things then!"

"All things have to die, honey. Even things we love."

Not exactly true, as it turned out. Not that day. For that was the day that Death's Door closed.

"Damn," said Shaheem, as he drove off. One dog down, but hopefully a human saved.

Then when he saw her on her apartment floor he wondered if it was in fact an even trade. The woman was at least ninety-years-old. About the size and weight of a wet raincoat.

He and his partner loaded her onto the gurney and were easing her down the stairs, when a familiar face appeared in the door below.

Is this a big story? Shaheem wondered. He recognized the face from TV. But there was no TV crew following. Ted Graeme was here to see about his mother.

"Mother?" Graeme said. He kissed her finely wrinkled face, aware that he was being watched. He was used to being watched. He was, after all, the anchor on the Nightly News.

"Mother?"

No answer. Not a flicker of interest or recognition.

Maybe this will be it, Graeme thought. It would be a blessing. She was his mother but everyone had their time, and she had been miserable since his father had died twelve—was it really twelve?—years before.

Tiny strokes had been chipping away at her, piece by piece. It was cruel way to go.

"Mother?"

Still no answer.

"You want to ride with her?" asked the EMS guy.

"It's okay," said Graeme. "I'll follow. You're taking her to Midcity, right?"

"Whatever you say, Mr. Graeme."

"We're running late, sir," said Hippolyte. He was the new producer of the *Nightly News*. Secretly, Graeme called him Still-Polite.

"I'm having a family crisis," Graeme said. "Did the warden call?"

"It's all set up," said Hipp. That was what his friends called him. He was a white man with dreadlocks, and Graeme had to remember not to smile whenever he looked at him. Times were changing. Times were always changing.

"I need to stay in the city," said Graeme. "I think Karin should go in my place."

Hipp looked surprised. "For real?"

"Definitely for real" said Graeme, picking up the phone. The most controversial execution in years, and he would have to miss it. "I'm calling her now."

"I'll prep her," said Hipp. "Meanwhile we have a big story. A plane went down outside Paris, at Charles de Gaulle."

"God. Not another Concorde?"

"Worse. A 777."

It was the one thing they weren't prepared for. Survival. As Jean-Claude poked through the wreckage he found bodies and part of bodies. The ones that were whole, or even partly whole, were still alive.

"My wife, my wife!" One man was cut almost in half; his entrails were falling out, all over his cheap suit, but he was still alive, asking about his wife in bad African French.

"We're looking for her," Jean-Claude said, even though it wasn't true. They were looking for parts of her; for parts of all of them.

"Bring her to me, *s'il vous plait.* Let me see her before I die."

"*Oui.*"

Jean-Claude waited for the man to close his eyes but he didn't. Jean-Claude resisted the impulse to reach out and close them for him. People were screaming all around him.

"They're all burned," said Bruno, his second in command. "They come to pieces when we pull them out, but they won't stop screaming."

"I'll help load them up," said Jean-Claude.

When he got back to the African, he was still alive, still clutching his entrails.

"Load him up," said Jean-Claude. "*Mon Dieu,*" he said to Bruno. "This is the worst yet. An air disaster with hundreds of survivors."

25

Karin had managed to sound concerned on the phone but Graeme knew she was pleased. Covering this execution was her big chance. He didn't mind. He would have felt the same. He had once been young and on the make.

He found his mother in the ICU.

"She's still breathing," the doctor said.

"She has a DNR," said Graeme, squeezing his mother's tiny, fluttering, birdlike hand. "It's on her chart."

"I know," said the doctor. "We haven't got her on life support. We couldn't anyway."

"What do you mean?"

"We have an overload today. Lots of serious injuries."

"A bad day?"

"No more than usual, it's just that everyone is surviving." He hurried off.

"I'll be back," Graeme said, kissing his mother's parchment cheek. He hurried out to the lot, beeping his car on the run. With Karin gone he would have to put together the six o'clock broadcast all by himself.

"She's suffering," Emily said to Henry when they were alone in the kitchen.

"Carnelia or Marge?"

"Both, damn it! Carny can learn about death without watching her dog die."

"Marge has a right to die at home, with dignity, and not in some vet's office," said Henry. "And as far as Carnelia's concerned, it's not just about learning. It's about going through the changes. She was terribly upset this afternoon. She'll grieve tomorrow. Right now she's fascinated. Death is fascinating as well as terrifying." "I work with death every day, remember?" Emily said. But she was coming around. She told him about her day while he cut up the salad, being careful to avoid his fingertips. Emily worked as a pediatric nurse in a preemie ward. "Today I thought death was on a holiday," she said. "Today not a single baby died."

"Not a one?"

"You get a day like that every once in a while," Emily said. "I suppose it's a reward for the others."

It was dark. She had expected the darkness, but not the light. The light was for the gullible, the light toward which you floated when you were dead. But here she was, floating toward it.

There were others, like herself. They were specks, sparks. So many. *I had not thought that death had undone so many.* Floating toward the light. They were rising together.

Then they were slowing. *So this is what it's like*, she thought. She was surprised. She hadn't thought it would be like anything.

Karin found herself eating too many doughnuts, provided by Krispy Kreme. Tasteless but tasty, she thought. Too tasty. You have to watch your weight when you're on TV. It shows up first in the face.

She put the doughnut away and followed the victim's family into the viewing room. Under the new protocol, the execution was set for sundown. It gave it the appearance of inevitability, almost of a natural death. She wondered if it made it any easier for the condemned.

The guards were already strapping Berry to the gurney. Karin wondered if he would get a cigarette.

Apparently not.

"Do you have any last words," asked the warden.

"You know I do," said Berry. He turned toward the window, which Karin had been assured was one-way. Still, she wanted to hide her face.

"You are murdering an innocent man," he said.

"Can you go on?"

The producer had heard about Graeme's mother.

"Sure," Graeme said, "but thanks for asking." As he sat down at his desk, an intern handed him the stories. Hipp had sorted them well. Start with the light, ease into the dark.

"Good news on the home front," Graeme began. "Billy Crystal came home from the hospital in Palm Springs, apparently recovered from the stroke that many thought spelled the end of the aging comedian's spectacular sixty-year career. Doctors are cautiously optimistic."

He turned the page.

"Rescue attempts are continuing in the Paris air crash. There are 255 casualties, passengers and crew, most with serious injuries but as yet, miraculously, no deaths. In India, UN authorities are investigating what appears to be the worst massacre in recent history . . ."

"You have prepare yourself for this," Krishna said.

"I have seen it before," said Paolo.

"No, you haven't," Krishna said.

He led the stocky UN rep through the gate into the

temple yard where the worshippers had been surprised. The massacre had been done the old way, with swords. People had been hacked to pieces. Arms and legs were lying on the ground, like spare parts. Bodies lay in heaps, their faces slashed into grim simulacrums of red mouths. But that wasn't the horror.

"Jesu!" said Paolo.

The horror was that they were all alive.

The warden himself pulled the switch. There was no sudden killer voltage, no sprung trap, just a slow IV drip—and a peaceful surrender.

The condemned man closed his eyes, and the small crowd sighed with pleasure. Relatives and colleagues of the man he said he hadn't killed. *Of course they all say that,* Karin thought; and as she did, she realized she had been holding her breath.

Berry kicked: one, twice; then lay still.

There was a long moment of silence, and then they all stood, reaching for their bags and the ID cards that would let them out of the prison.

Then, as one, they all stopped at the doorway and looked behind them.

The dead man had just opened his eyes.

The next morning Marge was still alive. Henry put his hand on her side, expecting cold, and felt her breathing. He considered for a moment telling Carnelia that the dog had died anyway, but she would insist on seeing the body before going off to school.

And there she was in the garage door. "Maybe she's going to be all right," she said, kneeling to pet the dog. "Don't die."

"She needs to die," said Henry. "She has massive internal injuries, her back is broken. She wants to be alone and die in peace."

"And you have to go to school," said Emily, gently pulling her daughter to her feet and leading her out of the garage.

"It was horrible," said Karin on her cell phone. "They had to administer the stuff twice, and he still wouldn't die. They made us leave. We're outside in the parking lot."

"That means there's no story," said Graeme. "Maybe you should head back."

"Not yet, please," said Karin. "They have to finish it somehow. That's our story. How's your mother?"

"Hanging in there," said Graeme. She had been moved into the ward with twenty others, all terminal; six of them with gunshot wounds.

"Did I tell you that I knew your mother? She was my English prof at Northwestern. She was a wonderful teacher."

"I know; you told me."

"She wouldn't let us call her Dr. Graeme. It had to be just Ruth. She made Milton come alive."

Coming alive is no longer the problem, thought Graeme.

"You may have to start with a hard story," said Hipp. "We have an earthquake in Lima, just coming off the wire. 7.6 on the Richter scale."

"Jesus," said Graeme, already reshuffling his papers.

So many lights. Sparks. They were still rising, but they had stopped up "above."

Above?

She floated into the cloud, a cloud of sparks. What had seemed like light now seemed like darkness.

Now she could see the light. It was a thin line, like a horizon. She had been watching it for what seemed hours, days? Years? If only she could remember her name.

The sparks were clustered around the bright line, like bugs around a light. She was one of them.

"I got this thing from the military," said Carlos in breathless Spanish. "It's like sonar. You can pick up sounds. In case anyone buried under the ruins is still alive."

"Not likely," said Eduardo. All around there was nothing but rubble, and the screaming of sirens. The business district had been leveled. *God knows what it's like in the* favelas. "What about the injured?"

"They're flooding the hospital," said Carlos. "More than we're prepared for. Central sent me to look for those who are buried alive, now that we have a way to locate them."

"Let's go, then," said Eduardo. "I've got two crews, and two backhoes. Just point us to the most likely."

"That's the problem," said Carlos, taking off the earphones.

"What do you mean?"

Instead of answering, Carlos handed Eduardo the earphones and scanned the pickup wand in a circle, around the ruined horizon.

Eduardo didn't even have to put them on. The noise was deafening. Knocks, screams, cries for help or at least mercy. It was as if an entire city had been buried—alive.

"A scooper," muttered Shaheem. He hated scoopers, and what was the rush?

But he was a pro; he turned on the light.

The police were gathered around the bottom of 122 Broadway.

The crowd was still there, held back by yellow tape. He had to push his way through.

"She stood on the ledge and took off her clothes," one of the cops told him. "A sure way to gather a crowd. The guys were trying to talk her down when she just stepped off backward, like this." He stepped back off the curb to illustrate.

Shaheem looked up at the ledge, twenty-two stories up. Two cops were still there: one taking photos, one just looking down.

The scooper had hit head first on the concrete, and blood was spattered around for twenty feet, some of it high on the plate glass of "Broadway Jewelry." Her head was flat on one side, as big as a watermelon, and when Shaheem knelt down beside her to unroll the body bag she whispered, "I'm sorry."

Carnelia had sat up with Marge until nine before going to bed. Henry was sure the dog would be dead by morning, but she was still breathing.

The blanket was stiff with blood that had leaked out of her mouth and nose and anus. Henry stuffed it into the trash, then went back into the house. He was surprised to find Emily dressed for work.

"I thought you had the day off. I thought you said . . ."

"None of the preemies are dying, but we have another problem," she said. "ER is overflowing."

"Overflowing?"

"Everyone they bring in is hanging on," she said. "The halls are filled with stretchers. Midcity has placed us all on call. It's worse than the stadium collapse."

After she left, Henry took a plastic bag out to the garage. Carnelia would be home from school in a few hours. He pulled the bag over Marge's head and sealed it around her neck with with duct tape. It moved in and out, slowly at first; then more and more slowly.

He didn't want to watch so he went back inside and turned on the TV.

The news was disturbing.

". . . unprecedented meeting of the Security Council with the International Red Cross," read Graeme, editing Hipp's clumsy copy on the fly. He had rushed in from the hospital where his mother was in a dim hallway with 126 other people, some of them screaming, others as quiet as herself.

". . . confirms that no one has died, anywhere in the world, for the past thirty-six hours."

He cut to the tape. "It's statistically improbable and medically impossible," said a talking head in a white coat. "People are surviving unsurvivable accidents."

Hipp nodded. Graeme came back on the air.

"And now we take you to Cold Spring State Prison, where our own Karin Glass is waiting for . . ."

Won Lee was taking a picture of Hong Kong harbor with his new digital camera when he felt the deck tip under his feet. Irrationally, it was his camera that he reached for as he began to skid across the deck. He almost caught a stanchion but the crush of falling, flailing bodies pushed him into the water.

It was cold and the camera was gone. It was dark and he held his breath for as long as he could, then gave up and felt the cold water filling his lungs, almost as satisfying as air. Then it wasn't so cold anymore. Drifting down was like flying. He spread his arms, or felt them spread. He felt himself slip into the soft muck at the bottom of the harbor.

He waited to die. He could see sparks, all around. Had the ferry caught fire? The mud was cold, then not so cold. It all seemed to be taking a long time.

Someone settled beside him. Was it his wife? There was no light but he could make out a face, the eyes wide open like his own. Was it a man or a woman?

It didn't seem to matter. Something was picking at his hand, uncovering little white bones. He watched and waited. It all seemed to be taking a long time.

". . . governor promises an investigation," said Karin. Her hands were shaking; she tried to hide it.

She had been allowed to see Berry, but not to speak with him. He was still in critical condition, not breathing.

". . . after the last minute arrival of the DNA test establishing his innocence," she said. She held up the microphone to pick up the chants from the demonstrators. "Meanwhile, the demonstrators outside the prison are calling for the DA's blood, in a dramatic and ironic role-reversal."

My best line, she thought. I'll bet that fucking Graeme cuts it.

There were so many sparks. The thin line of light was almost invisible. It was like Milton's blindness, she thought; there was plenty to see in the darkness. More than she had ever dreamed possible.

It had been a surprise, then a disappointment. Now she wanted to see what was on the other side. But there was no other side.

Only a thin line of light.

The sparks formed a cloud around it, like smoke. So many: *I had not thought that death had undone so many.* They were swarming and she was swarming with them, forward and back, filling the darkness so that the darkness was lighter than the thin line of light.

She wished she could remember her name.

"I'll be late," said Emily on the phone. "They're putting us on extra shifts."

"I know. It's on TV."

"Something very very weird is going on. The hospital is filled with people who shouldn't be alive. One man who took a shotgun blast in the mouth."

"It's a big story," said Henry. "It's on the news."

"Hey, I even saw what's-his-name, from the Nightly News. His mother is here. There's a whole hall filled with old people who have been taken off life support, waiting to die. Is Carny home?"

"Soon."

"Is Marge—over?"

"Yes. I'm sure." He told her about the plastic bag.

After he hung up, he went to the garage. He didn't want Carnelia to see the plastic bag.

The bag was no longer going in and out. It had been almost two hours.

He unpeeled the tape and pulled off the bag. He hid it under the blanket in the trash. Marge's eyes were closed. She wasn't stiff yet. He curled her as neatly as possible in the blood-stained box, and changed the blanket.

He was tucking it around her when she licked his hand.

"Berry's just one person," said Graeme. "We need you here."

"Please," said Karin. "This is the biggest story of the year. An innocent man almost executed."

"He's still alive?"

"He's on life support," said Karin, "Unlike all the others, who don't need it. Maybe he doesn't either. But I need to stay here for when he wakes up."

"Well OK, but stay by the phone."

She laughed. "The phone stays by me. How's your mother? Ruth?"

"I haven't heard from the hospital. They said they would call. Meanwhile we just got word from the pound that dogs aren't dying either. Cats, yes."

"Figures," said Karin, who had a dog. "Graeme, what in the world do you think is going on?

The Cedars was almost empty. The sound on the TV was off but the text scrolling across gave the story:

NO DEATHS, WORLDWIDE. NO REPORTED DEATHS IN . . .

"Weird, huh?" said the bartender, setting down a cold Heineken. "Where you been?"

"I've worked three shifts straight,' said Shaheem. "Who do you think is hauling all those people into the hospital? They used to wait for the guys from the funeral home."

"My girlfriend's into astrology," said the bartender. "She says it's a collusion or something of the planets, never happened before. Unpresidential."

"Unprecedented," said Shaheem.

"But that's fantasy," said the bartender. "Me, I'm a believer in science."

"Whatever that means."

"Science is numbers." The bartender pulled a magazine up from behind the bar. "Ever read *Discover*? This month is about the population explosion."

"Implosion, you mean," said Shaheem. "Guess I could do another."

The bartender set another Heineken on the bar. "More people means more deaths," he said. "It says here that more people die now every day than during World War II. Just of natural causes, plus all the little wars and disasters and shit."

"Not any more," said Shaheem. He told him about the scooper.

"Maybe death is getting behind," said the bartender. "Temporary overload. No way to process them all. Nowhere to put them."

"Does *Discover* tell you what to do?" asked Shaheem. He was not expecting an answer.

"Just wait," said the bartender. "It'll sort itself out. Things always do."

"You wish," said Shaheem. *I wish, we wish, we all wish.* "Ever thought you'd see the living waiting for death?"

The line of light was getting thicker. It was now a band of light. The sparks were flying through, extinguished by the light. She watched, breathless, bodiless, and saw that she was getting closer.

Or was the band getting wider? It was the same thing. So many sparks, all rising. She wished she could remember her name.

"It's for you," said Hipp. He handed the phone to Graeme as he picked up another.

The phones were all ringing at once.

"When is Karin coming back?" Hipp asked, over his shoulder. "We have to start putting the news together."

"I'll call her," said Graeme. "That was the hospital."

"Oh." Then Hipp saw that he was smiling.

"My mother just died."

Henry had quit smoking six months ago but he knew where half a pack was hidden, in his old coat. He smoked two waiting for Carnelia to get home.

There was something on TV but he kept the sound off. It was too weird. It was a worldwide crisis. But the most important thing was the crisis here at home.

Then he heard wailing and he realized that Carnelia had gone straight to the garage.

He found her wrapping Marge in the blanket. She dried her eyes with a corner. "Marge died, daddy. Can we bury her in the yard?"

Henry unwrapped the dog. Her eyes were open. There was no mistaking that peaceful look.

"Of course I will, honey."

"Will you dig a nice hole? Why are you smiling, daddy?"

"Because, Carny. I'm not."

So much light. There it was, all of a sudden, lots of it. Extinguishing the sparks, one by one, like rain drops in the sea.

Ruth, that was it!

Then it wasn't.

"Thanks for hurrying back," said Graeme, "I'm going to pick up my mother. I want to do it myself."

"I understand," said Karin.

"Lead with your big story," said Graeme. "The man they almost executed."

Karin was taking off her coat and combing her hair at the same time. "It's a bigger story now," she said. She held up her cell phone. "Berry died twelve minutes ago."

"Oh shit."

"I'll try and get a statement from the governor."

"And last words."

"He was in a coma," Karin said. "I'll go with the last words we had from the beginning: 'You are murdering an innocent man.'"

OPENCLOSE

Open.
Open.
Open, dammit.
Open, godammit.
O-pen!
O-pen, godammit!
Damn.

*

Call Beth.
Beth, are you there?
Beth, pick up if you are there.
Beth, call me as soon as you get this message. I'm at the airport and I'm locked out of the car.

O-pen.
O-pen you son of a bitch.
O-pen you god damned son of a bitch.
O-pen dammit if—
RIIING

✻

Finally! Beth, thank God.

Yes, he got on his flight. I guess—I saw him going through the security line. Now I'm double-parked by the curbside check-in and I can't get back into the car.

I don't know, it doesn't recognize my voice. Maybe the voice ID is busted, or maybe it's this cold. I just got out to help Dad with his bags. I'm lucky I didn't leave my phone in the car.

Of course I asked it nicely. Are you being serious? This is no joke, Beth. This is a security zone or whatever they call it and they are already starting to look at me funny.

I know you have to be in court, but I have an idea. You are on the voice ID too, so I will just hold the phone up to the lock.

Cool. Okay.

✻

---.

Try it again.

---.

More forcefully.

---.

That's better, No, it didn't open. I mean it sounded better. Try it again.

--- --- ---.

I'm not sure repetition is the thing.

_===!_

Shouting is not going to help.

No, I'm _not_ telling you what to do, I'm just making suggestions.

No, I can't leave it here, this is the airport for Christ's fucking sake.

I'm sorry, it's just that it's starting to rain and I don't have an umbrella.

All right, I _have_ an umbrella, but it's in my briefcase and my briefcase is locked in the fucking car and, look, Beth, please just try it one more time.

Good idea. I'll try the passenger side.

✳

Here we are. Slow and steady.

---.

Maybe if I hold it back a few inches.

---. ---.

STEP BACK. UNAUTHORIZED ENTRY ATTEMPT. STEP BACK FROM THE CAR.

Oh, shit.

OO WEE OO. STEP BACK.

That's the car, the alarm system. It thinks we are trying to break in.

OO WEE OO. OO WEE OO.

It gives you three or four tries, then it assumes you are a car thief doing voice impersonations, or something, I guess. Alarm, shut up! Alarm, it's me!

STEP BACK FROM THE CAR! UNAUTHORIZED USER.

There probably is a password but I don't know it. I never use it.

I _know_ I should have it, Beth. I'm sure I do have it. I'm

sure it's in my PalmPC which is in my briefcase which is in the fucking car.

OO WEE OO. STEP BACK.

I'm not freaking out, I'm just upset. I think that's understandable.

UNAUTHORIZED ENTRY ATTEMPT.

Now it's really starting to rain.

STEP BACK. OO WEE OO.

Damn. Maybe you should come out here, Beth. I know you're due in court at 2:00 but . . .

THANK YOU. CHIRP CHIRP.

✳

Hey, the alarm just stopped. And here comes the police. They must have a skeleton frequency or something. Maybe they will be able to open the car doors. They will probably give me a ticket but that's better than being towed.

Uh oh. It's one of those ashcroft vans.

STEP BACK FROM THE CAR, SIR.

Officer, it's my car, it's locked.

STEP BACK FROM THE CAR. KEEP YOUR HANDS IN PLAIN SIGHT.

Uh oh. It's not the police, Beth. It's Homeland Security. I just saw the twin towers logo.

PUT THE DEVICE DOWN, SIR.

They're not getting out of the van. I think there are two of them. I can hardly see through the glass.

PLACE THE DEVICE ON THE PAVEMENT, SIR.

It's not a device, officer, it's a phone.

Beth, you'd better talk to these guys. I have no fucking idea what . . .

SIR! PLACE THE DEVICE ON THE PAVEMENT AND STEP AWAY.

Officer, will you speak with my wife? She's a lawyer.

RIGHT NOW! PLACE THE DEVICE ON THE PAVEMENT.

I don't think they can even hear me, Beth. They won't get out of the van.

RIGHT NOW, SIR!

Okay, okay.

Beth, I have to go. I'll call you back. Don't go anywhere.

NOW STEP AWAY, SIR. RIGHT NOW!

Officer, that's my car. That's my phone. I'm a citizen. Here's my Homeland card.

HANDS AWAY FROM POCKETS, SIR! RIGHT NOW!

If you would just let me show you my card it would . . .

HANDS IN FULL VIEW, SIR! STEP TO THE REAR OF THE SECURITY VAN.

Officer, it's raining for Christ's sake!

SIR! RIGHT NOW!

I have to get my phone. I can't just leave it on the street in the rain.

YOU ARE IN A SECURITY ZONE. ALL UNATTENDED DEVICES ARE SUBJECT TO PREEMPTIVE DISASSEMBLY.

What!? You're going to crunch my fucking Nokia? What kind of shit is this?

PLEASE MODIFY YOUR LANGUAGE, SIR. APPROACH THE VAN SLOWLY.

So they *can* hear me. Motherfuckers.

PLACE BOTH HANDS IN THE EXTENDED SECURITY LOOP.

What for?

BOTH HANDS, SIR!

Hey! You can't handcuff me. I'm a citizen . . . Ow!

NOW STEP BACK FROM THE VAN DOOR, SIR. ONE STEP ONLY.

I need my phone. I have a right to call my wife.

YOU ARE IN A SECURITY ZONE. YOU WILL BE ALLOWED A PHONE CALL WITHIN 96 HOURS.

She's my lawyer. What about my car? It's her car too.

YOU ARE IN A SECURITY ZONE. ALL UNATTENDED DEVICES ARE SUBJECT TO PREEMPTIVE DISASSEMBLY.

It's not a device, it's a fucking car. It's *my* car!

WATCH YOUR LANGUAGE, SIR. STEP BACK FROM THE DOOR ONE STEP.

I have a right to call my wife. She's my lawyer.

OPEN.

What is this? Some kind of paddy wagon? No way!

STEP INSIDE THE VAN, SIR.

Ow! That hurts! Why are you shocking me? I'm a citizen.

SIT ON THE BENCH, SIR. KNEES TOGETHER.

I can show you my Homeland card.

SIR! WATCH THE CLOSING DOOR.

Dammit, you can't do this. I didn't do anything. I—

CLOSE.

SCOUT'S HONOR

On the morning of July 12, 20–, I got the following message on my lab computer, the only one I have:

MONDAY

Made it. Just as planned. It's real. Here I am in the south of France, or what people think of now (now?) as the south of France. It seems to the north of everywhere. If the cleft is at 4200 feet it means the ice is low. I can see the tongue of a glacier only about 500 feet above me. No bones here, yet, of course. It's a clear shot down a narrow valley to the NT site, about 1/2 mile away. I can see smoke; I didn't expect that. Wouldn't they be more cautious? Maybe they aren't threatened by HS yet and I'm too early. Hope not. Even though it's not part of the protocol I would love to learn more about our first encounter (and last?) with another human (hominid?) species. I do like to see the smoke, though. I never thought I would feel loneliness but here I do. Time is space and space is distance (Einstein). Heading down for the NT site. More later.

The subject line was all noise and so was the header. I was still puzzling what it was all about, for excepting the Foundation's newsgroup, I get no messages at all, when another came through the very next morning. The dates are mine.

TUESDAY

It's them all right. I am watching about 20 NTs, gathered in the site around a big smoky fire. Even through binoculars, from 50 yards away, they look like big moving shadows. It's hard to count them. They cluster together then break apart in groups of 2 or 3, but never alone. I can't tell the males from the females, but there are 4 or 5 children, who also stay together in a clump. Wish I could see faces but it's dim here. Perpetual overcast. I have been watching almost four hours by the clock on my com, and none have left the site. Separating one out may prove a problem. But I have almost 5 days (-122) to worry about that. Tomorrow I'll observe from a different position where I can get a little closer and the light may be better; above, not closer. I know the protocols. I helped write them. But somehow I want to get closer.

I began to suspect a prank, to which I enjoy a certain deliberate and long-standing immunity. But I do have a friend—Ron—and naturally I suspected him (who else) after the next and longer text came through, on the very day we were to meet.

WEDNESDAY

Totally unexpected change in plans. I am sitting here in the cleft with "my own" NT. He's the perfect candidate for the snatch, if I can keep him here for 4 days (-98). They are nothing like we thought. The reconstructions are far too anthropomorphic. This is NOT a human, though certainly a hominid. What we thought was a broad nose is more of a snout. He's white as a ghost, which I guess is appropriate. Or am I the ghost? He is sitting across the fire staring at me, or through me. He seems oddly unconscious much of the time, thoughtless, like a cat. What happened was this: I was heading down to observe the site this morning when I dislodged a boulder that fell on my left leg. I thought for sure it was broken (it isn't), but I was trapped. The rock had my leg wedged from the knee downward, out of sight in a narrow crevice. I couldn't help thinking of that turn-of-the-century Utah dude who sawed off his own arm with a Swiss army knife. I was wondering when I would be ready to do that, for I was in a worse spot than him: unless I made it back to the cleft in less than 100 hours, I was trapped here, and by more than a stone. By Time itself. The numbness scared me worse than pain. It was starting to snow and I was worried about freezing. I must have fallen asleep, for the next thing I remember "my" NT was squatting there looking at me—or through me. Quiet as a cat. Oddly, I was as little surprised as he was. It was like a dream. I pointed at my leg, and he rolled the stone away. It was as simple as that. Either he was immensely strong or had a better angle, or both. I was free, and my leg was now throbbing painfully and bleeding but not broken. I could even stand on it. I hobbl

Ron is a sci-fi writer who teaches a course at the New School. We meet every Wednesday and Friday, right before his class at 6. This is not by his plan or mine. It's a promise he made to my mother, I happen to know, right before she died, but that's OK with me. No friends at all would be too few, and more than one, too many.

"What is this?" he asked, when he finished reading the printout.

You oughta know, I said, raising my eyebrows in what I hoped was a suggestive manner. In accord with my own promise to my mother, I practice these displays in front of the mirror, and for once it seems to have paid off.

"You think I wrote this?"

I nodded, knowingly I hoped, and listed my reasons: who else knew that I was studying Neanderthal bones? Who but he and I had savored the story of the Utah dude so long ago? Who else wrote sci-fi?

"Science fiction," he said grumpily (having made that correction before). While we waited for his burger and my buttered roll, he listed his objections.

"Maybe it's a mistake, not intended for you. Lots of people knew about the Utah dude, it was a national story. And I am a little insulted that you think that I wrote this."

Huh?

"It's crude," Ron said. "He, or maybe she, uses 'oddly' twice in one paragraph; that would never get by me. And the timeline is all wrong. The escape comes before the danger, which deflates the suspense."

You didn't send this, then?

"No way. Scout's Honor."

And that was that. We talked, or rather he talked, mostly of his girlfriend Melani and her new job, while the people walked by on Sixth Avenue, only inches away. They were hot and we were cold. It was like two separate worlds, separated by the window glass.

Thursday morning I went in eagerly, anxious to get back to my bones. I scanned the Foundation's newsgroup first (rumors about a top secret new project) before opening the latest message.

THURSDAY

Sorry about that. I stopped transmitting yesterday because "my" NT woke up, and I didn't want to alarm him. Since my last truncated message we've been snowed in. He watched me build a fire with a sort of quiet amazement. God knows what he would think of this thing I'm talking into. Or of the talk itself. He only makes 3 or 4 sounds. I wait until he's asleep to use the com. After the NT freed me, he followed me up the hill. It was clear that he didn't intend to harm me, although it would have been pretty easy. He is about 6 feet tall if he stood straight up, which he never does. Maybe 250 lbs. It's hard to judge his weight since he's pretty hairy, except for his face and hands. I was in a big hurry to dress my leg, which was bleeding (OK after all). We found the cleft very different from the way I had left it. Something had gotten into my food. A bear? The follow box was smashed and half the KRs were gone. Luckily the space blanket had been left behind. I spread it out and he laid his stuff beside it: a crude hand axe, a heavy, stiff and incredibly smelly skin robe, and a little sack made of gut, with five stones in it: creek stones, white. He showed them to me, as if they were something I should understand. And I do: but of that later. He's starting to stir.

On Fridays I skip lunch so I will have an appetite in the restaurant. I wasn't surprised to find yet another message and I printed both Thursday and Friday to show to Ron. At the least it would give him something to talk about. I think (know) my silence is awkward for him.

FRIDAY

It's snowing. The stones are his way of counting. I watched him throw one away this morning. There are 3 left: like me, he's on some kind of schedule. We've been eating grubs. Seems the NTs hide rotten meat under logs and stones and return for the grubs. It's a kind of farming. They're not so bad. I try to think of them as little vegetables. Grub "talks" a lot with his hands. I try to reply in kind. When we are not talking, when I do not get his attention, he is as dead, but when I touch his hands or slap his face, he comes alive. It's as if he's half asleep the rest of the time. And really asleep the other half; the NT sleep a *lot*. His hands are very human, and bone white like his face. The rest of him is brown, under thick blonde fur. I call him Grub. He doesn't call me anything. He doesn't seem to wonder who I am or where I came from. The snatch point is still 2 days away (-46), which means that I get him to myself until then. An unexpected bonus. Meanwhile, the weather which was already fierce is getting fiercer, and I worry about the com batteries, with no sun to charge them. More later.

Ron and I always meet at the same place, which is the booth by the window in the Burger Beret on Sixth Ave. at Tenth Street. Ron shook his head as he read the messages. That can mean lots of different things.

He said, "You astonish me."

Huh?

"Don't huh me. You wrote it. It's very clever, considering."

I couldn't say huh again so I was just very still.

"The vegetarian business is what tipped me off. And no one else knows that much about Neanderthals. Their counting, the limited speech. It's what you told me."

That was common theory, I said. There was nothing new in it. Besides, I don't make stories. I write reports.

Even I could see that he was disappointed. "Scout's Honor?"

Scout's Honor, I said. Ron and I went to Philmont Scout

Ranch together. That was years ago, before he had entered the world and I had decided to keep it at arm's length. But the vows still hold.

"Well, OK. Then it must be one of your colleagues playing a joke. I'm not the only one who knows you do research. Just the only one you deign to talk to."

Then he told me that he and Melani were getting married. The conversation sort of speeded up and slowed down at the same time, and when I looked up he was gone. I felt a moment's panic, but after I paid the bill and went up to my apartment it gradually dissipated, like a gas in an open space. For me a closed space is like an open space.

The newsgroup was silent for the weekend but the scrambled-header messages kept coming through, one a day, like the vitamins I promised my mother I would take.

SATURDAY

The KRs are gone, but Grub drags me with him to look under logs for grubs. He won't go alone. Third day snowed in. One more to go. I have to conserve our wood, so we stay huddled together against the back wall of the cleft, wrapped in my space blanket and Grub's smelly robe. We sit and watch the snow, and listen to the booming of the icefall—and we talk. Sort of. He gestures with his hands, and takes mine in his. He plucks at the hair on my forearms, and pulls at my fingers, and sometimes even slaps my face. I'm sure he doesn't understand that I am from the far future; how could he even have a concept of that? But I can understand that he is in exile. There was a dispute, over what, who knows, and he was sent away. The stones are his sentence, that I know: Grub *feels* that about them. Every morning he gets rid of one, tossing it out the door of the cleft into the snow.

53

His sense of numbers is pretty crude. 5 is many, and 2—-the number left this morning—is few. I assume that when they are gone he gets to go "home," but he's just as desolate with 2 as he was with 5. Perhaps he can't think ahead, only back. Even though I'm cold as hell, I wish the snatch point wasn't so near. I'm learning his language. Things don't have names but the feelings about them do.

Saturday and Sunday I spend at the lab, alone. What else would I do? When else could I be alone with my bones? I am the only one who has access to the Arleville Find, which is two skeletons, an NT and an HS found side by side, which proves there was actual contact. The grubs confirmed my study of the NT teeth. Of course, this was just a story, according to Ron. Or was it? Sunday I found this:

SUNDAY

Change in plans: I want to alter the snatch point, put it back one cycle. I know this is against the protocols, but I have my reasons. Grub is desperate to get rid of the stones and return to the site and his band. These creatures are much more social than we. It's as if they hardly exist, alone. I'm getting better at communicating. There is much handwork involved, gesture and touch, and I understand more and more. Not by thinking but by feel. It's like looking at something out of the corner of my eye; if I look directly, it's gone. But if I don't, there it is. It's almost like a dream, and maybe it is, since I am in and out of sleep a lot. My leg is healing OK. Grub is down to one stone, and he's happy, almost. I am feeling the reverse: the horror he would feel at being separated from his band forever. Are we going to create an Ishi? What desolation. I am convinced we will wind up with a severely damaged NT. So we start our count at 144 again. Some peril here, since the com is getting low. But I have a plan—

Monday is my least favorite day, when I have to share the lab (but not the bones) with others. Not that they don't leave me alone. I scrolled down past the newsgroup, looking for the daily message and found it like an old acquaintance:

MONDAY

Made it. I am speaking this amid a circle of hominids, not humans, squatting (rather than sitting: they either stand, lie, or squat but never sit) around a big smoky fire. I quit worrying about what they would think of the com; they don't seem curious. Since I arrived with Grub they have accepted me without question, or interest. Maybe it's because I have picked up Grub's smell. They lay or squat silently a lot of the time, and then when one awakens they all awaken, or most anyway. There are 22 altogether, including Grub: 8 adult males, 7 females, and 5 children, 2 of them still nursing; plus 2 "Old Ones," of indeterminate sex. The Old Ones are not very mobile. The NTs grab hands and "talk" with a few sounds and a lot of pushing and pulling, plus gestures. Their facial expressions are as simple and crude as their speech. They look either bored or excited, with nothing in between. Lots of grubs and rotten meat get eaten. They put rotten meat under logs and rocks, and then come back for the grubs and maggots. It's a kind of farming, I guess, but it has all but spoiled my appetite. Perhaps any kind of farming does, seen up close.

All of this was interesting but none of it was new. Any of it could have been written by my colleagues at the lab, but I

55

knew it wasn't. They're in another world, like the people on Sixth Avenue, on the other side of the glass. Most of them didn't even know my name.

Tuesday

Something is happening tomorrow. A hunt? I sense fear and danger, and lots of work and lots of food. All these imprecise communications I got from the group as a whole. This afternoon they burned a bush of dry leaves and inhaled the smoke, passing it around. It's some kind of herb that seems to help in NT communication. Certainly it helps me. Between the "burning bush" and the grunts and pulling of hands I got a picture (not visual but emotional) of a large beast dying. It's hard to describe. I'm learning not to try and pin things down. It's as if I were open to the feelings of the event itself instead of the participants. Death, defeat, and victory; terror and hope. A braided feeling, like the smoke. All this was accompanied, I might even say amplified, by one of the Old Ones (more mobile than I thought!) spinning around by the fire, brandishing a burning stick. Later I amused the little ones (more easily amused than their elders) by cooking some grubs on a stick. Like cooking marshmallows. They wouldn't eat them though, except for one small boy I call 'Oliver' who kept smacking his lips and grinning at me as if it were me he wanted to eat. Even the little NTs have a fierce look that belies their gentle nature. The men (Grub, too) have been sharpening sticks and hardening the points in the fire. Now they are asleep in a big pile between the fire and the wall, and I am staying apart, which doesn't bother them. I can take the smell of Grub but not of the whole pile; that is, band.

Wednesday was a long day. I printed out the last five (including Wednesday) to show Ron. For some reason I was eager for a little "conversation." Maybe mother was right and I need to maintain at least one friend. Mother was a doctor, after all.

WEDNESDAY

This morning we were awakened by the children pulling at the space blanket. Grub had joined me during the night. Is it me or the space blanket that he likes? No matter; I am glad of his company and used to his smell. He was part of the hunt and dragged me along. He understood that I wanted to go. The others ignore me, except for the children. The party consisted of 7 men and 2 women. No leader that I could tell. They carried sharpened sticks and hand axes, but no food or water. I don't think they know how to carry water. We left the children behind with the Old Ones and the nursing mothers, and spent most of the morning climbing up a long slope of scree and over a ridge into a narrow valley where a glacial stream was surrounded by tall grass. There I saw my first mammoth, already dead. It lay beside a pile of brush and leaves, and I "got" that they had baited it into this narrow defile. But something else had killed it. It lay on its side, and for the first time I saw what I thought might be sign of HS, for the beast had already been butchered, very neatly. Even the skull had been split for the brain. Only the skin and entrails were left, with a few shreds of stringy meat. The NTs approached fearfully, sniffing the air and holding hands (mine included). I could feel their alarm. Was it the remnants of the smoke or my own imagination that gave me a terrified sense of the "dark ones" that had killed this beast? Then it was gone before I could be sure. The NTs went to work with their sticks, driving away 3 hyena-like dogs that were circling the carcass. Their fear was soon forgotten with this victory, and they started carving on the carcass, eating as they went. The kill was new, but pretty smelly. The NTs piled entrails and meat in a huge skin, which we had brought with us. By late afternoon we had a skin full, which we carried and dragged over the ridge and down the long scree slope. We were within a half mile of the site when the sun set, but the NTs hate and fear the dark. So here we are holed up under a rock ledge, in a pile. A long, cold, and smelly night ahead. No fire of course. They whimper in their sleep. They don't like being away from their fire. Me neither. I am beginning to worry about the com, which is showing a low power (LP) signal every time I log on. Not as much sunlight here as anticipated. None at all in fact.

"Scout's Honor?" Ron asked again after he had read the printouts, and I nodded. "It must be one of your colleagues, then. Who else knows this Neanderthal stuff, or calls them NTs. Did they really eat grubs?"

I shrugged. How would I know?

"Cavemen are full of surprises, I guess. And I have a surprise of my own. Friday's my last day of class. We're moving to California. Melani has an assistantship at Cal State. We're getting married in Vegas, on the way. Otherwise I would invite you to the wedding. Even though I know you wouldn't come."

I stayed home sick Thursday. And so I didn't check my emails until Friday morning, when I had two, after a lot of Foundation newsgroup gossip about a new project, which I skipped. It was mostly rumors and I don't like rumors. That's why I became a scientist.

THURSDAY

Dawn finally came, sunless. Something was wrong. I could feel it as we went down the hill, holding hands. The cave was filled with shadows, as before, but these were different in the way they stood and the way they moved. Then NTs saw them too, and fell to their knees, clutching one another with little cries. I was forgotten, even by Grub. The Dark Ones had come. The fire was less smoky, and the shadows moved like humans, like us, and chattering. Quarrelling, too. Many blows exchanged. They were butchering something. I drew closer before realizing, to my horror, that I was alone. The NTs had all fled. Before I had time to look around and see where they had gone, I was noticed by the dogs. The NTs don't keep dogs but the HS do. Perhaps they smelled the meat the NTs had dropped when they fled. They were barking all around me, nasty little creatures. Food or pets? Two of the HS came out of the cave toward me. They started to shout and I shouted back, imitating their sounds, hoping they would perceive that I was one of them. No such luck. They moved closer, shaking their spears, which were tipped with vicious stone points. Shakespear: they were acting, I realized. They were only interested in scaring me away. I took a step toward them and they shook their spears harder. They are completely, unmistakably human. Their faces are very expressive. Their skins are hairless and very black. I think they thought I was an NT because I was so white, at least compared to them. Nothing else in my gait or face or speech seemed to matter. I saw over their shoulders what the others were butchering. It was the boy who had dared to eat the cooked grubs, Oliver. His head was laid off to one side, opened for the brains. NTs have big brains, even the kids. I was almost sad, but didn't have the luxury. The two HS were shaking their spears, coming toward me one step at a time. I stepped back, still trying to talk, hoping that they would recognize me as one of their own, when something grabbed me by the ankle. It was Grub. He had come back for me. Come! Run! I scrambled after him, through the bushes, up the scree, toward the rocks and snow. The humans didn't follow us.

FRIDAY

Snowing again, harder than ever. We're in the cleft, Grub and I. I'm trying to save the batteries for the snatch connection (-21). No sun. Haven't seen the sun for a week. After my last (too long) com, we circled up into the high country, careful to avoid the HS—me as well as Grub. It's ironic that even here, at the beginning of human history, skin color trumps everything. Logical I suppose, since it is the largest and most evident of the organs. The band has gone over the glacier; we found the tracks leading up onto the ice. Grub wanted to follow them but I can't get too far from the cleft and the snatch. Luckily, he won't go anywhere without me. I maneuvered him back to the cleft, which was mercifully empty, and built a fire which seemed to comfort him—the building of it as much as the fire itself. I sat down beside him and he quit shivering and we slept under the space blanket, plus the skin. All we have to do is hole up here for another day and we will both be gone. Grub doesn't know that, of course. He is shivering and whimpering in my arms. His desolation floods me as if it were my own. And his fear. The Dark Ones! The Dark Ones! What would he think if he knew I were one of them?

"I really don't need to read any more," Ron said, tossing the printout aside. "Didn't you say that Homo Sapiens had originally come up from Africa?"

I nodded and shrugged. Nods and shrugs are "piece of cake" for me.

"So there they are, your dark ones. There will be a fight, and the Neanderthals, the NTs, will lose. It is clearly an amateur time travel story. If you ask me, and I suppose you have no one else to ask, I think it just bounced in off some anomaly in the Web. The Web has released all sorts of wannabe writers, sending stuff to one another and to

little amateur sites. This is a piece of a sci-fi story that got misaddressed in cyberspace."

SF, I said, but he didn't get the joke. There are ways to indicate that you're joking but I have never mastered them. Why me? I asked.

"I'll bet it's because you're on the Foundation server," Ron said. *"The one in New Mexico. Doesn't it use that new quantum computer, the one that received a message a few mili-seconds before it was sent? I read the story in* Science News. *Some kind of loop thing. But hey, it makes it the perfect receiver for a time travel yarn. Speaking of time—"*

He looked at his watch, then stood up and shook my hand. For the first time I understood his relief in saying goodbye. I tried to hold on but he pulled his hand away.

"I'll stay in touch," he said.

The people on the street were hurrying by. Sixth Avenue is one-way for cars but two-way for people. I didn't mind them through the glass. Scout's Honor? I asked.

"Scout's Honor."

I tried to take his hand again, just to be sure, but he was gone. My mother had finally set him free.

SATURDAY

Disaster. We missed the snatch, both Grub and me. We've been run off from the cleft. We were awakened—or rather, I was awakened by Grub. I was dragged out of the cleft and onto my feet, past the 3 HS with long spears at the cave door. Grub had smelled them before he had seen or heard them. They seized our supplies and the fire, and of course, the cleft, as we scurried up the rocks toward the ice above. They had no interest in following or harming us, just scaring us away. I can now see what happened in the Encounter: the HS didn't kill off the NTs—they only grabbed their sites, their food, their fires, and ran them off; and ate those of their children who fell into their hands. That was enough. Meanwhile, it is getting dark and Grub is counting on me to build a fire. I will make it a small one, to be sure.

I used to love Saturdays, I think, but now they felt sad, even at the lab. I wondered where Ron was, in the air somewhere. He likes to fly. Of course it was none of my business, not anymore. I almost wished my mother were still alive. I would have somebody to call. There are lots of phones at the lab. Sunday was the same.

SUNDAY

There was no snatch. Nothing happened. The HS who ran us off are still in the cleft, 2 of them. If I had left the com behind, you would at least have them. To their surprise. It was all I could do to drag Grub close enough to see. He's terrified. Me too. We're 144 hours from a new snatch, if it can be accomplished. I am going to try and keep these coms down to keep the batteries functioning as long as possible. Haven't seen the sun since I got here.

On Monday I had a personal eyes-only message from the Foundation. Attached was an e-ticket for a flight to New Mexico to discuss the new project. Don't they know I never fly? I scrolled on down and there it was, my next-to-last message, from the distant past and near future:

MONDAY

This morning Grub and I found 4 of his band, fireless and frozen in a small cave high on the ridgeline, above the ice. We buried them with great effort. No sign of the others, no more than 5 or 6. I have a dreadful feeling that they are in fact the last band, childless now. When the HS took their fire, they signed their death warrant, unless the NTs luck upon a lightning strike or a live volcano. Perhaps such events are not as rare "then" as they are "now." We'll see.

On Tuesday I went to the Burger Beret alone for the first time. It felt weird. Don't think I'll go back. Today's message, my last, cleared it all up. I now know who the messages are from. I also know that I will fly to New Mexico. I will have to "suck it up" and go. It is only one stop on a longer journey.

TUESDAY

This may be my last, since even the LP light on the com is dying. Giving up the ghost, I think is the term. We have other worries anyway. More HS have arrived in the site below. We see them in 2s and 3s, out hunting. Us? We aren't about to find out. Tomorrow we are going to cross the ridge and see if we can pick up tracks. Grub sleeps now but it was hours before he stopped shivering. His hands wouldn't leave hold of mine. Please don't leave me, he said with that NT mix of gesture and touch and speech, and I said I wouldn't, but I could tell he didn't believe me, and who could blame him? He was alone in the world, more alone, I suspected, than he knew. If his band is alive (and I doubt it) they are somewhere above us, childless, fireless, slowly dying of heartbreak and cold. I shiver to think of it. You won't leave me? he asked again, tentatively, all fingertips, right before he went to sleep. I put his fingertips on my lips so he would understand what I was saying and know that it was for him, Grub.

Scout's Honor, I said.

THE OLD RUGGED CROSS

One night Bud White had a dream. In the dream, he was hanging on the cross next to Jesus Christ, and the doors to Heaven opened wide, and a smiling little black girl in a starched white dress, the very girl he had raped and buried in the gravelly mud by the Cumberland River, welcomed him in.

Bud went to sleep a sinner, and woke up saved.

It so happened that the chaplain was on Death Row that very morning, counseling a Jehovah's Witness who couldn't, for religious reasons, be executed by lethal injection under the new Freedom of Religious Observance Act (FROA).

The scaffold or the electric chair? The condemned was having a hard time deciding. It was, he said, without a trace of irony, "the most important decision of my life."

The chaplain advised him to sleep on it. He had other things on his mind. The primer was dry on his 1955 Chevy 210 coupe, a Classic in anybody's book, and he intended to spend the evening sanding it again. It was ready to paint but he didn't have the money yet. $1225 for three coats, hand rubbed. You don't skimp on a Classic.

It was already almost noon. But on his way out of the tier, the chaplain passed by Bud's cell, and Bud called out, "'scuse me, Reverend."

The chaplain stopped. Here was a man who'd never had the time of day for religion or its representatives. All Bud did was watch TV.

"What can I do for you, White?" the chaplain asked.

Bud told the chaplain his dream.

The chaplain held his chin in three fingertips, like a plum, and nodded as he listened. A plan was already forming in his mind. He reached through the bars and placed a hand on Bud's plump knee. "Are you sorry, then, for what you did?"

"You bet," said Bud. "Especially now that I know there is a Heaven, and I'll go straight there." He looked as pleased as if he had just discovered a dollar bill in a library book.

"I'll do what I can to help," said the chaplain. "Would you like to pray with me?"

—————

That night instead of sanding his Classic, the chaplain made a phone call to his former professor at the divinity school. "Do you remember a lecture you gave twelve years ago," he asked, "on the medical mysteries of Our Lord's Passion?"

"Of course," said the professor. "I give the same lecture every year."

"What if there was a way to actually watch it happen?" the chaplain said.

"Were," said the professor, who also taught English Comp. "Watch what happen?"

"You know. The procedure and all. An actual crucifixion. What would it be worth?"

"To science or to religion?"

"Either, both, whatever," said the chaplain, who was beginning to wonder when the professor was going to get the point.

"It would be invaluable," said the professor. "It would be revelatory. It would settle once and for all the disputes over how long the crucifixion took, what was the actual cause of death, what was the pathology sequence. It would be marvelous. It would be worth a thousand pictures, a hundred thousand words; worth more than all the pious and vulgar . . ."

"No, I mean in dollars," said the chaplain.

"You have made an extraordinarily impressive conversion," said the chaplain when he met with Bud the next morning, at 8:45. "I want you to meet with my old professor."

"How old?"

"Former professor," corrected the chaplain. "He's a professor of religion."

"Professor of Religion!" said Bud, who had never realized there was such a thing.

"From my old, my former, divinity school," said the chaplain.

And Divinity School! It sounded to Bud like something good to eat.

After leaving Bud, the chaplain went two cells down, to see the Jehovah's Witness.

"Hanging," the young man said. He had apparently prayed all night. "The scaffold and the rope. Hemp and wood. It seems the most traditional."

"The hemp might be a problem," said the chaplain. (As it turned out, the wood was too.)

They prayed together and as he was leaving, as if it were an

67

afterthought, the chaplain asked, "Who's the lawyer who handled your FROA suit? Can you give me his phone number?"

It turned out that he was a she. The lawyer lived in a condo overlooking the Cumberland River, only half a mile from the mud bank where the little girl Bud White killed had been found.

"A prisoner's case? I can't afford any more pro bono," she said. But when the chaplain told her that the professor was financing it through a grant, she was more receptive. When he told her about the TV interest, she was positively sympathetic. That evening the three of them had dinner together, on the deck of a restaurant in downtown Nashville.

The chaplain had the fiddler with fries. The lawyer had the jalapeño hush puppies. The professor had the crab cakes and picked up the bill. He was going to see Bud the next day.

Bud White was watching TV when the guard brought his visitor. Bud watched a lot of TV.

"Are you really a professor of religion?" Bud asked.

The professor assured him that he was. "And I'm here to hear about your dream."

Bud hit MUTE and told the professor about his dream. "Jesus nodded at me," he said.

The professor himself nodded. "Your dream was almost certainly a sign," he said.

Bud wasn't surprised. He had heard about signs.

"The only sure way to go to Heaven is to follow in the exact footsteps of Our Lord," the professor said.

Bud was confused. "Footsteps?"

"It's a figure of speech," said the professor, realizing he should be more precise, more literal in dealing with Bud. "What I mean is, go the way he went."

"Go," repeated Bud, looking around his narrow cell. The word had a nice ring to it. But then Bud remembered the dream. "Is it going to hurt?"

"I'm not here to bullshit you," said the professor, placing his hand on Bud's plump knee. "It will hurt some, that's for sure. But think of the reward."

Bud thought of the little black girl. Her face and hair were clean, but her dress was muddy. He closed his eyes and smiled.

"The first step is to sign these papers making the chaplain and *me* your spiritual advisers."

"I don't *write* very good," said Bud.

"I'll help you," said the professor, guiding Bud's hand. "Now let the chaplain and me worry about the details. But I can tell you this: Cumberland Divinity has agreed to pay for everything."

"Divinity!" There was that candy sound again.

The professor rose to go. "Any questions?"

"What about my mother?"

"I didn't know you had a mother."

"I haven't seen her since I was a little boy, but she was there in the dream."

It was hard for the professor to imagine Bud as a little boy. Maybe it was the beard.

"I'll see about it," he said.

"This is outrageous," said the warden. "It's preposterous. It's impossible."

"We are prepared to concede the first two," said the lawyer. "But not the third."

"He wants his mother to be there?" the warden persisted.

"As his spiritual advisers, we can require it under FROA," said the professor.

The warden frowned. "Oh, you can, can you?"

The chaplain shrugged apologetically. "Jesus's mother was there."

The lawyer put her attaché case on her lap. She unsnapped it but didn't open it. "We didn't want to trouble you with a whole separate FROA filing. We'd like to work this out between colleagues. Between friends."

"Friends?"

They were sitting in the warden's office, in front of the huge, half-moon, barred window.

The lawyer leaned across the desk and presented the warden with her warmest (which was not as warm as his, and his was not warm) smile. "We needn't be adversaries," she said. "I am merely looking after my client's interest. You are merely obeying the law of the land. The chaplain and the professor here are merely fulfilling their spiritual responsibilities. None of us would choose what Bud White has chosen. But who would have chosen any of this?"

She waved a hand indicating the prison yard beyond the window. A few men lounged on rusted weight-lifting equipment, smoking cigarettes. Smoking was still allowed in the yard.

"I would have chosen it," said the warden. "In fact I did choose it. I dropped out of Law my second year and switched to Corrections."

"We're soul mates, then!" said the lawyer. "I dropped out of Police Academy to go to Law School."

"Ditto," said the professor. "I was studying for ordination when I decided to get my Ph.D. instead, in Biblical history."

"Okay, okay," said the warden. He rose from his desk to signal that the interview was over. "I won't fight you on the mother, but I'm not sure we can do the cross."

———————

"What's this Discovery Channel?" Bud's mother asked. "Hasn't anybody ever heard of ABC or NBC or even Ted Turner? What about Fox?"

"They didn't want it," said the professor.

"We tried them, in that order, as a matter of fact," said the lawyer.

"You should have come to me first," said Bud's mother, tipping a little more vodka into her Sprite.

"She's got a point," said the chaplain. He had positioned himself across the trailer so that he could see up her dress. "I say we cut her in for a full share."

"Cut me in? Just you try and cut me out! Who else is getting money out of this deal?"

"Other than the TV?" The lawyer tapped her attaché thoughtfully with a yellow pencil. "The professor and the chaplain split a stipend as Bud's spiritual advisers. I get my usual, plus a small commission on foreign rights. Oh, and the chaplain gets a finder's fee."

"Finder's fee? I gave birth to the sorry bastard!"

"It's only twelve-fifty," said the chaplain. "What say we make it twenty-five hundred and split it?"

The professor rolled his eyes, but it was only for effect. He had already decided to cut Bud's mother in.

"What about Bud?" she asked.

"What's Bud going to do with money?" asked the chaplain. "He would probably just leave his share to you anyway."

"My point exactly," said the mother. "Everybody else is double-dipping around here."

"Oak? Does it say oak in the Bible?" asked the carpenter.

"Bud can't read the Bible," said the lawyer. "He must have got that from TV."

"It's probably the only wood he's ever heard of," said the chaplain. "There's not a whole lot about wood on TV."

"He's never heard of pine?"

"Historically," said the professor, "it should be cypress."

They were meeting in the prison shop, just off the yard.

"Cypress is out," said the warden. "Isn't it endangered or something?"

"I think that's mahogany," said the professor.

"Cedar's nice," said the chaplain. "The boy's mother likes cedar."

"He's not a boy," said the warden.

"Under FROA, Death Row prisoners have the right to die in a manner consistent with their religious beliefs," said the lawyer, reaching for her attaché case.

"We should rape him and bury him alive in a mud bank, then," said the carpenter, a trusty.

"Shut up, Billy Joe," said the warden. He looked from the chaplain to the lawyer to the professor. "How about plywood?"

"I've researched this whole procedure," said the professor, "and the one thing we *don't* need is a doctor."

"You don't, but we do," said the producer. "Under *Kevorkian*, we are only allowed to televise a suicide if a doctor is on hand to prevent unnecessary suffering."

"He doesn't look like a doctor," said the lawyer. "No offense."

They were sitting in the warden's office, under the large, barred, half-moon window.

"None taken," said the doctor. "I'm what they call a para-doctor. I can stitch you up but I can't cut you open."

"It's not a suicide anyway," said the warden. "It's a state mandated execution, perfectly legal. Totally legal."

"And what's this unnecessary suffering business?" asked the professor. "In a crucifixion, the suffering is part of the deal."

"It's the whole deal," said the chaplain.

"Making it, by definition, not unnecessary," agreed the lawyer.

"Last Supper?" asked the warden. "Not a problem. That's on us, free of charge. Only we call it the last meal."

"He wants the Surf and Turf from Red Lobster," said the chaplain. "And he wants a long table, like in the frescoes. They must have showed the frescoes on PBS."

"Surf and Turf is technically two meals," said the warden. "The long table could be a problem, too. Unless it's in the corridor."

"What about the wine?" asked the professor.

"Wine's definitely going to be a problem," said the warden. "That's like the oak."

"We're trying to avoid a supplementary filing," said the lawyer, unsnapping her attaché.

"Maybe the Food Channel would pick up the cost of the Turf," suggested the mother. "Or the Surf."

"The Food Channel?" asked the warden. "When did they get in on this?"

"They're in the pool," said the producer.

"Scourging sounds okay," said Bud. It sounded sort of like deep cleaning. "But I don't like the part about the nails."

"The nails are an essential part of the experience," said the professor. He put his hand on Bud's plump knee and looked into his big, empty, brown eyes. "Our Lord didn't shop around, Bud. None of this 'want this, don't want that' stuff for Him. You have to take it as it comes. Render unto Caesar and so forth."

Bud was confused. "Sees who?"

"And we've arranged the Last Supper," said the chaplain. "We're all going to be there. Me and the professor and the lawyer. Plus the producer and the doctor, and even the carpenter."

"I like the carpenter," said Bud. "What about my mother?"

"Her too. Turns out she likes lobster."

"I thought we agreed on plywood," said the professor.

"No go," said the carpenter. "New environmental regs. Something about the glue. Toxic."

He was fitting together two steel framing two-by-fours.

The lawyer tapped one of them with the longest of her long (and they were very long) fingernails; it rang with a dull ring.

The professor was skeptical. A metal cross? "What about the nails?" he asked.

The carpenter, looking pleased with himself, pulled three wooden squares from a shopping bag. "Butcher blocks," he said. "Drilled and ready to bolt on. Ordered them from Martha Stewart™ Online. And check this out—they're cypress!"

"Billy Joe, you're a wonder," said the warden.

The little girl's grandmother lived in a neat duplex on Cumberland Road, only a few blocks from the Cumberland River.

"According to the Victims' Families' Bill of Rights, you are entitled to attend and observe the execution," the lawyer said.

"But I would advise against it," said the chaplain. "It's going to be ugly and take a long time."

"Why is it going to be ugly and take a long time?" asked the little girl's grandmother.

The professor explained why it was going to be ugly and take a long time.

"We'll be there," said the little girl's uncle, a uniformed security guard at the Cumberland Mall, who was the last person (except for Bud) to see her alive.

"The guidelines say all deliberate speed," said the warden. "I think that means we have to start early."

It was noon on Friday. Bud's execution date was twelve hours away, at midnight.

The warden, the lawyer, the chaplain, the professor, the producer, the doctor, and Bud's mother were in the yard, watching as the carpenter directed the four convict volunteers unloading the pile of stones that had been rented to make a small hill. Their names were Matthew, Mark, John and John. The professor had chosen them from the prison's roster. He couldn't find a Luke. Each was to receive a magazine subscription and a hooded Polartec™ sweatshirt.

"Golgotha wasn't very high," said the professor. "It wasn't a hill so much as a mound, a pile of rubble. So this will do just fine."

"How long is it going to tie up the yard?" asked the warden.

"We will definitely be out of here by dawn," said the doctor.

"Dawn!" said the warden. "You're not intending to drag this out all night, are you?"

"It's supposed to be slow," said the lawyer.

"Can't be too slow," said the warden. "The state has guidelines. All deliberate speed is one of them."

"The whole point of this procedure is that it's slow," said the professor. "Excruciating is the word, as a matter of fact."

"I'm just asking you to speed it up a little," said the warden.

"There's no way we can speed it up without violating the fundamental rights of the petitioner," said the lawyer, reaching for her attaché case.

"Whatever," said the warden. "Can you give me an ETA?"

The lawyer turned to the professor. "What does the Bible say?"

"Our Lord took three hours," said the professor.

"Okay, then it's simple," said the warden. "We start at nine."

"Set another place for the Last Supper," said Bud's mother. "I invited a friend."

"You can't bring a friend," said the warden.

"She's my lesbian lover," said Bud's mother. "Protected under—"

She looked at the lawyer, and the warden realized that this entire scene had been rehearsed.

"Under the Domestic Partners Extension 347 of 1999," said the lawyer.

"She's never gotten the chance to watch anybody die," said Bud's mother. "Particularly a man."

"I had no idea you were a lesbian," said the chaplain, after the warden had left for his rounds. This was in the days when wardens still made rounds. The chaplain sounded disappointed.

"I'm not," said Bud's mother, with a wink, followed by a nudge. "I just wanted to make sure she got in. She's from the *Tattler.*"

"That rag!?" exclaimed the professor.

"I tried to get the *Star* or the *Enquirer*, but they wouldn't return my calls," said Bud's mother.

"That's because Bud's not a celeb," said the doctor. "Wait till they start executing celebs, then they'll return your calls."

"They're already executing celebrities," said Bud's mother. "What about OJ?"

"He got off," said the lawyer.

"Again?"

"They're paper," said the guard.

"Feels like regular cloth," said Bud, pulling on his orange coveralls.

"No wine?" asked Bud's mother.

"No wine," said the guard, who was doubling as the waiter. "And no smoking, either."

The reporter from the *Tattler* put out her cigarette.

"I don't smoke!" said Bud. He grinned. "And don't kiss girls who do!"

"Pass the sour cream for the baked potato," said the doctor. "It's better and better for you than butter."

"Pass the butter," said the professor.

"Bud gets served first," said the chaplain, who was sitting at the Condemned's right hand. "Bud, you want steak or lobster?"

"Both," said Bud.

"That looks good, but it's time to go," said the warden from the corridor. "Any last words?"

It was 9:05.

"What's the hurry?" asked Bud, helping himself to the last of the frozen yogurt. "I thought it wasn't till midnight."

"It's not, officially," said the guard, as he snapped the plastic shackles around Bud's feet. "But they asked us to bring you around early."

"The whole thing could take hours," said the warden. "We decided to try and get you up on the cross by ten at the latest."

"I don't know if I like that," Bud said, holding his hands behind his back for the cuffs.

"There's nothing not to like," said the professor. "It's a necessary precaution since with this procedure death's not instantaneous."

"It's not? I guess that's good, then," said Bud. Instantaneous sounded painful.

They walked two-by-two, except for Bud's mother, down the long hallway toward the door that led into the prison yard. The warden and the lawyer went first. Bud and the guard were right behind them.

A man in a rubber suit stood by the door. He was holding a tank with a short hose and a nozzle, like a paint sprayer.

"Who's that?" Bud asked.

"Remember, we talked about the scourging?" said the chaplain. He and the professor were right behind Bud.

"That's why they gave you the paper coveralls."

"They don't feel right," Bud said. He had the feeling something bad was about to happen. He often had these feelings. Usually they were right.

"In order to duplicate the original procedure as closely as possible," said the professor, "there has to be a thorough preliminary scourging."

"So where's the whip?" the producer asked. He and the carpenter were next in line.

"It's going to be a chemical scourging," said the warden. "Whips are not allowed in Tennessee prisons."

The man in the rubber suit raised his mask, revealing himself to be the para-doctor. "This tank is filled with a powerful paint stripper," he explained. "It will traumatize the client before he is hung on the cross."

"Client," said the professor scornfully. "I can remember when the word was 'patient.'"

The para-doctor ignored him and lowered his mask.

"Otherwise," said the chaplain, placing a hand on Bud's plump shoulder, "You could hang there for days."

"So let's have at it, then, boys," said Bud's mother darkly. She was the only one walking alone. The reporter from the *Tattler* had already gotten sick and gone home.

"Turn around, Bud," said the guard.

Bud turned around. The guard stepped out of the way.

The para-doctor sprayed a foam onto Bud's back and shoulders. For the first split second it didn't hurt. Then the paper soaked through and began to smoke.

Then Bud began to scream.

"Is this legal?" the producer asked the warden.

"Is what what?" Bud's screams made hearing difficult. The producer repeated his question. The warden shrugged and nodded toward the professor. "Ask him. He's in charge from now until the actual MOE or Moment of Expiration," he said.

"Is that legal?" asked the producer.

"Is what what?"

The producer repeated his question. "Check your Bible," said the professor, with an air of mystery.

"There's a threshold requirement of religious authenticity," said the lawyer. "Otherwise none of this would be happening."

"Does that mean the client has been baptized?" asked the producer. Bud had quit screaming. He was rolling on the floor, which is hard to do in handcuffs, trying to get his breath back.

"You bet," said the chaplain, who had moved to the back of the line.

"You bet," said Bud's mother.

"You can't do that here," said the warden from the front of the line.

"Do what?" asked the chaplain and Bud's mother, in one voice.

"You two. That." They were holding hands.

"We lost the sound," said the little girl's uncle, who was watching from the Victims' Rights Closure Lounge on closed-circuit television. It was he who had found her, tracing her little doll to the muddy bank of the Cumberland.

Bud White had quit screaming. He was rolling on the floor of the corridor, trying to get his breath back.

"This ain't right," said the little girl's grandmother. Her name was Hecubah. The little girl had been named after her but hadn't liked the name. Her grandmother had always thought she would eventually come around, as children often do with unusual or Biblical names. But it was not to be, alas.

"We lost the sound," said the little girl's uncle. "Where's that guard?"

"That wasn't in the dream," said Bud. He was flopping like a fish on the cold concrete floor.

The doctor and the warden helped him to his knees. Then they handed him to the four convict volunteers, wearing rubber gloves, who dragged him through the door into the prison yard.

The rest of the party followed.

"Where's the cross?" asked Bud's mother.

A single steel upright stood at the top of a small hill of rubble.

The carpenter showed her the crosspiece which lay on the ground at the foot of the hill. "It gets assembled as we go," he said.

"It's almost ten," said the warden. "Let's get on with this."

The chaplain didn't want to drive the nails.

"I'm a man of the cloth," he said. "Isn't the state supposed to be sending somebody?"

"They are," said the warden, "but she won't be here till eleven. She usually just inserts an IV."

"With any luck, we could be done by then," said the carpenter.

"Let's hope not," said the professor, under his breath.

"Bud's ready to go," said Bud's mother. "Why drag it out? My boy is eager to get into Heaven, aren't you Bud?"

Bud was shaking his head and moaning. The convict volunteers were helping him out of what was left of his coveralls.

"And what is this?" asked the producer.

"It's a loincloth," said the professor.

"It's paper too," said the warden.

"Looks like a diaper to me," said Bud's mother.

"Here," said the carpenter, handing the doctor a nail gun. "Just pull the trigger. But get close. You don't want the nail flying out and hitting somebody. Somebody else."

"I've already done my bit," said the doctor, handing the nail gun to the professor. "I'm here to observe."

"Ditto," said the professor, handing it to the chaplain.

"Perhaps it should be a loved one," said the chaplain. He handed the nail gun to Bud's mother.

"No way," said Bud's mother. "He's mad enough at me as it is."

Bud was shivering even though October in Tennessee is rarely very cold. "I'm not mad at anybody," he said.

Nevertheless, Bud's mother handed the nail gun to the warden—who handed it back to the carpenter. "I'll owe you one, Billy Joe," he said.

Bud began to weep as the guard and the doctor laid him on his back over the metal crosspiece.

"Turn it up," said the little girl's uncle, who was watching from the Victims Rights Closure Lounge.

"Don't you dare," said the little girl's grandmother.

The guard turned it up anyway. He was the only one allowed to touch the 44-inch Samsung; it was state property.

"He's weeping because the metal's cold and his back is raw," said the doctor. "From the scourging."

"Sounds like a cleanser," said the uncle. "Looks like a diaper."

"This ain't right," said the grandmother.

"Not through the hands," said the professor. "That's a common misconception. Through the wrists. Aim for the little hollow."

"Which little hollow?"

"That little hollow right there."

Bud looked away. He tried looking toward the ceiling, then saw the stars and realized he was outside. It was the first time he had seen the stars in six years. They looked *as* cold as ever. "I don't remember any of this from the dream," he said.

"That's why I'm here," said the professor. "To make sure it's all authentic."

"It's going to hurt but it's supposed to hurt," said the chaplain. "Try and roll with it, Bud; try not to . . ."

BANG!

The chaplain didn't get to finish. Bud's body twisted almost comically as he tried to reach toward the wrist that had just been nailed to the left chopping block. But the four volunteers held his right arm in place.

"Look away," said the carpenter. He was talking to Bud.

BANG!

"Let's take him up," said the professor to the warden, who nodded toward the four convict volunteers.

Matthew and Mark lifted the cross-piece over their heads and into the slot in the upright. Bud White was hanging from it. Meanwhile, John and John guided Bud's feet, which were still shackled together, toward the cypress block near the bottom of the upright.

Bud was screaming again. "I wouldn't have picked him for a screamer," said the warden. "Is that in the Bible? All that screaming?"

"How am I to know," said the professor. He was tired of the warden and his lofty attitude.

"Put the one over the other," said the carpenter, as Bud's feet were held against the lower block.

BANG!

Nailed in three places, Bud raised up and drew a breath, and screamed again.

"What's he smiling about?" asked Bud's mother.

"Probably just a reflex," said the chaplain, putting his hand, and then his arm, on her shoulder.

"I don't mean Bud," said Bud's mother. "I mean the professor."

"Wish they'd turn the sound up," said the little girl's uncle.

"You're done wishin'," said the grandmother.

She grabbed her youngest son by the arm and yanked him out of the Victims Rights Closure Lounge, brushing past the producer, who was just entering.

"What's with them?" the producer asked the guard. He was carrying a plate of pimento cheese sandwiches. He had hoped to get a few shots of the family.

"Weak stomach," said the guard.

"Want a sandwich?" asked the producer. "Hate to see them go to waste."

Bud was making a sort of honking sound. "Like a goose," said his mother.

"Or a car," said the chaplain. He had already shown her his Classic, newly painted, in the prison parking lot.

"It's 10:41," said the warden. "How long is this supposed to take?"

"Not less than three or more than four hours, if all goes well," said the professor.

The warden looked at his watch. "We have a shift change at 11:30. That's less than an hour from now."

The watch, a Seiko, was a gift from his father-in-law, also a warden.

To breathe, Bud had to raise up on his feet. The nails made it painful; very painful; more painful than he had ever imagined anything could be.

Not that Bud was big on imagining things.

But the body's yearning to breathe, he learned, cannot be overriden, even by pain.

When he stood up was when he made the honking sound.

Stand, honk, breathe, honk.

His head turned from side to side.

"It looks like he's looking for somebody," the carpenter said.

"Who?" asked the professor.

"Bud."

"No, I mean who's he looking for?"

"Isn't that your department?" said the carpenter.

Bud was. Looking for somebody.

Somebody was missing.

"Professor," Bud said. "Professor!"

The professor looked up.

Bud raised up for air. Instead of honking, this time, he asked, "Where is He?"

"Who?"

"Jesus."

"Jesus Christ!" said the professor.

"He's not here in person, Bud," said the chaplain,

reaching up to pat Bud's plump knee. "That was a long, long time ago."

"It's not required," said the lawyer.

Bud groaned and honked.

"Bud's like a lot of people," the professor said to the warden, "in that he takes things too literally."

Bud White groaned. He was supposed to be getting to Heaven pretty soon.

He hoped Heaven wasn't anything like this.

He found he could still wiggle all his fingers but two.

From his high perch he could see the professor and the warden and the lawyer standing side by side.

The doctor and his mother and the chaplain stood right behind them.

The TV producer and the four convict volunteers, none of whom Bud knew, were milling around a small catering table.

Bud had never hurt so bad. When he had been shot, right before his capture, it had hardly hurt at all. The bullet had gone in and out of the flat part of his neck.

Bud's eyes filled with tears. He felt sorry for himself, and for everyone around him. They were all just flesh and bone, like himself. They were only alive for a few precious moments. Like the little girl herself.

"Bud? Bud White?"

He blinked away the tears and saw Jesus, hanging on the next cross, one over.

"Yes, sir?"

"You're in luck, Bud. See the gate?"

Bud looked up. The sky swung open, and swinging on it, there was a little girl in a muddy white dress.

She stuck out her tongue but Bud knew that she didn't

hate him. Even though he had cracked her little neck with his hands, like a rabbit.

Her dress was muddy. The wind lifted it when she swung forward, and he could see her little blue panties.

She wore little gold shoes.

She stuck out her tongue again—just teasin'! Her lips said "Bud White!" She took his hand, both hands, and pulled him up, not down, peeling him off the nails like a sticker.

Boy did that hurt!

But it was worth it, 'cause—

"We could borrow a guard's club and crack his shins," said the doctor. "That way he couldn't stand up to breathe."

"The Romans often did precisely that," said the professor. "They had great respect for quitting time. But when they went to do it to Our Lord, they found that he had already expired."

"We're in no hurry," said the new guard. "We're just starting our shift. We're good for the darnation."

"He means *du*ration," said the warden. "But shouldn't somebody check Bud? He's stopped honking."

Sure enough, Bud was silent. His big head drooped to one side.

"I don't like the diaper," his mother said. "And I never liked the beard."

"It was Bud you never liked," muttered the carpenter, who had grown to like Bud, a little.

"You watch your mouth," said Bud's mother. "When I want some stupid redneck opinion, I'll read the *Banner.*"

"He's not raising hisself up anymore," said the chaplain.

"Him-self," said the professor.

The warden shook his watch, which had mysteriously stopped at 12:04. "Anybody got the time?"

It was 12:19, according to the producer. Amazingly, according to the professor, the re-creation had taken almost exactly the same time as the original Passion.

The Discovery Channel provided the ambulance as part of the deal. It pulled up in the yard. "You'd think whoever thought of a nail gun," said the carpenter, "would've come up with a better way to pull them."

He used a short crowbar which he called a "do-right." He had to use a block, since Bud's hands were soft. Hands get soft on Death Row. He gave one of the nails to Bud's mother, who wiped it off and put it into her purse. He gave one to the professor and kept the other for the warden.

The guards slid Bud into the back of the ambulance, feet first. He was headed not for a graveyard, but an Autopsy Center.

"You want to ride with him?" the warden asked.

"No, no, no," Bud's mother said. "I'd rather ride with the chaplain. He's the spiritual adviser for the entire family, you know."

"What about the butcher blocks?" asked the producer.

"If you turn them over, they're still good," said the carpenter.

"I'll take one, too, then," said the professor. He was already planning where to send his paper. First he would mount the précis on the World Wide Web—a necessary first step these days.

"You can quit sulking, Luke," said the little girl's grandmother. Her youngest son was sulking because he had been dragged away from the Victims Rights Closure Lounge.

"Yes, ma'am."

"And you can go to church with me tomorrow."

"Yes, ma'am."

The two of them were in her gray '97 Hyundai, heading east on the interstate, toward Nashville, where the grandmother taught, and still teaches, school. Sunday School, too.

A car passed them doing about eighty, also heading for town. A one-handed driver with a woman tucked close by his side. A Chevy; a 1955 210 coupe, cherry red, three coats, hand rubbed.

A Classic in anybody's book.

COME DANCE WITH ME

. . . who called to say "come dance with me"
and murmured vague obscenities.
It isn't all it seems—at seventeen."

—from AT SEVENTEEN, *Janis Ian*

"Not so tight," Billy said. "I can't breathe."

I was like, isn't that the whole idea? But I didn't say anything, I just loosened his rope and straightened it. I never had a boyfriend before, but straightening a tie is something every girl knows how to do, from watching *Friends* and *The Creek*. And this was sort of the same.

"That's better," Billy said. "I still have to do you— Amaranth."

I love it when boys call me Amaranth. Amaranth is my real name, my secret name, the name I chose for myself. I closed my eyes while Billy put my rope around my neck and pulled it tight. It was rougher than the string, that's for sure, but I didn't worry about it leaving a Frankenstein mark. They could do me like they did that other girl and cover it with a high lace collar at my funeral.

"Scared, Amaranth?"

I'm like, No! Billy clickety-clicked the cuffs on my hands behind my back, then ratcheted his own together and dropped the key onto the desk. It rang like a bell when it hit. We were standing on a metal desk in the junked-up office of an abandoned skating rink on New Circle Road, Roller Heaven. There's a joke if jokes are what does it for you.

They say sounds get real loud when you're fixing to die, but you couldn't prove it by me. I listened for a bird, maybe a nightingale, but there weren't any. Maybe they don't like night after all. Maybe it's just another phony name. The best I could do was a dog barking and a horn honking somewhere. Pluto in his little car, picking up his girl friend. Good-bye cruel world!

I heard a gagging sound like somebody trying to puke. At first I thought it was Billy trying to say good-bye, so I opened my eyes for one last smile-try, and then I saw he was stretching, trying to use his feet to reach the key. I don't know how he planned to pick it up, unless there was some magic gum on the bottom of his shoe, and even if he did, then what? Go home to our happy homes? That made me mad, after all my hard work. I kicked the fucking desk over. That's one thing big legs are good for. That and keeping boys away.

Billy was in, right away. As soon as I kicked the desk over, his mouth popped open and his eyes got the look you get when you enter the Realm for the first time. His legs were doing a little dance. My own eyes closed on their own even though they were wide open, which was weird. But OK. I couldn't breathe, but what did I care? I could see the stairs under my feet, and I could see somebody in front of me, running down the steps. I figured it must be Billy—who else? I reached out and grabbed his coat but it wasn't exactly a coat. It wasn't exactly leather. It was cold and slick, and when I tried to pull him back it slipped through my fingers, and he went on down, around the corner. Something was hitting the door. BAM then BAM, like those little rams on *Cops*. There was a light, pulling at me, like another rope. It was so bright I closed my eyes, which was like opening them, everything being reversed, which makes sense, if you think about it. I was looking into a flashlight and I felt two hands under my tits, lifting me up. Mommy, I groaned, but it was a black woman.

I heard her say "This one's breathing," and then she stepped away and somebody else strapped me to a stretcher. Meanwhile EMS came in and cut Billy down. I barely opened my eyes so they wouldn't see that I was seeing. I could tell Billy had made it all the way into the Realm and I was glad, even though I hadn't. It's like in those movies when the guy dies happy because he has saved his girlfriend's life, only reversed. It's gross to see the way they handle people when they are dead. It's not like what you see on TV, believe me. "Can you hear me?" The black woman was back.

I was like, of course I can hear you, you're hollering right in my fucking ear.

"Why did you do it?"

I said, to get out of class, and she goes, "Huh?"

I said, everybody gets out of class when there's a kevorker. Usually there's an assembly. She goes, "Good God, girl," (Have you ever noticed how some people are always calling you girl?) and gives me a shot, which you're not supposed to do without permission, I'm pretty sure. Don't make jokes with cops. Or EMS personnel, which are the same thing. I woke up in jail. You know where you are right away, because of the bars.

I sat up and groaned. There was a fat white lady sitting outside the bars reading a paper. *Suicide watch*. I felt better already. They brought me pancakes for breakfast, with a plastic fork. I acted like I was trying to stab myself with the fork, but the lady reading the paper didn't seem to think that was funny. It was the *Star*. Did you know that the *Star* and the *Enquirer* are put out by the same company? When I found that out, it was like the last straw. After a while two cops wearing suits came and took me upstairs to a little Interview Room, just like *NYPD Blue*. One cop was black and one was white. Everything at the jail is perfectly integrated. There was another man waiting for them in the room, wearing a less cheap suit.

"I'm your lawyer," he said. "I was engaged by your father."

Congratulations, I said (on his engagement) but he didn't get it. Instead of paying attention to me, he laid a briefcase on the table and unsnapped the two snaps, and they were so loud I thought: maybe I'm dead after all; everything is so loud. But no such luck. The white cop told me I was going to be charged with murder, and could possibly face the death penalty if I was tried as an adult. I'm like, Hooray, I feel better already. The black cop pulled out a palmtop, the kind that records onto a flash-card, and set it on the table in front of me.

"Eleanor," he said. "Can I call you Eleanor?"

I shrugged and said, Why not. Everybody else does.

"Here." He took a pack of cigarettes out of his cheap generic sport coat.

"You can't give her that," the white cop said. "She's underage."

"So what," said the black cop. They were playing good cop/bad cop. "You are going to charge her with murder and you won't even give her a fucking cigarette?"

"It's not established yet that they intend to charge her with murder," said the lawyer; "my" lawyer.

The black cop, the Good Cop, tapped a Marlboro out of the pack and lit it for me with his orange Lakers lighter. I took a drag even though I don't actually smoke. I saw a woman smoke once through a hole in her neck. She was dying of cancer. It was cool. He said, "Can you tell us why you did it?"

I told him so we could have assembly, the same thing I had told the EMS lady. That didn't go over too hot. The white cop looked disgusted. The lawyer looked pissed. The black cop took a drag on his own cigarette, and then squinted at it and put it out. You can always tell when somebody's trying to quit. The lawyer pushed the ashtray as far away as he could without pushing it off the table and said, "Her father tells me she likes to be called Amaranth." "Amaranth," said the black cop. "Why don't you tell us the truth."

I'm like, Okay. The truth, if that's really what you want. The truth is that there really is a Life After Death. But it's only for teenagers who kill themselves.

The assembly thing wasn't totally a joke. They call them Healing Assemblies. The first one was in November, right after I transferred to Oakmont. A boy and a girl kevorked in her garage using his dad's car exhaust. They left the radio on and died listening to WFFV, soft rock, the kind of folky stuff my original mother liked. According to the papers they were "popular," and it was a "mystery" why they had done it, and it was all true, I guess. They were definitely more popular dead than alive. Who isn't? The next two were in January, and they were part of the goth crowd. They did it at the old skating rink on Outer Loop. They hung themselves with electrical cable. Their names were Gail and Gregory. The two Gs made it easy to remember.

There was another Healing Assembly. Afterward, there were all these girl-hugging clumps in front of the school, like they like to show on TV. I was just about the only girl standing off by myself, as usual, which is maybe why they wanted to interview me. They don't usually interview fat girls. Maybe it was the goth thing. The TV lady was all set up with a camera guy following her, and a sound guy following him, and a battery guy following them all, like the *Wizard of Oz*. She stuck a mike in my face and said, "Were they friends of yours? Why do you think they did it?"

Well, yes, I think they did it to get out of class, I said. She frowned and switched off her camera and they all stomped off together. By now I was in the middle of a circle of kids. They all walked away too, looking disgusted, like I had let an enormous fart. But Billy looked back. I had already noticed him because he was wearing a black string around his neck. Some skinny girl was holding his hand and she pulled him away.

Even though I don't smoke, I can fake it. The next day I went to Marlboro Country outside the lunchroom where the goth types hang out and bummed a cigarette. Pretty soon there he was. William Winston Lamont was his full name. I had checked it in the Yearbook database during English.

"It's no joke," he said. "There really is a Life After Death."

Cool, I said. Finally my father has put me in a school where I can learn something. I shook out my sleeve so he could see the scars on my wrist.

"What's your name?"

I said, they call me Amaranth, my first actual lie. There wasn't any "they." But I had just moved to Oakmont from Edgefield, all the way on the other side of Columbus, and why not start over?

"Know what this means?" he said, pulling down his collar, like I hadn't already seen the black string tied around his neck.

I said sure, just guessing. But you're not really going to do it.

"What do you mean?"

Guessing again, I said, your girlfriend won't let you. Miss Teen Queen.

He stepped on his cigarette and said, "Fuck you," and walked away.

Okay, I said.

"What did you say?" he said. He stopped.

I said OK, I said. I said, are you hard of hearing?

Later that afternoon, my father and my latest mother came to the jail. It was upstairs again to the same Interview Room. Same two cops but they waited outside. Same cheap suits. Same lawyer, too.

"She's a minor," my father said. "She's barely seventeen."

The lawyer shook his head. "They say she's going to be tried as an adult." They talked about me like I wasn't there so I pretended I wasn't. The lawyer said the murder charge was because the Arresting Officer saw me kick the table over. He had watched the whole thing. "He waited to knock the door down so he could catch them in the act."

"Then he's the one who killed that boy, isn't he?" my father said. "Isn't that entrapment?"

"I took the liberty of engaging a psychiatrist," the lawyer said. I said congratulations again, but he didn't get it again.

"We're getting you out of here tomorrow," my father promised.

I'm like, Is that a threat?

"I'm not sure she wants to go home," the good cop said. I hadn't noticed him back in the room.

"Is that true?" my father asked. If I closed my eyes, he wasn't there. I could almost see Billy going down the stairs. *Wait!* What happens now, since you can only enter the Realm in twos. Did he make it? Why didn't I?

"Is it a boy, honey?" my latest mother asked.

What's with the honey shit? I'm wondering.

"Damn it, open your eyes," my father said as they led me away in handcuffs.

I made Billy pick me up at the Kwik-Pik since my father has a thing about boys with tattoos. About boys, actually. "Where do you want to go?" he said. I said, second base. He looked at me funny, then parked by this old lake. He started to unbutton my blouse and I cut him off and said, Let's talk.

"Okay." He lit two cigarettes and handed me one. He still hadn't figured out that I don't actually smoke. "What do you want to talk about? If you're talking about Susan, we're sort of broken up, but I'd just as soon she didn't know about this."

I said fuck Miss Teen Queen, I came here to talk about the club. He's like, "What club?"

The Kill-Yourself Club.

"That's not the name of it," Billy said. "The name is a secret. The Kevorkians."

Like my name I said. Amaranth.

The car had power windows. I hit mine to throw out my cigarette but it went all the way down. Special setup for tolls. Then I let him get to second base, which boys appreciate. He's like, "Amaranth." I didn't let him go below the waist and after a while he was ready to talk again.

"Tell me about Hell first," I said.

"It's not Hell," he said. "It's called the Realm. It's like a

Web site but you can only get there with the right music. You know Hard Hate?"

Of course, I nodded.

"You know how with really great music you go somewhere, I mean, really go somewhere? Well, if you do it the right way, with the computer, it takes you somewhere really real. It's like a Web site but it's really real. Another guy in another high school showed it to Greg. He moved here last year from Colorado."

Colorado, I nodded. Of course. This is Ohio. Everything always comes from somewhere else.

"Greg showed it to me, and now Greg is there, so I know it's real. We have two couples in the Realm now. That's the only way it works, we have to do it in twos."

I said, there are rules? I didn't like that. One good reason to be dead is because of all the rules.

"There aren't any rules once you're in the Realm," he said.

How do you know?

"Greg told me. I talked to him last night."

I'm like, Sure you did.

He started the car. Was he taking me home? Buttoning my blouse I said, You have to drop me at the Kwik-Pik. But he said, "I'm not taking you home. I'm taking you to my house, but you have to be quiet."

It was a Volvo, the safest car in the world. A real going-to-Hell kind of car.

The psychiatrist was a nice lady in a nice suit with a nice smile. All nice as hell. The two cops were there, to protect her from me, I guess. We went through the cigarette thing again, and then she said, "Why don't you tell me all about it."
I told her what I had told the cop: There is a Life After Death,

but it's only for teenagers who kill themselves. I figured the best way to confuse them was to tell the truth. But she was more interested in Billy than in my amazing news. "Do you always sleep with guys on your first date?" she asked.

Only, I said, if they call me by my real name. "What is that?" she said, pecking away on her little laptop, and I said, None of your business. Unless you want to fuck me too.

She closed her little laptop. "I don't think she's crazy," she told the lawyer. "I think she's just a nasty little bitch." "Amen," said the white cop. The black cop gave me another cigarette. I was beginning to wish he was my boyfriend instead of Billy, who had left me behind, although they were all saying it wasn't his fault. I wasn't so sure. I needed to check with him.

The lawyer came in, and they stood me up to take me back downstairs. I could hear him on his Nokia with my father. They were arguing. I knew my father didn't want me home. The lawyer was telling him that since I was a juvenile they couldn't hold me unless I was a danger to others, or crazy.

What about the murder charge, I said.

"Unfortunately, you are still a minor," said the lawyer.

Surprise—Billy lived in a big new house in the big new house part of town, only about four blocks from "my" house. Nobody seemed to be home. We went in through the three car garage and down a few steps to the basement without ever going through the house. He had his own room with his own door. There was a wooden guitar in the corner. On the walls it was all heavy metal and topless girls, with long, skinny legs.

Billy sat down in front of his computer and put in a CD.

The screen saver was fish with skulls for heads, swimming back and forth. The CD was Hard Hate, *Stairway to Hell*.

"The music has to be playing," he said. "It does some kind of interactive thing with the processor or something."

Whoever said boys all know all about computers hadn't met many boys. Billy told me to close my eyes while he typed in the secret URL, then got up and gave me his seat. "There, it's ready to go. Just hit RETURN."

I hit RETURN.

The skull-head fish were gone. Now the screen had a picture of stairs. The steps were wide and they curved in from gold bannisters on each side. They looked like the casino stairs in Las Vegas that I saw when I went there with my father, right after my original mother died. My father told me she had a heart attack, but I found out later this was a lie. There wasn't any ceiling or any floor. People were standing on the stairs, all couples, holding hands. They were all just outlines. There was a red carpet down the middle of the stairs and everything else was gold. The bannisters, the steps, even the shadows were gold.

"See?" said Billy, sounding excited. Hard Hate was playing the same two-guitar intro, over and over. The same four chords. It was like the CD was stuck. "This guy from Colorado found it and showed it to Greg, who showed it to me. That's them, on the stairs, they are all there now. Click on the title."

I clicked on Realm.

: : Enter User Name

"It doesn't have to be your real name. But it has to be a name you are prepared to use for all eternity." He put his hand on my shoulder, under my blouse, on my bra strap, like we were lovers.

I typed in *Amaranth*

: : **Enter Password**

"K-E-V-" Billy began.

I typed in *kevork* without waiting for him to finish.

"Now hit return."

I hit RETURN. All the legs started moving and the couples moved down. But just one step, the same step, over and over. "Click on any one," said Billy.

I'm like, Any one what? Any one couple? How do you click on a couple? Do you click on the space between them? None of them were even holding hands.

"Any one person."

I clicked on a girl outline. A face filled the screen. It was the girl who had killed herself last week. It was the picture that had been in the newspaper. She was wearing a Sunday dress, but she had a black string around her neck, which hadn't been in the paper. I thought that was pretty neat.

"HELLO, AMARANTH" she said. Her lips moved funny like a cartoon. Her voice was whispery under the music—still the two guitars, over and over.

I said Hello.

"No, you have to type it in," said Billy.

I typed in *Hello*

"Her name is Gail."

I'm like, I know. I read the papers. I typed in *Hello Gail*

"Ask her a question," said Billy.

I typed: *How the Hell are you?*

"GREAT."

"It's not a joke," Billy said, taking his hand off my shoulder. "Don't you want to know what life after death is like?"

I typed: *What is Life after Death like?*

"IT'S GREAT HERE."

"Click on Greg," Billy said. "Next to her."

I clicked on the boy next to her. Her face went away and his came up. He was wearing a suit and tie. It was the picture that had been in the paper, except for the black string. His lips were moving funny like a cartoon. I started to get up so Billy could sit down but Billy put his hand back on my shoulder.

With his other hand he reached down and typed,

Hey Greg it's me

Greg's voice was deep and tinny, under the two guitars: "HELLO, AMARANTH. WOULD YOU LIKE TO JOIN US IN THE STAIRMASTER'S REALM?"

I typed in, *I guess*

"GREAT," he whispered.

I typed: *What's it really like?*

"IT'S REALLY GREAT."

I typed: *Want to talk to Billy?*

"BILLY WHO?"

"I don't want to talk to him anyway," Billy said. "It's late."

We logged off, which was all right with me. I let Billy get to third base on his bed, under the poster girls. He was so proud he walked me home. Sneaking in was easy, since my father and what's-her-name go to bed right after *Seinfeld*.

My father waited until 3:30 the next day before he came to the jail to take me "home." I guess he thought it was like school. He took me out the side door. He even brought a coat to throw over my head to protect me against the reporters, of which there weren't any.

It was understood that I wasn't supposed to go out. I

said, where would I go? I told him I wanted to do some homework. He believed that, even though I hadn't been to school since the week before. As soon as he left, I logged onto the internet and typed in the URL, which I remembered even though I wasn't supposed to have seen it.

http://stairmaster.die

I hit RETURN. Nothing happened. No welcome, no stairs. After a while there was a beep and a box came up.

: : File not found

I tried a search under kevork, under death, under stairmaster. I got lots of sites but none of them were right. No Stairmaster's Realm. No Billy.

Then I remembered the music. I looked under my desk for my CDs but they were all gone. No Toxic Waste, no Hard Hate, not even Sperm Dogs or Hole. My father had thrown them away! Luckily, there was a box of my mother's old CDs in my closet, with her broken guitar. Bob Dylan, Janis Ian, Joan Baez, Laura Nyro, soft rock. The Beatles. It wasn't the right music but on a hunch I kept sticking them in and popping them out until I got one that worked.

One guitar but the same four chords, over and over, and there they were: the golden stairs with the red rug.

There were the outline couples, hand in hand.

: : Welcome to the Stairmaster's Realm

: : Enter User Name

None of the outlines looked familiar. But then how familiar did Billy look to me? I typed in my secret name, *Amaranth*.

:: Enter Password

I typed in *kevork* and one of the couples in the background moved. I clicked on the boy's face and it was Billy, wearing a suit and tie, just like in his newspaper picture. There was the string. My heart was pounding as I heard his voice, all tinny and small: "HELLO, AMARANTH, HOW ARE YOU?"

I didn't make it. They cut me down

"IT'S REALLY GREAT HERE."

They put me in jail

"ARE YOU PLANNING TO JOIN US HERE IN THE STAIRMASTER'S REALM?"

I guess. But how?

"Eleanor? Amaranth!?" My father was knocking at the door.

Help

"COME DANCE WITH ME."

I'm like, huh? But it wasn't Billy, it was the record. And my father at the door, banging and shuffling around.

"Amaranth? Who are you talking to? I thought you were doing homework. Your mother has fixed a nice dinner, to welcome you home. Your favorite, macaroni and cheese."

Macaroni? I thought, hitting PAUSE. Don't think so!

The kids at school call the corner where the cool kids hang out, Marlboro Country. I waited there, with one black string on my wrist and another on my neck, pretending to inhale. Billy appeared and said, "Now do you believe?"

I always believed, I said. But I told him I didn't understand how the music thing worked.

"It's interactive," he said, as if that explained anything. "You have to go in twos, you have to have the right music—"

Hard Hate, I nodded.

"'Stairway to Hell.' That's the way we got it from Greg, and he got it from Colorado. Now I'm next in line but the question is, who gets to go with me. Not everybody is willing to go all the way."

I'm like, Like your girlfriend?

"She doesn't get it. She thinks they are dead. She doesn't understand that there is eternal life and that they will live forever in a place without rules. There aren't many who are willing to go all the way."

Is this a proposal?

He didn't get it but that's OK. There's lots of things boys don't get. That night I let him go all the way in his father's Volvo. The next night he picked me up at Kwik-Pik and took me to the old roller rink on the north side of town, and you know the rest.

May I be excused? I asked politely, getting up from the table. Homework, you know.

My father beamed like a fool. I ran back to my room. The stairs were still on the screen, and my mom's music was still playing: soft rock, like before. The same four chords as "Stairway" but not electric. It was spooky.

: : you have been disconnected

I logged back on, same music, soft rock, and when the chords started repeating I knew I was there. But this time I couldn't get the outline figures to move. I clicked on Billy. His face came up but he wouldn't say anything. He looked dead. I clicked on the girl outline next to him but no face came up. It was spooky, but it made me feel better.

I knew that spot was saved for me.

I put the computer to sleep and crawled under the covers until I heard my father and my latest mom go to bed. As I passed their bedroom I could hear them talking, or rather, him talking and her listening. "Tomorrow," he was saying, "She will go back to school and see the shrink twice a week," etcetera, etcetera.

I'm like, Sure. As silent as a cat, I went down to the kitchen and got a plastic bag and a flashlight, checked the batteries, and let myself out, clicking the door shut softly behind me.

The garage at Billy's was open. I sneaked in and went down to his room. It was just like the last time I had seen it. There were the girls on the wall. The guitar in the corner was wood, like my mother's before I broke it. The computer was on, but asleep. It was covered with a white sheet, like a veil, or rather a shroud.

I didn't need the flashlight after all. Hard Hate was still in the computer's CD slot. I popped it out, then popped it back in, thinking, why not? There was no one awake, probably no one home. It was better than "my" house.

While the two-guitar intro was playing I typed in the URL and hit RETURN. Again it was like the CD was stuck, playing the same four chords over and over. Yes! There were the stairs and the welcome logo. I tried to log on but all I got was

: : incorrect user name

I tried *Billy* since it was his computer, and it worked. I pulled the plastic bag over my head and hit RETURN. All the legs started to move. When I clicked on Billy, he looked confused in his suit and tie.

"HELLO, BILLY," he said. His voice sounded whispery under the music.

It's me, Amaranth, I typed in. *I can't breathe.* I thought he would like that.

"THAT'S NICE. WOULD YOU LIKE TO JOIN US IN THE STAIRMASTER'S REALM?"

I can't breathe

"IT'S REALLY GREAT," he said. The guitars were getting louder and louder.

I can't breathe

My body kept wanting to breathe, even if I didn't. I touched Billy's face on the screen. I couldn't find his hands.

"I'M FINE," he said. "IT'S REALLY GREAT HERE, BILLY."

I sucked the plastic into my mouth, like a dentist's thing, and all of a sudden there I was, on the steps. I was running down, I had made it through. The music was gone but I could hear the scraping of my shoes, some new kind of shoes. Leather on stone.

What happened to the rugs? I was on concrete stairs. No gold, no bannisters. The walls were gray, rough and cold. It was like the stairs at the airport parking lot. Suddenly I felt very sad, thinking of my poor fat body laying there like an empty house. I was at the airport when he told me my mother died.

I stopped. I tried to turn around but I couldn't. I could hear voices down the stairs.

I yelled, BILLY! But it didn't come out as a yell. It came out as a whisper. I must have taken another step down or turned a corner, because he was right there beside me. I was sitting on a landing.

BILLY, I whispered. WE MADE IT. I reached for his hand but it wasn't exactly there, not so you could hold it.

"WHO IS IT?" he said.

AMARANTH.

"AMARANTH WHO?"

JUST AMARANTH, I said.

"WELCOME TO THE STAIRMASTER'S REALM."

You don't cry when you're dead, even when somebody hurts your feelings. It's just like when you're alive. I looked around. So this was it.

I THOUGHT IT WOULD BE NICER, I said. Sort of said.

"WE ALL DID. WHY ARE YOU PULLING AT YOUR FACE?"

I hated the way my skin felt. WHERE'S THE RUG AND THE . . . THE BANNISTER?

"IT DOESN'T LOOK AS NICE FROM THIS SIDE."

WHERE'S THE MUSIC?

"IT DOESN'T LOOK AS NICE FROM THIS SIDE."

I tried to turn around but I couldn't. "WE GO DOWN BUT NOT UP," some girl said. I hadn't noticed her before. She was sitting two steps down, trying to light a cigarette. The matches wouldn't work.

WHAT ABOUT THE NO RULES?

"IT'S NOT A RULE," said Billy. "IT'S JUST THE WAY IT IS."

I'm like, WHATEVER. There were other girls on the steps below. Some boys too. They were just sitting. They were not in couples at all. I tried to look up the stairs but I couldn't.

WHAT HAPPENS NOW?

"NOTHING," said Billy. I sat down beside him. The concrete steps were cold. I was wearing a sort of dress with no back, like a hospital gown.

NOTHING? We sat there for a long time.

NOTHING.

We sat there for a long time.

Come dance with me.

I'm like, What's that?

"WE'RE FINE," said Billy. "HOW ARE YOU?"

CAN YOU HEAR THAT? I asked. I could hear music, but

not Hard Hate. The same four chords, though. How long had I been sitting here, on these concrete steps? It seemed like forever. My hands and butt were cold.

I stood up. The music was louder. I looked behind me, up. The steps led around a corner that went two ways at once. It was weird. No rug, no gold.

"WE DON'T GO UP," said Billy. He was holding my hand but my hand was still cold.

Come dance with me.

I JUST WANT TO SEE.

"SHE DOESN'T KNOW ANYTHING," said some girl.

I went up one step. Billy's hand slipped through mine. Around a corner, there was a girl. Sort of a girl. She was young like a girl but old like a teacher at the same time. It was weird. She was singing and I knew the song. It was one of the folky songs my mother had left behind. Soft rock. I suddenly wondered: had she intended to leave them for me?

WELCOME TO THE STAIRMASTER'S REALM, I said. I sounded exactly like Billy. It was not really my real voice.

Come dance with me, she said, and I took another step. She was holding Billy's guitar.

I'm like, THAT'S BILLY'S. Plus, she was too old to be there. This was our place.

I don't think so, she said. It's my place too. I come here when I sing this one song. I've been coming here for years.

LIKE HARD HATE.

I don't have to kill myself, she said. Sometimes I die on stage. She laughed. That's a joke. Every time I sing this song, I find myself here. Back here. I know this place well. I have known this place for years.

THIS IS HELL.

She's like, Think I don't know that? It's only for kids but we singers get to come and go. At least I get to play my old

D-18. She knocked on the guitar, like knocking on a door.

Music makes space, she said. And since the universe includes every space, every new space is a new universe. No matter how small.

IT'S REALLY GREAT HERE, I said.

She just shook her head. She held out her hand but still played the guitar at the same time, a neat trick. *Come dance with me.*

I followed her up the stairs. One step, two. It felt weird. I'm like, WHERE ARE WE GOING?

I'm not going anywhere. She laughed. Song's over, hear that thunder? I'm outa here, girl. She handed me the guitar and I knocked on it, like knocking on a door. Then she was gone and I heard sirens, pulling me like a rope. I dropped the guitar, but not on purpose. It made a big noise on the steps. "She's still breathing," somebody said.

I opened my eyes. It was the same black woman as before. A woman was standing behind her with tired sad kind troubled eyes. "Mother?"

"Oh honey, no, I'm Billy's mother. Was Billy's mother. Now what have you done?"

It was weird; she was holding my hand. I closed my eyes and looked for Billy, but he was gone. It was all gone: the steps, the guitar, the girl singer. It was all gone and the weird thing was, I was sort of glad.

"Here, kid." It was the black cop in the crummy suit. He offered me a Marlboro. "Your dad's on his way."

"Hooray," I said, and I let him light it with his Lakers lighter, even though I don't smoke. And then, for some reason, maybe because he was trying so hard to be nice, I started to cry.

SUPER 8

Look. We were all so pretty. And we knew it, shooting everything we did, and one another, turning our present into instant past, and future too, loaded into memory: Super 8. Cars, faces, clothing, places, mugging and vamping, boy-girl romps in dry leaves and on city streets, ripped off from *A Hard Day's Night*, and *Jules et Jim*. How much we take from movies! Once, they say, it was the other way around. This first dim (poor light? cheap film?) jerky memory of us all together shows the playful ascent of a small mountain (big rock!) in Central Park, hand-in-hand up a steep trail. Laughing. The circle is small, only four of us so far, all boys but one. Two of us are "comic artists" (cartoonists), debuting in a new magazine put together by the scion of a well-known but never-mentioned-aloud family. There's Mason, regretting his slick-soled cowboy boots. There's John, who doesn't need boots to look cool. The scion, Si, leads the ascent. Our oldest, almost thirty, he unpacks the food, the grass, the wine, the rest of us laughing at his formal picnic basket until he laughs too, the shy, self-effacing laugh of the uncomfortably rich. No beard yet, but already thinking about it. And Wendi, our one and only girl, long legs, small breasts, expensive shoes. (This is before B.J.'s long legs, big breasts, funny shoes.) It's cold and windy at the top, but it was cold and windy at the bottom too. It looks like late November, the leftover leaves fluttering around like ghosts, looking for a place to rest, hopefully together. Ghosts already! Each of us takes a turn with Si's Super 8. John mugs, thinking it's cute, and Mason broods, more careful of his dignity. And Wendi, our Wendy, already telling us our story. She talks into the camera as if it could be persuaded to record her words. Fast Forward to Park Avenue and the disapproving doorman and the dark apartment, as big as a small deserted city, where Si's grandfather, even then, is never home. The circle is small. Sitting on the Persian rug, reluctantly admitted to be a gift of the Shah, sharing a joint. Does Wendi know that John as well as Mason can see her panties? Expensive, like her shoes. We are surrounded by unwanted treasures. Rockwell Kent on the wall: it is said that he once sat in this chair. John tries on a fur coat from a dark, forgotten closet and Si tries to mask his disapproval, unsuccessfully. FF to another larger circle, a high meadow upstate. B.J. bursts from a pile of leaves, like Venus emerging from the sea, new-born, nude, and simply beautiful. Look how happy she seems. John must have taken this shot. But not this next one. FF, night, watchful shadows around the dome, silver in the moonlight, watching it burn—

"Oh!"

"What's the matter?"

"I don't know. I had a dream."

Mason sat up in the bed. Through the big window, the moon looked in, like a wondering face.

"A nightmare?" Constance rolled over. She looked old without her makeup. Funny. Mason remembered the days when he hadn't wanted her to wear makeup. Now he wished she did.

"More of a dream. It was a dream about—something."

"Something."

"It was about the old days, back in New York. It was weird. It was—"

"I'm sure. Can we go back to sleep?"

"It was in Super 8."

"Okay. Now can we go back to sleep?"

Look! Here we are headed south, to DC, for the big antiwar protest of '68. Si's VW bus is covered with Peter Max swirls and militant slogans. We knew how to paint it but not how to fix it, but it doesn't matter, for when we break down, a bearded VW mechanic, also headed for DC and the demo, pulls over and has us moving in less than twenty minutes. "These little forty-horses are hell on points." We nod as if we know what points are. Vince (his name is Vince) won't take Si's twenty, but he accepts John's fat-rolled joint with a beardy grin, and we're off again. Farewell! Where is Vince today, but here, in our collective memory? Our bus is one in a caravan of crusader children, grins and peace signs in rear windows. FF to the demo itself, a swirl of pretty faces, young, angry only for show, filled with joy at our new-found power. We are the future! Tear gassed, still laughing as we puke. Hey, hey, LBJ! When SDS runs through the crowd under red flags we follow (who wouldn't?), whooping with happy rage. Mason, who had just last week done his first cover for

Si (a Frazetta imitation), sucks on a huge joint with a huge grin. We are in free territory, among our own, for the first time. Mason passes the joint to Si, who passes it to John, who sticks his tongue out at the camera: a puppy, with all (and only) a puppy's charm. Wendi in her designer dress, spattered with mud and smelling of tear gas, passes up the camera as she takes the joint. The Super 8 with its blinking light, passed in a circle, hand to hand, is the only one of us we never see. FF and the circle grows larger, but tighter too. Now Will is one of us, face and hands, headband and all. We are standing around a small geodesic dome, all but B.J., who is in the doorway, while the flames lick at the Celotex skin, casting a yellow light on hers—

"Damn."

Wendi sat up alone in her big bed. Through the window the lights of Manhattan shone like stars, each inhabited.

"Second night in a row," she said to herself. She checked the clock: 2:00 A.M. Too early to get up, yet she didn't want to go back to sleep.

She wished there was someone she could call.

There was always Mason, but it would be midnight in California.

There was always computer solitaire.

Look. Autumn in New York. You can tell by the light. You can tell by the water tanks, stalking the horizon like shy wooden beasts, that we are on the roof of the loft, in what is now Soho. Then it was just the edge of Little Italy, with live chickens for sale on the corner of Broome and

West Broadway. See the neon chicken, nodding, day and night. Mason must be holding the camera, for it was he who found the loft, and the chicken is his totem. Here's Si, spreading cream cheese on a bagel (Sunday morning) while John inserts a joint into his mouth. There's Wendi, talking as usual, our Wendy, telling us a story, and we can tell what story it is, for there are five of us, not four. As the camera goes around the circle, we see an extra hand with no face to go with it. Will. No face, not yet. But there's the bandaged hand, and Fast Forward and there's Will, struggling with a posthole digger, putting in the floor of the dome. See the lordly Hudson in the distance, through the trees, like a broad steel road. FF and there's the dome, almost completed, B.J. opening the triangular doorway, her perfect figure outlined by the flames—

―――――――

"Are you OK?"

It was the stewardess. Rather, the flight attendant. In first class they are always attentive.

"Just a bad dream," said Si. He didn't mention that he hadn't slept in three nights. They weren't paid to be that attentive.

―――――――

Look. Wendi is in a long silk dress ($1400) sitting in the dusty light from West Broadway, telling us a story. The Super 8 loves her dancing, weaving hands. Wendi is a scion too. Her father was a writer for *The New Yorker*, and when he smoked himself to death, he left her with no money but a rich circle of connections. It's not hard to get a job at *Vogue* when the Editor knew you as a schoolgirl. Wendi gathered stories uptown and brought them downtown to us. Listen, she says. She and Si were at a party when a well-known rock critic beckoned them into a quiet corner and asked, what do you know about the Underground Expressway? Enough, they said. It was a way out of the military for those who hated the war, and who of us didn't? Wendi scribbled an address on a matchbook (from '21,' or was it the *Four Seasons?*), and sure enough, the next afternoon, a dark, intense and *faceless* young man showed up at the door with his clothes in a paper bag, saying Si and Wendi had sent him. Mason and John took him in. No pictures of that, of course. FF, and he's one of us, walking with B.J. up the hill, into the Upper Meadow, hand in hand, both nude, of course. This is our world, opening like a flower in the sun. FF and Si is handing a shovel to Wendi who doesn't want it, who angrily tosses it into the leaves drifted against the pilings of the dome, narrow locust leaves, smoldering, then bursting into flame—

"You're up already?"

"Couldn't sleep."

"Again?"

"I've been having these dreams." Will didn't tell Emma that he'd had these dreams before. Years before. And found his way from them, into her arms long and small. *And therewithal sweetly did me kiss . . .*

"Why don't you stay home from work today and get some sleep?"

"Good idea. I have some calls I want to make anyway."

Three, no four nights in a row. Mason thought about it all the way to work, in his new Audi A6.

Traffic on the Bay Bridge was brutal; normal, that is. He idled through the obligatory Monday morning meeting (the latest glitch in the OS) and at noon he retreated to his bright corner office, telling his "administrative assistant" (secretary) he would be meditating for an hour, and called a number that he hadn't called in so long that he almost had to look it up.

"Renee, you know I don't take calls during lunch crunch."

"I told him. But he said you'd take it. Said to tell you it was Mason."

"Oh. Give it here, then. But you'll have to watch the front for me."

"Yes ma'am."

"And quit ma'am-ing me. I'm not that damned old yet. Mason?"

"Wendi."

"My God. Where the hell are you?"

"At the office. San Francisco. I know you're busy, I just had to call you. I had this weird dream last night."

"I know. So did I."

"Super 8. So you're having it it too."

"Four nights in a row."

"Shit."

"Weird, right? Listen, can I call you back? This is my money hour. How late can I call tonight? This coast to coast time thing—"

"Call tomorrow. We're going to the opera tonight. Benefit thing."

"The opera?"

"You don't want to know. Tell you what, I'll call you in the AM. How early can I call?"

"I'm the one on the East Coast, remember?"

"I'll call you at nine. Six my time."

Wendi's *New Yorker Luncheonette* was hardly a luncheonette, though it looked like one, until you opened the menu and saw the burger prices. Dinner however was easy and over by ten.

At her apartment, Wendi found a message on her machine: "I know this will come as a surprise. Or maybe not. Can you call me back tonight? We need to talk."

Will, too? She wished now she had taken Mason's call. She wanted to talk with him first, before she dealt with Will. She wished she still drank. She didn't want to shut her eyes and go to sleep, but finally she did.

And wished she hadn't.

Look. Our hair is longer, and here we are in Si's grandfather's big, empty Park Avenue apartment. Wendi is dressed to kill, as always; she has just come from the *New Yorker* Christmas party, to which she has a standing invitation. Si is cooking, as always. Mason and John are lighting a joint. The circle grows: there's Nelson, Si's brother, who is always sour but wants to be part of the gang (but isn't) and his latest, a young (eighteen, or so she said) California girl who came to New York to be a model. He continually puts her down and everybody minds but her. B.J. seems eager not to notice. FF to the Persian rug, littered with money, like leaves. We have decided to buy a farm upstate. Everyone is throwing in, but of course it is Si who will actually put up the money to buy the land. His family owns land upstate but this is to be a new start. Mason has a couple of grand from his last FlashKomix contract. Wendi tosses in her father's silver lighter, which she tells us we can sell, since it was given to him by Robert Benchley. We don't; it is still in her purse today. B.J. startles us with a ten. And a shy wave. Part of our circle now, she takes up the Super 8, and we get our first look at Will's face, for which B.J. is scolded, gently, and only later told why. FF to the building of the dome. There's Mason on the scaffold, clowning. B.J. tosses him a hammer, and he leans out to catch it and almost falls. No sound but we can read his laughing lips. "A brush with death." Ah, death. FF to Wendi, weeping, holding a shovel, her tears as bright as jewelry in the orange light of the flames—

"God damn."

John sat up. Through the filthy window of the trailer, he could see the dome in the moonlight, like a saucer that had landed in the meadow and never taken off again.

Fire. Five nights in a row. He almost wished he had a phone.

"Fuck."

Wendi couldn't go back to sleep. She pulled on a long T-shirt, one of a drawerful given to her by a liquor supplier, and padded around the apartment, not drinking, waiting for the sun to rise, always a long process in midtown Manhattan.

Having friends on the West Coast was good, at night. In the morning it was a drag. At 7:30 it was still 4:30 out there. Wendi lay back on the couch and folded her hands over her neat, small breasts, looking straight up; closed her eyes and went to sleep, deliberately; she could do that sometimes. It was like a little, a practice death.

Not always.

The phone rang. She opened her eyes. It was 8:55.

Finally! "Mason?"

But no. "Wendi. It's Will. Did you get my message?"

"Will. How many years has it been. You too, huh?"

"Super 8," he said. "Five nights in a row. So we're all having the same dream again."

"But different. It always ends with fire. It always ends with B.J.."

"I'd rather not talk about all this on the phone," said Will. "Have you heard from any of the others?"

"Mason."

"And Si? Aren't you in touch with Si?"

"Of course. But he's flying to Alaska, taking pictures of the pipeline for the *Times*. Won't be back until the 14th. That's a week from yesterday."

"Must be nice being rich."

"It's a job, Will. You have a job too."

"Let's don't fight, Wendi. I'm thinking of coming down, into the city tonight. Can I meet you?"

"You know where to find me. Gotta go. I have another call."

It was gone but she knew who it was. She dialed Mason's home number.

Big mistake. "Hello?" It was Constance. "Hello! Who is this, damn it?"

Wendi hung up without saying anything. She and Constance had never gotten along. The phone rang immediately.

"Mason?"

"Wendi? I called at six but your line was busy."

"I was talking to Will." No need to mention Constance. "Where are you?"

"In the car, on the Bay Bridge. Will too, huh? That means we're all having the same dream again. After all these years."

"Seems so. He sounds worried."

"What else is new?"

"Tell me you're not worried."

"Have you heard from Si?"

"He's in Alaska." Wendi put out her cigarette in the ashtray that had held her father's butts at the *New Yorker* for forty-one years. It had been given to her by Tina Brown.

"What does Will want to do? Will always has a plan."

"I don't know. He's coming down here tonight. We're meeting after work."

"Where?"

"At the restaurant, I guess, why?"

"Because I'm going to be there too."

The traffic on the Westside Drive was terrible, as usual. Four-wheel drive was no help. Will got to the restaurant at 9:45, and saw Mason at the bar, nursing a Kirin. "Well, I'll be goddamned," he said. "Where'd you come from?"

They hugged stiffly: old friends. Old rivals. The two somehow the same.

"I flew in this afternoon," said Mason. "Jet Blue. I talked to Wendi this morning."

"Me too. You too?"

"Super 8. Four nights in a row. We're all having the same dream again."

"Nightmare," said Will.

"Well, that's the thing, isn't it? A dream brought us together. A nightmare brings us back."

Wendi approached from behind, and put one hand on each.

"Just like old times," she said. "Give me another half an hour, then Renee can close. What are you drinking?"

"Kirin," said Will. "So this is your new place."

But she was gone already. He looked around at the tables, still half filled with yuppies, all in couples. All untroubled by dreams. Or nightmares.

"I hear you got married," said Mason.

"Eleven years ago next week," said Will. "Emma and I are both practicing law in Albany. Death penalty appeals."

"I heard. Good for you."

"And I hear you're a millionaire."

"Only on paper," Mason said. "One good thing about owning your own company, you can get away whenever you want to."

"Or need to," Will said as the bartender set two Kirins on the bar. "Have you talked to Si? Or John?"

"John? I haven't talked to John in years."

"Me neither," said a voice from behind. They both turned and saw a bearded man in an orange parka, out of place in the black-on-black of lower Manhattan.

"Si!" they both said at once.

"I've been having them too," Si said, as the bartender brought another Kirin.

"In Alaska?"

"On the way. I caught a plane back. Just got in an hour ago. I thought I might find you all, us all, here."

"Si!" said Wendi, hugging him from behind. "Thank God. Let's get the fuck out of here. Renee can close."

She was already pulling on her coat: an oversized black motorcycle jacket. Does that mean she has a boyfriend? Mason wondered, as glad for her as he was sad for himself.

They took Will's SUV uptown to 34 Park Avenue. No one had anything to say until they were upstairs, and inside. The old apartment looked the same.

"Here, where it all began," said Will, while Si opened the drapes to let in the starlight from the street. But those weren't stars. They were windows, all looking out.

"This place was in the dreams," said Mason. "Broome Street, too."

"It started for me here," said Will. "That night you decided to buy the Meadow, last night's dream—we all had it, right?"

They had all had it.

"That was when I realized I belonged with you guys. That I didn't have to run away to Canada after all."

"Did you ever have to do any time?" Mason asked.

"Six months probation. And an undesirable discharge. Thanks to Jimmy Carter."

"So we needn't have worried?" Wendi asked. Trying not to sound accusatory.

"That was years later. After the war was over. At the time—"

"At the time it was all serious," said Si. He was carrying little coffee cups out of the kitchen on a silver tray. Always the host.

"Coffee?" said Wendi. "It's midnight, Si."

"Do we really want to sleep?" asked Mason, taking his cup.

"It started up on the Meadow," said Wendi, declining hers. "The dreams, anyway. They began when we started building the dome. The first night, after we put in the pilings for the floor."

"Circles," said Si. "I remember that morning. We all looked at each other, and John—it was John, I believe, who said, "Hey, am I crazy or did we all have the same dream."

"And he wasn't crazy," said Wendi. "Not then anyway."

"I don't even remember what the dream was," said Will.

"I do," said Mason. "We all dreamed we were standing in a circle around the dome, watching it build itself."

"It was spooky," said Si. "That was where I got the idea for the hubs. Making them out of PVC pipe."

"It seems spooky now," said Wendi. "We didn't think it was spooky then."

"I did," said Will. "Still do."

"I didn't," said Mason. "I thought it was fucking wonderful."

"Magical," said Wendi. "And logical, too. We were living the same dream in the day, and having the same dream every night. It seemed right."

"It was right, for a while," said Si. "Until it turned into a nightmare."

"In Super 8. It brought us together, then it tore us apart," said Wendi. "Then back together again. What now?"

"To sleep, perchance to dream," said Mason.

They all fell silent. Had it really been thirty-five years?

"Maybe it was the mushrooms," said Si. "Remember Shroom, the first time he brought them up the road? We all thought he was the cops. Because we had blasted the postholes. A scare."

"Shroom," said Will. "He *is* a cop now, I think. John told me he was still around. The eternal townie."

"You see John?" Wendi was surprised.

"Once, a few years ago," said Will. "And the dreams were long gone. Why are they back? That's the question. Why are we all here, having the same dream again?"

"Maybe we're here to end it," said Wendi. "Besides, it wasn't the mushrooms. It was the dome. The postholes. The circle. Completing a circle."

"It's B.J.," said Si. "She's in every dream."

"We're all in every dream," said Mason.

"It's not the same," said Will. "Look, we all know it's not the

126

same. And every dream ends in fire. What's that all about?"

Wendi was pulling off her jeans. Mason was trying not to notice. "Let's don't go there," she said. "Not yet. Maybe the dreams are telling us a story."

"Anybody got any dope?" said Mason. "I came on a plane."

"Don't smoke much anymore," said Si.

It was two in the morning. They slept in a star, heads together, on the musty Persian rug in the big living room. Mason was still on West Coast time and he stood at the window as the others went to sleep, looking down on the cabs on Park Avenue, trolling for stragglers.

Perchance to dream, he thought.

Finally, fearfully, he too lay down and closed his eyes. And wished he hadn't.

Look. Here we are, where we always wanted to be, on a high meadow on the side of a mountain, overlooking the Hudson. It must have been John who shot this sequence, showing the dome going up, in stop time. First just a circular platform, then the struts, all numbered, attached with PVC hubs and strap. We were all so pretty. B.J. especially. No longer looking over her shoulder, west. Here comes a Jeep, psychedelic colors. Shroom. Si is brewing tea, looking stage-evil, like a witch in Shakespeare. The dome is the center of it all. The circle. FF to B.J. again, framed in light, like an angel. But no, it's fire, fire again. Her outstretched hands are black.

"Shit."

"You too?"

127

"Of course. We all had it, the same, right?"

They were all sitting up, nodding.

"It's not going to go away," said Si. "We're being called. Summoned."

"We might as well get going," said Wendi, pulling on her jeans. She had slept in her T-shirt and underpants. Mason tried not to stare at the little white triangle, once so familiar, so dear.

Will pulled his car keys from his pocket. "I have to move it anyway," he said. "You can't park on Park after seven. And it's 6:30."

"I should call Constance."

"I have a cell phone," said Wendi. "You can call her from the highway."

"Everybody has a cell phone," said Will.

The Westside Highway. The Henry Hudson. The Saw Mill, The Taconic. They were silent, more or less, until they reached the first ridge of the little mountains that marched across the Hudson, from New Jersey, north toward New England.

New means old, thought Mason. He leaned up over the seat and popped in a CD.

"All Along the Watchtower." *Two riders were approaching . . .*

"There's got to be a logical explanation for all this," said Will.

"Logical?" Si said. "Dreams are not logical. Neither is memory. It's memory we share. We created a group memory, and it exists independent of each of us. Even when the group is gone."

"A hive mind," said Mason.

"A what?"

"A hive mind. Made out of all of us, but independent. We off-loaded all our memories into the Super 8. And then the memories started accessing us. They only existed when we were together. And we are only together when we sleep."

"Thank you, professor," said Will.

"What about the time zones?" asked Wendi.

"No time in dreams," said Si. "Asleep we are in the same time zone, maybe."

"Maybe," said Mason. "Anyway, it went away and now it's back. What has changed?"

The leaves had changed, or were changing. That's the only thing I miss about the East, thought Mason. That and the little triangle.

"It's calling us back," said Wendi. "It's B.J. calling us back," said Wendi.

"Unlikely," said Will. He was an expert, a businesslike driver. "Let's talk about what's real."

"The dreams aren't real?" Si asked.

"What's real is that the dreams are back, after thirty-five years. What's real is that we're all having them. Again. After we thought we had managed to get rid of them."

"We couldn't get out of there fast enough," said Si.

"To get rid of them, we had to separate," said Wendi. "Go our separate ways. And it worked. At least for a while."

"Thirty years," said Mason. "That's quite a while."

"Thirty-five." Will pressed on. "Secondly, they have a theme. They all end at the same place. With fire."

"And B.J.," said Wendi. "Fire and B.J.."

"Third, we are all responding. Here we are. We're all here because we are scared."

"Maybe it's guilt," said Wendi. "Remember guilt?"

"Fourth, we all know what to do."

"We do?" Mason asked Will.

"We're here, on the Taconic, aren't we? Heading north. After all those thirty-five years."

Will took the Route 55 exit off the Taconic.

"You remember the way," said Mason.

"I've been back, once, six or eight years ago. To check on John. To make sure he wasn't bringing the pigs down on the place. He wasn't particularly glad to see me. He was growing dope, living here alone. Looked like a mountain man."

"That was always his dream," said Wendi.

"That was then," said Si. "This is now."

"What do you mean?"

"I mean none of our dreams are our own anymore. Or haven't you noticed?"

"Finally get to use this four-wheel drive," Will muttered. They were all silent as the big Pathfinder rocked and lurched up the dirt track, through the narrow gate.

Somebody, it could have been anybody, stepped out of the woods with a shotgun in his hand.

"John!" said Wendi. He looked so old. They were all as shocked as she was. He had been the youngest, the puppy.

"Welcome home," John said with a grim sort of grin.

"What happened to your hand?"

"Fire," said John, opening the shotgun to show it wasn't loaded before getting into the Pathfinder. Wendi slid over to the middle of the front seat to let him in.

"Fire?" Si asked.

"Of course," said Will. "We all saw it in the dreams, didn't we?"

"You should know better than to stick your hands into a dream," Si said to John.

"Yeah, well—"

"How'd you know we were coming?" said Wendi.

"I mean, right now, up the road."

"Alarm," said John. "That box on the gate is a laser, sets off a dinger up by the trailer. But I've been expecting you all, since the dreams started up again. Or some of you. I didn't expect the whole crew. Cool. Wendi."

She accepted a kiss on the cheek. "What fire?"

Then as the SUV pulled up the last steep stretch, through the little grove of locusts, into the clearing, she saw.

They all saw.

"My God," said Si.

The dome had burned. It was a circle of charred boards with the blackened two-by-four struts still standing. The PVC had melted but the straps still held the struts together.

They stood and looked in silence, then walked around it.

"Happened last night," said John. "Went up like a bomb. Luckily it was raining, and it didn't spread. I burned my hand trying to get stuff out."

It was starting to rain again, a little.

"Stuff," said Will, sniffing the charred wreckage. The dome was twenty feet across, ten feet high. The Celotex covering had burned away completely, and only the charred struts were left, like a dream of a dome.

A bad dream, thought Mason.

"Meth!" said Will, angrily.

"Huh?"

"A fucking meth lab. Are you crazy, John? You've gone from growing dope to cooking crystal meth? You turned the dome into a meth lab?"

"A guy's got to live," said John, heading toward his trailer, trailing his shotgun. "You guys want some coffee? I'll put a pot on."

The trailer was an ancient plywood Windwalker; it stank of mold and socks and cigarettes. They all slipped out of their shoes, even though the floor was gritty with old mud, and found places to sit while John fired up the wood stove and stirred grounds into a coffee pot.

"Cowboy coffee," said Wendi with a comic grimace.

The meth lab didn't bother her. She sipped her coffee and studied John. It was hard to believe that this narrow-eyed old man had once been the beautiful boy who had come between herself and Mason. And then herself and Will.

"Have you seen a doctor?" Si asked, taking John's arm and peeling back the bandage.

"It'll heal," John said, rewrapping it. "Besides, it was just last night."

He went from wrapping his arm to rolling a joint. John always rolled the best joints.

"I was getting out of the business anyway," he said. Nobody believed him.

———

But it was OK. The sun had come out and the Meadow had the old magic, completing the circle. They all drifted out of the trailer into the sun.

"Hard to believe we were once so young," said Wendi. She and Mason walked up the hill to the spot where they had once planned to build their cabin.

"Maybe you're right," Mason said. "Maybe the dream is just a signal, to bring us back together one more time. A summons."

"From who? B.J.?"

"That makes it a ghost story."

"Maybe it always was a ghost story, all along."

"What do you think would have happened if it hadn't been for B.J.?" He reached for her hand.

She let him take it. "Do you mean, would we have all stayed here and lived happily ever after? I doubt it, Mase. But it's nice to think so, isn't it?"

"Having the same dreams."

"It wasn't so bad. It wouldn't have been so bad, would it?"

Mason sat on the grass and Wendi lay down beside him, at ninety degrees, with her head on his lap. Just like old times. It felt weirdly, irreversibly, irretrievably right.

She closed her eyes. And wished she hadn't.

Look. It's dark outside but there's a light in the dome. One of us, it's Wendi, pulls open the heavy door and there, in the light of three candles on the floor, is B.J., twirling slowly, hanging by the neck from a rope tied to the high center hub. How did she get it up there? Now we see the ladder, kicked over on the floor, amid the boxes and junk that fill the dome. B.J. spins around and we see her face. She is mouthing words, silently, but we can all read lips, in memory at least. "Help. Help me." Then she spins away, into the gathering fire.

"Whoa!"

"What's wrong?"

"I fell asleep."

"I know. Just like the old days." Mason was smiling. Wendi wasn't.

"I had the dream." She scrambled to her feet, tucking her skirt up under her knees.

"By yourself? Just now?"

"We were all in it. Let's go."

"Where?"

"Back down. To the trailer. The others."

Always the others, Mason thought, following.

They were halfway down the hill when they heard John's warning bell: *ding ding ding*.

Then again: *ding ding ding*.

A Jeep Cherokee was pulling up the last part of the hill, slipping in the mud. On the side it said Orange County Deputy Sheriff. A portly man got out and started up the hill toward Si and Will. John came out of the trailer with his shotgun. Mason and Wendi joined them from the hill above.

"Shroom!" said Wendi.

"Goddamn, John!" said Shroom, touching the brim of his deputy hat as if for luck. "Put the fucking gun away. You're running a meth lab here? I told you, man!"

"Not loaded," said John. He opened the gun to show him, then set it down beside the trailer steps. "Accidental fire."

"Bullshit," said Shroom. "Is that you, Will? I'll be damned. And Si. Remember me?"

Of course. They all shook hands.

"And Wendi too. And Mason. Man! Everybody but B.J.. What ever happened to her?"

"You don't want to know," said Wendi.

"Probably not," said Shroom. "I always had a crush on her."

"You had a crush on us all," said Wendi. Our townie.

"Somebody saw the fire from the river last night," said Shroom, accepting a cup of tea, brought from the trailer by Si. He took a drink then spat, politely. "I had to investigate.

Now you've compromised my ass, John. A little grass is one thing, but a meth lab—"

"There's no meth lab here." John spread his hands. "Just some ashes of an old hippie dome."

"No meth lab, said Will. "Just an accidental fire. Civil stuff. No need for you to take note."

"Well, you're all full of shit, and I'm glad to see you all," said Shroom. "And believe me, I don't want trouble for anybody." As he spoke he was unsnapping a leather case, one of several on his belt.

A gun? Wendi wondered, curious but curiously unconcerned. Whatever would be would be.

It was a roll of bright yellow tape.

"But you guys have put me in a spot. The sheriff sent me up here, and if he doesn't like my report he will come up here himself with the fire marshall. Insurance and all."

"We don't have insurance," Si pointed out.

"I have to cover my ass, just in case," said Shroom. He was wrapping a long piece of CRIME-SCENE tape around the burned dome. It took the entire roll.

"This is *not* a crime scene," said Will. The others were silent, letting him talk. He who had been their outlaw was now their lawyer.

"It's the only tape I have," said Shroom. "I can't help it if anybody goes in and removes any incriminating stuff, especially if I don't know about it, especially if they don't fuck with the tape. I would hate to see anybody get in trouble but I have to cover my ass."

"Understood," said Si.

"Then we're square," said Shroom. He shook hands all around and headed back down to his Jeep. "By the way, the sheriff's an asshole," he called out the window as he backed down the hill, not bothering to turn around. "And John, you're an asshole too!"

"Well, now we know," said Mason, watching the Jeep back down the hill toward the gate, like Fate rewinding.

As if Fate could rewind.

"Know what?" Will asked. "Know John's an asshole?"

"Know why we're here. Don't you see? We have to move B.J.. Before they start poking around."

"Shit," said Wendi. "That's it. He's right."

"This is some spooky shit," said Mason. It was raining again outside. "Here we all are, after thirty-five years."

The rain beat on the trailer like a drum.

"B.J. was calling us," said Si. "Protecting us. Warning us. She doesn't want us to get into trouble."

"Please. If she didn't want us to get into trouble she wouldn't have killed herself," said Will.

"She wasn't thinking that far ahead," said Wendi. "She never did." She looked at John.

He stared back. "What?"

"You found her," Wendi said. "I remember the night. You were hollering from inside the dome. We all came running."

"So?"

"So. What did you find?"

"What do you mean?" John asked.

"Was she dead when you found her?"

Si made tea. Coffee seemed inappropriate. John sat on the stained, the broken, the filthy couch, either trying to cry or trying not to cry. It was hard to tell.

"B.J. was so crazy," he said. "She was spinning, still kicking."

"Why didn't you cut her down?" said Mason. "You had a knife. A fucking handmade knife."

Wendi had given John the knife for his twenty-first birthday.

"I still don't know why," said John, his voice small. "I just didn't."

"She was pregnant, wasn't she," said Wendi. It was a statement, not a question. None of the men would look her in the eye.

"It's too late to lay blame," said Si. He was the only one who hadn't slept with her.

"Poor B.J.," said Wendi. "Poor Betty Jean." A moment of silence followed. They all knew B.J.'s story. Raised in a trailer park (Mission Oaks) in Riverside, her first boy friend was her uncle Roy. Her Playboy figure was her ticket out. Away. East.

"It never felt right to leave," said John.

"You did leave, though," said Wendi.

"I kept coming back," said John. "Then I just sort of stayed. It was like it was my job to watch her grave."

"You even fucked that up," Will pointed out.

"Doesn't matter," said Mason. "We still have the same job, why we're here. We have to move her."

As soon as the rain let up, they hauled the blackened remnants of the meth apparatus up the hill and buried it under a pile of old trash; John's trash. The dome floor was charred but not burned through. The floorboards would have to be pulled up, and it was raining again, halfheartedly. They returned to the trailer for spaghetti from cans. Si's suggestion that he drive to town for food was vetoed.

"We have until morning," Will said. "It's getting dark anyway. And are we planning to sleep?"

Nobody wanted to sleep.

"It's like we've been dreaming B.J.'s dreams," said Wendi.

"But B.J. was in the dreams," said Will.

"So? I'm always in my own dreams."

"From the outside?"

"We've been dreaming our collective memory," said Si. "Watch out what you wish for. That was once our wish, to be as one. It was what we got."

"Only in our dreams," said John. Was it supposed to be a joke? No one could tell. He had finished crying: that was for sure.

"Except one of us is dead," said Mason.

"Murdered," said Wendi. If she wanted John to wince, and she did, she was disappointed.

"We're all murderers," said Will. "Accessories to murder."

"You made us that," said Wendi.

"We had no choice," said Will. "I wasn't just AWOL. I was a deserter. Plus I had burned that bus. That was probably treason."

"They never got you for that anyway," said Mason.

"They had lost interest. They would have been interested if they had caught me in 1970, believe me."

"It's done," said Wendi. "We all agreed not to call the cops, or anybody. What could it have done for her anyway? We were her people. There was no one else."

"The rain," said Mason, at the window. "It's quit again."

"We need a crowbar," said Will. The floor boards were charred but still intact.

"There's one in my truck," said John. He got it and pulled up the boards while the others watched. The old nails squealed. Soon the boards were laid aside. The dirt under the dome was bare and clean, as if there had been no fire, no intervening thirty-five years.

"An unmarked grave," said Wendi.

"Quite otherwise," said Si. "Marked with the dome itself. Our dreams for the future."

"Now gone," said Mason. "Give me the shovel. I'll do the honors since nobody else seems to want to."

They all stood in a circle and watched as Mason dug. The shovel cut into the damp earth like a knife into flesh, and Wendi flinched with every slice.

Mason felt it too. *Careful.*

Only two feet down, he hit the sleeping bag. It was gray, no longer green. He didn't want to touch it.

"Let me," said Si. He pushed the dirt back with his hands until the zipper was uncovered. It was brass, still bright. He didn't want to touch it.

"Let me," said Wendi. She knelt between the standing Mason and the kneeling Si, while John and Will looked on. "Rolling away the stone," Mason said, as she pulled the zipper down.

Then wished he hadn't.

The sleeping bag was empty.

"Look. She's gone." John.

"Impossible," said Wendi. She pulled the sleeping bag out of the long, shallow hole and held it up and shook it.

"She's gone," said Mason. "Maybe that's the point."

Something lay in the bottom of the grave. "My camera," said Si. "I thought it was lost."

"I thought so too," said John.

"I put it in the sleeping bag with her," said Wendi. "I didn't put it in the grave."

"Why didn't you tell me?" Si picked it up. It was corroded into a lump of brushed aluminum, caked with mud.

"Because I knew you would want it back. I thought it would put an end to the dreams."

"Well it didn't," said Will. "What about the film?"

"I kept the film," said Si. "All transferred to video, long ago."

"Our collective memory," said Mason. "Maybe that explains the fast forward."

"Where's B.J.?" Wendi asked, looking for the first time as if she were about to cry. "Poor B.J.. Who called us here?"

"I say we split," said Mason. "It's not even midnight yet."

"And leave me here to deal with the sheriff alone?"

"Then come with us," said Wendi.

"You're all going to different places," said John. "Different worlds."

Wendi rolled up the sleeping bag and started back toward the trailer. "I'm cold," she said.

"This is impossible," said Will.

"Poor B.J.," said Mason. "Did we dream it all?"

"Huh?"

"There's no body. She's as gone as ever. More gone. Maybe it never happened. Maybe it was like the dreams."

No one believed that. They shared a glass of tea, with whiskey from John's half-empty plastic jug of Jim Beam.

At midnight they went to sleep. All on the floor. Mason and Wendi slept side by side for the second time in thirty years. "I'll call Constance tomorrow," Mason said. "Meanwhile, it's kind of nice, to all be together here. Back home."

"The crime scene, you mean," said Will.

"Our only crime," said Wendi, yawning, "was dreaming of a better world."

"And not cutting her down," amended Will. The last to close his eyes.

Look. It is always sunny, Super 8. Our collective memory. Perhaps that's just because no one made films in bad weather. Or perhaps memory has become imagination.

Imagine if it had all worked! Our collective mind imagines what our individual memories couldn't, didn't dare, even then. Here we are, older, wiser perhaps, walking around the ruins of the dome that was our first collective project. Our first and last. Our only. It's in ruins but we are still standing.

There are Mason and Wendi, hand in hand, in old age. Will, free at last. Si, still holding things together, still making tea. Even John, having survived heroin and meth, abashed as always, but with a grin. With a knife and a gun and a circle of friends, his oldest unacknowledged, irretrievable, impossible dream. We all look worried, but less worried than the young, who are afraid of losing their youth, as if it is a country to which they will never return.

We got over that one.

"I thought it was dead," says John, cleaning the camera with a toothbrush. "But there's a light on the side."

"That's just the sun."

"Blinking?"

The rain is gone. We are sitting in the sun, on boards and stumps, since the inside of the trailer was cold.

"No sheriff, anyway." John seems pleased.

"It's only ten," says Will, consulting his watch. "Ten-ten."

Mason opens the door of the Pathfinder, so we can all enjoy the music floating across the long brown autumn grass. "All Along the Watchtower."

Look. Wendi is hanging the sleeping bag on a line. It looks brighter, greener in the sun than it did in a hole in the earth.

Ding ding ding

Mason looks up. "Two riders are approaching."

Ding ding ding

"Shit," says Will. "Shit," says John.

We all stand, and peer down the road, to where the sheriff's car will appear between the knotty, ash-gray locust trees.

Si and Will hurry to make sure that the CRIME-SCENE tape is still secure. The dome is a circle of ash, a pile of boards around a hole. Maybe we should have nailed the boards back. Or scattered them over the hole.

"Should've been here by now."

"Maybe he got stuck. Road's still pretty wet."

"Someone's coming." Wendi points.

Look. There is no car. A woman is walking up the road. Short gray hair, tall, wearing coveralls and funny shoes. A little boy walks beside her, holding one hand.

She waves with the other. A little shyly.

"Look, Mase." Wendi reaches for and finds his hand. It feels right in her own.

After a moment's hesitation we all wave back. And wait.

ALMOST HOME

1. THE OLD RACETRACK

Troy could hardly wait until supper was over. He wanted to tell Toute what he had discovered; he wanted to tell Bug; he wanted to tell somebody. Telling made things real, but you had to have the right person to tell. This was not the sort of thing you told your parents.

He fidgeted at the dinner table, ignoring his father's gloomy silence and his mother's chatter. She was trying to cheer him up and failing, as always.

Troy cleaned his plate, which was the rule. First the meat, then the beans, then the salad. Finally! "Excuse me, may I be excused?"

"You don't have to run!" his father said.

I know I don't *have* to run, Troy thought as he hit six on the speed dial. Toute's line was busy. He wasn't surprised. It had been busy a lot lately.

He dialed Bug's number. "Excuse me, Mrs. Pass, may I speak with Bug, please?"

"Clarence, it's for you!"

"Bug, it's me, listen. Guess what I found out. You know that white fence at the old racetrack? That broken down fence by the arcade?"

"The one with all the signs."

"That one. I just discovered something today. Something really weird. Something really strange. Something really amazing."

"Discovered what?"

"Well—" Suddenly Troy was reluctant to talk about it on the telephone. It seemed, somehow, dangerous. What if the grownups were to hear, and what if for some reason they weren't *supposed* to hear? It was always a possibility. Every kid knew that the world was filled with things that grownups didn't know, weren't supposed to know. Things that were out of the ordinary worried them. Worrying turned them into shouters. Or whisperers.

"Well, what?" Bug asked again.

"I can't talk about it now," Troy said, lowering his voice, even though his parents in the next room obviously weren't listening; they were having one of their whisper-arguments. "I'll tell you tomorrow. Meet me at the usual tree tomorrow, the usual time."

"I have practice."

"Not till afternoon. We'll have time to do some fishing."

★

The usual tree was at the corner of Oak and Elm; the usual time was as soon after breakfast as possible, allowing for the handful of chores required by Life with Parents: in Troy's case, garbage take-out and sweeping (for some reason) the crab apples and leaves from the driveway.

The old racetrack was at the edge of town, where the houses gave way to fields. There was no new racetrack, only the old one, long abandoned. It was just a dirt oval around a shallow lake that was all grown over with lily pads and green scum. Troy and Bug called it Scum Lake. That is, Troy called it Scum Lake and Bug went along. Bug generally went along.

The racetrack could have been for horses, but there were no stables. It could have been for cars, but there were no pits. No one seemed to remember who had built it or what it was for.

As they rode their bikes toward the track, Troy tried again to tell Bug what he had discovered. "You know the white fence along the infield, the one with all the signs on it? Well, yesterday, after you left for baseball, I climbed up into the stands, and when I looked down. . . ."

"The stands! You climbed up there? They're so rickety, the whole thing could fall down!"

"Well, it didn't, and it won't if you watch your step. Anyway, here we are. I'll show you."

They parked their bikes by the chain-link fence. They didn't have to lock them. Nobody came by the old racetrack, and nobody stole in their town anyway. Sometimes Troy wished they did.

"Come on, and you'll see!" Troy led the way through the hole *something* (not they) had dug under the fence, and then through the dark tunnel under the stands, lined with dead soda machines. Bug carried his backpack with his ball glove in it, and Pop-Tarts for lunch. Usually they just headed across the track for the infield and the lake; but today, after they emerged into the bright sunlight, Troy led the way up into the stands, using the board seats for steps.

Troy knew Bug didn't like high places, but he knew he would follow. The planks wobbled and rattled and boomed with every step.

"The cheap seats," Troy said, sitting down on the top plank. Bug sat beside him, with his backpack between his feet. From here, they could see the entire track, with the lake in the middle; and beyond the backstretch, fields of beans in long straight rows; and beyond them, the dunes.

"I stayed yesterday, after you left for baseball," Troy said. "I like to come up here sometimes and read, or just look around. You know, imagine what it was like when there were cars on the track, or horses, you know?"

"I guess," said Bug, who was a little short on imagining things.

"Anyway, look at the fence from here." A white fence followed the track halfway around the infield side. It was broken into two parts, which met at an old enclosed plywood food arcade near the start/finish line. The fence opposite the grandstands was almost straight, but the part that led toward the lake wandered crazily, left and then right. Parts of it were fallen, and other parts were still upright.

"What's that fence for? It doesn't keep anything out or in. And see how both ends come together at the arcade. Don't they look like two wings of a bird, but broken?"

"I guess," said Bug. "But. . . ."

"Plus, have you ever noticed how they aren't really very strong. They're made out of slats and wire and canvas, that white stuff."

"That's because they're just for signs." Bug read them aloud, like the answers on a test: "*Krazy Kandy, Drives You Wild. Buddy Cola—Get Together! Lectro with Powerful Electrolytes. Mystery Bread.*"

"Maybe. But maybe not," Troy said. "Maybe they are wings."

"Huh?"

"You can only see it from up here. See? They look like the wings of an airplane—an old-fashioned airplane, an *aero*plane, all wood and wire and canvas. The wings meet at the arcade, which would be the fuselage." Troy was proud of his knowledge of airplanes, which he had gotten entirely from books. "The front end of the arcade, there, by the track, would be the cockpit."

Bug was skeptical. "So where's the tail? An airplane has to have a tail."

"The outhouse," said Troy, pointing to an old wooden outhouse at the far end of the arcade that had turned over and split into two parts. "It makes a V-tail, which some planes have. Everything looks like something else, don't you see? If it was a crashed airplane, that crashed here a long time ago, and it was too big to move or get rid of, they would've just built a racetrack around it so that nobody would know what it was, because that would give away the secret."

"What secret?" Bug asked.

"The secret that it is an airplane," said Troy.

"I guess," said Bug, picking up his backpack and starting down. "But now it's time to go fishing."

✫

With Bug, it was always time to go fishing. Fishing in Scum Lake was sort of like ice fishing, which neither of them had ever done, but Troy had read about in a magazine. You made a hole in the ice (or scum) that covered the lake, then dropped in your line and waited. But not for long. The little bluegill were so eager to get caught that they fought over the hook; they would take worms or cheese, but worms were better.

Troy and Bug climbed down from the stands, rattling the planks, and walked across the track to the infield. They slipped through a fallen section of fence, or wing, and followed the short path through the reeds to the lake. Their fishing poles were under the dock, where they had hidden them. Digging under an old tire, they found worms.

They sat on the end of the dock and caught bluegills, then threw them back. They were too little to eat, but that was okay; there were plenty of Pop-Tarts. Troy caught eleven and Bug caught twenty-six. Bug usually caught more. Troy was careful taking out the hooks. He wondered if it actually hurt the fish.

He was beginning to suspect that it did.

The bluegill weren't the only fish in Scum Lake. There was also a catfish as big as a rowboat. Troy had seen it once, from the end of the dock, when the light and shadow were just right. Bug had seen it, once, sort of; at least he said he had.

After he had caught his first "rerun," Troy quit fishing. He left the line in the water, just to make Bug happy, but left off the worm. It was fun just to sit in the sun and talk about things. Troy did most of the talking, as usual; Bug was content to just listen. "Didn't you ever wonder how everybody got to our town?" Troy asked.

"In one little airplane?"

"It's pretty big. Then they multiplied. Didn't you ever wonder why they are all so much alike?"

"I guess. But I have to go to practice."

They hid their poles and started back toward the stands. On the way, Troy walked off the two ends of the infield fence. The two sections had different signs—*Buddy Cola, Krazy Kandy, Oldsmobile*—but were exactly the same length. Didn't that prove that they were, in fact, wings? And the arcade where they met definitely could have been the fuselage. It was about twenty feet long, with a flat roof; one side was open above waist-high counters.

"I'm going in," Troy said, climbing over a counter on the open side. Bug grumbled but passed in his backpack and followed. The roof and the floor were plywood. The roof was low enough to reach up and touch. They had to duck under a three-bladed ceiling fan. Troy reached up and spun it with his hand.

"It stinks in here," said Bug, wrinkling his nose.

"Mouse droppings," said Troy.

"What's that?"

"Mouse crap. Mouse shit," said Troy. "Let's look up front."

"All right but it's getting late."

The plywood floor creaked as they walked, bent over, toward the front of the arcade, where a dirty glass window overlooked the track. Under the window, there was an old-fashioned radio, filled with dusty vacuum tubes of all different sizes. It sat on a low shelf next to an ashtray filled with white sand.

"Here we have the cockpit," said Troy. "The control center. Why else would there be a radio?"

"Announcers," said Bug. "Anyway, I have to go to practice."

"Okay, okay," said Troy. He climbed out and helped Bug with his backpack. He stopped at the entrance to the tunnel and looked back. Even from the ground now it looked like an airplane. He didn't need to be up in the stands to see it. It just took a little imagination.

"What about a propeller?" said Bug. "An old airplane, made out of wood and canvas, would have a propeller."

True, thought Troy, as they descended into the tunnel. But not true in a way that opened up possibilities. True in a way that closed them down; not the kind of true he liked.

☆

They rode together to the usual tree, before riding off in different directions. Bug lived in the old section of town, with all the trees. Troy lived in one of the new, big houses on the way to the mall.

"See you tomorrow," said Bug.

"I may not make it tomorrow," said Troy. "I have to go to the mall with my cousin."

"The bent girl? She's so bossy!"

"She's okay," said Troy.

☆

2. The Bent Girl

Toute was Troy's cousin but more like his sister, especially since he didn't have a sister. When they were kids he and Toute had slept together and even bathed together, until they got old enough for the grownups to realize that, hey, one's a boy and one's a girl.

Toute was eleven, almost a year older than Troy. She got her name because when she was little, her mother had taken her to Quebec for treatments, and she had learned to say "Toute" for everything.

Toute means everything in French, which was funny, Troy thought, because Toute got hardly anything. First her mother died. Then she got more and more bent until she could hardly walk, and couldn't ride a bicycle at all. Once a week she went to a special doctor in the mall, and Troy went with her so they could pretend it was a trip for fun. But it wasn't much fun. Usually Toute was worn out from the treatments, and sometimes she looked like she had been crying.

The next morning Troy rode his bike to Toute's house, which was not far from the usual tree. There was an extra car in the driveway. The door was open. Toute's father and two strange men were in the living room, talking in whispers.

Toute was sitting on the stairs. She looked gloomy but she smiled when she saw Troy. "I had a dream about you last night," she said. "I dreamed you had your own airplane and you took me for a ride."

"No way!" said Troy. He sat down beside her and told her what he had discovered at the racetrack. Now he was more convinced than ever that it was real.

"Get my backpack," Toute said. "It's up in my room. Let's go."

"Don't you have to go to the mall for that treatment?"

"They're discontinuing it," Toute said emphatically, as if *discontinue* were something you actually did instead of

stopped doing. "So I'm free all day. Get a bottle of Lectro out
of the fridge. We can leave a note for my dad."

Toute sat on the crossbar of Troy's bike. She could
sit okay, though she couldn't stand without holding onto
something. They rode by the usual tree, just in case—and
there was Bug.

"Where did she come from?" he asked Troy. "I thought
you said you and her had to go to the mall."

"I want to see the airplane," said Toute.

"She wants to go fishing with us," Troy said.

"She doesn't have a fishing pole," Bug pointed out.

"She can use mine," said Troy.

They parked their bikes against the chain-link fence and
crawled under. Toute was pretty good at that part; then she
had to hold on between the two boys as they walked through
the tunnel, past the dark abandoned drink machines.

Troy was wondering how he was going to get Toute up
into the stands. It turned out not to be a problem. As soon
as they emerged from the tunnel into the light, Toute blinked
twice and said:

"Definitely an aeroplane."

"Huh?" said Bug.

"Aer-o-plane," she said, pronouncing each syllable. "More old
fashioned than an airplane. All wood and canvas. Let's look inside."

"It's just some old plywood," said Bug, but Troy and Toute
were already heading across the track.

The boys helped Toute over the counter on the open
side, and climbed in after her.

"Smells in here," said Toute, wrinkling her nose.

"Mouse droppings," said Bug.

"Here's the cockpit," said Troy. He tried to wipe the
window clean but most of the dirt was on the outside.

"And here's the main power control," said Toute.

"That's the radio," Troy said.

151

"It's a receiver," said Toute. "It can draw power out of the air. There's a lot of radio waves flopping around out there that never get used. Turn it on."

Troy turned the biggest dial, in the center, to the right, then to the left. "Nothing."

"And here's why. This battery is bone dry," said Toute, stirring the white sand in the ashtray. "Hand me my Lectro, Bug. It's in my backpack."

She was too bent to reach into her own backpack. Bug grumbled but did it for her, handing her the plastic bottle. She poured a narrow stream of clear liquid into the white sand ashtray, making a damp spiral in the sand.

"What does that do?" asked Troy.

"Lectro has powerful electrolytes," Toute said, as she handed the bottle back to Bug. "You can put this back now."

"Thanks," Bug said sarcastically as he put it back. "Isn't it time to go fishing?"

★

Bug caught twenty-one bluegills, and Troy caught sixteen. Even Toute, a girl, caught eleven, on a handline.

Troy quit when he caught his first rerun, but Toute kept going. "I don't know why everybody feels sorry for the fish," she said. "I feel sorry for the worms."

"You get over feeling sorry for the worms," said Bug.

Toute was so bent that she had to sit sideways on the dock. "What I really want is to see this giant catfish you are always talking about."

"It's best on a cloudy day," said Troy. "Then the light doesn't reflect off the surface of the water, and you can see all the way to the bottom."

Just then a cloud passed over the Sun. They all three crawled to the edge of the dock; Troy made a hole in the scum with his hands. They could see all the way to the bottom, the little waving weeds and a few small fish, examining an old tire. But there was no giant catfish.

"It may be an urban myth," Toute said.

"What's that?" asked Bug.

"You're forgetting one thing," said Troy. "I saw it myself."

"Bug, did you see it?"

"I think I did," Bug said.

"I want to see it myself," said Toute. "Troy makes things up sometimes."

Troy felt betrayed. It was Toute who had showed him the Teeny-Weenies who lived in the roots of a tree in her yard. He tried to remember if he had really seen them or just wanted to see them. He couldn't remember.

Bug had two Pop-Tarts in his backpack, which they shared three ways. They had to take their lines out of the water to eat, because the fish were so eager to get caught.

They were just finishing the Pop-Tarts and putting their poles back into the water when Troy heard something strange. "What was that?"

"What?" said Bug.

"Sounds like groaning," Toute said.

"The wind," said Bug.

"I don't think so," said Toute. "Better go see."

Troy left his line in the water and went to investigate. The infield section of fence was tipped over until it was almost flat on the ground. The other side, along the track, had fallen, too. Lying down, the fence looked more like a wing than ever.

"The wind probably blew it over," said Bug, when Troy returned.

"There isn't any wind," Troy said.

"There may be at the other end," Bug suggested. "The fence is all connected. And anyway—"

"There it is again," said Troy.

They all three heard it this time: a groan, a rattle, a

splintering sound like a branch breaking.

"Sounds like the mating call of a tyrannosaur," said Toute.

They put away the poles and went to investigate, all three this time. Toute walked between the two boys, an arm around each shoulder. Her feet barely touched the ground.

Both fences were now completely flat. The front of the arcade was now sticking out onto the track; it had dragged the ends of the fences with it.

"The wings are swept back, like a jet," said Troy.

The outhouse on the back had tipped so that now it looked more like a V-shaped tail than ever. They could enter the arcade through it without climbing over the counter.

"Ugh, it stinks," said Toute. "It's like the butt."

The tubes in the radio were glowing. Toute held her hand over them, palm down. "It's warming up," she said. "Bug, the Lectro. In my backpack."

"You don't have to be so bossy," he said, even as he was opening it.

"Sorry," she said (though she didn't sound sorry). "You'd be bossy too if you were so bent you couldn't reach into your own backpack."

"No, I wouldn't," said Bug. He handed her the Lectro, and she poured half the bottle into the sand.

"What happened to the fan?" asked Troy, looking up. The ceiling fan was gone.

"I have practice," said Bug.

Toute gave Bug the Lectro to put back in her pack. They helped her out over the counter on the open side, because she didn't like the smell in the "butt." None of them did.

They walked around to the front. "Whoa, there's the fan!" said Bug. "Now it does look like an airplane."

"Aeroplane," said Troy. The ceiling fan was on the front of the fuselage, just under the front window. It was turning slowly, even though there was no breeze.

Troy stopped it with his hand. When he let go, it started up again.

"This is getting weird," he said.

"We're going to get blamed for this," said Bug. "Let's get out of here."

"Blamed for what? Blamed by who?" asked Toute.

"For making things different."

"Don't be silly," she said. But even she seemed uncomfortable. She got between the two boys and they started through the tunnel.

Troy stopped for one last look. Was it his imagination, or had the aeroplane turned, just a little, so that it was starting to point down the track?

"It's growing, like a plant," Toute said. "Can we come back tomorrow and see what it's grown into?"

"I guess," said Troy.

"I have practice every day this week," said Bug.

☆

"What did you kids do today?" Troy's father asked that night at the table.

"Nothing much," said Troy. "I took Toute for a ride on my bike."

"That's nice," said Troy's mother. "You should take her again tomorrow. Her father has discontinued her treatments, and she. . . ."

"Claire!" said Troy's father sharply. Then they started one of their whisper-arguments.

"Can I be excused?" asked Troy. He wanted to go to his room and think about the aeroplane. He was wondering if it would still be there the next day; wondering if it would fly.

3. INTO THE AIR

The next morning Toute was waiting on her front steps, with her backpack on.

"Don't go in," she said. "It's chaos in there." Chaos was one of her favorite words.

She perched on Troy's crossbar and they rode to the usual tree and picked up Bug. "I brought three Pop-Tarts today," he said.

They left the bikes in the weeds and crawled under the fence and hurried through the tunnel.

They emerged into the light—and there it was. Bug was the first to speak.

"It moved."

The aeroplane—for there was no longer any doubt what it was—was halfway on the track. The front of the arcade, the fuselage, was angled across the start/finish line, pointing up the track. The outhouse was split into a V-tail. The right wing was still in the infield, but the end of the left one drooped onto the hard clay of the track.

The ceiling fan on the front, under the windshield, was turning, very slowly. There were two spoked wheels under the front of the fuselage, though the back still dragged in the dirt.

"It even has wheels," said Troy. He noticed that two wheels were missing off a tipped-over hot dog cart nearby.

"Of course," said Toute. "It wants to be what we want it to be. An aeroplane."

"Maybe it's some kind of car," said Bug.

"With wings? Give me a boost," said Toute. They lifted her through the side window into the plane, and then followed after her. The plywood creaked under their feet.

The tubes in the radio were barely glowing. Toute stirred the white sand with her fingertips. "Needs more Lectro."

"Turn around, I'll get it out of your pack," said Troy.

"I forgot to bring it," said Toute.

"I thought you always carried Lectro," Bug said.

"I forgot it," said Toute. "Just because I don't have practice doesn't mean I don't have a lot of things to worry about."

"There's a Lectro machine in the tunnel," said Troy. "But it's dead."

"Not exactly," said Bug.

"What do you mean?" Toute asked.

"If I get you your Lectro, can we go fishing?"

"Deal," said Toute.

★

Toute and Troy watched from inside the aeroplane while Bug climbed out and crossed the track, and descended into the tunnel. "Aren't you curious?" Toute asked.

"I guess." Troy climbed out and followed Bug at a distance, like a spy.

At the bottom of the tunnel, where it was darkest, the drink machines sat against one wall. There were three of them. Troy had always thought they looked like lurking monsters.

Bug walked up to the center machine and, after looking both ways, kicked it at the bottom.

A light inside came on, illuminating the logo on the front of the machine. *Lectro! With Powerful Electrolytes!*

Bug looked both ways again, then hit the machine once with the heel of his right hand, right under the big L.

A coin dropped into the coin return slot with a loud *clink*.

Cool, thought Troy. Bug had hidden talents.

Bug dropped the coin into the slot at the top of the machine and hit a square button.

A plastic bottle rumbled into the bin at the bottom.

Troy stepped out of the shadows, clapping.

Bug jumped—then grinned when he saw who it was. "I didn't know you were there."

"You have hidden talents!"

"Just because you never notice them doesn't mean they're hidden," Bug said, starting up the tunnel, toward the daylight.

☆

"It's warm," said Bug, as he handed the bottle through the big side window into the plane.

"That's okay," said Toute. She poured half the bottle into the sand. "It's not for drinking. Look."

Troy could see the radio under the front windshield. The tubes were starting to glow, just a little.

He reached for the fan. It started to turn on its own, before he could touch it. He pulled his hand back. Weird!

"I thought we were supposed to go fishing," Bug said.

"Deal," said Toute. "Just give me a hand out of here."

☆

Bug caught twelve and Troy caught nine and even Toute, the girl, caught six. Then they ate their Pop-Tarts. Bug had brought one for each of them this time.

"What's that noise?" said Bug.

They all heard it: a low groaning sound, from the racetrack.

"I'll go see," said Troy.

"I'm going too," said Toute, grabbing his shoulder.

☆

The plane was all the way on the track. The wings were straight, no longer swept back; they drooped at the ends, so that the tips touched the clay. The fan, in the front of the fuselage, was turning so fast that Troy couldn't make out the individual blades.

"This is too weird," he said.

"Or just weird enough," said Toute. "Give me a boost." He helped her inside and followed after her. The tubes in the radio were glowing. Troy put his hand over them; they were warm, like a fire.

"What are you doing?" he asked Toute.

"What do you think?" She was pouring more Lectro into the sand. The fan was turning faster. A weird creaking came from under the floor. Troy knew what it was without looking— the wire wheels turning.

The plane was moving slowly down the straightaway toward the first turn. The fan turned faster and faster, but never as fast as a real propeller on a real airplane. Troy could still see the blades, like a shadow, under the front window— or rather, windshield.

"That's enough!" he said. Toute put the cap back on the Lectro bottle. There was only about an inch left.

"Wait!" It was Bug. He was running alongside, trying to carry his backpack in one hand and grab the wing with the other. "Slow down!"

"No brakes!" Troy hadn't realized the plane was going so fast. And it was going faster all the time. The wingtips were off the ground. "Throw me your backpack," he said.

Bug threw his backpack in through the big side window, then scrambled in behind it. "Careful!" said Toute. "Don't kick a hole in the wing!"

"Ooooomph!" said Bug, landing with a loud thump on the plywood floor. "How do we stop this thing?"

"Why would we want to stop it?" Toute was in the front, by the radio, staring straight ahead, down the track. "Troy, come up here! You have to steer."

"Me?" Troy tried to walk. The plane was lurching from side to side. The wheels were squealing and the plywood was creaking and rattling.

"It's your plane," Toute said. "You discovered it."

"I just found it, that's all," said Troy, joining her at the windshield. "Uh oh!"

The plane was almost at the first turn. It was going to run off the track and into the grass. Maybe, Troy thought, that would be best. It would bounce to a stop and—

"Try the knobs," said Toute.

There were three knobs on the radio. The one in the center was the biggest. Troy turned it to the right, and the plane turned to the right, just a little.

He turned it more.

The plane lumbered on around the first turn, the left wing tip just brushing the weeds at the edge of the track. Troy turned the knob back so the notch was at the top. The plane started down the back straightaway, going faster and faster.

"Fasten your seat belts!" said Toute.

"I don't like this," said Bug.

Troy couldn't decide if he liked it or not. The trees and weeds seemed to speed past, as the plane bounced and rattled down the track. It seemed to Troy that it was the world that was sliding backward while the plane was standing still. Well, almost still; it was bouncing up and down and weaving from side to side.

The little fan was spinning soundlessly under the windshield. Troy had read enough about airplanes to know that it was not nearly big enough to make the plane move. But the plane was moving.

It was not nearly big enough to make the plane fly.

But—

"Whoa!" said Bug.

"We're flying," said Toute. "We're in the air."

It was true. The wheels were no longer squealing and the plywood floor was no longer bouncing up and down. Troy looked down. The track was dropping away, like a rug being pulled out from under them. They were approaching the finish line, where they had started, but this time they were almost as high as the stands—and getting higher.

"Okay, now make it go down," said Bug, looking out the side window.

"Hold on!" said Toute. "Everybody hold on."

Bug made his way to the front and squeezed in between Troy and Toute. "Okay, now make it go down," he said again. "Seriously."

Troy turned the center knob to the right, and the plane banked, following the curve of the track. He started to straighten it for the back straightaway, but Toute pulled his hand away.

"Leave it," she said. "Circling is good."

★

The circles got wider and wider as the plane got higher and higher.

Below they could see the whole track, with Scum Lake in the center, bright green. There was the chain-link fence, with their bikes in the weeds beside it.

There were the streets, the houses, the trees: all in miniature, seen from above.

Troy checked the wings, to the right and to the left. They were straight, then bent upward slightly at the tip. The canvas was stretched tight, except for a few wrinkles that flapped in the wind.

"We're going to get in trouble," said Bug.

Troy and Toute said nothing. What was there to say? They stood on either side of Bug, looking out of the front of the plane as it circled wider, leaving the track behind. There was the usual oak, and Toute's house, with several strange cars in the driveway.

"Doctors," she said scornfully. "Big meeting today."

There was the school, shut down for the summer. The baseball diamond in the back was empty. "At least you're not late for practice," said Troy.

"Not yet," said Bug. "Can't you make it go back to the track?"

"It seems to know where it wants to go," said Troy. "Like a horse or a dog."

"I never had a horse," Toute said wistfully. "Or a dog." Then she clapped her hands. "But this is better!"

The circles got wider and wider and higher and higher. They flew over the center of town. The clock on the courthouse tower said 12:17. A few cars scooted through the streets, under the trees. It was so quiet below that they could hear a screen door slam. They heard a dog bark.

A few people walked on the sidewalks, but they never looked up. *People in our town never look up*, Troy thought. And it was a good thing, too. What would they see? A plywood plane with long, square-tipped, white canvas wings, soaring higher and higher.

At the edge of town, Troy could see the bean fields and a couple of run-down farmhouses; and then the green fields gave way to yellow dunes, some of them as high as a house.

It was just as Troy had always suspected. The town was surrounded by a wilderness of sand. There wasn't a road or even a path leading in or out, as far as he could see.

Troy turned the knob back to the left, so that the notch pointed straight up.

The right wing creaked and came up, the left wing dropped, just a little, and the plane flew straight toward the edge of town.

"Whoa," said Bug, looking alarmed. "What are you doing?"

"Leveling off," Troy said, "Straightening up. Don't you want to see what's out there?"

"No way."

"Out where?" Toute asked.

"Past the town. Past the fields. On the other side of the dunes."

✭

4. Across A Sea Of Sand

The plane flew straight, soundlessly.

It flew straight past the courthouse, between the water tower and the church steeple.

The trees gave way to fields, edged with fences. The last street became a dirt road. Someone was riding a bicycle; someone who didn't look up. The road ended in a field of grass, and the grass gave way to sand.

"I don't think we're supposed to fly out here," said Bug.

"We're not supposed to fly, period," Toute pointed out.

The dunes lapped like waves at the edge of the grass. At first there were patches of grass in the hollows between them; then that green, too, was gone, and all was sand, yellow sand.

"Nothing but sand," said Toute. She looked almost scared.

"Just as I always suspected," said Troy. "Though nobody talks about it, ever." The dunes went on and on as far as he could see. He leaned out the side window and looked back. The town was an island of trees in a sea of sand. It looked too impossibly tiny to be the town where they had all lived, until this very moment.

And it was getting smaller and smaller.

"Time to turn around," said Bug.

"Not yet," said Troy. "Don't you want to know what's out here?"

"No."

"Nothing but sand," said Toute. "A sea of sand."

The plane flew on. Troy stood at the front, at the controls, with his hand on the knob. There was nothing but yellow desert in every direction as far as he could see.

He looked back. The town was just a dark smudge against the horizon. Maybe it was time to turn back.

He turned the knob to the right.

Nothing happened. He turned it back to the left, but the plane flew on, straight. He wiggled the knob from side to side.

Nothing.

"What's the matter?" Toute asked.

"Nothing."

Troy turned the knob each way again, then straightened it with the notch at the top. No need to tell the others; not yet, anyway. It would just worry them.

He stood at the front with his hand on the knob. The sand looked the same in every direction. There were a few smudges of grass, an occasional dark spot where a dead tree poked up through the drifts. But no roads, no houses, no fences.

The plane flew on, tirelessly, soundlessly. Troy stuck his face out the left side, into the wind. The air was hot. It felt like they were going a little faster than a bicycle; a little faster than a boy could run.

"We don't have any food or water," said Bug.

"I have food," said Toute. "Look in my backpack."

Bug pulled out a Pop-Tart. He handed it to Toute, and she sat down beside him and broke it into three pieces.

Troy put his piece on the shelf beside the radio. He was too nervous to eat. He was afraid that if he let go of the knob, the plane would spin to the ground, or fall, or lose its way. He took his hand off the knob, as an experiment; nothing happened. But he felt better at the controls.

"What about water?" said Bug.

Toute passed him the Lectro. "Just a sip," she said. "We may need the electrolytes for power."

"None for me," said Troy.

He looked back toward the town and saw that even the smudge was gone.

He didn't tell Toute and Bug. He didn't want to alarm them. They were sitting on the floor, finishing their Pop-Tarts. The next time he looked Bug was asleep, with his head on Toute's bent, bony little shoulder.

Troy wanted to tell Toute not to worry—or was it himself he wanted to reassure? No matter: when he started to speak she smiled and put her finger to her lips. The next time Troy looked back, she was asleep too.

The dusty vacuum tubes still glowed hot. The fan was turned steadily, a circular shadow pulling them silently through the air.

Troy studied the dunes, looking for landmarks, anything that would mark their way back. Airplanes don't leave tracks. The dunes were like waves, featureless. He searched to the left and the right, but he couldn't even find their shadow passing over the sand.

There were a few shapes in the distance, dark moving specks that might have been rabbits, or horses, or antelopes. It was hard to tell their size or shape.

Then they, too, were gone.

And it was just sand, a sea of yellow sand.

★

5. ANOTHER TOWN

"Look!"

Troy opened his eyes, wider. Had they been closed? Had he been sleeping?

Toute was standing at his side, holding onto his shoulder. Her grip was so strong it almost hurt.

"There's something up ahead."

Bug scrambled to his feet and joined them. Below the windshield, the fan was spinning away. The plane was flying smoothly, silently.

Ahead there was a dark smudge against the horizon.

"Did you turn around?" Toute asked.

"No, why?"

"Because!" Because the smudge ahead looked familiar. The dark was trees. Streets, houses. As they grew closer they saw the water tower, the steeple, the courthouse.

"We're back," said Toute. She sounded disappointed. "You must have turned the plane around."

"I didn't turn anything," said Troy. "Maybe it's like Columbus. You know, all the way around the world."

"Columbus didn't go all the way around the world," said Toute. "And besides, the world is a lot bigger around than that. I hope."

"There's the courthouse," said Bug. "Fly past it so I can see what time it is. Maybe I won't be late for baseball."

"I'll try," said Troy.

As the sand gave way to fields, and then tree-lined streets, the plane responded to the turning of the knob. Troy turned it to the right, and the plane banked right; left, and it banked left. Very gently. Troy was careful to keep it headed for the racetrack, now barely visible on the other side of town.

"Where's the clock?" Bug asked.

There was no clock on the courthouse tower.

"That's weird plus," said Toute, as they flew past.

Everything else was the same. There was the downtown, with a few people walking around. The same people? They were so small, it was impossible to tell.

There was the school, shut down for summer. The baseball diamond was no longer empty though. There were a few ballplayers, hitting flies.

"Whoa, I'm late," said Bug.

"It looks like they're just starting," said Troy. "You can still make it."

"And there's my house!" said Toute. The driveway was empty, except for her father's Windstar.

"Looks like all the doctors have gone," said Troy.

"Good. You should hear them talk. They all talk in big whispers."

Bug was silent, grim, looking worried. Troy ignored him and concentrated on the old racetrack, still far ahead. It seemed that the plane was going slower. It was starting to descend, toward the treetops.

He put his hand over the tubes. "They're not as warm as they were."

"We're losing altitude!" said Bug, pointing at the treetops, getting closer.

Toute opened the Lectro bottle. There was an inch left. She poured it into the sand.

The tubes responded instantly, glowing brighter. The plane nosed up slightly, just clearing the last trees before the old racetrack. Troy turned the knob to the right and the plane started to circle over the track, going slower and slower.

"It knows how to land," Troy said. "It's like a horse; it knows where to go."

He hoped it was true. Toute and Bug didn't look convinced.

Lower and lower they went. The fan was turning so slowly that Troy could see the individual blades, flashing in the sun.

He kept his hand on the knob but the plane followed the track on its own, gliding down over the stands.

The fan was spinning slower and slower; the tubes were glowing dimmer and dimmer.

"Fasten your seat belts," said Troy.

"What seat belts!?"

"It was a joke, Bug." Troy held onto the edge of the shelf that held the radio; Bug held onto the edge of the side window; and Toute held onto both of them as the plane hit the clay track—

It hit, bounced, hit again, bounced. The left wingtip scraped the track, raising a little cloud of dust. The plane hit again, rocked from side to side, rolled—

And rolled to a stop.

Troy opened his eyes and saw Toute just opening hers. Her face was filled with a big grin, a grin that was bigger than she was. She started to clap her hands and Troy joined them, finally realizing that they were not applauding him but the aeroplane.

Bug opened his eyes and joined in.

"Hooray," said Troy.

"But we're on the wrong side of the track," said Bug.

It was true. They were on the back side of the lake, in the middle of the back straightaway.

"So what?" asked Toute.

"How will we explain how it got here," said Bug. "On the wrong side of the track?"

"Who cares?" said Troy. "No one knows we did it."

"They'll know now," said Bug.

"Then we'll taxi," said Toute. She shook the last few drops of Lectro into the sand. The tubes glowed warm again.

The fan, still spinning, spun faster, and the aeroplane moved off at a walk, lumbering around the track with the wings dragging and the wheels creaking. The tubes died again and the plane stopped exactly where it had started, in front of the stands at the start/finish line.

"Later!" Bug tossed his backpack out the side window. "I have my glove in my backpack," he explained, climbing out after it. He stopped and looked back in. "Can you make it okay?"

"I'll help her," said Troy.

"I can make it," said Toute. "Go on ahead."

Bug waved and disappeared into the tunnel, running for his bike.

"So here we are," said Toute. "But. . . ."

"But what?"

"Doesn't it look a little different?"

"The stands," said Troy. They seemed smaller. And there was no wheelless, tipped-over hot dog cart.

"Maybe it's just my imagination," said Toute. She put her arm around Troy's shoulder and they climbed out the back, through the outhouse/tail. It didn't stink as badly as before.

The stands definitely seemed smaller, thought Troy. Some of the board seats were missing. He decided not to mention it; it seemed best not to notice.

With Toute hanging onto his side, they went through the tunnel. It was as dark as before, and there were the machines, lurking in the darkness like waiting monsters. Two of them; hadn't there been three? Troy wasn't sure, and again, it seemed best not to notice. They hurried on through, into the sunlight on the other side.

"Uh oh," said Toute.

The chain-link fence was gone—and worse.

Bug was kicking the weeds, his fists clenched. "My bicycle is gone," he said. "Somebody stole my bicycle!"

True. There was Troy's bike, in the weeds where he had left it—but all alone.

"Maybe somebody found it and took it home for you," said Troy. Even though he didn't believe it.

"Yeah," said Toute. "Everybody knows your bike." It was a Blizzard Trailmaster, with front and rear shocks.

"Let's go," said Troy. "You can still make it to practice."

They walked to Toute's house, pushing Troy's bike between them, with Toute on the handlebars; they dropped her off, and continued to the usual tree.

"Go ahead and take my bike to practice," said Troy.

"It's okay," said Bug, who clearly thought it wasn't. "It's too late anyway."

True: it was getting dark. Bug waved good-bye and started walking home dejectedly.

Troy felt bad. But not too bad. Missing practice seemed a small price to pay for such an adventure. *Bug will get over it*, Troy thought. *He'll remember this and thank me someday.*

☆

Troy rode on home, through the darkening streets. His house was lit up when he got there. And there was a visitor. A little red sports car was parked in the drive. It was a Miata; or rather, almost a Miata. The rear end looked different, and the grill was painted instead of chromed. Maybe a custom?

Troy started around the side of the house, toward the back door—and then stopped.

There was his father in the kitchen, talking to his mother, who was standing at the sink in a yellow dress. But he was smoking a cigarette! And he had a little mustache.

Troy reached for the doorknob—then stopped again. The woman at the sink had turned around. It wasn't his mother at all. She was wearing his mother's yellow dress, but she was younger, with shorter hair and bright red lipstick.

Troy backed up, into the shadow of the trees, almost tripping on the crab apples that littered the ground—the same crab apples he had raked up just the day before. There was a smell of weeds and rot. He watched while his father lit a cigarette and passed it to the woman—not his mother!— who took a drag and then laughed.

A strange laugh, Troy thought, even though he couldn't hear it through the glass. His father gave her a pat on the bottom and they both left the room.

Troy was frozen. He couldn't move and couldn't think. He didn't know where to go or what to think. It was his house, and yet it wasn't. It was his father, but it wasn't; and it was not his mother at all. The kitchen, he noticed for the first time, was painted a different color, although it was the same kitchen.

He tried to remember what color it had been. Yellow, like the strange woman's dress. This kitchen was more the color of sand.

I'll knock on the door and demand to know what's happening, he thought. No, I'll slip upstairs to my room and . . . No, I'll run away, back to the racetrack, and. . . .

And what? He was just starting to get upset when he heard a sound from the trees across the street.

Who-hoot.

Who-hoot.

It was a hoot owl call. Troy stepped out of the shadows and looked toward the street.

There was Bug.

"I found my bike," he said in a loud whisper.

"Where was it? Where is it?" Bug was on foot.

"At home. But something is weird!"

"I know," said Troy. "Here, too. My parents are strange. And my mother is not my mother."

"Come on," said Bug. "Ride me on your bike, back to my house. I'll show you what I mean."

They rode silently through the empty streets to Bug's house, on the other side of town. They left the bike on the street and went around to the back of the house. Through the window, they could see Bug's parents sitting down to dinner. There at the table was—Bug.

"Uh oh," said Troy. "That's you."

"Not me," Bug whispered. "I'm right here."

"Who is it, then?" The boy at the table looked exactly like Bug except that he was wearing a red shirt that said X-Treme. Bug's T-shirt said Go Ahead, Have a Cow.

"I think it's my brother," said Bug.

"But you don't have a brother."

"I did, though. I was supposed to," said Bug. "When I was born I had a twin, but he died. I never knew about it but my mom told me once."

"And that's him?"

"She even named him," said Bug. "His name was Travis, after my dad. That's why I wasn't named after my dad."

Bug's real name was Clarence. He had always hated it.

They crept around the side of the house, by the garage. "And there's my bike."

It was leaning against the garage door. A Blizzard Trailmaster with front and rear shocks.

"Well, get it and let's go," said Troy. "Let's get out of here. This is not our town. Something is wrong."

They rode through the dark, empty streets to Toute's house. They sneaked around to the back, but they couldn't see anything. Toute's house didn't have a kitchen window.

"Just go to the door," said Bug.

"I'm afraid to," said Troy.

"You started all this. Plus, you're her cousin. Nobody will think it's weird if you knock on the door."

Bug hid in the bushes while Troy rang the bell. Instead of the usual ring it played a little song, twice.

Toute came to the door. She was wiping her mouth with a napkin. "Fried chicken," she said.

"Something is wrong," Troy said, whispering.

"I know," said Toute. "I knew it was you. Here." She handed him something wrapped in a greasy paper napkin.

Bug came out of the bushes. "What's that?"

"Fried chicken!"

"We're in the wrong place," said Troy. "My parents are all strange. And Bug's too."

"I know," said Toute. "Mine, too."

"Who's at the door?" a voice called out from inside.

"Just some friends," said Toute. She dropped her voice. "That was my mother. My mother is alive here. She cooked fried chicken! And look, I can walk." She walked in a little circle. "A little sideways, but I can walk."

"That's great, but we've got to get out of here," said Troy.

"We're in the middle of dinner," said Toute. "I'm coming, Mom!" she yelled. Then she whispered again: "You guys have to wait at the plane. I'll come in the morning."

"In the morning? We have to go home!"

"This is my only chance to see my mother," said Toute.

"Can we come in and use the bathroom?" Bug asked.

"No!" Toute whispered. "You'll ruin everything. Besides, boys can pee in the bushes."

She shut the door.

"What if I don't just have to pee?" Bug grumbled.

★

They rode back to the old racetrack, avoiding streets that might be busy, even though few streets in their town were busy after dark. *This isn't our town*, Troy kept reminding himself; *not really. What if we got stopped by a cop? How would we explain who we are?*

They left their bikes in the weeds and entered the track through the tunnel. It was easy without the chain-link fence.

The tunnel was darker and scarier than ever at night, but they knew the way and hurried through, without a word.

Troy felt a moment's fear—what if the plane was gone? How would they ever get back home?

But there it was, right where they had left it, shining in the moonlight.

"What if it rains?" Bug asked. "Look at those clouds."

Troy looked up. He had only thought it was moonlight. There was no Moon, but the clouds high overhead were bright. It was as if they were lighted from the ground. *Even the clouds here are weird*, he thought.

"We'll sleep in the plane," he said. The plane was the only thing that seemed normal, unchanged. The fabric on the right wing was torn where the wingtip had hit the track. The fan in the front was still. Troy spun it with his hand; it spun, then stopped.

They entered the back, through the old outhouse. It still stank, a little. "You can't use this outhouse," Troy said.

"Huh?"

"Didn't you say you needed to—you know?"

"I didn't say I needed to. I said, what if I needed to."

The inside of the aeroplane was just as they had left it. Troy was relieved. The vacuum tubes were cold. The sand in the ashtray was dry.

Bug threw his backpack onto the floor. "I'm hungry," he said.

"Look." Troy unwrapped the greasy napkin Toute had given him. There were two drumsticks inside. They each had one and threw the bones outside, through the side window.

"I'm still hungry," said Bug. "Aren't there any Pop-Tarts left?"

"There's this one." Troy found the third of a Pop-Tart he had left on the shelf by the radio. They shared it sitting on the floor of the plane.

"I wish we had something to drink."

"Well, we don't."

"I'm cold," said Bug.

"It's not cold," said Troy.

They tried using Bug's backpack for a pillow but it was too small for both their heads. Bug took out his glove; it just fit the back of his head. Troy used the backpack. It was lumpy, even empty.

"Why is everything so weird?" Bug asked. They lay side by side, looking up at the plywood ceiling. "If that's my twin, does that mean I'm dead and he's alive?"

"Don't think about it," said Troy.

"What about your mother?"

"Don't think about it," said Troy. It was funny. It had always been his job to make things interesting, but now he felt it was his job to make things as normal as possible. "Just go to sleep. Let's don't talk about it. In the morning maybe it will all look different."

He didn't believe it, but he felt that he had to say it.

★

6. Good-bye! Good-bye!

Morning. Troy woke up wondering where he was, but only for a moment. The plywood ceiling of the plane brought it all back.

He sat up. Where was Bug? Troy was all alone in the plane. But someone was outside, tapping on the windshield.

"Who's there?"

He stood up and saw Bug, outside, sitting on his bike.

"Bug?"

"Who's Bug? Is he the one who stole my bike?"

Troy got it. "Wait a minute," he said. He climbed out the side window. The boy on the bike—Bug's bike—looked exactly like Bug, but Troy knew it wasn't Bug. He was wearing an X-Treme T-shirt.

"He didn't steal it," Troy said. "He just borrowed it."

"I found it out in the weeds. You guys are in big trouble. My dad's a cop."

"So is Bug's."

"So what? Who is this Bug and who are you, anyway, and what is this, some kind of airplane?"

"Aeroplane," said Troy. He introduced himself. He held out his hand for a handshake, but Bug's twin acted like he didn't see it.

"I'm Travis Michael Biggs," he said, "and my father's a policeman, and you are in big trouble if you think you can just steal my bike."

"I told you, we just borrowed your bike," said Troy. "And I can explain."

But where to begin? He was wondering how much he should tell this different, more assertive, and slightly obnoxious Bug, when the real Bug came around the side of the plane, carrying a string of tiny fish.

"Bluegills!" Bug said. "We can build a fire and. . . ."

Then he saw his twin.

"Whoa," he said. "It's me. I mean, you."

"Whoa," said the twin. "Who in the hell are you?"

"I'll find us some firewood," said Troy, "and let you two sort it out."

When Troy got back with enough wood to build a fire, the two were cleaning fish, as if they had known each other all their lives.

"My dad's a cop, too," said Bug. "His name is Travis."

"That's my dad, too," said Travis. "I'm named after him. This is just too weird. You mean there's another town just like this one?"

"Almost," Bug said. "Do you play baseball? What position?"

"First base."

"I'm a pitcher," said Bug. "Sometimes. Sometimes a catcher, too. What's your coach's name?"

"Blaine," said Travis. "He's a jerk."

"Same guy," said Bug. "I'm afraid he won't let me pitch next week because I missed practice."

"No-excuses Blaine," said Travis. "Same guy. But maybe flying in an airplane is a good excuse."

"*Aero*plane," said Troy. "And no grown-ups must know about this. They would go nuts. We have to get back before they find out about any of this."

"So, it actually flies?"

"It does. Do you have a match?"

Once the fire was going, they cooked the tiny filets on sticks. Each boy got half a fish. Cooked down, they were no bigger than candy bars.

"They need salt," said Bug.

"You're not supposed to eat them anyway," said Travis. "I just catch them and throw them back."

"So do we," said Bug. "But I was starving. Still am."

"Have some Pop-Tarts then."

They all looked around. It was Toute. She was reaching into her backpack. "I only brought three, but I already ate breakfast."

"Me too," said Travis, unwrapping the Pop-Tart she gave him. "But I'll have some more."

Toute seemed to notice him for the first time. "And who in the world are you?" She frowned. "Isn't one Bug enough?"

Bug explained, and Troy told what he had seen at his parents' house. Toute nodded as if she understood. *And maybe she does*, Troy thought. Weird was beginning to seem normal.

"How did you get here anyway?" he asked.

Toute grinned and pointed to a bike lying on the track in front of the plane. It was a pink and white girl's bike Troy had never seen before.

"You can't ride a bike," Bug pointed out.

"I can here. Plus, I have a mother, plus—" Toute's grin was almost too wide for her narrow face. "I can walk! I'm not bent. Not so bent, anyway."

She walked in a little circle, just like the night before. She still limped, and dragged one foot, but it was true: she could walk.

"That's great," said Troy. "But we've got to get out of here." He climbed back into the airplane. Toute followed, limping in through the tail.

The tubes were cold. Toute dragged her fingers through the sand in the ashtray. "It's dry," she said. "Plus one of the wingtips is broken."

"The fabric ripped when we landed," said Troy. "Maybe it'll still fly, though."

"Better to fix it," said Toute.

Troy followed her out the back of the plane. She limped to the wingtip, reaching into her backpack as she walked. Troy watched, amazed. She had never been able to do either before.

She pulled out a tube of glue.

"Girls are always prepared," she said. Troy held the fabric tight while she glued it to the wood.

"Good going," he said. "But we still need Lectro. Do you have any left?"

"You saw me shake out the last drops," Toute said. She put the glue away and pointed toward the two brothers, who were sitting on the ground examining a ball glove. "I guess it's up to the Bugsy twins."

They followed Bug down into the tunnel. There were only two soda machines, not three, but nobody except Troy seemed to notice, and he didn't point it out. Things were weird enough as it was.

First Bug hit the bottom of the machine, which should have made the light come on. But it didn't. Then he slammed his fist into the center of the machine, which should have dropped a coin into the coin return. But it didn't.

"You're not doing it right, Clarence," said Travis.

"It's Bug."

"Bug, then. Watch."

Travis kicked the machine on the side and the light came on. Then he slapped the big L above the coin return, and a coin dropped down.

"Let me see that," said Troy.

Travis tossed him the coin.

"There's no hole in it!"

"Of course there's no hole in it," said Travis. "It's real money. Gimme."

Troy tossed it back, and Travis dropped it into the slot and pressed a square button.

A bottle fell with a *thump*.

"It's not Lectro!" said Bug.

"What's Lectro?" Travis opened the bottle and took a swig. "It's Collie Cola—gooder than good." He held out the bottle. "It's warm, though. Here, we can share."

Troy grabbed it. "No way. That's our ticket home. If it works."

"It'll work," said Toute, grabbing it from Troy. "It's like everything else here, the same only different."

★

Troy climbed into the plane and Toute handed him the bottle of Collie Cola through the side window. He poured a thin stream of brown liquid into the sand.

Nothing happened.

"More," said Toute.

He poured in half the bottle.

"Now stir it."

Troy stirred the damp sand with his fingertips. The tubes started to glow.

"See? It's working," Toute said. She touched the fan and it started to spin—slowly at first, then faster.

"Come on, get in, you guys!" Troy said.

"This thing actually flies?" asked Travis.

"That's the idea," said Troy. "Come on, Bug, Toute. Get in. Let's go."

Bug was standing beside his twin on the clay racetrack. Except for their T-shirts, they looked even more alike than ever.

They both looked confused. They both spoke at the same time:

"I wish you would come. It would be cool to have a twin brother."

"I wish you would stay. It would be cool to have a twin brother."

Troy and Toute both laughed. Bug and Travis didn't.

"What I mean is, you could come too," said Bug.

"No way!" said Troy. "We don't know if this thing will even fly again with this stuff. How do we know it will carry four?"

"You could stay here, then," said Travis.

"What about my mom and dad?"

"Same problem here," said Travis.

"Maybe we should switch for a day. But wait, I'm supposed to pitch on Sunday."

"Not if you miss practice," said Travis. "No excuses!"

"Forget switching," said Troy, pouring another inch of Collie Cola into the sand. The fan was turning faster and faster. "There's no way to know we could ever find this place again."

The wheels creaked; the floor lurched under Troy's feet—the plane was starting to move.

"Whoa!" Bug scrambled in through the side window, and Travis passed him his backpack.

Then Travis took off his X-Treme T-shirt and tossed it to Bug. "Swap," he said. Bug took off his Go Ahead, Have a Cow T-shirt and tossed it to Travis.

"What is this, a striptease?" said Toute.

"If you ever want a brother, just look in the mirror," said Travis.

"Cool," said Bug. "I will."

"Come on, Toute!" said Troy. The plane was starting to roll slowly down the track. The wingtips were bobbing up and down.

Toute walked alongside, shaking her head. "I don't think so."

"What!?"

"I'm staying here," she said, picking up her bike.

"You can't stay here! You don't belong here. This is not our real town."

"Yes, it is. It's just as real. And here I can ride a bike."

As if to prove it, she got on and started pedaling alongside the plane.

"Toute, no!" Troy pleaded. The plane was going faster and faster. "If you stay here, what about me? I'll never see you again. I can't come back to get you. I'll get in trouble. They'll say I left you here."

"Left me where? Nobody knows where I am. They probably think I'm at the mall. Nobody knows I'm with you."

"What about your dad?"

"He'll get over it. Plus I have a mother here, remember? And my dad is here."

"Not the same dad."

"Pretty much the same."

"You can't do this!"

"Why not!"

"Because—" Troy could think of a hundred reasons: Because you are part of me. Because we are like brother and sister. Because I love you. But none he could say. "Because you just can't!"

"I have to," said Toute. "I can walk here and ride a bike. Back home, it's just getting worse and worse. I can hear them whispering all the time."

"Don't!" The plane was picking up speed, lumbering toward the first turn.

"Steer, Troy!" said Bug. "We'll hit the wall."

"I will miss you," Toute said, pedaling faster and faster. "You are my best friend. But hey, maybe there's a you here."

"There isn't! There's not!"

"If there is I'll find him. But you have to steer, Troy, look out!"

The left wingtip was scraping the weeds at the side of the track.

Troy turned the knob to the right, and the plane angled into the first turn, still picking up speed.

"Good luck!" said Travis, catching up on his bicycle. "Good luck in the game."

The floor stopped bouncing. The plane began to rise off the ground.

Toute was pedaling faster and faster. Troy was impressed. But she was falling behind—

"What do I tell your dad?"

"Nothing," said Toute, out of breath. "I've already told him. Good-bye, Troy. I'll never forget you, ever, even if I do find another you. And thanks."

"Thanks?"

"For discovering the aeroplane!"

"Bye, Travis!" Bug yelled. "Bye, Toute." They were rising off the track, leaving Travis and Toute behind. When they circled back around, higher and higher, they could see them, standing in the center of the track by their bicycles, looking up and waving.

Then the plane made a broad circle out over the town, and they were left behind, too small to see.

☆

7. Flying Home

Troy remembered that flying in he had followed a line from the courthouse to the racetrack. So he left the same way, flying between the steeple and the water tower, past the clockless courthouse, straight over the town.

They left the streets and trees behind, then the fields. Soon they were flying over trackless dunes again.

"Are you sure this is the right way?" Bug asked.

"Sure," said Troy. He wasn't. And Bug knew he wasn't. They both just wanted to hear him say he was. So he said it again. "Sure I'm sure."

The desert was just sand with an occasional stretch of bare rock, scarred as if by huge claws. The tubes glowed, the fan whirred silently, and the plane flew along at a slow, steady pace, not much faster than a bicycle.

"We should have brought some Pop-Tarts," said Bug. "What if we crash? We'll starve."

"You don't starve when you crash," said Troy. "You just crash. It sort of ends everything."

Troy kept the notch straight up. He was pretty sure this was the way home. But what if the wind blew him off course?

There seemed to be a wind. Below, he could see little puffs of sand along the tops of the dunes. And the occasional bush, in a hollow between two dunes, was shaking as if angry.

And there was a yellow wall of clouds dead ahead.

"It's a storm," said Bug.

"Sandstorm," said Troy. As if calling it by its right name would make it any better.

"Can we go around it?"

Troy shook his head. "I'll lose my bearings."

He kept the notch straight up; they flew straight into the storm. It was all around them, blowing not water and rain but gritty yellow sand. The plane was rocking from side to side. Bug was holding onto the bottom of the window, trying to keep his balance.

He gave up and sat on the floor. "I think we're going to crash," he said. "I still wish we had some Pop-Tarts. What if we survive?"

"Shut up," said Troy. He could barely see out of the windshield. It seemed that the plane was going slower. The wingtips were shaking slowly, up and down. The fabric was rippling, though Toute's repair seemed to be holding.

Then he couldn't see the wingtips anymore. He couldn't see the fan. Everything was yellow, yellow sand. The tubes were looking dim, or was that his imagination? He looked at the Collie Cola bottle. There was less than half a bottle left. A lot less.

Suddenly there was a break in the yellow cloud, and Troy saw white rocks, dead ahead. Was it a mountain, or were they going down? He poured the rest of the brown liquid into the ashtray.

The tubes glowed more brightly, and the front of the plane picked up. The right wing dropped, and the rocks were gone.

"We're turning," said Bug.

Troy wished he would shut up. Bug was becoming the bearer of bad news. "I know."

There didn't seem to be any point in standing at the controls, since the plane did what it wanted to do anyway. And it was hard to breathe. Troy had sand in his eyes, and it gritted between his teeth.

Bug was on the floor, looking like a bandit, with the collar of Travis's X-Treme T-shirt pulled up over his nose. Troy sat on the floor beside him, and covered his nose with his own T-shirt, which didn't say anything. He could breathe but he could hardly see.

There was nothing to see anyway. He closed his eyes. The plane circled higher and higher, shaking, creaking and groaning, through the storm.

Then all was still.

★

Troy opened his eyes. Bug was asleep. The sand was gone, except for the grit in his eyes and on the floor and between his teeth.

He wiped his eyes and stood up.

They were still circling, in calm cold air. The stars shone high overhead like little chips of ice. "I'm cold," said Bug, waking up. He joined Troy at the controls.

The sandstorm was like a yellow smudge far below. It was still daylight down there. For some reason, Troy found this encouraging.

He tried the knob, left, then right. The plane dipped its wings, left, then right. Troy centered the knob and it straightened out. They were flying straight again—but straight to where?

Then Bug, the bearer of bad news, brought some good news. "Look!"

Far off to the left, there was a dark spot on the horizon. *Our town?* Troy wondered.

There was only one way to find out. Turning the knob to the left, he headed the plane toward it.

"Think that's our town?" Bug asked.

"For sure," Troy lied.

The boys held their breath, waiting and watching.

Hoping.

The plane was descending.

The smudge on the horizon grew into a blur of trees and streets and houses, looking more and more familiar. There was the courthouse, and the water tower, and the church steeple.

Still descending, the plane flew past the courthouse. Both Troy and Bug were relieved to see that it had a clock.

It was 1:37.

"I can still make it to baseball," Bug said.

"A day late," Troy reminded him. As soon as he said it, he wished he hadn't.

"Maybe Blaine won't notice," he added lamely.

There were a few people on the street, but they didn't look up as the plane flew over. *If they did, what would they see?* Troy wondered. The wings, white, with ads for bread and candy, cars and cola. The fuselage, a long square plywood tube, open on one side. Wire wheels spinning slowly in the onrushing air. A V-tail, slightly cockeyed, and the propeller, a ceiling fan, turning slower and slower as they descended.

"There's your house, Toute," said Troy. Then he remembered that she was no longer with them.

"Look at all those cars," said Bug.

Toute's driveway and the street in front of her house were packed with parked cars.

Troy saw what looked like his father's car—not the little sports car, but the big white Olds. He looked down at the crowd of people at the door, trying to see if his parents were among them. It was hard to tell. They were all dressed alike, in suits and ties.

"Hey! Pay attention," said Bug.

Troy looked out the front. The plane was too low. It was not going to make it over the last row of trees before the old racetrack.

Troy turned the dial to the left, and then to the right, banking the plane between two trees. He leveled off with the stands dead ahead. With the last drop of Collie Cola, he brought the nose up, barely missing the top row of seats.

"We're going to hit the lake," Bug said. "And drown."

"It's not deep enough," said Troy. "Shut up and fasten your seat belt."

He spun the dial and dropped the left wing. The wingtip scraped the track and the plane landed sideways, skidding, teetering first on one wheel, and then on the other.

CRUNCH!

☆

Everything was dark. It's always dark like this down among the roots, Troy thought, where the Teeny-Weenies live. It's okay, though. Toute knows the way. "Let's go back up," he said to her. "It's too dark."

"You go on," she said.

"I don't know the way."

"Sure you do."

"Come on!" said Bug.

Huh?

It was light. Bug was dragging him out of the back of the plane.

"Hey! You're getting splinters in my butt!"

"You crashed us!" Bug said. "It's going to burn!"

187

"Let go of me! It's not full of gas, it runs on water and sand. How can it burn?"

"I guess you know everything," said Bug, dropping him. "I was trying to save your life."

"Sorry. Thanks." Troy stood up, his feet slipping. The track was muddy. The ground felt funny, after the air.

The plane was a mess. One wing had come off and landed in the mud along the infield, where it looked like a fallen fence.

The other was still attached to the fuselage, which was half in and half out of the infield. The tail was tipped over, like a fallen outhouse.

"Looks like there's been a storm here, too," said Troy. "Are you okay?"

"I'm okay, but I'm late." Bug was already heading for the tunnel, his backpack over his shoulder.

Troy followed him across the track and into the tunnel. They splashed through water at the bottom. The drink machines were dark, like sentinels. There were three of them. Outside, the hole under the chain-link fence was filled with water from the storm.

They climbed over instead of under.

Their bikes gleamed in the weeds, looking like they had just been washed. Bug got on his Blizzard and bounced the wheels, as if making sure it was real. "I can still make practice if I hurry."

"Go, then."

"What are you going to tell them about Toute?"

"I don't know. I'll think of something."

But the fact was, it was hard to think of anything. The place where Toute had been was like a hole in Troy's thoughts as he rode toward home. Her memory was like a dark patch he couldn't look into—but couldn't look away from, either.

★

"Where have you been!" Troy's father demanded, when he opened the door. Troy couldn't look at him; he kept remembering the little mustache. He looked away.

"It's okay." His father squeezed his shoulder in that way that fathers do. "I know you are upset. Your mother is over at William's house now. I was there all day."

William was Troy's dad's brother, Toute's father.

"Toute—" Troy began.

"Toute died peacefully in her sleep," said Troy's father. "William was waiting for it. He was prepared. She was prepared, too. She knew for a week, he said. I'm surprised she hadn't said anything to you. You two are so close. Were so close. Anyway, get dressed. Your mother is already there, and we are expected for the memorial. She laid your suit and tie out on your bed. Get dressed and I'll help you tie your tie."

✦

8. ALMOST HOME

Troy hardly recognized Toute at the funeral, she looked so still and so straightened out. He tried to cry because everyone else was crying, but he couldn't. So he just sat with his eyes almost closed. It was like getting through a sandstorm.

In the days that followed he missed her, but he knew where she was. He even knew what it was like there, and what she was doing: riding her bike. Eating fried chicken.

Troy was in far less trouble than he had expected. He was surprised to find that his parents thought he had spent the night with Bug. Nor was Bug in trouble, either. He told his parents he had spent the night with Troy after they had been caught in the storm. Luckily, the phone lines had been down all night.

It was several days before the two boys met at the usual tree and rode to the old racetrack on the outskirts of town. The drink machines still lurked like monsters in the tunnel, but when Bug kicked the center one, no light came on.

"The rain must have ruined it," Bug said. He was wearing the X-Treme T-shirt. No one had noticed, he said.

Troy wasn't surprised. "Grown-ups never really read T-shirts," he said.

The aeroplane was in pieces on the track and in the infield. The track was still muddy in spots.

One good effect of the storm: the scum was almost all gone from the lake. *We may have to change the name*, Troy thought. It wasn't Scum Lake anymore.

While Bug went to get worms, Troy lay face down on the end of the dock. He could see all the way to the bottom. There was a concrete block, and a tire. Then, as he watched, a great blunt shape swam out of the shadows and stopped, right under him.

He started to call Bug, but didn't. It was better to be silent and watch. He wished Toute were there to see it. She would have liked it. She always liked it when weird things got real.

GREETINGS

Most things may never happen:
This one will . . .
                    —Philip Larkin, Aubade

ONE

It started out with a tangle, which should have been a sign. Tom's first concern, after his initial raw animal terror, was how to break the news to Ara; so he called Cliff and asked for help, telling him not to tell anyone, at least until he got there. But Cliff was already on the phone with Pam, who was meeting Arabella at the farmers' market, and so by the time Tom got to Cliff's (walking across the golf course, even though it was prohibited) "the girls" had already dropped their bikes in the yard and were waiting in the kitchen.

They were all best friends, old friends ("At our age," Tom liked to joke, "all your friends are old.") and so Tom wasn't surprised or, after he thought about it, even annoyed to see them. It made it like an event, a ceremony of sorts, which seemed proper. And the terror had receded to a dull dread: a fear no less animal, but more domesticated, which he was to learn to live with over the next ten days, like a big, ugly, dun-colored dog.

"What's this, Cliff, an intervention?" he asked.

"Don't make this into a joke," Arabella warned. She was known for bursting into tears but only for the little things: a fender bender, a dropped dish, a goldfish floating on the top of the water. Her hand was damp as it found Tom's under Cliff and Pam's old-wood kitchen table.

"Start at the beginning," said Cliff, who was a lawyer, though he didn't practice anymore. "Guess he finally got it down," Tom liked to joke, though he didn't feel like joking this morning. It was 11:25, almost lunchtime. It was mid-October, and most of the leaves that were due to go that year were gone.

"It's pretty simple," Tom said, though *pretty* wasn't exactly the word. "I got it an hour ago, when I checked my mail. Certified. Here, I printed it out."

He laid it on the table, flattening it with the heel of his hand. Under the official US logo, it read:

GREETINGS Thomas Aaron Clurman (401-25-5423)
YOU HAVE BEEN CHOSEN BY LOTTERY FOR INDUCTION INTO THE OREGON SUNSET BRIGADE. CONGRATULATIONS ON YOUR SACRIFICE. YOU ARE TO REPORT TO CASCADE CENTER 1656, 18767 WEST HELLEN ST, AT 10 AM, OCTOBER 22, 20—. IF YOU WISH TO DISCUSS OTHER ARRANGEMENTS, AS PROVIDED BY LAW, PLEASE CALL 154 176 098 8245.

"That's only ten days from now," Pam said. "The bastards."

"They don't want to give you time to think about it," said Cliff, who was serving coffee to everyone.

Arabella burst into tears.

"Come on, honey. What am I, a goldfish?"

"I don't get it," said Cliff, sitting down. The coffee was imported directly from the growers in Costa Rica. "I thought they weren't drafting anyone under 75."

"Guess now they are." Tom folded the notice and put it into the pocket of his L.L. Bean chamois shirt. "The law says three score and ten, doesn't it?"

"The bastards," said Pam.

"That's the Bible, not the law," said Cliff. "Maybe it's the death rate in Africa. I read where some new vaccine has lowered the infant mortality rate by 34 percent."

"Whatever," said Tom, suddenly irritated by Cliff's interest in world events. "At any rate, last summer we talked about what we would do, remember? No way I'm marching off with the Sunset Brigade, so I'll need your help; Ara and I will need your help." He squeezed Arabella's hand.

Arabella was slow in squeezing back.

"Well, of course," said Pam. "But isn't there something we need to do first, some. . . ?"

"There's no appeal process," Cliff said. "There are options, of course. And we're with you a hundred percent, Tom. We all feel the same way you do."

Do you really? thought Tom. "Right. Anyway, maybe Arabella and I should talk first, and see you guys later."

"Yes, later," said Pam. "Tonight's card night anyway. Come early for dinner."

"Should we bring anything?" asked Arabella.

"Just yourselves," said Pam. "The bastards."

✳

Walking home, around the golf course, Tom and Arabella were silent. He walked her bike, which was, he thought, sort of like holding hands. Now, when there was everything to talk about, there was nothing to say. How come the world looks so bright? Tom wondered. So various, so beautiful, so new . . .

"You and Cliff were stoned that night at Holystone Bay," said Arabella. "It isn't all that easy to, you know, do-it-yourself."

"Stoned but sincere," said Tom. "What do you want me to do, join the Brigade?"

"I don't want any of it. There must be something we can do. We should call the kids."

"Not yet," said Tom. "It's not their problem. Besides, Gwyneth was just here last week. Thomas is another matter altogether."

"Thomas always was."

※

That night Pam cooked pasta. Cliff brought out a bottle of wine from his own vineyard.

"It must have been Africa," he said. He showed them the article in *The Economist*. A new vaccine had reduced the infant mortality rate and therefore, it was speculated, adjustments would have to be made in the death rates in the "developed" countries.

Tom had never had a problem with this before. Neither had Cliff. America had reaped the benefits of selective underdevelopment for hundreds of years. Now they were making up for it.

But tonight, drinking Cliff's Willamette Valley *pinot noir* and looking out over the golf course, Tom found it alarming that someone else's good fortune was his bad luck. Did this mean that life was a zero sum game after all; and that the humanistic, liberal philosophy that had guided him and Cliff for most of their fifty-odd years as friends, was false; based on a false premise—that the greatest good for all and the greatest good for one were in some sort of deep, unwritten, unspoken but unbreakable harmony? Now the world, lopsided or not, was about to spin on without him.

It was, quite literally, unimaginable.

"I think they're after the opposition," Pam was saying. "The bastards."

"We're hardly the opposition," Cliff pointed out. "In fact you might recall we're among those who supported the hemlock laws as a progressive move; a willingness to think and act in global terms."

"But not the Brigades," said Tom. "Not those smiling marching fuckers with their little flags."

"What about the Resistance?" Pam asked.

"That's an urban legend," said Cliff.

"Wishful thinking," said Tom. "A token opposition at best. Look, there's no point in talking about how to beat this. We're not kids. I'll be seventy-one in August. I've had my three score and ten."

"So has Cliff," said Pam, who was sixty-six herself. "I still say there's something fishy about it. How many friends do we have who've gotten Greetings?"

"Guy Frakes, from the firm," said Cliff.

"Not exactly a friend. And he was almost eighty," said Pam.

"Seventy-seven," said Cliff.

"That's what he told you."

"You're not going to get that many anyway," said Cliff. "The Brigades are just a symbol, showing our willingness to adjust the death rate rationally. Most of the quota is made up by DNRs and end-term care reductions."

"And it's all guys," said Tom. "That was a great victory of the women's movement."

"Huh?" said Pam, showing her teeth.

"Look, it's a law of nature. All this does is put us into some sort of compliance," Tom said. He was amazed, listening to himself, at how self-assured he sounded. "Besides, we already decided what to do about this. Remember? We talked about it."

"You mean last summer, at the beach house," said Pam. "You guys were stoned."

"What does being stoned have to do with it?" Cliff protested. "It was after we watched that PBS special on the Brigades, before they had their weekly show."

"It was disgusting," said Tom. "Enlightening, really. All those geezers in their orange uniforms marching off into the sunset."

"Some were even volunteers," said Cliff.

"Cancer patients," said Tom. "They joined for the last cigarette."

"I don't see why you have to make a joke of it," said Arabella.

"It's no joke," said Tom. "It's my life and I want to go out like I lived, with my friends, with dignity. With some dignity, anyway. At home. Listening to Coltrane, or Bob Dylan."

"And stoned," said Cliff. "Why not. I'll take care of that part."

"We'll all do our part," said Pam. She reached out for Arabella's hand. "You can count on us."

"Me too," said Tom. "I'll check out. End of story. That'll be it."

It. They were all silent. Tom reached for the wine bottle, and saw that it was empty.

"It's just that we never really thought it would happen," said Arabella.

"No, but how many people live to be this old anyway? Better than dying of cancer." Although Tom wasn't as sure as he sounded. At least cancer didn't give you a date.

"It's even legal," said Cliff, "not that that matters. Oregon has a law making it legal to do it at home. Every state except Kentucky and Arkansas has them—it was a rider that defused some of the opposition to the Brigades."

"So what do we—do?" Arabella asked, pouring herself the last few drops of wine.

"We open another bottle," suggested Tom.

"I checked out the law at lunch," said Cliff. "All you have to do is show the Greetings, and you get the hemlock kit. It can all be done at the drugstore."

"How convenient," said Pam. "The bastards."

✳

Two

The next morning, Tom, Pam and Arabella went to Walgreens for the kit. They were sent to the pharmacy counter at the back of the store.

The pharmacist was a young man of about forty-five. He had a Sunset Brigade Certificate on the wall: a picture of his father, the former owner of the store, saluting a sunset. *Living Forever In Our Hearts*, it said.

"Can I help you?" he asked.

Tom seemed to have lost his voice.

"We need one of those kits," Pam said, because Arabella wasn't speaking up either. It seemed that she had lost her voice too.

"One of those what?"

Pam took the induction notice from Tom's hand; she unfolded it and spread it out on the counter. "They sent us back here to get it."

"Oh, the home kit." The pharmacist looked at Tom. "It's $79.95."

"Jesus," said Pam. "Eighty bucks? What do you get?"

"You get an IV rack," the pharmacist said. "You get the three chems; the sharps and the sterile solution; cotton swabs; death certificate; plastic bags . . ."

Arabella looked sick. "I'm going to wait in the car," she said.

Tom started to follow her but something held him back. *This is my show.* The pharmacist reached under the counter and set a beige box on the counter. "There's a DVD, too," he said. "Do you have a DVD player?"

"Everybody has a DVD player." Tom's voice was back.

"Well, there's a DVD that comes in the kit. And this 800 number here on the side is for the monitor. But you don't have to worry about that, he'll be calling you. As soon as I make this sale, your number goes into the database."

"Monitor?" Pam sounded suspicious.

"There has to be someone there from the government," the pharmacist said. "You're using lethal drugs."

"But they're supposed to be lethal," said Tom.

"Doesn't matter," the pharmacist said. "It's the law. It's not an extra cost. Although I hear some people tip him."

"Ring it up," said Tom.

Arabella was waiting by the car, in the parking lot. "Cliff just called," she said.

"And?"

"Better let him tell you." And she burst into tears, for the second time.

✳

Cliff had gotten his notice at the office. He went in two days a week. He wasn't practicing but mentoring a younger attorney.

"This makes things simpler," he said, spreading it out on

his kitchen table. It looked exactly like Tom's, except that the date was three days later.

GREETINGS William Clifford Brixton III (401-25-5423)
YOU HAVE BEEN CHOSEN BY LOTTERY FOR INDUCTION INTO THE OREGON SUNSET BRIGADE. CONGRATULATIONS ON YOUR SACRIFICE. YOU ARE TO REPORT TO CASCADE CENTER 1656, 18767 WEST HELLEN ST, AT 10 AM OCTOBER 25, 20—. IF YOU WISH TO DISCUSS OTHER ARRANGEMENTS, AS PROVIDED BY LAW, PLEASE CALL 154 176 098 8245

"Simpler!?" said Pam.

"I mean now it's unanimous, or something."

"Like, we don't count?" said Arabella.

"That's not what I said," said Cliff. "Not what I meant."

"Do you really want to count?" Tom asked. "I mean, this is one battle the women's liberation movement didn't want to win."

"Leave the women's liberation movement out of this," said Pam. "So what do we do now?"

"The same thing we were already doing," said Cliff. "Same time, same station. Another kit."

"Jesus! Isn't one enough?" Tom asked. "We've always shared everything before."

"And we're sharing this," said Cliff. "But it's the law. You have to have one for each—inductee."

✱

THREE

The next day, a Wednesday, Tom went with Cliff and Pam to picked up the second kit at the drugstore. This time they got another pharmacist; a more sympathetic, older man—African-American.

Was it just a convention of the movies, or were African-Americans always more sympathetic? Tom wondered. It was always either that or angrier, never both at once, as in real life.

Real life. It has a beginning. It has an end. It's almost over.

"There are several alternate-exit program DVDs," the pharmacist was saying. "Made to coordinate with the official kit. You can get them at Tower Records or order them from Amazon. Or your church may provide one. It's more personal."

✳

"Two by two," said Cliff, laying the two kits side by side on the kitchen table. "Like Noah's ark."

"Not exactly," said Tom.

The woman were away, at the Aerobics for Seniors class that they shared. Life had to go on, after all.

It will go on, Tom thought. Without me. It was, quite literally, inconceivable.

"Let's smoke a joint," said Cliff. He pulled out the silver cigarette case he had received after twenty years at his law firm. In it were six neatly rolled joints, the finest *sinsemilla*, a week's supply.

That afternoon, as luck would have it, the Brigades had their weekly show. It was afternoon TV; not quite ready for prime time. The celebrity guest was introduced to do the invocation. It was almost always a woman.

This week it was Hillary Clinton.

The Sunset Brigade, in rose-colored coveralls, were lined up on a hill overlooking the sea. Their eyes were shining; their jaws were firm. The veterans got to wear their military braid. The theme was a French horn/piano concerto especially written for the Brigades by Randy Newman.

Tom turned off the sound.

"You get an extra four days," he said, looking at Cliff's induction notice.

"Three," said Cliff. "I'm not going to take them, though. We'll go together. It'll be easier on the girls that way."

"You think so?"

"I know so." Cliff passed Tom the joint. Hillary got thin, scattered applause. The Brigade saluted the flag and started up the hill. Judging from the vegetation, this induction was taking place somewhere in the East. Massachusetts? New Jersey? The East, like the West, looked all alike.

There was nothing to distinguish the draftees from the volunteers, except for the few who were in wheelchairs with IVs on little masts. They marched (or rolled) off, shoulder to shoulder in their rose uniforms and easy-off slippers, following the color guard off to the departure site, which was always over a hill and never seen. They carried little individualized flags their wives and grandchildren had made. The flags would be returned to the loved ones.

When the last of the men disappeared over the hill, Cliff turned the sound back on. The closing theme was by Elton John: another version of "Candle in the Wind."

Tom turned it off.

"Better to do it our own way," said Cliff.

"Anything is better than that clown show," said Tom.

"What are you guys watching?" Pam asked, bursting through the door like Kramer, as she always did.

Always, thought Tom. Always was almost over. For him, anyway. And for Cliff, too.

"Nothing," said Cliff, turning off the TV. "Some dumb reality show."

✳

Tom had Arabella had never had trouble making love, even though the frequency had dropped. Once they had gone for a whole year. But when he turned sixty-five Tom had decided that they were going to set aside a day every two weeks for sex play, like it or not. It turned out that they liked it; liked being freed of the need to think about it and initiate it. At least he did.

But today something was wrong.

"Not a problem," said Arabella. "Easy for you to say," said Tom.

Ara saw no point in arguing. She got out of bed and dressed, pulling on her regular panties, the ones he hated, the ones that made her look like an old lady. "How about I make us some coffee?"

"Later," said Tom. "First I got to go see Ray."

✳

Ray was Tom's lawyer. His office was in a trendy new shopping center overlooking the Rose Garden. His desk top was of recycled barn wood. Odd, thought Tom, how many things in the new world get more valuable as they get older.

Everything but us.

"What can I do you for?" asked Ray.

They were old movement comrades, if not exactly friends. They had once been adversaries, since Ray was of the electoral persuasion, and Tom and Cliff were Direct Action.

But that was long ago.

Tom unfolded his induction notice and flattened it along Ray's desk, looking out for splinters.

"Jesus fucking Christ," said Ray. "Are you sure this isn't a mistake?. I thought they weren't calling anyone under seventy."

"I'm seventy," said Tom, refolding the paper. For the first

time he noticed its color and shape, like a tiny tombstone. "So are you."

"Well, you get certain advantages," said Ray. "There's the bonus. And there is no probate, which means you won't have to worry about Arabella. I mean, in terms of the house and stuff."

"We don't get the bonus," said Tom. "We're not doing it."

"Not doing it?" Ray looked uncomfortable.

"Not doing the Brigade thing. There's a provision in the law that allows you to do it yourself, at home. We're going to do it at our summer place, down at Holystone Bay."

Ray nodded. He had done the paperwork on the partnership twelve years before, when Tom and Ara had bought the house with Cliff and Pam. Ray had provided for every possible disagreement. There had been none. If anything, the two families were closer now than they had been then, when they had been cautiously, consciously, determinedly recovering from Cliff and Arabella's foolish, brief, unhappy affair.

"I want you to make sure Arabella is covered. And one other thing. I want you have my Steve Earle records."

"Jesus, man. That's huge. But what about Cliff?"

"Cliff too. Cliff's going with me."

"Jesus fucking Christ. Cliff too! I've always hated these Brigades, even though I agree with the idea, I guess. But this stinks."

"I don't know why you say that," said Tom. "We've always felt that it wasn't right for the developed countries to use all the resources. Well, here it is, population control. It's not abortion or infanticide. It's voluntary. Or sort of, anyway."

"Nobody fucking volunteers," said Ray. "Not for—this."

"Well. Let's not abandon all our principles just because our number came up."

Ray was silent. Tom realized he had been lecturing him. It was an old habit he had never managed to lose. "Sorry," he said. "I was on a high horse."

"It's OK," Ray said. "I've always rather liked your high horse. And now—"

He blushed and shuffled through a stack of papers.

"You need to sign a power of attorney for Arabella," he said. "I have one on boilerplate. It will avoid probate. Especially since you and Arabella aren't actually married."

"What about the domestic partners law?"

"They still contest that occasionally," said Ray. "What if they wanted to get even."

"For what?"

"For doing things your own way. Here. You sign it and I'll get Arabella's signature after. I mean, later."

Tom signed the papers and got up to leave. Ray came around his desk and stopped him at the door.

"I don't know what to say, man."

"I'm sorry I lectured you. It's just, a shock, you know."

"It is to me, too. I don't know what to say, man."

"That's OK. Just so long, I guess."

"It's been great knowing you."

"Likewise," Tom said. And he meant it. It was his first goodbye. "So long."

✳

When Tom got home, Cliff and Pam were at the house. Cliff laid a ticket on the glass-topped table. It had a red-white-and-blue border.

"What's that?" asked Tom.

"Your airline pass," said Cliff. "I figured you might want to see your kids."

"What about your kids?"

"We just saw them last month," Pam said.

The pass was good for one round trip in the continental U.S.A.

"I thought we didn't get them if we did it ourselves."

"I fooled them," said Cliff. "I turned my kit back in, told them I'd changed my mind."

"You didn't—"

"No, no. I'll go back and get it again. Change my mind again. I have ten days to decide, remember?"

"I could have done that," said Tom.

Cliff shook his head. "You're not a good liar," he said. "I'm a lawyer, remember? Or didn't you notice that big car parked outside?"

After Cliff left, Arabella asked: "Who are you going to see?"

"Thomas," he said.

"I thought so," she said.

✳

FOUR

Tom and Arabella had two kids. Thomas, from Tom's first marriage, was a loan officer in Las Vegas. Thomas and his wife Elaine had two kids. If it had been possible, they would have had 1.646, thought Tom—the national average. The only child actually born of Tom and Arabella was Gwyneth, thirty, a kindergarten teacher in San Francisco.

She was Tom's favorite but he had seen her just the week before. She knew he loved her.

Thomas was more of a problem.

On Monday, with four days left to go, Tom caught a flight for Las Vegas. It felt strange to be leaving Arabella, this close to the end of everything. Tom, who used to be terrified of landings, noticed as the plane descended that he wasn't nervous anymore. Everything in the world looked so temporary—-what was a plane filled with people, more or less?

He was a little disappointed when the landing, like the twenty-three that had preceded it that day, or the 223 that had preceded it that week, went off without a hitch.

Thomas met him at the gate, looking worried. "Something wrong?" he asked.

"Why should something be wrong?"

"You don't usually come and visit us here except on holidays," said Thomas. "In case you didn't notice. And Arabella usually comes with you."

"I just felt like seeing the grandchildren," said Tom. "And you and Elaine, of course."

Traffic in Las Vegas was even slower than Tom had remembered. The leather seats and quiet ride of the big Mercedes made it worse, not better.

Thomas and Elaine put him in the guest room, which had its own bath.

"Makes it feel like a motel," he said to Arabella, on his cell phone.

"It's their world," said Arabella. "People want to have their own bathroom. Sharing a bathroom seems old fashioned, and probably a little unsanitary, I guess."

"Makes it feel like a motel," Tom said again.

"Just be nice," she said, "and hurry home."

✳

The next afternoon Tom took his grandchildren to the zoo.

Tara wanted to see the gorilla that had died the month before. She naively thought its body would still be on display. Eric wanted to talk about his day at school. Tom was impressed—how many kids want to talk about school? Until he heard what it was.

"We got a visit from the Sunset Brigade," Eric said. "Two men came by the school in their uniforms and told us to take good care of the planet because they were leaving it to us, to take good care of it. We got a signed certificate. It was cool."

"I'll bet," said Tom.

"Will you join the Brigade when you get old, grandpa?"

"I'm already old," said Tom. "And I think the Brigades are horse shit."

✳

"Grandpa said the S word today," said Tara at the dinner table, right after Thomas had said grace. "Pass the mashed potatoes."

"Say 'please,'" said her mother, Elaine.

"I was overexcited," said Tom. "It must have been the gorilla."

"There wasn't any gorilla," said Eric.

That evening Tom gave the grandchildren a good-night kiss and Thomas took him to the airport to catch the red-eye back to Portland. There is always a red-eye to everywhere from Vegas.

"Dad," said Thomas. "The kids aren't old enough to share your values. I mean about the Brigades and the government."

"They may never get that old," Tom said. "You didn't."

"You may recall, I was never given the chance," said Thomas. Tom had abandoned his first family when he had gone underground with the Red Storm.

"That was my mistake," said Tom. "It doesn't mean I don't love you today."

"I know, Dad. And I know how you feel about the Brigades."

"You do?"

"Sure. It's how you feel about everything. Resistance. Rejection. Rebellion. Is there something you wanted to tell me?"

"Just that—I am proud of you, you know. You're a much better father than I ever was."

"Not such a stretch," said Thomas; then he laughed and clapped his father on the shoulder, a glancing blow. "I noticed you didn't say 'better man.'"

"I meant that too."

"I know, I know. Well, Dad, this is as far as I can go without a ticket."

They hugged and parted. Tom had taken great pains not to show his son his red-white-and-blue ticket. He waved good-bye and disappeared down the tunnel, through the gauntlet of bored security guards.

✳

FIVE

"Wainwright is opening the house," said Pam, when she met Tom at Portland International. "We're all set up to head down tomorrow."

"Tomorrow?"

"Well, we all thought we could go down early and get a day at the beach before, you know . . ."

"Before we do *it*," said Tom. He was finding a perverse pleasure in reminding others what this was all about. Even Arabella. Even though he didn't want to say what "it" was any more than the others did.

He slept late. When he got up, Ara was packing groceries, tears running down her face.

"We knew this had to happen," he said, putting his arms around her from behind.

"That doesn't make it any easier," she said.

While she finished packing, he found himself walking through the rooms, saying goodbye to the Salter Street house. It wasn't as hard as he would have thought. He had said goodbye to lots of houses in his day. And this house was more Arabella's than his anyway, even though they had bought it together, almost twenty years before.

It was Ara's garden he found hardest. She made sure it was all watered before she left. These plants will continue to grow, he thought. They will still be growing in their mindless, stupid way, while I will be no more.

No more.

"Heere's Johnny!" said Cliff, pulling up in his yellow Cadillac.

The drive from Portland to Holystone Bay was three hours, over the dark, tangled ridges of the Coast Range. It was a quiet drive. The four of them, who had talked nonstop about everything for twenty years, couldn't think of anything to say.

It was raining when they crossed the last ridge and saw the ocean with the great holed rock that gave the bay, and its smattering of a town, its name. The house was cold. The wind rattled through the boards. Tom fired up the wood stove while Cliff hauled in the groceries and Arabella and Pam put them away.

"Brrrr," said Cliff. "This house was never designed for winter."

"It's fall," said Pam.

"It was never designed for any of this," Tom said grimly.

"Well, it'll have to do," said Cliff. He set the beige box on the table, which was made of driftwood planks, salt-whitened—like bone, Tom thought.

"Stop it," he said, to himself.

"Huh?" asked Pam from the kitchen door. "What?"

"Nothing."

There was knock at the front door. Tom opened it, and stepped back—shocked at the figure on the stoop.

Death, in a yellow hood. No—

Not yet.

A young woman was on the stoop, dressed in a yellow raincoat, hood up, dripping wet.

"Can I help you?"

"I'm Karin," the young woman said. "With an I. Your midwife."

"Midwife?"

"I mean M-monitor," she said, standing first on one foot and then the other. "Monitor. For the induction."

"That's not until tomorrow," said Cliff.

"I know, but I thought I . . ."

"Come in out of the rain," said Arabella from the kitchen door.

Tom closed the door behind her and she stood, dripping all over the rag rug. Arabella took her raincoat and gave her a towel. Instead if drying her hair with it, she put it around her shoulders like a shawl. She was very tall and thin.

"You must be Arabella," she said, using two fingers to squeeze the rain out of her stringy blond hair; it fell, hissing, onto the wood stove. "I know all your names from the social security database. My name is Karin, with an I. I know it's not until tomorrow—"

Even *they* call it *it*, thought Tom, with a certain grim satisfaction.

"—but I came early, because I have never seen the Oregon coast," she said, "and I thought I would make it sort of a little vacation. The state pays for three days for out-of-the-way places. I'm staying up the road at the Spyglass Lodge."

"The only place around," said Cliff. "Wainwrong's place."

"How did you get here?" asked Pam, looking outside for a car.

"I walked. They don't give us a car. They give us cab fare but there are no cabs. There's no anything here."

"You got that right," said Tom.

"I didn't mean to intrude," Karin said. "I just came by to say hello and introduce myself. I don't usually do . . . this sort of thing."

"We don't either," said Tom.

"Sit down," said Pam. She set an extra place for dinner. Ara cooked frozen shrimp imported from South Carolina, and Cliff opened a bottle of Willamette Valley *pinot noir*.

"This is my government service," Karen said, after she had stopped shivering. "I still have eight months to go. I haven't done too many of these."

"Then we're even," said Tom.

"What's this about being a midwife," Arabella asked. "Is that what they call it?"

"Oh, no, no!" said Karin with a laugh, which she quickly stifled, turning it into a polite cough. "I was training to be a midwife when they called me up. That's what I still hope to do full time. This is very good wine for Oregon."

"*Pinot noir*," said Cliff. "I own an interest in the vineyard."

"An interest!" Pam said, with a bitter laugh. Cliff had invested a hundred thousand in the vineyard; he often joked that the wine was twelve hundred dollars a bottle. It was Pam's least favorite joke.

"Let me guess," said Tom. "You're from California."

"Los Angeles. But my boyfriend is from Oregon. He told me it was beautiful here."

"It's a lot nicer here in the summer," said Arabella. "But we like it all the time."

"Does it always rain like this?"

"No, no. Sometimes it rains sideways," said Tom.

They finished the bottle and Cliff opened another. The presence of the girl at the table made it somehow easier to talk. She was a dishwater blond with sallow skin but perfect, if slightly small, teeth. Her eyes were a washed-out blue.

"We bought this place for twenty grand twenty years ago," said Cliff.

"Twenty-one five," said Pam.

"We were in the army together," said Cliff. Tom, Arabella, and Pam all looked at him, puzzled. "The anti-war army," he said. "Back in the day."

"He told me all about you, the man at the motel," Karin said.

"Wainwrong," said Cliff.

"Wainwright," said Karin, looking confused.

"Cliff's little joke," said Pam. "He has several of them. Anybody want to play cards?"

"We're not allowed to play cards," said Karin. "And I guess I should be heading back."

It had almost stopped raining, so they let her walk. Her raincoat was still wet but her hair was almost dry. It was only a quarter-mile up the steep, slick, empty street, to Wainwright's Spyglass Lodge.

✳

SIX

Sunrises are sneaky in Holystone Bay. The sun lingers behind the fog-topped ridges to the west until the world is lit by a gradual pearly glow, and then it appears unannounced and unheralded, except by shadows, and somehow less than surprising. Two long shadows on the sand announced the arrival of the sun over the ragged line of Georgia-Pacific Ridge, named after the company that owned it.

My last sunrise, thought Tom, and I missed it. He and Ara were walking on the beach. It was too cold and windy to talk. They stopped and stood, holding hands, watching the sea patiently enlarging its hole in the great stone offshore. One, two, three: it was like watching a clock.

"Do you think we should call Gwyneth?" asked Arabella.

"Let's leave her in peace," said Tom, "till after. I know her, she'll feel something is required of her, and it isn't."

"Maybe it's something required of us," said Arabella.

"Let's think about it for another day or so," said Tom. "Look, isn't that the girl?"

It was indeed the girl, stringy blond hair and all.

"What are you doing here?"

"Just taking a walk," Karin said. "I didn't mean to intrude on anyone."

"You're not intruding," said Arabella. "This is a public beach."

"Does this job always make you cry?" asked Tom.

"I'm sorry, it's not you," Karin said. "It's me. A personal loss. My boyfriend. We just broke up."

She lit a cigarette—an American Spirit. She offered Tom one, but Arabella turned it down for him.

"He doesn't smoke."

"I'm thinking of starting again," said Tom.

"Can I use your phone?" asked Karin. Tom's was in a mesh pocket on his windbreaker. "I can't use mine because I don't want him to know where I am. I promised myself I wouldn't call him. But he broke every promise to me. I can break one."

"Then make the call, dear," said Arabella, handing her Tom's phone.

"Feel free," Tom said. "I have some extra minutes I'm never going to use."

"You shouldn't be so hard on her," said Arabella, as they watched her walk away, dialing. "She's exactly Gwyneth's age."

"How can you tell?"

"A mother can tell."

✻

213

When Tom and Ara got back to the house there was a car pulled up in front. A Ford Expedition, the ice-blue Shackleton model, with a blue light on top.

"Oh no," said Tom. "Wainwrong."

"Do you want me to tell him to go away?" asked Arabella, taking Tom's hand again; she had dropped it back on the little wooden stair that led up the last dune.

"No, of course not."

Waiwright was in the kitchen, having a cup of coffee with Cliff. Pam was scowling at them both.

"Wainwright wants to handle the arrangements," she said.

"The what?"

"The arrangements," said Wainwright, standing up and extending his giant paw. "In addition to being the mayor and the head Homey, and of course the handyman and hotelier, I operate the only licensed funeral home on this section of the coast. But aren't we getting ahead of ourselves? I came by to extend my sympathies to you all. And to offer my services, of course."

"Of course," said Tom. "How did you find about about this, anyway?"

"The girl," said Wainwright. "It's a terrible thing. It's on the Homeland Security database, too. All this stuff is tracked."

"We don't need any services," said Tom. "We're handling this on our own."

"Of course you are, " said Wainwright, pulling at his beard. "But you can't do everything by yourselves. If you don't go through the Brigade, the government doesn't cover the funeral costs."

"No funeral," said Tom. "We're saying our good-byes as we go."

"No funeral, then. But what about cremation? You can't do that yourself."

"He's right, Tom," said Cliff. "He already gave us a price. It makes it easier on the girls."

"There are no girls here," said Pam.

"I want to be as helpful as I can," said Wainwright. "This is a courageous thing you're doing."

"What's courageous about it?" said Tom. "We have no choice."

"But to do it alone, like this."

"I'm not doing it alone," said Tom. "I'm with my family and friends. And Cliff is doing it too."

"Cliff!" Wainwright looked at Cliff, shocked. "I had no idea. She didn't tell me that. You're both sidetracking the Brigade, giving up the bonus?"

"Side*stepping*," said Tom. It sounded like a dance.

"I don't need no stinkin' bonus," said Cliff. "I'm a wealthy lawyer. Perhaps you haven't noticed my car, parked just outside."

"You already gave us a price," said Pam.

"That was for one," Wainwright said. "The problem is, there are regulations. Even if I could technically stuff two . . ."

"Can we talk about this later," said Arabella.

"Of course," said Wainwright, brightening. "I'll see what I can do. Meanwhile . . ."

"Meanwhile, we who are about to die salute you," said Tom, lifting Cliff's coffee cup.

Wainwright shuffled toward the door. "Meanwhile, there's a big storm coming on. There's a pressure dome moving in. I have to get back up to the lodge and look after the shutters. You should close yours."

"One of them is broken," said Cliff. "On the oceanside. Remember, you were going to fix it?"

After Wainwright had driven away in his Ford Expedition, Tom turned to Cliff. "You never got the hemlock kit?"

"One is enough," said Cliff. "They still think I'm showing up at the Brigade. I want to surprise them."

"For real? For sure? You still want to go early with me?"

"Come on, of course for real. Isn't that what we decided? Case closed. Where are you going?"

"Give me the card to your Caddy. I'm going for a drive."

✳

Arabella stayed to help Pam with lunch while Cliff closed the shutters, all but the one that was broken. Tom drove out to the headland and parked, and watched the sea through the windshield, like a drive-in movie.

Tomorrow that stone will still be here, and so will the sea. So will the seagull, floating on the wind, looking for something to eat. While I will be—

Something to eat.

No more Tom. No more nothing.

All hole and no stone. Over. Finis.

He started the car. If there was a storm coming, it wasn't showing yet. The waves were smaller than usual, moving the tangles of seaweed in and out, like a big mop. *A big fucking mop.* Tom decided to skip lunch. He drove up the coast six miles toward Seal Cove, the first real town.

There was hardly any traffic. Tom passed a state trooper. As always, he felt illegal, today more so than ever. Do they know I'm going to die tonight? he thought. It gave him a great freedom: *It's like, I can do anything. The ultimate outlaw, beyond the reach of the law.*

He resisted the impulse to wave.

He was thinking of calling Gwyneth, dreading it. Had he left his phone with the girl on purpose? He even stopped and swiped his card at the phone on the edge of the parking lot of Seal Cove Liquors. She knows we love her, he said to himself. Then he hesitated. Why add this to her troubles?

Then he dialed anyway. He was relieved when he got Gwyneth's machine. "If you don't know what to do now, you have no business using a phone."

"Gwyn, honey," he said. "It's your dear old dad. I'm calling from Holystone Bay. Your mother and I are here at the house with Pam and Cliff. It's beautiful."

It wasn't particularly beautiful, especially not in the parking lot of Seal Bay Liquors, but honesty was not among Tom's purposes.

"I just called to say that I'm thinking of you, and I love you. Your mother too. Bye!"

There. That done, he went inside and rewarded himself with a pack of American Spirits, the brand the girl had smoked. And on second thought, a bottle of whiskey.

When he got back to the house, the afternoon was almost gone. Cliff and Pam were playing a version of two-handed solitaire Pam had invented.

"Old Grandad," said Cliff admiringly. "What's the occasion?"

"Very funny. Where's Ara?"

"She went for a walk," said Pam.

✳

The wide beach was empty and the sea was strangely still. There was no surf at all, just a smooth glassy plate rising and falling, in and out. A windsurfer heading toward the stone was the only solid thing—his sail was transparent, so that he looked like a walker on the water, striding the waves like the gulls strode the wind.

The sea is calm tonight. The tide is full, the moon lies fair upon the straits. The Sea of Faith was once—

He couldn't remember the rest of the words. It didn't seem to matter. There was no moon anyway. It was the ending he remembered: *Ah, love, let us be true to one another!*

"There you are. I found you."

It was Arabella. He had gone looking for her, and she had found him. As usual; as always. Looking at her slight form in her sweatshirt and jeans, heavy breasted, narrow in the hips, her short hair faded gray but still full, he felt a tremendous rush of love, even more powerful than the sexual desire that had drawn him to her thirty years before when he had first seen her across the room at a World Bank protest.

Thirty-two.

Is this what love is? he wondered. Not what's left after sex, and sex's promises, and sex's betrayals, but what grows from them all, like a bright plant from dark soil.

"I called Gwyneth," he said. "And left a message. OK?"

"Does that mean I have to call her tomorrow?"

"I guess."

"She'll be angry."

"Maybe that's the best way," said Tom. "Anger." He skipped a stone across the glassy sea. "Funny. There are no waves today."

"It's the pressure dome," said Arabella. "Wainwright says it means a storm is coming."

"Wainwright's a weatherman too?" The waves that usually boomed through the rock, cutting the hole bigger every day, every year, every century, were lapping gently. The rock was getting the evening off. The windsurfer cut through the hole, an unheard-of maneuver. "He looks like a jesus bug," said Tom. "Walking on the water."

"A what?" Ara took his hand.

"A jesus bug. When I was a kid there were lots of jesus bugs on the pond behind my grandparents' barn. I used to shoot at them with my BB gun. I didn't think anything about it."

"He made it through," said Arabella. The windsurfer caught the wind again, and headed out to sea.

"Good for him." Tom had forgotten the American Spirits.

He opened the pack and lit one, while Arabella looked on disapprovingly.

He waited for her to say something.

"It's all organic," he said finally. "Indian-approved."

"Are you OK?" Ara asked.

He looked at her sharply and exhaled, then said, "No."

"Me neither."

"I love you," he said finally. "I really do."

"I know."

"You and me, Ara, we've had a great run. I don't regret a bit of it. I mean that. Not even the hard parts. I mean that."

"I know," she said. "There've been some hard parts."

"That's OK."

"This is one of them."

"Oh, honey." She was crying. "Maybe we should go back to the house."

"This one is different," she said. "This one we can't make better."

He sat with her on a rock while she cried softly. He held her hand, but after a while he felt nothing. He was like the stone on which they sat. When you throw a stone into the water it disappears without a trace, as if it had never been.

"It's getting dark," he said finally. "Let's go in."

✳

SEVEN

Theirs was the only house in the row of beach houses that was lighted. The lighted window drew Tom and Arabella like a beacon—a little spot of life on a dark, silent coast. And as they approached, the light went out.

It was Cliff, nailing a plywood sheet over the window.

"Wainwrong's back," he said. "Bearing plywood, and other gifts."

Wainwright was was in the kitchen with Pam.

"I brought some lasagna," he said. "From the restaurant. Mirta made it special. And the plywood, to replace the broken shutter. By the way, have you seen the girl?"

"Karin?" asked Pam. "No. Not since this morning."

"I was supposed to give her a ride down here, but I couldn't find her."

"She likes to walk on the beach," said Arabella.

"She's got my cell phone," said Tom.

"Well, I hope she's got her raincoat too," said Wainwright. "There's a massive pressure dome off the coast. That's why there are no waves. It'll bring a big storm later tonight."

"You mentioned that already," said Tom.

"Well, I just felt the need to remind you. And I brought you this." He held up a DVD.

"A going away present?" Tom asked.

"It's called EZ-Exit," Wainwright said. "It replaces the DVD in the kit, which is sort of religious. With this one, you can make it the way you want it to be. There are eight programs on the disk. Different kinds of music, visuals . . ."

"You've tried them?" asked Tom, taking the plastic case and setting it on the coffee table next to the plain beige box. The DVD's cover showed an angel in a tie-dyed smock, playing a guitar. He looked a lot like Jerry Garcia.

"I was curious," said Wainwright. "I inherited it from York."

"Yorick?"

"The uncle who left me the funeral home. He had cancer so he did himself in. Some of them are pretty cool. My favorite is number four, which is all Jerry Garcia."

"The Dead."

"It's a solo thing. But you get the idea. They are designed to be combined with acid, or dope, or maybe even heroin, the Garcia one, who knows. I'm not saying this officially, of course."

"Of course not," said Cliff. Wainwright was the local Homeland Security Chief.

"We need to be getting ourselves ready," said Pam.

"Ever hear of the Last Supper?" asked Tom.

"I understand," said Wainwright, standing. His gray ponytail almost brushed the little house's low ceiling. He held out his big hand, first for Cliff, then for Tom. "If anybody could turn water into wine, it's you guys. I mean that."

"Thanks," said Tom.

"Thanks," said Cliff.

"It takes real courage to laugh in the face of death."

Death. There was a long silence. It was the first time anyone in the house had said the word.

"Well," said Wainwright. "Don't let the lasagna get cold. I had Mirta make it special. And Cliff, I hope you nailed that plywood down good. This is what they call the calm before the storm. You probably thought that was just a saying."

"Like death and taxes," said Tom.

"I'll never forget the last time we had a pressure dome off shore like this. It was back when Doc Azarov's boat was in my marina. Remember that Boston Whaler? That old son of a bitch had it insured for twice as much as . . ."

"Good night, Wainwright," said Pam, opening the door. Outside, the night was strangely still. "Thanks for the lasagna."

"And the plywood," said Cliff.

"And the Grateful Dead," said Tom.

"It's solo Garcia," Wainwright corrected. "But great stuff. There's also some jazz, is that's your thing. And Yanni. Yuck. Meanwhile, before I go, can I ask one question?"

"Shoot," said Cliff.

"You guys have never been really sick or anything, have you? Like a heart attack or cancer or something?"

Tom and Cliff both shook their heads.

"I didn't think so. You're lucky you can laugh."

"What do you mean?" Arabella asked.

"Because death is not just some abstract nothing," Wainright said, stopping in the doorway. "It's not like a hole you fall into. It's a thing. I learned that from York. It comes after you. It's like a mad dog. It's irresistible."

"Thanks and good night," said Pam, shutting the door in his face.

"Wow," said Tom.

"What was that?" said Arabella, pouring herself another Old Grandad.

"An asshole," said Pam.

"*Quod erat demonstrandum,*" said Cliff. "What say we retire to the deck and watch the sunset?"

"Wow," said Tom, again.

❋

The wind had come up and the sea was getting choppy. Big slow rollers boomed. The windsurfer was long gone: even the birds were gone. Cliff poured everyone a double shot of Old Grandad, and they arranged themselves facing west. Tom and Arabella shared one chair.

The sunset wasn't a disappointment like the sunrise had been. It was in fact a winner. A huge, and hugely distant, ball of fire sank slowly into a black band of cloud, turning it rose, then bright red, like a bloodstain. They watched silently until the wind came up. The waves were back. The hole in the rock looked like a wound, red against the black of the stone.

Cliff poured another round. "Quite a show," he said. "Don't guess we get to ask for an encore."

Nobody felt like talking. They just sipped their drinks

and stared at the red streak where the sun had been, growing darker and darker. The wind came up, cold and smelling of rain.

Tom lit an American Spirit. It took three matches.

"I wish you wouldn't do that," said Ara. Tom threw the cigarette away and wrapped his arms around her. The first raindrops arrived, one by one, sounding like stones hitting the plywood.

Pam stood up. "It's about that time," she said.

Both Tom and Cliff looked up, suddenly, like two deer caught in headlights.

"For supper, I mean, before the lasagna gets any colder."

✳

Supper was surprisingly easy, almost normal. Cliff opened a twelve hundred dollar bottle of pinot noir and they ate with a candle on the table. It was almost like the old, good times. Yesterday.

The lasagna wasn't bad, either.

"Here's to good friends," said Cliff. He twirled his glass and watched the wine slip down from the sides. "Can I get serious?"

"Beats me. Have you ever tried?" Tom immediately wished he hadn't said it when Cliff took his hand. They had been friends for twenty, no, thirty years but they had never held hands.

"There's something I want to say," said Cliff. "Which is, thank you. It has really been a privilege to be part of this foursome. I truly love you guys. My family. All of you."

"And we love you," said Arabella.

"And we love you," said Tom. He took Pam's hand; she was crying. "It's hard to leave this sweet old world. But the hardest thing is leaving friends."

"I still don't think it's fair," said Pam, breaking the circle and standing up. "I'm not going to pretend it's all right."

"No, it's not all right," said Arabella, pouring herself another drink.

"The undiscovered country," said Tom, lighting a cigarette. "Funny how we think of it that way. And yet it's the most familiar thing of all. We spend a third of our lives unconscious, in that little death called sleep."

There. He had said the word.

"We have been dead since Time began, for half of eternity, and alive for a only a few brief moments, and yet we fear what we know better than life itself. A kind of going home, back, to what we always were."

Ashes.

"That's a pretty speech," said Pam. "But you still can't smoke in the house."

"Pam!" said Cliff.

"It's OK," said Tom. "I want to step outside anyway, and watch the storm come in."

Cliff joined him. They stood in the lee of the house, out of the rain, almost.

"Are you scared, Tom?"

"I wasn't. I really wasn't. Until now. Now I'm scared shitless."

"Me too. But we can't let the girls know. We can't lay that on them, too."

"No, no. Cliff, are you sure you want to do this?"

"I got the greetings, too, remember, buddy?"

"I mean now, tonight, with me."

"Sure. What's three days?"

"It seems like a lifetime from here."

"Damn, it does, doesn't it? But no, I'm too scared to do it alone. And can you imagine the girls having to do it twice?"

"They probably make it easy in the Brigade. I mean, with

the group dynamics and all."

"Fuck that. Don't we have group dynamics here? What, are you saying you want to go join the geezers? Or that I should?"

"Neither."

"So shut the fuck up, please. What are you, chain-smoking?"

"Why not? Want a drag?"

"Why not. Jesus, what is this shit! No wonder the Indians died out."

"Better not let Pam hear you say that."

"I may be old but I'm not stupid. They'll be all right, won't they, Tom? The girls?"

"They'll be fine," said Tom. "That's the one thing I'm sure of. If it was them leaving us, we would stick together and survive wouldn't we?"

"I just worry about Pam. Arabella is so level-headed. Pam is always lashing out at one thing or another."

"Ara will keep her on track. They're good together. They were always the real couple, you know. You and me were just the support system."

Cliff looked hurt. "That's sort of true, isn't it?"

Tom put his arm around Cliff's waist. "No. But we have to do our best and trust them to do the same. Right?"

"Right," said Cliff. "Stiff upper-lip."

"Absolutely colonial," said Tom. "And now I'm getting wet. Let's go inside, buddy."

*

Pam and Arabella were doing the dishes. "You guys get the night off," said Pam. It was her first attempt at a joke, and they all honored it with a laugh.

Arabella dried her hands and poured another Old Grandad. The bottle was half gone. Tom lifted it, worried. "I thought you were leaving the bourbon alone," he said.

"I thought you didn't smoke," Arabella said. She gave him a peck on the cheek; it was almost girlish. "Don't look so worried, it's just for tonight. I am not about to become an old drunk."

"I have something better anyway," said Cliff, sitting back down at the table and opening his silver case. "Enough talk about death—"

There, thought Tom. We have both said it. Suddenly it seemed easy.

"—Let's talk about life!" Cliff lit a joint and passed it to Tom. "All our favorite things. Ice cream, whiskey, good friends, good dope."

"This is certainly good dope," said Tom.

"Lawyer dope," said Cliff.

Tom passed the joint to Pam while Cliff put a CD in the player. Coltrane: *My Favorite Things*.

Pam passed the joint to Arabella, but she waved it away.

Tom was relieved, until he saw her fill her glass again.

"What were your favorite things?" Cliff asked.

Past tense already?

"My favorite thing was sunrise from the top of Mt. Hood," Cliff said, exhaling a huge Jamaican-style cloud toward the ceiling.

"You never went there," said Pam. "You only talked about it."

"Just knowing it was there was enough. What a run. What a stage on which to strut."

Cliff got up from the table and went into the living room. Remembering the beige box on the coffee table, Tom got a chill. "Where are you going?"

"I'm looking for my Shakespeare. There's an index."

"He's going to look up Death," said Pam, groaning.

Now they had all said it; all except Arabella.

"I don't need no stinkin' index," said Cliff, coming back into the room empty-handed. "'Out, out damned spot!'"

"That's not about death," Tom said. "That's about murder."

"So?" said Pam, suddenly serious. "So? Everything in *Hamlet* is about death," said Cliff. "Good night, sweet prince."

"That's from *Macbeth*," said Arabella.

"I beg your pardon!" said Cliff.

"I mean the spot," said Arabella, giggling. "I know because my grandmother used to say it when she was washing the dishes. She was an actress until she met my grandfather. They were married for fifty years. Can you imagine?"

"Almost," said Tom. He pulled her down beside him on the couch.

"Well, it's a *Macbeth* sort of night," said Cliff. "'To be or not to be'. 'The undiscovered country.'"

"That's from *Star Trek*," said Tom, to lighten the mood.

"Quod erat demonstrandum," said Cliff. *"Habeus corpus* and all that. Listen to that wind howl."

They fell silent and listened to the wind howl. It was not a pretty sound.

"We have time for one more game of cards," said Pam. She knocked the cards on the table three times, preparing to shuffle.

As if in answer, there were three raps on the door.

Pam froze; they all froze.

Had it been imagined? There was no sound but the shrieking of the wind and the rattling of the rain on the plywood.

Then there it was again: RAP RAP RAP

"Fucking Wainwrong's back," said Cliff.

You wish, thought Tom. He got up and opened the door. Who would have thought Death would appear as a tall, skinny girl in a yellow hood, carrying an attaché case instead of a scythe, and asking:

"Can I come in? Are you ready?"

*

Eight

Karin took off the slicker, which made her look a little less like Death, and dried her stringy blonde hair with the towel Arabella provided. She was wearing a forest-green uniform: Youth Service Corps. It didn't do much for her figure. While Pam made sassafras tea for everyone, Karin set her attaché case down on the coffee table, between the beige kit and the EZ-Exit DVD.

"What's this," she asked.

"Your *hotelier* gave it to us," said Cliff. "It replaces the DVD in the kit."

"This is all new to me," said Karin. "You'll have to forgive me, all I know is the medical procedure."

"We'll forgive you," said Tom. *Forgive them, Lord, they know not what they do.* "Want a cigarette? I have your brand."

"I can't smoke in uniform," said Karin.

"You can't smoke in the house anyway," said Pam. "Do you want some sassafras tea?"

Tom opened the beige kit. It contained a bottle of pills, a DVD in a plastic slipcase with an angel (not Jerry Garcia) waving an American flag, and a red-white-and-blue death certificate.

"This is all you get for $79.95?" he said. "They could at least give you a little gun."

"No guns in the house," Pam reminded him.

"The kit is really just for the death certificate," said Karin. She didn't seem to mind saying the word anymore; in uniform, she was all business. "Where's the other one?"

"It's in the mail," Cliff lied smoothly. "They said you could write in both names on that one."

"I didn't know you could get them by mail," said Karin, unlocking her attaché. "Anyway, I have everything I need here." She took out a little plastic device that looked like a toy pipe organ. It was three upright plastic tubes in ascending sizes, each one filled with a fluid: one pink, one amber and one yellow. "The amber one is a tranquilizer. The yellow is a muscle relaxant, very powerful and smooth-acting. The pink contains the actual . . ."

"We don't need to know the details," said Pam.

"That's true," said Karin. "Sorry." Each tube was connected to a clear plastic IV line; the lines were tangled. Karin set the little device on the piano, which had come from Arabella's grandmother's house in Corvallis, and began the process of untangling the lines.

Meanwhile Cliff put the EZ-Exit DVD into the player, and started navigating through the menu. The first image that came up was clouds, and the Yanni soundtrack.

He skipped to Track Two: Jerry Garcia facing a huge crowd in a sunny meadow. "Was Jerry Garcia at Woodstock?"

"It was raining at Woodstock. See what the next one is," said Tom.

Arabella poured herself another bourbon. Pam was sipping sassafras tea.

Track Three was Coltrane: "My Favorite Things" over a picture of dunes and the sea.

"Let's do the dunes," said Tom.

"Done," said Cliff, hitting pause. "Now what?"

Karin arranged them on the couch, girl-boy-boy-girl. Tom and Cliff were sitting side by side, between their two wives. Cliff held the remote, and laid it on his lap while he pulled a fat joint out of his silver case.

"I don't think that's allowed," said Karin.

"I think it is," said Cliff. "I'm a lawyer, or haven't you seen my car outside?" He lit the joint and passed it to Tom. "It comes under medicinal, and we're all terminal here, right?"

"Well, I don't know," said Karin, who was still trying to

untangle the IV lines. She looked, to Tom, like Penelope undoing her weaving. Is that what death is like? he wondered. Instead of your life flashing before your eyes, a string of classical references.

"Don't we get a few minutes to say our good-byes?" Pam asked.

Karin shook her head. "We're already in overtime," she said. "This was supposed to happen at sunset."

She pulled two syringes from her attaché case. She swabbed each man's arm with alcohol.

"Wouldn't want to get an infection," said Tom. He closed his eyes as Karin put the needle in his arm. Cliff left his open.

When both needles were inserted, she hooked the IV lines up to a coupler, which connected both men to all three lines. The lines were still tangled, but the loose ends were free, and each one found a connection.

Karin seemed satisfied. "Now before I release the fluids, I have to note the exact time. Does anybody have a watch?"

"Aren't you supposed to have that?" asked Cliff. "Here, take my Rolex. But you can't keep it. Pam gets it in my estate."

"Rolex!" said Pam. "Don't let him make you nervous. He bought it on Canal Street in New York last year."

They were all nervous. Karin's hands shook as she slipped the watch onto her skinny wrist. Tom felt suddenly sorry for her. Arabella was leaning back on the couch with her eyes half-closed. I'm glad we've said our good-byes, Tom thought. The whole point of all this is to make you eager to get it over with. "Let's get it over with," he said.

As soon as Karin had turned her back to write down the time, Tom felt Cliff tapping his hand.

He looked down and saw an orange tab of LSD in his palm. "Wainwright?" he whispered.

"No way, man. Clifford select. I've been saving this for a special occasion. I think this qualifies."

Cliff swallowed his.

Tom squeezed Cliff's hand but didn't take the acid. He pretended, and dropped it into his pocket. "I'm with you, man," he said.

"All I have to do is push this plunger down," Karen said. "It's better if I'm behind you and you aren't watching. The idea is . . ."

RIING

Karin jumped and pulled a cell phone from her pocket.

"That's my phone!" said Tom. He had forgotten it. He reached for the phone but Karin pulled it back.

"I don't think . . ."

"Better answer it," said Cliff, grinning. "It might be the governor."

Karin reluctantly handed Tom his phone.

"Daddy?"

"Gwyn?"

"Daddy! What are you doing!"

"Gwyn, honey . . ."

"I can't believe this. This is crazy. You can't do this!"

Tom got up from the couch. He looked at Arabella. "It's Gwyneth. I want to take this outside."

Even more reluctantly, Karin unhooked Tom's IV from the coupler, and he stepped outside the door. The wind had dropped. He lit a cigarette.

"Daddy!" Gwyneth's voice sounded far away. "This is crazy. You can't do this."

"How did you find out what I was doing?"

"Thomas called me after your visit. He thought you were acting strange. Daddy, you can't do this. There are other ways."

"You mean the Brigade?"

"No! There's an underground. A Resistance! I thought you of all people would know enough to know about that. I called them. They are on their way. They can help."

"Help with what? Honey, this is already happening." Tom looked down at the needle dangling from his arm. "We're already into the procedure."

"Fuck the procedure," Gwyneth said. "You can't just abandon us this way. We have a right to be there."

"Gwyn, honey, believe me, you don't want to be here. This isn't *Little House on the Prairie*."

"This is too cruel. Let me talk to mother."

"Your mother is OK. She's—busy," said Tom.

"She's drunk, right? I can't believe you let her start drinking again! I can't believe you two!"

Tom looked up. They were in the eye of the storm. A few stars showed overhead, and among them, a single blinking light—a plane far overhead, coming from Japan, bypassing Oregon, heading for Chicago or Toronto or New York or . . .

"Put her on, maybe I can talk some sense to her," said Gwyneth. "This is just too ZZXXXZZZ"

"You're breaking up," said Tom. The stars overhead seemed cold and far away. They were lost in a sea of blackness. Floating in a sea of death.

It's all death out here. Come and join us.

He felt it pulling at him. But the tiny spark of life was still pulling harder. Wainwright was wrong. Death wasn't a mad dog; it was more like gravity—everywhere, but weak. Nothing escaped it in the long run but everything, even a few cells, could resist it for a while.

For a while but time is up. "I have to go back in," he said.

"You can't do this to me," Gwyneth said. "Are you saying I'll never talk to you again? You're my father! You can XXZZXXZZX—"

"You're breaking up," Tom said again. "I love you, honey. I'll always love you." *A lie. Always was all but over.* He clicked his phone shut and walked back into the house.

"Gwyneth," he said, putting the phone on the table.

"Let me talk to her," Arabella said woozily.

"She says she'll call you tomorrow," said Tom, sitting back down on the couch and holding up his arm for the connection. "Let's get on with this."

"Let's get it on . . ." Cliff sang; he was smiling. The acid, Tom thought. *Maybe I should have taken it too.* While Karin reconnected the lines to his IV, he leaned over and gave Arabella a kiss. Her lips were cold. Her eyes were closed. She seemed as far away now as she would ever be.

"It's been a pleasure working with you all," said Karin. "Thanks for all your help."

"Think nothing of it," said Tom. "Should we start the DVD?"

"Go," said Karin.

Cliff was holding the remote. Tom leaned over and pressed PLAY. The TV showed a picture of the dunes, wavering, like from a rocking boat. The tall grass was dancing to the familiar sounds of "My Favorite Things."

The camera was a handheld, lurching through the dunes, toward the bright blue sea. Maybe I'm getting a rush, Tom thought. It was almost as if he had taken the acid. There was Coltrane, then Bill Evans. No, it was the triads of McCoy Tyner.

These are a few of my favorite things . . .

"You will feel sleepy," said Karin, from far away. "Whatever you do is OK now. Just relax, go to sleep if you want to."

Sleep? Is that what they call it?

The camera was a handheld, bobbing up and down through the low, no, high dunes. Ocean and sky met in a faraway blue/blue line. Ahead, there was something sticking up. It was bright orange. The trick, Tom thought, is to pretend to walk, to pretend to be there. He pretended to run toward the top of the dune but the sand was soft and his feet were numb with cold, and clumsy. He slowed to a walk and there it was, a small hang glider with a seat hanging under it. It was already in the air, hovering. He sat down on the seat and scooted over to make room for Ara, and someone was beside him. Too heavy, though; it was Cliff. Tom pushed off with one foot and the glider soared upward, over the dunes. The clumsiness was gone, though his feet were still cold.

My favorite things.

"Hey this is great," he said to Cliff, but it was Pam who answered. "Cliff is gone."

Where was Ara?

The little glider was sailing higher and higher and higher, caught in an updraft. "I can't turn this thing," said Tom. Leaning from side to side did nothing; it was if he had no weight at all.

Higher and higher.

The dunes were gone and it was all sea and sky.

Coltrane, soprano, blue blues blue. My favorite things.

Tom squeezed Arabella's hand and she squeezed back. She had never understood his thing about music, about Coltrane, but she was getting it now, at last.

"Oh, honey," Tom said, but she was gone again and he was alone on the wide underglider seat, descending.

It was going down.

The water looked solid, like a sheet of blue light.

There was an island ahead, tiny but getting bigger. He tried to turn, but the glider was heading straight for it. They know what they are doing, Tom thought.

The island had a hole in it, like a little pond. Someone was standing beside it, waving him in.

Ara?

The glider tipped and he hit the water and the water was hard. Tom closed his eyes and they opened instead. He was on the floor, looking up at the low, patched ceiling of the summer house he had bought twenty years ago with Arabella and Cliff and Pam. The IV stung in his arm, and his arm was bleeding. Karin was on the couch, kneeling between Pam and Cliff. She was pulling a plastic bag over Cliff's head. Arabella was slumped over sideways.

Tom gulped for air but nothing came. He clutched his face and it was covered with clear plastic. He ripped off the plastic bag. The rush of air felt like water, waking him.

"Hey!" Karin was taping the plastic bag around Cliff's neck. Cliff's hand was raised, bobbing up and down, as if he were hoping to be called on.

Objection, Your Honor.

"Hey!" Pam sat up and started beating on Karin's back. "What the hell are you doing?"

"It's not working right," Karin cried. "I must have crossed the lines."

Tom stood up and pushed them both aside and ripped the bag off Cliff's head. "He can't breathe! You're trying to kill him!"

Cliff's mouth was lopsided and he was drooling. His right hand was still bobbing up and down.

"Do something!" Pam was hitting Tom in the back now. "He's had a stroke. Do something!"

"I'm trying," said Tom. He pushed on Cliff's chest but Cliff just sank deeper into the couch.

"We have to continue the procedure," said Karin. "We can't stop now."

"Somebody do something!" said Pam.

Tom stood back, confused. Where had the island gone? Ara was sleeping peacefully on the couch, her head to one side. She was the only one in the room who looked dead.

Karin traced the tubes into Cliff's arm. "Oh no!"

"What?" asked Tom and Pam together.

"I misrouted the tubes," said Karin, pulling two more plastic bags out of her case. "We have to use the bags. They're the backup."

"What do you mean, misrouted?" Pam stopped her with a strong hand on her skinny little arm.

"He got two of the relaxants," Karin said, pointing at Cliff. "Double yellow. The whole thing has to start over."

"What?" Tom looked around the room. It was like waking up. He was in the beach house he had bought twenty years ago with Arabella and Cliff and Pam. He had survived Death. He wasn't dead at all.

He stood up, reaching down to the coffee table to steady himself. "Everybody slow down," he said calmly. "Let's all have a drink of sassafras tea—or whiskey."

"She can't drink on the fucking job!" said Pam. "All she can do legally is kill you."

"We've run out of time" said Karin, looking at Cliff's watch. "The deadline was nine o'clock!"

Deadline.

"Give me that," said Pam, grabbing at the watch. It slipped off Karin's wrist and hit the floor with a loud *crack*.

"The whole thing was supposed to be over twenty minutes ago," Karin said, starting to cry. "I messed it up entirely. Now I'll lose my certification for sure."

"Tough shit," said Pam. "I'm calling 911. We need an ambulance. Tom, where's your phone?"

"On the table," said Tom. He pulled the IV from Cliff's arm, then pulled Cliff down from the couch, onto the floor. He knelt over him and pushed down on his chest.

"Your IV is bleeding," said Karin. "There's not supposed to be any blood. That means it's out of the vein."

"It's out for sure now,' said Tom, pulling his needle free.

"You can't do that!" said Karin. "You're not medical personnel."

"Personnel?" Tom had always hated the word. "Nobody's personnel here," he said, tossing the IV to the floor. "But Pam's right about one thing, this whole business is over. Now we have to get Cliff to a doctor."

"Nobody's going to any doctor," Karin said grimly. She was rummaging around in her attaché case. For what? Tom wondered: Instructions? A noose? A gun?

He grabbed her arm. "Sit down!"

"You can't order me around!"

"I can't?" He pushed her down on the couch beside Arabella. "Because I'm dead? Well, I'm not dead anymore. In fact, I've lost all interest in being dead. Arabella!"

He slapped her face, gently at first, then harder. "Wake up, it's over."

"It's not over!" said Karin. It was in fact a gun. She pulled it out of the attaché case—a tiny 9mm automatic, matte-black, as black as a little hole in the universe.

"He's choking!" said Pam. She was kneeeling over Cliff, banging on his chest with her fists.

"It's the muscle relaxant," said Karin. "Let it do its work. It relaxes the diaphragm." She pointed the gun at Pam, then at Tom. "I'm sorry, but I can't allow you to interfere."

"Give me that," said Tom. He reached for the gun and she handed it to him, surprising them both. It fit into his hand just right. He pointed it at her. "Now do something for Cliff."

He clicked the safety off, then on again. Karin hadn't known that it was on.

"This is all wrong," said Karin, kneeling down over Cliff and pushing Pam aside. "It's his diaphragm, it's not his lungs. You have to press down, here, hard."

Cliff gasped, then took a single loud breath.

"It was supposed to be yellow to yellow," said Karin. "But the pink looked yellow in the tubes. The light was bad!"

She pressed down on Cliff again and he took another breath. "Now we have to start over."

"No way," said Tom. "This show is over. "

"What do you mean?"

"What I said. Over. We have to get Cliff to the doctor in Tillamook. No point calling an ambulance. That will take forever."

"I can't allow this," said Karin, standing up. "I have already signed the papers."

"Shut up," said Pam, pushing down on Cliff's diaphragm. "It's not working. He's not breathing again."

"You do it," said Tom.

"I can't," said Karin. "If we just let the muscle relaxant work, it will . . ."

"It will kill him, I know," said Tom. "But we don't want to kill him anymore, do we? What you have to do is help him breathe."

"No."

Tom clicked the safety off, then on again. It made a wicked little noise, like a gun on TV. "Yes."

Karin knelt back down on the floor. She pressed down on Cliff's diaphragm and he took another breath. "You're making a big mistake," she said. "I'm a federal employee on duty. This is terrorism."

"Terrorism is about innocent people. I don't see any of them here. Pam, see if you can wake Arabella up. She's passed out from the fucking whiskey. Then we have to get Cliff into the car; do you have the card?"

"You do," said Pam, dragging Cliff by his armpits toward the door.

The storm was back. When Pam opened the door, a flood of rain and wind filled the room. Tom felt a moment's nostalgia for the peaceful sea he had been flying over. It had been replaced by a raging storm.

Arabella got to her feet on her own. "What's going on?" she asked. "Tom?"

"It's over," said Tom. "Get in the car. We have to get Cliff to the doctor."

"I can't allow this," said Karin. "It's terrorism."

"Get in the car!" said Tom. He pointed the gun toward the open door.

"No."

"Stay here, then." Each taking an arm, Pam and Tom dragged Cliff out the door, into the rain, across the gravel drive, to the yellow Cadillac.

"The card, the card," said Tom.

"You have it," said Pam.

They dragged Cliff into the back seat while Ara wobbled woozily around the car and into the right front seat. "Going for a ride in the car car . . ." she sang.

Jesus! thought Tom. The rain was pounding down and he was soaked. Karin was standing on the doorstep in her yellow raincoat, hurriedly punching numbers into Tom's cell phone.

"She's calling the police," said Pam.

"You were about to call them a minute ago," Tom reminded her. "Get in the back with Cliff."

Tom got into the driver's seat and slipped the card through the slot on the dash. The Cadillac started with a smooth whine.

"Let's go, let's go! He's not breathing again!"

Dead again.

"I'm going," said Tom. "But first—"

He got out of the car and grabbed Karin by the arm. "You're going with us," he said, dragging her toward the car.

"No!" She pulled away, holding onto the doorknob of the little house they had bought twenty-five years ago. *It was raining then, too . . .*

"Let her go!" said Pam. "Get back in the car. Cliff is barely breathing. Are you sure you can drive? Your arm is still bleeding."

"Only a little," said Tom. "But I'm woozy." When he closed his eyes he could still see the island perched on the edge of earth and sea, and the glider descending. "Hell, I was dead a little while ago."

"Let me drive," said Pam. She got out of the car and put Tom into the back with Cliff. Then she got into the driver's seat.

Tom leaned forward over the seat back. Rain was streaming down the windshield, outrunning the wipers. "It's raining," Arabella said, opening her eyes.

"No shit," said Pam, slipping the Cadillac into gear. She started out the drive, then slammed on the brakes. Karin was standing in front of them, carrying her raincoat wadded up, like a yellow ball. "What's that crazy little bitch up to now?"

"Crazy little bitch," said Arabella, giggling.

"I'm going too," said Karin, pulling the back door open.

"No way!" Tom pushed her away.

Karin threw her wadded-up slicker into his lap as she fell backward and sat down heavily in a puddle on the drive.

"Go!" Tom said.

"I'm going, I'm going." Pam floored the gas and the Cadillac spun out onto the highway, spraying gravel and mud behind it, and roared up the hill toward the meager lights of the town.

✳

Nine

Pam raced through the town's single street. "Where are we going?" she cried.

"Tillamook, Tillamook," Tom said. The word was like a mantra. It was the biggest town around; it would have a hospital with an emergency room.

"Uh oh!" A Ford Expedition sped past them with a blue light flashing. "Wainwright," said Pam.

"Where's he going?"

"After us," said Pam. "That little bitch called the cops, remember? Well, that's includes him. He's got his Homeland Security light on."

Tom looked back. The Ford's taillights were bright. "He's stopping, he saw us."

"Of course he saw us!" said Pam. "How many yellow Caddies are there around here this time of year? Now what?"

"He thinks we're going to Tillamook. Step on it till we're out of sight, then turn right."

Pam understood perfectly. She topped the hill, then slowed, skidding on the wet asphalt, and turned into a narrow street leading up into the pines.

"Now stop and turn off the lights. Put her in PARK and take your foot off the brake."

"Why are cars always 'her?'"

"You should be flattered."

They watched out the rear window, through the streaming rain, holding their breaths as the Ford Expedition raced past on the highway, heading for Tillamook.

"Dumb shit," said Pam. "How's Cliff?"

Cliff was slumped against the door. "He's breathing. How's Ara? I've seen her drunk but I've never seen her drunk like this."

"I gave her a tranq," said Pam. "She must have taken two. They interact with the whiskey, making me the designated driver. Now what?"

"I'm thinking." Tom shook an American Spirit out of the pack and fished through his pockets for a match.

"Wainwright will figure out we're not ahead of him," Pam said. "He'll turn around and come back. They've probably got the state troopers out too, by now."

"I know, I know." Tom found matches in Karin's slicker, next to a lump that might have been a phone—or another gun.

"You can't smoke in the car," said Pam.

"Oh, for Christ's sake!" Tom shoved the slicker onto the floor. He rolled down his window and lit the cigarette, taking two drags before tossing it out into the rain.

Another car sped by on the highway. A state trooper, blue light flashing, heading down the hill toward the beach and the house.

"Damn that little bitch," said Pam. "She must have called every cop in the country. What do we do now?"

"We can't go to Tillamook. We have to stay off the highway. Go to the end of this street and turn left. We'll go to Azarov's."

"That quack?"

"He'll have to do. Cliff's breathing but only about once or twice a minute."

"Damn that little bitch." Pam put the car into gear and roared off, spraying gravel—no lights. "This is Bonnie and Clyde time."

"Clyde?" asked Arabella, sitting up. "Who's Clyde?"

"Nobody, honey," said Tom. "Fasten your seat belt."

✱

Pam drove without headlights, from streetlight to streetlight through the dark town. She saw Azarov's driveway almost too late; she barely made the turn, and skidded to a stop in a circular gravel driveway behind a Boston Whaler on a trailer, white as a ghost in the steel-gray rain.

A light came on, revealing a stubby unpainted porch.

The door opened, and man stepped out, holding an umbrella.

"Doc, it's Cliff, he's . . ."

"I know, I know," said Azarov, a middle-aged Iranian with a pepper and salt beard. A blonde woman was standing in the doorway behind him, talking on a cell phone.

"I cannot treat him," said Azarov.

"He's having trouble breathing!"

"You do not understand," said Azarov. He walked out to the car, under his umbrella, and bent down to the open window. "I can not treat him. There is an all-points DNR out on him, and on you too, Tom."

"Nice to see your ass, too," Tom muttered.

"You must go now, before the authorities get here!"

"They don't know where we are."

"They will puzzle it out. I am the only doctor for miles."

"Chiropractor," said Pam.

Azarov ignored her. "It is on the TI-hotline, Tom. Assault, terrorism, kidnapping."

"Kidnapping?"

"But the main thing is the termination. Interfering with a termination is a federal offense."

"We didn't interfere; she fucked it up."

"Emily is on the phone with Homeland Security right now," Azarov said, pointing back over his shoulder. "They will be all over you like fleas in shit."

"It's flies *on* shit," said Tom. "At least take a look at Cliff."

The doctor shook his head. "If I even look at him, I will have to put a bag over his head. Yours too, Tom. Try Portland. Take the old highway. They may not be watching that."

"Damn!" said Pam.

"Just go!" Azarov pleaded.

"Let go of the car, then," said Pam. "It must look like I am trying to stop you. Go!"

Pam hit the gas and turned sharply around the Boston Whaler. Azarov went flying, into the shrubbery by his porch.

Was that for real? Tom wondered. Or for show?

✳

The old highway was a concrete slab, cracked and patched in so many places that it looked like an asphalt highway patched with concrete.

It was dark in the pines. Pam turned on the headlights. The rain slacked up but there were wisps of fog, tangled in the trees like ghostly Spanish moss. The road was slick with leaves and an occasional tiny, battered corpse.

Road kill. We are the universe's road kill.

In the car, there was silence. Pam drove; Arabella slept; Tom watched the road grimly, with his gun in his hand; and Cliff breathed, once every mile or so.

They were almost at the top of the pass when they saw the roadblock. The road was filled with lighted flares and plastic cones.

"Shit."

Two figures stood beside a blue Ford Expedition, waving lights in the air. One of them wore a trooper hat over a ponytail.

"Wainwright!" said Pam, slowing. "And his homies. How did they find us here?"

"Slow down," said Tom. "Stop. I'll talk to him."

"Are you kidding? They'll shoot."

"Not if we stop. Just do it." Tom pulled Karin's little gun out of his pocket as Pam rolled to a stop. He rolled down the window. The flares hissed. "Wainwright, is that you?"

"Tom, Cliff? Step out of the car, please." Wainwright started toward them, a stun gun held across his chest. He looked stern.

Tom stuck the pistol out of the window and fired twice into the air.

BAM BAM

Wainwright hit the ground rolling, just as he'd been trained to do. Pam stepped on the gas without being told, scattering flares and cones.

"He'll be right behind us," she said, as she rounded the first curve, into the trees.

"Not him. He'll leave it to the state troopers now," said Tom. "Let's just try and get to the interstate before they block it."

"How's Cliff?"

"Still breathing."

The road corkscrewed down the mountain, and followed a rocky little creek. Pam drove expertly; Tom could feel the rear end of the Cadillac sliding on the turns, but always returning to true.

Cliff was slumped against the door. His eyes were open. He looked terrified.

"We're taking you to a doctor," Tom said.

"What?" asked Pam from the front.

"It's Cliff. His eyes are open."

"Habeus corpus," said Cliff.

"What?" demanded Pam.

"He's talking in his sleep," Tom said. "Just drive!"

Pam drove. The road left the creek bed and switchbacked up another long hill. They were almost at the top when they saw the SUV parked across the road—another Ford Expedition.

Pam slowed. A man got out of the SUV and stood on the highway in the rain, waving his arms. He wore a ponytail under a wide brimmed hat.

"Wainwright," said Pam. "How the hell did he get ahead of us?"

"That's not Wainwright," said Tom. "That's a Tilly hat. And that's not the Shackleton model."

"Must be one of his homies," said Pam.

"Just go around him."

"I hear you. Hang on! The shoulder looks soft."

It was indeed soft. As soon as the Caddy hit it, it crumbled.

"Uh oh." In the back seat, Tom could feel the rear of the car sliding sideways, off the edge. Pam over-corrected with the wheel, and the car nosed down, into a grove of trees so black they looked like they had erased the world. Tom closed his eyes and heard wood snapping, first small branches, then bigger and bigger; then nothing at all.

✳

Tom was surprised to find eyes behind his eyes. He opened them both. He was looking up out of a car window. It was like when he was a kid and lying in the back of his father's Oldsmobile watching the long riverbottoms pass under the wide Indiana sky. Except he wasn't a kid anymore.

He was seventy-one.

He sat up.

There was darkness and leather all around. He was between the seats; they were jammed together.

Cliff's door was open. He was out of the car; only his feet were up on the seat. One shoe was missing. Then both feet were gone, and Cliff had slipped away.

Passed away.

Arabella!

"Ara!" Tom tried to get up but he was wedged tightly. He wriggled free, out Cliff's door, and tried to open Arabella's door.

It was jammed. He climbed back into the car and leaned over the back of the front seat.

Pam was slumped against the window, which was

smeared with blood. Arabella was leaning forward with her head in her hands, as if in thought. Tom put his hand on the back of her head. Her hair was wet and cold. His hand was sticky. "Ara!"

"Tom," said a voice. Someone was pulling at his arm. "There's no time. Come on."

"No!" said Tom. *No time?* Someone had him by the arm, pulling him out of the car. He jerked his arm free and tried to stand and fell to his knees on cold, wet stones. "Who are you? What are you doing here?"

"A friend."

"Arabella," Tom said. There was blood on his hand; he wiped it on his shirt. *So much blood!*

He tried to get to his feet and fell again; then he felt something cold—a cold, soft, wet rag, like a dirty diaper— pulled across his mouth and nose.

"Ara," he said out loud, and the night went gray, then white: a brilliant cold bone-white.

✳

TEN

The island was a hole of sand in a wall of water. Tom was circling down toward it, down, down, down. The island was bright, too bright; sunny, too sunny.

The lawn chair swung under the glider's wing but the wing was too square, like a door or a window.

Tom opened his eyes. He was in a lawn chair, but inside, by a window. The window was bright, too bright.

"Arabella?"

She was gone. The car was gone, the night was gone, the rain was gone.

He looked at his hand. The blood was gone.

"Habeus corpus," said a familiar voice.

It was Cliff. He was sitting in a wheelchair, between two single beds. They were in a motel room. The wallpaper was a black and white pattern of interlocked birds flying in two directions at once; an Escher, wall to wall.

Cliff's right arm was lifting and dropping, lifting and dropping. His face looked weird; his mouth was slack. Tom panicked for a moment; then he looked into Cliff's eyes and saw that he was still there.

"Cliff, you're alive," he said, amazed. "We're both alive."

Shit, he thought meanwhile. He's had a stroke or something. And where are the girls?

Then he remembered.

He remembered it all, from the scene in the beach house, to the chase, to the crash.

"Where are the girls?" He got up, unsteadily. He was wearing pajamas. "Where are we?"

"Habeus corpus," said Cliff.

"You're awake," said a woman's voice.

Tom stood and turned and saw her standing in the doorway, all in white, like an angel. It was not Arabella, though.

"Who are you?"

"You can call me Tanya," she said. She was young and skinny, with limp blonde hair, like Karin, the Angel of Death. "Don't worry, you're safe here. But I think you're not ready to be walking around yet."

She was right. Tom felt dizzy. "Where's my wife? Is she here?" He sat back down. The lawn chair creaked.

"The Super will explain it all," Tanya said. "In the meantime, you get some rest. You're not ready to be walking around yet."

"What day is it?"

But she was gone. Tom turned back to Cliff. "What happened? Where are the girls?"

"Habeus corpus," said Cliff. He lifted his arm and dropped it, twice.

"How long have we been here?"

"Habeus corpus," said Cliff.

Shit, man. Is that all you can say? Cliff looked bad, but that was to be expected. What about Pam? What about Arabella?

Tom got up, still dizzy, and opened the door. Looking out, he saw a long hallway past other doors, most of them closed. He could hear shouting at the far end of the hall. Steadying himself against the wall, he walked toward the sound.

A TV was blaring in a room filled with old people; it was a small room and it only took six to fill it, four of them in wheelchairs, like Cliff.

The shouting was a talk show. A fat white girl in a halter top was shouting at a skinny black man with three gold teeth. He made the ancient, universal, hands-up gesture of helplessness, but it only made her shout louder.

Maybe we're dead after all. And here we are in Hell.

"Tom!" It was the woman in white, Tanya; she was feeding an old man with a long spoon. "You should wait in your room. I'll bring your lunch there."

Tom didn't have to be told twice. In Hell you do what they tell you.

He shuffled back to his room and sat down and closed his eyes. He didn't want to look at Cliff. His mouth was too slack and his eyes, though bright, were too wide. He looked like an old baby.

✳

"You can call me Tanya."

Huh? Tom opened his eyes. The woman in white was feeding Cliff with a long spoon; the same long spoon. It was a terrible spoon. "Are you hungry?"

Tom shook his head, too hard: it hurt.

"You probably still have the chemicals in your bloodstream. We thought there for a while last night we were going to lose you."

"Please," said Tom. "Start at the beginning. What happened? Where am I? Where's my wife, Arabella."

"There was an auto accident," said Tanya. "The Super is checking our sources, trying to find out about your wife. I told her of your concern. In the meantime, just relax and let your body heal itself."

"What about Cliff? Is his body healing its fucking self?"

"He has apparently had some kind of stroke. The doctor will be here tomorrow to look at him. I can understand why you would be upset. Meanwhile, you are safe here with us."

"Who is us?

"I'm not allowed to talk about that. But you know who we are. You know you do."

The Resistance? "This is all a mistake," said Tom.

"There." Tanya wiped Cliff's chin and stood up, smiling. "Meanwhile, don't worry about a thing. The Super will let you know as soon as she finds out something."

"The Super?"

"You can call her Dawn." Tanya left, closing the door behind her.

Dawn. Tom felt strangely relieved. Maybe it *was* all a mistake, *my* mistake, he thought. Maybe his memory of Arabella and her head all sticky with cold blood was a dream. He checked his hands again. They were clean.

Maybe I just dreamed I saw Arabella dead.

"Cliff, do you remember anything about the wreck?"

"Habeus corpus."

Shit. Poor fucking Cliff. Tom lay down on the bed closest to the door and closed his eyes, determined to search his memory ruthlessly and confront whatever he found. Instead, he went to sleep.

＊

When Tom woke up, it was dark. He turned on the light beside his bed and studied the wallpaper birds. Were they landing or taking off? He was still trying to decide when there was a knock at the door.

"Tom? Do you mind if I call you Tom? We like to call everyone by their first names. You can call me Tanya, remember?"

She was at the door, all in white, like an angel.

"I remember." Tom closed his eyes. The last thing he wanted to see was an angel.

"I'm afraid I have bad news. Your wife and her friend have passed away."

"Passed away? What?"

"There were fatalities in the accident. The Super asked me to tell you, since I'm a more familiar face. She will be here in the morning to speak with you directly, if you want to know the details."

"Arabella? Passed away." Tom couldn't bring himself to say the word. The word would make it real.

"I'm so sorry," Tanya said and closed the door again.

Tom swung his feet off the bed. He tried to stand up but he was dizzy; he sat back down.

He could reach the door from the bed; the room was that small. He put his hand on the knob but he didn't want to open it. Not now, not yet. Through that door, Arabella was dead.

Maybe this is the dream. He lay back down and closed his eyes and willed the world to go away, and before very much hateful time had passed, it did.

＊

ELEVEN

When Tom woke up, light was streaming in the window. It was morning. He was alive.

Arabella was dead.

He stood up. Cliff was asleep on the other bed. *Just as well.* Tom wasn't dizzy any more. He looked for his clothes and found them in a paper bag at the foot of the bed. They smelled of smoke and rain. His hands were shaking but he managed to put on his shirt and button it. One sleeve was stiff with dried blood.

Arabella's? *Better not to think.* He had to sit down to pull on his pants, first one leg and then the other. Arabella had always hated these pants. *Arabella—*

"Habeus corpus," said a calm, untroubled voice.

Cliff wasn't asleep after all; his eyes were wide open and his hand was plucking at the covers. In the morning light, he didn't look like an old baby anymore. He looked like an old man.

"Back in a minute," Tom said. "I'm going down the hall to figure out what's happening."

"Habeus corpus," said Cliff in the same calm voice as before, but his big eyes were brimming with tears.

He knows.

"It'll be all right," Tom said. *What a stupid fucking remark!* "Be right back." He squeezed Cliff's hand and slipped out the door, into the dark hallway.

Tanya was in the dayroom, feeding one of the old folks through a tube. It was thicker than the IV tubes Karin had tangled. "Tom, good morning" she said. "Where are you going in those clothes?"

"The Super. Her office?"

"You really shouldn't wear those clothes around here, they're covered with blood and dirt."

Tom nodded. "Sure thing. Where's her office?"

The Super's office was another motel room off another hallway on the other side of the TV room. Instead of beds, it had two desks and two swivel chairs. A woman sat in one, at a computer screen. She looked up when she saw Tom in the doorway.

"You must be Tom." She also wore white.

Tom nodded.

"I'm sorry to say your wife has been in an accident."

"I know. I was in the same goddamned accident. And who the hell are you anyway?"

"You can call me Dawn. I'm the Super of this site. Look, I'm on your side, OK? Why don't you sit down so we can talk."

Tom sat down in the other swivel chair. The wallpaper was the same Escher birds, either landing or taking off.

"I know this is all a shock. This whole operation has been difficult."

"You can say that again. Who are you people anyway? Where am I?"

"You know who we are, Tom. We feel the same way you do about the Brigades, the kevorkians, the involuntary suicides. We have devoted our energies to doing something about it."

"This is all a mistake," Tom said. "None of this was supposed to happen."

"Of course not," Dawn said, shaking her head sympathetically. She had long hair tied back in a ponytail, like Wainwright's. She looked to be in her mid-forties. "We know that you didn't volunteer for the brigade; that's why we intervened. We don't intervene when there is a terminal illness or a voluntary cessation."

"Nobody intervened in anything. You must have picked me up on the highway, after the accident. My wife—"

"I'm afraid your wife didn't survive the accident," said Dawn. "Nor did her friend, Cliff's wife."

"Pam," said Tom. "Pam and Arabella." Saying the names somehow made them more alive. Less—dead.

"I'm sorry for your loss," said Dawn.

"I need to call my daughter," Tom said. "This is a family emergency."

"I understand, certainly, but that's not possible right now," said Dawn. "You are still under the influence of the drugs and we are in a crisis situation here. There's an all-points out on you and your friend."

"And he needs to see a doctor."

"That's going to happen. We're doing the best we can in the face of a Homeland Security Blue Alert. Usually they ignore us; this is a new development. But with any luck the doctor will be here tonight. He's the one who rescued you, in fact. But delete that; I'm not sure you're supposed to know that."

"He's the doctor who treated Arabella? My wife?"

"I really can't say," said Dawn. "I'm sure we'll know more by tonight. Can you wait until then?"

Tom suddenly felt very tired. He was relieved to be relieved of the necessity of doing anything. "Sure," he said, getting up. "But Arabella—"

"There's nothing any of us can do for her now. And one other thing. Please don't wear those clothes here. They will freak out the others."

✻

On his way down the hallway toward his room, Tom passed a door that opened to the outside. He opened it and saw a yard of yellow clay with patches of grassy sod, like hairplugs. Beyond the yard was a dark forest of shaggy pine trees. They were moaning, as if in a wind, though their limbs were still. The sky overhead was filled with thin, high clouds. At the coast the clouds were low and thick; here they were wraiths, like ghosts.

He found the American Spirits in his shirt pocket. Matches too, all crumpled and black with blood. He lit one; there was no one to tell him no.

Arabella is gone.

The taste was sweet. Almost like a friend. Or a betrayal.

He looked down at his hand. It was wrinkled and old. He could almost see right through it, to the ground. He was seventy-one. He was old.

"Tom? That door's alarmed." It was Tanya, all in white.

"Alarmed?"

"You can look out, but don't go through. It's not to keep people in, it's to keep intruders out."

"OK."

"Plus, you can't smoke here, you know. The others."

"I understand," he said, taking a long drag. He flipped the cigarette out and hit a bare spot. An easy shot, since most of the lawn was bare.

✳

Cliff was lying on his back, looking up at the ceiling and the birds.

Tom sat on the bed beside him and took his hand so that it stopped fluttering.

"It's bad, Cliff," he said. "We didn't think it could get any worse but it did. Ara and Pam were killed. There was a wreck. Both killed. But you already knew, didn't you?"

"Habeus corpus."

"You remember everything that happened, don't you?" Tom was surprised at the anger in his voice. Was he mad at Cliff for understanding or for not understanding?

"Habeus corpus."

Tom had never felt so alone. He laid down on the other bed and closed his eyes.

It was afternoon when he awakened. He could tell by the shadows, even though he didn't know which way was east and which was west. There was something about the shadows, about the slow dropping of the birds . . .

"That's it," he thought. I can tell time by them. In the morning they are taking off and in the afternoon they are dropping back down. It was easy. Everything was easy; too easy.

He fell back asleep. He dreamed of Arabella. He was walking in big circles on the sand, looking for her.

He awoke in a panic. Arabella was gone.

Cliff was gone.

He found Cliff down the hall in the TV room, lifting and dropping his arm. How did he get back and forth? Did someone push him?

"That's better," said Tanya.

Huh? Then Tom realized she was referring to his outfit. He was wearing pajamas. Someone had changed his clothes while he slept.

"Would you like to join us?"

No he wouldn't. But he did. She brought him some tuna salad on a tray. He hadn't realized he was hungry before. It tasted good.

On the TV a judge was berating an overweight man for allowing his dog to ruin his girlfriend's carpet. The judge and the defendant were black; the girlfriend, also overweight, was white. The dog was white. Tom watched for a while, then went down the hall to the motel room/office where Dawn was pecking at a keyboard.

"The doctor?" he asked hopefully.

"He's on his way," she said. "I can't give you an arrival

time because we're not in contact. Too dangerous. The phones are all monitored, and a call would lead them here. But don't worry, he will be here, and he will have news."

News? Tom went back to the TV room hoping to watch the news. But there was nothing on except judges and game shows.

"Is there anything to read?" he asked.

"Of course," said Tanya. Her smile and her tone made it clear that she approved of reading. She gave him a stack of magazines. One was about golf; another was about yachts for sale. He never got to the others. He must have fallen asleep, for when he opened his eyes he saw the lights of a car on the window; that's how he knew it was dark outside.

He heard a car door slam. That's how he knew the doctor had arrived.

"Where are you going?" Tanya asked. She was playing checkers with an old woman, moving for both of them.

"The office."

"It's right down the hall."

"I know where it is."

There was a man in the office in Dawn's chair. He had a ponytail like Wainwright's, and he wore a Tilly hat. Tom recognized it from the *New Yorker* ads.

"You must be Tom," the man said. "Come in and sit down."

"That was you," Tom said, as he sat down in Dawn's empty chair. "Flagging us down."

"Sorry I'm late," the man said. "I had to take a circuitous route to get here. They're on us like ticks on a hound. I'm afraid I don't have much to tell you yet. I'm trying to get through to certain people. Everybody's gone to ground. The homies are swarming like bees."

"Are you the doctor?"

"One of them. You can call me Lucius. We don't use our real names here. And of course I can't tell you where you are. I'm not even supposed to know myself. As you have probably determined, you are safe here with the Resistance. I'm sorry about your wife."

"Where is she?"

"She didn't make it out of the wreck. There was nothing we could do for her and we barely had time to pull you and Cliff free before the homies got there."

"No, I mean where is she now?"

"That's what we're trying to find out."

"We thought you were the homies. We tried to get around."

"The shoulder was soft, from the rain. The embankment gave way. You went all the way down into the ravine."

"You caused the wreck," Tom said, standing. "We were getting away."

"The rain caused the wreck," Dawn broke in. She was standing in the doorway. "The government and its inhuman policies caused the wreck."

"You only thought you were getting away," said Lucius. "They had roadblocks up all over the place. Still do. DNR and APB and whatever else they can think of. And you still had Karin's GPS sender in the car." He saw Tom's confusion. "Oh, yeah. It was in her raincoat; that's how I was tracking you, too."

"Karin? The monitor? She was in on this?"

"Not that she knew of."

Tom sat back down. "You are the boyfriend. She told Arabella you had broken up with her."

"It was she who broke up with me. She learned that I was using her to track the involuntary kevorks. I think she was pretty ambivalent about the whole business anyway."

"She was just doing her job. Not too fucking ambivalent, either. She tied a plastic bag over Cliff's head, which is why he's the way he is now. Are you going to do something for him?"

"I'm going to look at him while I'm here. But don't expect too much, Tom. The muscle relaxant knocks out the blood supply to the brain; stroke symptoms are fairly common among survivors."

"I have to find my wife. Is there a phone? I have to speak with my daughter."

"That can happen," said Lucius. "Your daughter knows about all this; she's the one who called and put us on the trail. Gwyneth? But it can't happen yet. You have to give it a few days."

"Days?"

"Come, I have something I have to show you, so you know the situation, the real deal."

The real deal. Tom followed Lucius and Dawn into the TV room. Lucius took a remote from a drawer under the TV (so that's where it was hidden!) and switched to CNN. If the old folks staring at the screen noticed the change, none of them showed any sign of it. Only Cliff seemed interested, with his bright eyes and his right hand fluttering up and down.

"It's been on all the networks," Lucius said. He sampled through memory, backing up through the evening news, until a familiar face filled the screen.

Tom's own. His mouth was open, as if he were about to speak. It was a picture Gwyneth had taken last summer on the deck. Wainwright must have picked up the picture in the house. Had they left it open? But of course, Wainwright had a key. The homies had a key.

"Sought on terrorism charges, plus attempted murder and flight to evade prosecution," said the broadcaster. "Shoot-out in a sleepy seaside resort town of—" The words were unconnected but powerful.

There were pictures of rotating lights and a wrecked car being winched up a steep embankment, onto a rain-dark highway.

Then a Brigade, marching under an American flag. A sturdy, weathered face, looking resolutely into the sunset.

Then Tom's face again. He was surprised by how decrepit, how depraved, how old and wicked he looked. Could they have tampered with the photo? Did they need to?

"Aggravated terrorism and kidnapping—"

"Terrorism? Kidnapping?" Tom said. "All I did was pull an IV out of my arm!"

"And take a shot at a federal employee on duty, according to them. Which makes it a Homeland Blue Alert."

"Wainwright? I shot in the air and the idiot hit the dirt. He's just a fucking handyman anyway."

"He's a homie on alert," said Lucius. "Or maybe they meant Karin, who knows."

"I never shot at her. She pulled a gun on me!"

Lucius shrugged. "Whatever. The kidnapping charge may refer to Cliff here. Apparently he's still under Brigade induction. You guys didn't even get your paperwork right."

"I've seen enough," said Tom. "I need to call my daughter and tell her where I am."

"We're taking care of that," said Dawn. "We're trying to get through to her. It has to be done in a secure way that doesn't endanger the others."

The others again.

"You have to understand," said Lucius. "It's not really you they are after. It's us." He tapped himself on the chest. "By putting out an APB-DNR on you, they are admitting that we exist."

"That there is alternative to involuntary suicide," said Dawn. "That there is an active, effective Resistance."

"I still need to contact my daughter. Are the cops looking for her too?"

"I'm sure she's being watched," said Lucius, "in the hope that she will lead them to you—and to us. That's why the important thing now is to lay low and remain cool. Surely you of all people can understand that."

"What do you mean?"

"I mean, we know about you and Cliff and your history in the movement. We know we can trust you to maintain security until this cools down."

"If it ever does," said Dawn. She raised her chin slightly, as if prepared to take a blow.

Lucius shot her a look. "Meanwhile I need to take a look at Cliff and you need to go back to your room and relax until morning. I promise to let you know as soon as we find out anything. OK?"

"OK," said Tom.

✳

TWELVE

Tom's clothes were still in his room, in the paper bag. He knew better than to put them on. He fished out the American Spirits. There were only four left in the pack; they were all bent. And there was something else in the bottom of the bag, something heavy.

It was Karin's little matte-black 9mm automatic. He wrapped the shirt around it and put it back.

He straightened out one of the last American Spirits and took it down the hall to the outside door before lighting it.

The stars looked very cold and very small and very far away.

Tom wondered how he would ever get to sleep with Arabella gone, lost, closed up in a morgue drawer somewhere.

"Tom? Do you mind if I call you Tom?"

It was a girl in white, a black girl, not Tanya. She was pushing Cliff through the hall in his wheelchair. "You can call me Butterfly. You know, you can't smoke here."

"Sorry," said Tom. He threw away the cigarette and followed them to his room.

*

The next morning Dawn's office was closed. Breakfast was pancakes, with sausage. Some of the old folks in the TV room even smiled when they smelled the sausage.

Tanya's replacement had a sweet, wide smile and fluttering hands that almost matched Cliff's. "You can call me Butterfly," she said.

"I know," said Tom.

She was combing Cliff's hair over his bald spot, tenderly. Tom helped put the breakfast dishes away and checked the office again. Still closed.

He was watching a morning talk show when Lucius came in and pulled the remote from the drawer. "The Resistance is no longer a myth," he said, switching to CNN.

The TV showed two young people in chains, a man and a woman. They were both smiling and holding up their fists as they were led to a waiting Homeland Security van.

"This story has broken the silence," said Lucius. "Now the whole country knows there is a Resistance and it is active. The government has stopped trying to hide it. They are of course trying to paint us as murderers and criminals, but the people will know the difference. Most of them anyway."

"How about Cliff?" Tom asked.

Lucius shook his head. "Not so good. I examined him last night. There's no change and there's not likely to be change. We can take care of him, of course. That's why this place is here."

"He doesn't want to be here," Tom said. "Neither do I. We need to be with our families."

"I understand how you feel," said Lucius. "But you can't really speak for Cliff, can you? It would be suicide for you or him to leave here, and we can't allow that. Plus, it would endanger the others. Wait until you have thought it over and things have cooled down a little."

"What would your wife think?" It was Dawn, in the doorway. "I'm sure she wouldn't want you to throw away your life after all the efforts that have been taken to save it. Think of the thousands who are risking their own careers to put up a resistance to the involuntary suicide and judicial murder that is the Brigades and the kevorkian laws."

"This has all been a mistake," Tom said again. "We appreciate what you are doing but . . ."

"Not a mistake," said Lucius. "An inevitability. Sooner or later they would have to realize we existed. Now the fight has been joined. It's more important than ever that we keep you hidden and help you survive this assault."

"Let me call my daughter, at least."

Lucius put a hand on Tom's shoulder. "I understand and we're on it. We have to patch in the call from the Netherlands, so they can't trace it. We've gone from symbolic resistance to real Resistance. We need your total cooperation."

"Doing what?"

"Laying low. Being cool. *Chilling*, I believe was once the word."

✳

Tom spent the morning "chilling" in the TV room with Cliff. The morning was filled with talk, then with games where people won money and then leaped about.

After a particularly big win, with much leaping about, Tom went back to his room to get an American Spirit out of the paper bag. There were three left, all crooked. The black gun was still safe, wrapped in the shirt in the bottom of the bag.

He unwrapped it and put on the shirt. The blood on the sleeve cracked off and fell to floor as dark powder.

He went back down the hall to the open door and lit the cigarette. The forbidden taste, the betrayal, was sweet—but where was the betrayed? *Arabella, I didn't mean to leave you there alone. I didn't mean for any of this to happen.*

The long bare lawn, with a few patches of grass, ended abruptly at a row of shaggy pines; dark, thoughtless, still-living trees.

Tom tried to remember Arabella's face, her voice, but they both were dim. Like seeing through fog.

"Remember, Tom, you can't smoke here."

It was Butterfly, Tanya's replacement. Darker skin, brighter eyes, all in white like—

"Oh, yeah, I forgot," said Tom, flipping the cigarette out onto the lawn, hitting a bare spot. "What's that noise out there?"

"What noise? Out where?"

"Beyond the trees. I thought it was the wind but there's no wind."

"A highway, I think," Butterfly said. "I don't know which one, of course. We come here blindfolded, for security. That way if we're arrested, like the ones this morning, we can't betray anything because we don't know anything."

"I thought it was the wind," Tom said. A highway was better.

✱

When Tom got back to the room, Cliff was there, sitting in his wheelchair by the window. Tanya was feeding him lunch with a long spoon. "There's a sandwich for you on the bed," she said. "I'm sorry we're out of juice."

"I thought you had gone," Tom said.

"We're all stuck here until the alert is lifted," she said. "We can't *all* get arrested, can we?"

She made it sound like a privilege. As soon as she had wiped her spoon and left, Tom unwrapped his sandwich and ate it. Tuna fish.

"This is fucked," he said. "It's an old folks home. Assisted living. We go from assisted dying to assisted living. Fuck!"

"Habeus corpus," said Cliff.

"It's a bunch of kids taking care of old people. But I'm talking to Gwyneth this afternoon. I'm going to figure out a way to get us out of here."

"Habeus corpus," said Cliff.

"I don't know where. Just somewhere. Anywhere."

Tom lay down on his bed and closed his eyes. He wanted to see the island again but he couldn't find it, even in his imagination. Sleep wouldn't come; it was neither morning nor afternoon. He opened his eyes and watched the birds, caught in the wallpaper's beige universe, neither landing nor taking off.

Finally he got up and went down the hall to the TV room. The old folks were dozing, tomato soup dribbling down their chins. On the TV a judge was listening to the excuses of a black man whose dog had ripped down the wash from a neighbor's line. "He didn't know it was wash, Your Honor. Who hangs out wash anymore?"

The judge seemed unsympathetic. Just as she was about to announce her verdict, Tom felt a hand on his shoulder. He jumped, startled; he had been imagining he was the defendant.

It was Lucius, looking pleased. "Tom, your call. As promised."

Tom followed him to the office down the hall. "Make the best of it," Lucius said. "It took a lot of doing. We have people in Europe too. We learned a lot from you and Cliff."

"From me and Cliff?"

"From your generation. From people with a personal history of resistance. From all those who would not go gently into that good night. There's the phone. Remember, it's international."

He turned and left the room.

Tom was both eager and reluctant to pick up the phone. "Gwyn?"

"Dad!"

"It's me. Are you all right, honey?"

"Yes, they can't prove anything. Oh, it's so good to hear your voice."

"What do you mean they can't prove anything? Have you been arrested?"

"Only detained for an hour or so yesterday. They're so stupid."

"What about your mother?"

"She's at Wainwright's."

Tom felt a moment's surge of hope. Then he realized what she meant. "Funeral home?"

"He won't release her body. They say it's evidence."

Her body. It used to mean something else.

"I'll take care of it, Dad. I promise. It's what mother would have wanted."

"What? That?"

"For you to be OK. Don't do something foolish like I know you're thinking about."

"Like what?"

"Everyone is looking for you. You and Cliff are heroes. You have to lay low."

"Heroes, hell. Gwyneth, this is no good. This is an old folks home."

"What's wrong with that?"

"Nothing but I'd rather have joined the fucking Brigade.

Cliff is here too. He's had some kind of stroke."

"Daddy, talk sense. It's not fair to Mom. It's not fair to me!"

"You're breaking up," Tom said. "I love you."

"I don't want to be an orphan!"

"I love you," said Tom, hanging up.

"She's right, you know," said Lucius. He was standing in the doorway.

"What the hell do you know! You were listening to my phone call?"

"Of course not." Lucius sat in the chair across from Tom and placed his two thick hands between his knees. "But I know what she was saying. I know this place looks bad. We have people here who were injured by the kevorkian chemicals. But you don't belong here. At the other centers, in California and back East, you will find people you will want to be with. Maybe even work with. You may even want to work with us. Now you have a choice. That's the whole point."

"What about Cliff?"

"He belongs here. He'll have to make his own choices. You can't make his choices for him."

And you can? "What about my wife? They won't release her to my daughter."

"And they sure as hell won't release her to you. Tom, you're a wanted man. You're part of the Resistance whether you like it or not."

"Ara wasn't supposed to die."

"Tom, you have to give her up. She was ready to give you up. Can't you do the same for her?"

"I don't want to talk about it," said Tom, getting up.

"I understand," said Lucius. "You've been through a lot. Get some rest and think about it and we'll talk tomorrow."

❋

THIRTEEN

Outside, the sun was going down. Tom found Cliff in the TV room. He pulled the remote out of the drawer and found CNN. The rest of the old folks either didn't notice or didn't mind; most of them were dozing.

"Arrested in Eugene and Northern Washington," said the announcer. The TV showed four young people in chains, being loaded into a red-white-and-blue ashcroft van. They were smiling and holding up their fists.

"More arrests," said Dawn. She was standing in the doorway again; she seemed to like doorways.

"How many of there are you?" Tom asked.

"I don't actually know," Dawn said. "And of course I wouldn't say if I did. The Resistance is nationwide. Some are medical students, some are religious activists, some are volunteers like Tanya and Butterfly. We come from every sector of society, just like the opposition to the death penalty, or the right-to-life movement in your day."

"But those were two entirely different sets of people, and politics," Tom said.

"Things change. The enemy of my enemy is my friend. We unite all those who are dedicated to fighting a society that discards old people when their usefulness is done. We fight for the dignity of old age and the rejection of suicide as a social policy. Surely you, with your history of political activism, can understand that."

"Not exactly. I supported the idea of voluntary termination at first," said Tom. "It seemed like a socially desirable thing, especially since the life span is so long in the developed world."

"Isn't that a little racist," said Dawn, with a tight smile. "Isn't suicide itself a little arrogant, with a hint of *noblesse oblige*? It's not just about you anyway. The Resistance is more than just a haven for those who are escaping the kevorkian laws. It's a mechanism for those who want to put their principles into action, like the Underground Railroad."

"But the Underground Railroad wasn't set up for the benefit of those who ran it," Tom protested.

Or was it? He looked up and she was gone.

✳

Cliff was getting stronger. His arm was rising farther and and falling more slowly. His eyes seemed brighter, more— understanding.

"Where are you taking him?" asked Butterfly.

"For a walk," said Tom. "Is that allowed?"

"Of course, but don't go outside. We don't know who might be watching through the fence."

"There's a fence?"

"It's not to keep people in," said Tanya, who was helping with the evening feeding. "It's to keep people out. Security."

Tom rolled Cliff down the empty hall. He stopped by their room and got the next-to-last American Spirit out of the bag. Then he smoked it, half in and half out of the open back door, while Cliff looked on in his now customary silence.

"It's all backward," said Tom. "More than backward. Twisted almost totally around."

"Habeus corpus," said Cliff.

"Young people dedicating their lives to keeping old people alive. Risking their lives, or at least their freedom, so . . . what? So we can watch talk shows and eat tuna? Most of us don't even know what we are watching on TV. Or maybe we do. That's worse."

"Habeus corpus," said Cliff.

"They see this as their big shot. By repressing them, the government is finally taking them seriously. And in a weird way, they dig it! I can see it in their eyes, hear it in their voices. Remember all the people in the movement who didn't care about winning, who just wanted to fight the good fight?"

"Habeus corpus."

"You can't win and therefore you never have to take responsibility for actually changing anything. You just get to feel good about making the fucking effort. Moralism in arms. They're not fighting the Brigades, they're fighting Death itself. Moralism's ideal strategy: pick a fight you know beforehand you can't possibly win. But what am I saying, it's not just them. All our lives, we are fighting Death. That's what life is, I guess, a slow holding-action against entropy."

"Habeus corpus," said Cliff.

"Tom, you know you can't smoke here." It was Butterfly. "Think of the others."

"They can't smell it," Tom said. "They don't know what the hell's going on anyway. Tell me, Butterfly, why do you do this?"

"This?"

"All this. Taking care of all these old people. Of us."

"Old age deserves dignity," Butterfly said.

"No it doesn't," Tom said, throwing out his cigarette and closing the door. "Take it from one who knows."

❋

Tom was alive, in a motel room. Arabella was dead, in a drawer.

It was backward. Worse than backward. But what could he do? He was a prisoner here, and Dawn was right, it was the fault of the government. The whole business was fucked.

He lay down on the bed and closed his eyes. He had a gun, in the bag. He could end it for himself and Cliff. But what would that do to the kids here, who had saved them; or who thought they had saved them? It would be worse than betrayal.

He was trapped. He was in a drawer like Arabella.

Only worse: alive. With no one to talk to, except Cliff, who had forgotten how to talk back.

It was over but it still went on. It was just as his grandfather had said, back in Indiana: "The problem is, life goes on after it's over."

He closed his eyes, hoping the world would go away again, like before. But it didn't. Tom was no longer tired, no longer dizzy. He tried counting sheep, and it was going OK, until suddenly someone pulled at his sleeve.

"There you are. I found you."

He opened his eyes. He was in the bed alone. But it was Arabella's voice. He started to cry, for the first time in years, and closed his eyes.

"I found you," she said again.

✳

FOURTEEN

There was a quarter moon. The clouds continued their march eastward, into nothingness. They dissipated over the unseen desert, leaving not a trace: no rain, no shadow, and finally, no cloud.

Tom stood in the doorway smoking the last American Spirit, all the way down, until it would have burned his fingers if it were not for the filter. He tossed it away and went back inside and put on his clothes, stiff shirt and all. There was the gun, in the bottom of the bag. The safety was off. Had it been off all along?

271

He switched it on and stuck the gun into his belt.

He felt like an outlaw. An American Spirit Outlaw. An old fucking outlaw.

"Habeus corpus," said Cliff.

"You awake? We need to talk," said Tom. He sat down on the bed and took Cliff's hand. "I have to get out of here," he said. "I have to deal with Gwyneth and with Arabella, and Pam too. Everything is fucked. They don't need me here. You don't need me here."

"Habeus corpus," said Cliff.

"Gwyneth will help me. I will come for you when all this is over. I'll try. I'll do what I can. But first I need to get far enough away so if I get caught they can't trace me back to these kids."

"Habeus corpus," said Cliff.

He knows I'm lying, Tom thought. Then he saw that Cliff was looking at the gun in his belt.

"It's the one I took from Karin," he said. "With an I. Don't worry, I'm not going to use it. If I can get to the highway I can trade it for a ride to Portland."

"Habeus corpus."

"Seattle, then. Hell, Eugene. I know we're in Oregon, somewhere on the western side of the Cascades; I can tell by the clouds." He put his hand on the doorknob. "So long, buddy. So long again."

Cliff raised his arm and held it, almost steady. A salute? A plea? "Habeus corpus," he said.

Tom took his hand off the door. He couldn't go through. Not alone, anyway. "OK, OK," he said.

✳

If the alarm went off, Tom didn't hear it. Perhaps the alarm had been a bluff, he thought, as he pushed the wheelchair through the door and onto the long, patched lawn. Then he turned it around: it was easier to pull than to push. Cliff was facing backward, saluting or waving steadily, as Tom pulled him into the woods.

Just inside the trees, there was a steep bank. At the bottom was a chain-link fence, taller than a man, with three strands of barbed wire at the top. Beyond the fence there was a dirt road. Tom could barely make it all out in the moonlight.

He heard a bell ringing behind him.

"Habeus corpus," said Cliff.

"The alarm," said Tom. "I thought they were bluffing."

"Tom? I know you're there!" Lucius was speaking through a bullhorn. "I'm on your side. I want to bring you back safely, in a way that doesn't endanger you or us. Is Cliff with you?"

Tom didn't answer. That meant they couldn't see him, even in the moonlight. He heard a door open and shut; he heard muffled voices.

"We know he's with you. That's OK. Just don't go any farther. There's a fence. It's electric."

You're bluffing, Tom thought.

"It's not to keep you in. It's to keep them out. Come back before you bring the homies down on us all."

Tom studied the fence. There was no way he was going to get through it with a wheelchair, even if it wasn't electric, which it probably wasn't. Plus the bank was too steep here; there was no way down.

"Tom, it's me, Lucius. I'm coming to bring you back."

Tom pointed the gun straight up, toward the sky, and pulled the trigger. He had forgotten the safety was on. He clicked it off and pulled the trigger again.

BLAM!

"Whoa! What was that?"

He fired again: BLAM!

"Damn, Tom, I hope you're not shooting at me," Lucius shouted through the bullhorn. "Because I'm not going to shoot back, if that's what you want."

Tom decided it was best not to answer.

"Habeus corpus," Cliff whispered. Tom was surprised. Had he been able to whisper before, or was this a new power? Cliff was leaning forward in his wheelchair, his right hand plucking at the rim of the right wheel. Suddenly Tom realized what was happening.

Too late.

Before he could grab the chair, Cliff had rolled it over the edge of the bank. It pitched forward, spilling him out and rolling down on top of him. Cliff and the chair hit the fence at the same time.

There was a crackling sound, and a wad of dry grass burst into flame.

"Shit! It *is* electric!" Tom slid down the bank, holding the gun in one hand and slowing himself with the other.

The grass was still burning but the fence was no longer crackling.

Cliff was half in and half out of the chair, wedged between the bottom of the bank and the fence. The wire was sparking where it crossed the spokes of the wheel. Cliff's arm was rising and falling rapidly.

Tom grabbed Cliff's hand, and it shocked him.

"Damn!" He tried it again; this time it was barely a tingle. He grabbed Cliff's wrist and pulled him out of the chair. But there was nowhere to go. They were both wedged in the tiny space between the steep bottom of the bank and the fence.

"Habeus corpus," said Cliff.

"I know," said Tom. "It wasn't supposed to be like this, old buddy. We did our best didn't we?

"Habeus corpus."

Tom could hear doors slamming in the distance. Floodlights came on, lighting the tops of the trees, high above.

"Tom, don't do this! You're giving us no choice."

No choice? Tell me about it.

He could see silhouettes at the top of the bank. They were looking down. A light shone in his face.

He raised the gun and fired again.

BLAM!

The light went out.

"Go ahead, you old fool," said Lucius. "I can wait till morning. You're trapped there. We tried to work with you, but you're determined to put us all in danger. Well, we can wait you out."

Tom thought it best not to answer. At least the light was out. He tried to move the chair but it was wedged against the fence. His hands tingled again when he touched it. It wasn't a shock, really; more of a warning.

Cliff was folded up in a fetal position on the ground. His left leg was moving in unison with his arm, back and forth.

Shit. Tom turned over and lay on his back and looked up.

The clouds swept across the moon like cotton swabs, big and incredibly beautiful, faster and faster—eastward, toward the still faraway dawn. They disappeared behind the trees.

"Habeus corpus," said Cliff.

"I know."

Tom put the gun against the side of Cliff's head. It wasn't supposed to be like this but no one had to look. He could keep his eyes closed.

"So long again, old buddy."

BLAM

"Tom! If you're firing at me, you're wasting your shots. I won't fire back."

Tom put the gun against his own temple. As he searched for the familiar little indentation he saw the island again, finally. There was one tree on the center, just like in the cartoons. The hang glider was descending, too fast. There was Arabella, all in silhouette, all in black, but sweetly familiar.

"I found you."

Then there was nothing at all.

This grave partakes the fleshly birth,
which cover lightly, gentle earth.
                    —Ben Jonson

Dear Abbey

Lee and I were never really friends, and never is saying a lot if you are covering all the way from late October to the End of Time. We were office-mates, initially; colleagues, as it turned out; comrades, if you insist. And traveling companions, to be sure.

If it seems odd to you that a Distinguished Professor of Higher Mathematics should share an office with an American Studies Associate, you have never worked at a community college; much less Southwest Connecticut Community College, which is, due in small part to its central location on the BosWash Corridor, and in no small part to its liberal hiring policies, a brief and unceremonious stop for Eastern Seaboard academics on their way down, or out, or both. Lee had brought his exalted title with him from MIT, from which he had decamped after an undisclosed (and, as it turned out, almost entirely diversionary) conflict with a department head.

But hey, we all have our little secrets. I, on the other hand, like most of my other colleagues at "Swick" (as we called it on the rare occasions when we spoke among ourselves), had been hired sight-unseen, no-questions-asked to fulfill some obscure bureaucratic quota, and could count on being let go when I came up for review in a year or so.

Not that I frankly my dear gave a damn. I was only passing through.

But enough about me. Did I mention that Lee was Chinese? Sixtyish, which meant old enough to be my father (if you could imagine my old man with a doctorate, or even imagine my old man, but that's another story) and a political refugee from mainland China, which could mean, or so I then thought, anything.

Lee was somewhat of a campus celeb since at MIT he had been shortlisted for a Ballantine (the math MacArthur). His post-postdoc from Rice had apparently carried no language requirement, since he spoke a coarse pidgin with a brutal and bizarre Texas drawl. It was as if he had learned English from a "You Know You're a Redneck If" phrase book.

A shared office at SWCCC meant one desk, one chair, one TI line; the two of us weren't supposed to be in the office at the same time. It was a time share, which is ironic, I suppose, considering. We each had our own shallow drawer. I kept a pint of bourbon and a few books in mine. Lee kept—who knew?—a time machine in his.

⁕

The day it all began was a Friday—the last day of classes before the long holiday weekend, when the "Swick" campus was due to become even quieter and deader than usual.

Since when did Halloween become a college holiday? As much as I hated teaching, I hated holidays even worse. Especially this coming weekend. I had promised to stay away from the apartment while Helen picked up her stuff, mainly the extra uniforms and the little wheeled bag that fit perfectly through the carry-on templates. It was, like her underwear, and indeed her personality, a pricey and initially fetching example of minimal design. And there was of course her little dog. But enough about her. I finished my last class (Nineteenth-Century Slave Narratives), of which two-thirds had escaped on that underground railway that spirits students away before holidays, and stopped by the office to have a drink and puzzle out a way to kill the evening. No big deal. Welcome to Moviephone.

When I opened the office door and saw a pair of cowboy boots on the desk, my heart skipped, as they say, a beat. Did Connecticut, like New Jersey, have sheriffs? (Turns out it does but they are not Chinese.) But it was nothing so serious. It was only my rarely-seen office-mate, Won "Bill" Lee, leaning back, reading, a paper cup in one hand and a book in the other.

"Dr. Cole!" Lee said, sitting up and spilling the contents of the paper cup down the front of his never-iron (and never-really-white) white shirt with its plastic pocket protector filled with pens. I could tell by the smell it was my Jack Daniels. "Lay in wait!"

The book was mine too: *The Monkey Wrench Gang*.

"Just Cole is okay," I said. "But hey, Lee, keep your seat. I'm only passing through. What are you doing here this late on a Friday afternoon, anyway?" I reached for the phone, but while I was dialing 777-FILM, Lee cut me off with one finger.

"Lay in wait," Lee said again, standing up. "You and me, pardner."

"Me? What can I do for you?"

"Like the good book says," Lee said mysteriously. He replaced the book and the bottle in my drawer and pulled a Palm PC out of his own. Then he grinned, suddenly and rather incongruously, and pointed toward the door. "Round on the house? Wet the whistle? Happy Hour?"

I figured, Why not? Halloween comes only once a year, Thank God.

※

Lee was small, even for a Chinaman, with black hair that managed to look short and uncut at the same time. He wore a hideous L. L. Bean safari jacket over his no-iron shirt and pen protector. And shoes, you don't want to know. Since the campus was, quite literally, in the Middle of Nowhere, and I had no car (don't believe in them: which was only one of Helen's well-documented complaints), we rode in Lee's rather surprising Prius to a little place a block from the Sound called, ominously, it seems in retrospect, The Pequod. "Two Jack," Lee said, and two amber shots of B grade bourbon appeared on the bar.

I am always amazed that foreigners think Jack Daniels is an A bourbon. I drink it strictly in honor of my Tennessee grandmother. But what the hell, it seemed as good a way as any to kill an evening. "Cheers," I said, raising my glass. "To Chinese-American friendship."

"China-merica no-no," Lee said, shaking his head with a sudden seriousness. Then he smiled, like an actor changing moods. "Dear Abbey yes! Monkey Ranch Gang yes!"

Dear Abbey? I was startled, suspicious even. But no, no way—I decided to let it go. "It's 'wrench,'" I said, draining my glass and signaling for another. "But why not? Here's to old Ed Abbey."

Lee smiled and toasted back. Then he winked. "To the Jersey Kaczynski."

"Whoa!" I looked around. We were alone in the bar except for a couple in the far back, by the jukebox. "Where'd you hear that?"

Though it was no secret how I had lost my position at Princeton, I hadn't exactly advertised it at Swick. It had been almost five years before. I had done eleven months for refusing to testify about the firebombing of some ski lifts in the Poconos, with collateral damage. No direct connection had been proven, or even officially alleged. Since then I had, rather strategically, distanced myself from the environmental movement.

"Pell," said Lee. "Smell the beans. No problem."

"Spill the beans," I said. "And it *is* a problem because this Pell should learn to mind his own business and keep his mouth shut. I didn't know you ran with that crowd anyway."

Which was true. If Lee was Green, this was the first I had heard of it. The Greens (at Swick, anyway) tended to be all white and ostentatiously boho, neither of which fit Lee's profile; or, for that matter, my own.

But I felt (as usual) compelled to say more. "The Jersey Kaczynski thing was all bullshit anyway. I had no connection with EarthAlert or with the individuals who were later captured. I happened to be an easy target because I had assigned Kaczynski's 'Unabomber Manifesto' in an American Studies class. The feds came after me because they were too stupid or too lazy to find the individuals they actually wanted."

Not exactly true but close enough for The Pequod.

"They needn't have bothered anyway," I said, getting wound up in spite of (or perhaps because of) the fact that Lee could barely understand me. Or so I thought. "The environmental movement is a joke. It's way too late for talk. Peat fires in the Arctic tundra. In Africa, the elephants are dying in heaps. The sea level is expected to rise two to four feet in the next hundred years. Do you have any idea what that means?"

"Every any idea," said Lee, nodding. "Lamentation river stage flood." What that meant, he explained, and I pieced together, as we shared another round and I began to understand Lee's fractured Texas English, was that China's infamous Yellow River Dam project had reached reservoir level one week before, inundating the last of the ancient, doomed villages. Either Lee's English or my understanding, or both, got better with the whiskey, and I learned that Lee had worked as an engineer on the project for eleven years before comprehending what a disaster it would be. He had then opposed it publicly and clandestinely for two years before being forced to leave the country just two steps ahead of the secret police.

"Bare excape," he said with an enigmatic smile, effortlessly nailing the authentic Texas pronunciation. I looked at my colleague with new respect. Eleven months in Allenwood Federal Correctional Facility was a piece of cake compared to what they do to you in China, if they catch you. And I had been lecturing him!

"So here's to Ted," I said. I didn't bother to whisper. Except for the two in the far back, by the jukebox, Lee and I were the only people in The Pequod besides the bartender, a mournful Connecticut Yankee who politely kept his distance while he wiped glasses and watched the "news" on TV, as if the routine murders of inner-city drug dealers were news.

"Ted?" Lee asked, raising his tiny glass.

"Ted Kaczynski. Because the crazy fucker's right, unfuckingfortunately," I explained, signaling for another round. "Because we're in the middle of what E. O. Wilson calls the Sixth Extinction. Because the ongoing, relentless, merciless, and mindless destruction of the planet overrules whatever small progress might have been made against racism, nationalism, greed or ignorance or all of the above. Because they can't even make a fucking gesture of a deal to stop global warming; because they deny it's even happening; because—"

"So why not Pell? Why not Greens?"

"Because, Lee, what's Texan for a day late and a dollar short?"

"Why not Monkey Ranch, then, Cole? Why not Dear Abbey indeed?"

"Whoa!" I said, aloud this time. There it was, Dear Abbey, again. This time it was no mistake. It was deliberate. I could tell by Lee's suddenly inscrutable smile.

Some kind of cop: that was my first thought. I set down my empty glass. "I beg your fucking pardon. What in the world are you talking about?"

"What he's talking about is what we've all been talking about for the past two and a half years," said a familiar voice from the back of the bar, by the jukebox.

※

I was suddenly sober, or so it seemed to me. My heart, or what I have been told passes for a heart, was pounding as I turned and faced the two who were walking toward me out of the shadows in the back of the bar. One was Pell, of course, I should have guessed; and right behind Pell was my most valued, most troublesome, and least expected friend.

Justine?

There's always a problem when you run into somebody who's underground, especially when they're with someone. Even when it's clearly not an accident, what do you call them? What do *they* call them? Who knows who and who knows what? Adding to the confusion, there's never any time to think.

"Justine?"

"Actually, it's Flo these days," she said. "Don't I get a hug?"

"Of course," I said, complying, "but what the hell are you doing here? And with—"

There was no way to cast a look toward Pell without seeming rude. I cast a look toward Pell.

Pell smiled and nodded. Smug? Stupid? Both. He went and stood beside Lee at the bar but didn't, I noticed, order a drink. Of course not. He was on duty.

So was Justine, or rather, Flo. If you're looking for a description, you won't find it here. You probably don't need it. She looked exactly the same as she had looked on *America's Most Wanted*, except for the hair color. Six million people saw that, thanks to the two teenagers, both boys, who had broken into the Skyline Lodge looking for cell phones to steal.

Teenagers usually kill themselves and one another. They don't ordinarily depend on environmentalists to do it, even as collateral damage. But I digress . . .

"Good to see you, Cole," she said, checking to make sure the bartender was out of earshot. "Though this isn't exactly a social call."

"Why am I not surprised," I said. "Good to see you too. I hope things are going okay. I haven't heard much. That's good in itself, I guess."

"That's good," she confirmed. "Things have been quiet. We've been laying low. Laying off the 'stupid stunts.' I'm quoting you here, Cole. I knew you would approve. Bartender?!"

"Thought this wasn't a social call."

"It's not but don't worry. The bourbon is part of the deal, believe it or not. I wanted to introduce you to Dr. Lee, and this seemed the easiest way."

"Introduce? He's my office-mate."

"Yes, quite a coincidence, *n'est-ce pas?* I meant introduce politically. You are also comrades, as you have been discovering."

"Quit beating around the bush, Justine. What does he know about Dear Abbey? Is that why we're here?"

"It's Flo. And yes, my friend and comrade, yes it is."

✳

By now either you know, and everyone knows, or you don't, and it doesn't matter any more, that Dear Abbey is a radical, long-range plan for saving the environment that will make Ted Kaczynski look like Mother Teresa. It involves an alarmingly complex but theoretically possible piece of genetic engineeering that will, let us say, severely inhibit the ability of humans to degrade the environment. Severe is the operative modifier. You can't call it terrorism because no one will be killed, directly at least, and no one will even know for sure what is happening until it has been operating for almost a decade, by which time it will be too late to undo it. The human cost will be high but not nearly as high as the cost of doing nothing, or of simply continuing with the kind of pointless stunts for which the environmental movement is known.

Dear Abbey was the only thing that still connected me to EarthAlert. I hadn't come up with the idea but I had been among the first to embrace it and argue for it. I had lost interest only when it became clear that it couldn't be accomplished any time soon; the technology was still decades away. As far as I was concerned, these were decades the world didn't have.

"Dear Abbey has aroused a great deal of interest in China," Justine, or rather Flo said. "As drastic and as necessary as Dear Abbey will be here, it is even more drastic in Asia. And more necessary."

"Aren't we forgetting one detail? That it can't be made to work yet?"

"Tell that to the Chinese. They say they can make it work. They say they have found the missing link. Which is where our friend comes in."

I felt a surge of hope, so sudden, so unfamiliar and so welcome that I distrusted it immediately. "Impossible! I was told it would take a whole new gene-sequencing technology based on a mathematics that's not even . . ."

She cut me off with a smile and a shrug. "Lee has found a fix. A way to access tomorrow's technology today." "Right. Time travel."

"You needn't look so smug, Cole. No, it's not science fiction, but yes, according to Lee it does involve some kind of quantum uncertainty math thing. The Chinese are way ahead of us. Isn't Lee the guy who won that award for the computer program that executes commands nano-seconds before they are given?"

"Yes, nano-seconds, but . . ."

"Yes, but nothing. You and Lee are supposedly using some see-into-the-future computer program to pick up a gene-sequencing patch that will make Dear Abbey work. The missing link. The trigger. The one thing we don't have, and for some reason it's a two person operation."

"Time travel. Science fiction. But why me?"

"We wanted to be involved, and the Chinese requested you. Maybe it's their idea of promoting racial harmony. Maybe it's the prison thing; maybe they think it means you can be trusted. Maybe it's because you are already hooked up with Lee, in a way, although I wonder if that was entirely coincidence."

I was wondering too. "When all does this happen?"

"Tonight. In less than an hour. At nine."

"Surely you jest."

"No, Cole, I don't surely jest. Maybe it's you that surely jests. Maybe you were jesting when you told Big Bird that when we needed you for Dear Abbey, you would be there, no questions asked."

Big Bird was EarthAlert's central committee. "Here I am, aren't I?"

"Then don't ask so damn many questions. Think of it

as the inscrutable Orient, and all that." She looked around to make sure Lee wasn't listening; he and Pell were at the bar, with their backs turned. "This whole thing sounds a little woo-woo to me too. Maybe it's nothing but a make-nice between Big Bird and the Chinese; a little hand-holding to flatter a nutty professor. So what? If Lee's for real, and this works, which I'm told it could, we have Dear Abbey now, when we need it. And even if it's bullshit, which it probably is, you've gained us an ally and wasted an hour."

"And gotten arrested or worse. What if this is some kind of stupid second-story job?"

"I doubt it. Lee got out of China and into MIT, didn't he? Just go along with Dr. Lee and see where it goes, Cole. Your presence represents their trust for us; that in itself is a breakthrough. It'll all be over in an hour, OK?"

I had already decided to go along with it. "OK. But first, you have to answer me one question."

She looked at me warily. "What?"

"Where'd you come up with Flo?"

※

I finished my drink while Lee and Justine, or rather Flo, made their final arrangements. She looked as imperious, as mysterious as ever. Lee no longer looked the least bit woozy, but who knew how a whiskey-drinking revolutionary Chinese math-wizard was supposed to look? Pell looked the same as always: insignificant and untrustworthy. But who was I to argue with Big Bird? Decisions had been made. When organizations are underground, and under attack, as EarthAlert certainly was in those days, decisions are not made democratically. The less one knows, the better.

Flo was looking at her watch. "Time," she said. "Good luck, Cole." Then she kissed me on both cheeks and split.

"What is this, the Resistance?" I said, as much to myself as to her, as she and Pell exited through the back. The only part of my life that made sense, and she had whittled it down to a point. A very sharp point. I set my empty glass down on the bar. It made a very loud noise.

"Dr. Lee, I'm your guy. Let's do this thing."

"Follow me." The Chinaman was all smiles.

※

1

Lee and I exited through the front. Lee was carrying a briefcase decorated with formulas that accentuated his nerdy look. His cowboy English got better, explaining technical things. "According Barbour, Hawking, Liu Hsun," he said as we folded ourselves into his Prius, "Time is illusion. We live eternal present, in each moment coexist. Separate Universe, like beads on string."

"I've heard that story," I said. "We're the beads, Time's the string. But what does that have to do with anything?"

"Time string loops," Lee said, rather mysteriously.

"Whatever." I was not exactly drunk but not exactly sober either. I wondered where we were going but knew enough not to ask. My role was just to ride shotgun, the token Westerner, so to speak.

The Prius was unexpectedly noisy. It was the brick street. We were heading back toward the campus. I could barely hear Lee, who was explaining that since Time was relative, the algorithm had to be accessed by two people because of what he called the "subjective factory."

"What algorithm?" I asked, just to be polite.

"See tomorrow math."

"So this time travel has something to do with math?"

"Straight shooting," Lee said, turning into the campus.

"I see," I said, as the little car bounced over the first speed bump. Do the Chinese think they mean speed up? The return to campus was a surprise, and a reassuring one. It fit right in with the nutty professor theory. It meant a wasted hour in familiar surroundings; a favor done for Big Bird; and a promise to Helen fulfilled. I had promised I would stay away from the apartment until ten. At least now I had something to do. *Never mind, Moviephone.*

The next surprise was less reassuring. Lee drove past the Faculty Extension and parked at the Student Union, a building I rarely visited. Even though classes were done for the holiday, and only a few students were around, the SU was filled with thumping music, rap, advertising the thuggishness of Swick's student body, as if it weren't obvious already from the appearance and demeanor, if it can be called that, of the few that were left on campus.

The next surprise was, Lee had a key to the basement.

He closed the door behind us and turned on the light. We were in a large, windowless bare room with a concrete floor, like a church basement from the Tennessee half of my childhood. It even had a big wall clock like the one I had watched—and watched and watched—as a kid.

It was 8:47. Still early in what turned out to be, by far, the longest evening of my life.

※

In the center of the room was a familiar if unexpected sight. It was a "glider," the old fashioned metal kind that served as a swing on my Tennessee grandmother's porch. It was painted dull orange and blue-gray, and it hung in a low, square frame that kept it level, or almost level, which is the difference one supposes between a glider and an ordinary swing.

I thought it was for a flea market or an antique sale. Then I saw Lee's inscrutable smile.

"This is it?" I gave it a push. It squeaked. "This is your time machine?"

"No way, José." Lee pulled a Palm PC out of his briefcase and tapped its tiny screen. "PC see tomorrow math. Glider just seat."

Thinking this could turn out to be a rather long hour, I sat down and started to swing. I remembered the squeak from my childhood. More of a squeal. I used to think of it as an army of mice.

"Subjective factory," Lee said. He set the briefcase on the floor beside the glider, then sat down beside me. "Sit same metal. Field equations matched. Move but staying still. All good for see-tomorrow math."

See-tomorrow math. "Whatever," I said. "So what do we do, swing?" I kicked the glider higher.

"Hold horses," Lee said, dragging his feet, so that the glider twisted, then stopped. He pointed at the clock. "Loop at nine."

"Whatever." It was 8:56.

"Hold horses, Jersey Kaczynski!" Smiling, he reached into another pocket of his hideous safari jacket and handed me what I thought at first was a Zippo lighter. It was a tiny (and rather lovely) brushed aluminum digital camera.

"Have a look-see!" Lee said.

I slipped the camera into my pocket and shrugged. According to the clock on the wall, it was 8:58. I figured that if I played along for an hour, until ten, everyone would be happy, and I could go home. I knew what the place would be like without Helen. I was wondering what it would be like without her little dog.

Lee was noodling with numbers on his Palm PC, moving things around on the tiny screen. "Three ways," he said, not looking up. "Three maybe happens. One, algorithm not work, in which case nobody lost or gain. One probably most probable. Two, see-tomorrow algorithm too good, in which case we pull too far, all way to End of Time. Or three, algorithm work right, in which case pull through multiverse a microsecond, then larger slice, then larger slice, ekcetera (he pronounced it Texas style), until three . . ."

"Whoa," I said. "The End of Time?"

"Not likely," said Lee. "Only if square root of the square root of the first Infinity Progression divisible by the third integer of the under-equation, which here doubt. No problem."

No problem? It was 9:00 according to the clock on the wall. "So, okay, let's do it." I kicked the swing to start it going, just enough to squeak.

"Hold horses!" Lee took my hand. "Hold hands! Subjective factory."

Hold hands? But before I could complain Lee hit RETURN on his Palm PC. The screen filled with numbers, dancing, swapping places.

Lee kicked the glider higher, and I kicked to even it out (just as I'd had to do with my grandma), and there they were: the army of mice, squeaking in regular time.

The numbers went faster and faster, until Lee's little LCD screen was a multicolor blur. We were swinging back and forth, glider style: no up, no down, no arc. There was a flickering, either in the room's lights or in my eyes. I couldn't find the clock on the wall. I couldn't find the wall. Then suddenly the squeaking stopped although the flickering kept going. There was a sudden pain in my knee, and an old, familiar smell . . .

Then the swing was squeaking again, slowing, and the screen on Lee's laptop was empty, except for a blinking cursor dead center, which I noticed, because it was an odd place for a cursor to be. I looked around and everything looked totally unfamiliar, the way even your own room does when you suddenly wake up from a deep sleep in the afternoon.

The clock said 9:55.

Whoa! I pointed at the clock. "How did you do that?"

Lee was smiling. That inscrutable, enigmatic . . .

"What happened!?" I asked, pulling my hand from Lee's. The pain in my knee was gone. The smell was still there, but fading fast, like a dream. It was familiar, almost identifiable, then gone.

☀

+1

"Beats me, " Lee said. "But OK." He was already moving numbers around. "Try other slice quick."

Before Cole could register his disagreement with this strategy, Lee hit RETURN and the screen started filling with numbers again. He grabbed Cole's hand and pushed off with one foot.

Cole added his little kick to even out the glider, and there was the army of mice again. Squeaking in cadence. The clock had no hands and then there was no clock. The walls were flickering again. Cole tried closing his eyes. There was the old, almost familiar smell, and then it was gone. And the same sudden, sharp pain in his knee . . .

The glider stopped squeaking. Stopped moving altogether at the back of its swing. The world was tilted just slightly . . . but the swing was still.

Cole looked for the clock but the wall was gone. He saw something in the distance like the spine of a dinosaur, and felt a moment of terror until he realized it was the Sill, the little basalt outcropping that runs through the campus of Swick.

"Picture," said Lee. Of course he said it Texas style: pitcher.

Cole had forgotten he had the little camera. It had a zoom but it was too dark to see anything but the jagged outline of the rock. He snapped two pictures, hoping for the best. "Where are we?" he asked Lee.

"Beats me!" Lee's voice sounded far away, as if he were speaking through a tube.

"How did we get outside? What's going on?"

"Sill!" Lee said, pointing. The air was cold. Cole sniffed, looking for the smell, but it was gone. He realized they were swinging again. He could still see the Sill. Then it was gone. Lee had let go of his hand, and he was looking at the basement wall.

The clock said 9:07.

"Okay, what's going on?" Cole asked again. He was beginning to sound stupid, even to himself. "Now the clock is right again." Or had he misread it before?

"Sill." Lee pointed at the camera. "Pitcher?"

There was a display on the back of the camera. Cole hit a button and there was the Sill, just a dark stegosaur silhouette.

But how? "Lee, what the fuck is going on? What happened to the wall?"

"Future!" Lee shrugged. "Maybe no wall. Or see through time slice, like propeller. Beats me."

"Whoa. No building? What if they replace it with a parking lot and we end up in solid concrete?" Cole seemed to remember something like that from an old Superman comic. His Tennessee grandmother hadn't allowed them, but he had kept his stash in Brooklyn. His mother didn't care what—or if—he read at all.

"No sweat!" Lee picked up Cole's hand again. Cole tried

to pull away but Lee's grip got tighter; he was like a Chinese puzzle. Hell, he was a Chinese puzzle. "More slice quick. Get three!"

"Wait!" Cole liked it less and less the more it dawned on him that they actually had actually traveled in time. But Lee had already hit RETURN, and there was the army of mice, back again. They were swinging. Cole straightened the glider out, as best he could.

This time he recognized the pain in his knee. It was what he called an old football injury, from high school. Actually he had fallen off a ladder decorating the gym for the Homecoming Game. The smell was more elusive . . .

It was cold. They were stopped again. There was silence; no squeaking, nothing at all. The wall, the clock, the basement room itself had all disappeared, and they were hanging in cold, dark air. Cole could see snow—he could smell it in the air. He heard a popping, and thought of the way swing chains used to pop when he was a kid, but gliders don't have chains.

The strangest thing was, none of it seemed strange. The snow, the clocks, the traveling in time. "We're actually traveling in time," Cole said. It was no longer a question.

"Always travel time," said Lee. "Only no back and forth."

"So where are we?" Then Cole saw the Sill again. Had he been looking at it all along? The world was sort of drawing itself in, taking its time. There was a sunset behind the Sill, red as fire, and a wailing/barking sound like sirens, far off.

He started to take a picture but Lee stopped him. "Down there!" Lee pointed with his free, his right, hand.

They were looking at a wall—no, a window. Someone was coming through, feet first. First a plastic boot. Then a gun in a broad, gloved hand; then a helmet, arms, shoulders.

It was a man, a short white man with a short black beard. He took off his helmet; his bald head gleamed with sweat.

Looking down on it, Cole realized that he and Lee were off the floor, somewhere near the ceiling.

The bald man set down the gun—it was plastic, and oddly shaped, but clearly a weapon. He took off both gloves. Remembering the camera, Cole took a picture.

The man looked up. He was Asian, like Lee, but with a little beard. Had he heard the click? He looked straight at Cole but showed no sign of seeing him. He pulled a piece of white paper from his breast pocket and unfolded it. It was covered with numbers, neatly handwritten. He held it up in both hands, and Cole realized he was supposed to take a picture. Just as he was about to snap it, the man's head nodded abruptly to one side and a spray of blood came out, blood and bone, white and red, on the wall and on the floor.

The paper fell from his fingers and fluttered into the dust and rubble on the floor. Cole almost dropped the camera, barely caught it in Time. . . .

"Oh Goddamn!"

Was that me, Cole wondered, or Lee? Lee was leaning forward, reaching down, too far. Cole pulled him back. They were swinging again, and there was the army of mice. The lights in the room were flickering, then steady. They were back. The clock on the wall said 9:11.

"Damn!" Lee said, snatching the camera from Cole's hand and scrolling through the display. "Damn!"

"Damn what? Was that it, on the paper? Where were we? Where are we?" Cole got out of the swing and hopped in a tight circle on the concrete floor. He could hardly walk. His knee was stiff. The clock was back to normal: 9:12. Had he just imagined it was 9:55 before? Rap music was booming vaguely from upstairs: just the bass; the accompanying doggerel was mercifully lost in the ether. Everything seemed normal, except—

They had actually traveled in time!

"No picture!" Lee was bent over his laptop. "Lost number. See-tomorrow math!"

"Let me see," Cole said. He picked up the camera and scrolled through the display. There was the Sill; there was the man, coming through the window; and then—nothing.

"Lee, what's going on here?"

He was about to hand the camera to Lee when the thumping music from upstairs suddenly got louder. The door opened and Parker stuck his head in. Cole called him Porker, only to himself of course. Parker was the campus security chief, an overweight black man with the kind of elaborately tasteless hairdo favored by Latrell Sprewell fans. A big, dimwitted Rent-A-Cop who carried a Stephen King novel in one hand and a flashlight in the other.

"Dr. Lee!—Mr. Cole?" Parker openly despised Cole and always called him "Mister," presumably to show his contempt for a non-science, non-business degree. "I thought I heard something. What in the world are you two doing here this time of night? I mean, are you. . . ?"

"Justice chickens," said Lee, in his peculiar Texas twang. "No problem?"

"Well, I guess," said Parker, deferring to the tenured professor. "But I will have to lock up at ten."

"No problem!" said Lee. But then he turned to Cole as soon as the door was shut. "Some fuck up!"

"No shit!" Cole said. "Lee, where the hell were we? Was that paper Dear Abbey, the formula, the patch we are supposed to get?"

"Future. Fumble. All fuck up."

Future fumble all fuck up—as if that explained everything. And it did. Cole had seen the future and the big surprise was that there were no surprises. It was business as usual.

The Sixth Extinction. The doomed, lost, murderous world, chewing off its own foot. And the irony was, of course, that it looked just like today. Just another murder.

"We actually traveled in time. And we blew it, didn't we?"

Lee nodded grimly, studying his Palm PC.

Cole handed Lee the camera; made him take it this time. "I've seen enough. We actually traveled in time. How far? What year?"

"Three? Six?" Lee muttered mysteriously, dropping the camera into one of the many pockets of his hideous safari jacket. He held up his Palm PC and shook it. "Numbers fucked. But come on, one slice to go."

"You said there were only three trips. We've done three. And besides, we blew it."

"Numbers fucked," Lee said. "No formula." He pointed at the blinking cursor on his Palm PC. "Let's ride."

"I've seen enough," Cole said, But Lee grabbed his hand and pulled him down to the glider, beside him. Maybe Cole should have pulled away harder. Maybe he was curious. Probably he could have, should have, pulled away. But according to Helen (and others, including his grandmother) he'd never been resolute, never been decisive. And Time was like a rip tide, drawing them away from the shore, dragging them from the crumbling banks of the Present into the maelstrom of All That is Yet to Be.

※

1+

There they were, the army of mice, and the clock on the wall was gone.

The wall was gone.

Cole looked down at Lee's Palm PC but couldn't find it. Everything was flickering. Nothing looked wrong but nothing looked right. He felt a cold wind and there it was again, the old, familiar but unidentifiable smell and the pain in his left knee. The flickering stopped, faded really, and he thought, Good! It was all a mistake and we haven't gone anywhere, because he could hear the stupid thumping rap beat from upstairs . . .

But wait! That couldn't be right. He saw snow whirling in the air. They were somewhere outside, on a low hill overlooking a long gray plain, and the thumping sound was . . . A drum.

Mournful and regular as a heartbeat.

Boom. Boom. Boom.

The room was gone and there was the Sill, behind them, black against the sky. The sky was sort of a yellow gray. The air was cold and sweet, and now Cole recognized the familiar smell. It was the smell of mud; the smell of the sea when the tide was out. It was the smell of death.

Small death.

"Where are we now?" It was Cole, now, who was squeezing Lee's hand. Lee didn't seem to mind.

"Beats me," Lee said, staring at his Palm PC. "Some ride. Numbers wild!"

"I hear a drum."

Lee pointed without looking up. What had looked to Cole at first like a fence, or a line of trees in the distance, was a line of riders, single file. The line passed from horizon to horizon, from yellow-gray fog on the right, to the vague line in the distance where the gray plain met the sky.

The camera had a zoom and he used it like a little telescope. He could see two walkers for every rider. He couldn't tell what kind of people they were or what they were wearing. They were carrying long poles with black flags and black banners. Black birds circled overhead.

He clicked, then gave Lee the camera. "Some kind of mourners," he said.

"Dark age," Lee said, looking through the zoom. "World go back. Mud is sound."

Cole thought that last was one of Lee's Texas non-sequiturs; then he realized that they were looking at Long Island Sound. And it was dry.

"Does that mean there's ice to the north? So what happened to global warming?"

"Beats me," Lee said gloomily, handing Cole the camera and turning back to his little Palm PC.

The glider was stopped but Cole couldn't reach the ground with his shoe. He couldn't see anything close at hand; only far away, where the riders were fading into a thin mist, blowing down from the north.

Boom Boom Boom

The wind was cold. Cole had to pee but he wasn't about to get up. They were in the future, no doubt about it. He had passed all the way from amused, contemptuous skepticism to belief, without stopping by amazement. Lee's algorithm, whatever it was, worked. And it was all depressingly real. The future was exactly what Cole had feared it to be.

Never had he so hated being right before; it's an unfamiliar feeling for an academic. But looking into the future was like watching a nine-year-old with a Glock. Humanity was like the kid down the street who had found his crackhead uncle's "nine" under the sofa and proceeded to blast away his friends and family, expecting they would get up and dust themselves off when the show was over, just like on TV.

Well, the show was over and nobody was getting up.

Cole felt like crying. He looked at Lee and Lee shook his head as if he knew what Cole was thinking. "Everything too late," he said. This was the world that Dear Abbey, with all its horrors, had been intended to prevent.

Cole looked up and saw vapor trails far above, three of them, in formation. That unexpected sign of a still-extant technology depressed him even more; he shivered, remembering the days when commercial jets flew alone through untroubled skies. Most of the time, in most of the world, anyway.

He took a picture of the vapor trails. Was this it? There was nothing else to photograph. Just mud and mourners. Just desolation. "Let's go," he said. "There's nothing here for us." He kicked but the glider wouldn't budge. It felt as heavy as a car.

"Hold horses," Lee said, holding up the Palm PC. "Wait for cursor."

Cole waited. Two of the riders had pulled out of the line and stopped. Had they seen them? Even through the zoom, Cole couldn't see faces, just silhouettes. But he could tell they were riding his way, slowly at first, then faster . . .

"Lee . . ."

And then there they were, like the cavalry to the rescue, the army of mice. The glider was moving; the sky was flickering and then it was no longer sky, just white space.

Cole breathed a sigh of relief, on his way "home" to his own sad and sorry time.

Or so he thought.

※

+500

Something was wrong. There was the pain again, in Cole's knee; there was the sweet, small death, sea smell. The mice screamed their chorus as the glider slowed, and stopped, but. . . .

But the glider was still outside.

In a mist. A cold, thin fog. Outside, on a long, sloping lawn of rough grass, unmowed but short. Cole smelled salt and heard waves. The glider squealed to a stop and he shivered.

This was not the Student Union. "Where the fuck are we now?"

"Dr. Lee? Mr. Cole?"

Cole turned and saw the Sill in the distance, and closer, the crumbling walls of a ruined building. Two people were approaching at a fast walk across the tufted, gray-green grass. One was smiling and one was frowning, like the twin thespian masks of Comedy and Tragedy.

"Whoa!" Cole said aloud as they got closer and he saw that they were masks—stylized, with fierce eyes and wide mouths. One was turned up in a sketchy grin somewhere between have-a-nice-day and Hannibal Lecter; the other turned down in an elaborate, hideous scowl that suggested blind hatred more than tragedy or sadness.

The scowling mask held back a step. The smiling mask approached, bowed at the waist, and spoke again.

"Dr. Lee?" A man's voice.

He held out his hand to Cole.

Cole took it without thinking and was startled to find that it was solid, cold—but real. Had he expected a ghost?

"I am Lee," Lee said beside him, his voice shaky.

"Bienvenido!" The masked man shook Lee's hand and then Cole's again. He spoke slowly, with a Spanish accent. "You must be Cole, then. And you are African!"

"So?"

"You are Black! You are Negro!"

"So? It's Dr. Cole," Cole said. "And so what? So fucking what?"

"Well, we did not know," the man in the mask said. "That is all. It is a surprise. Perhaps there is much that we do not know. Now you are here." He touched the chin of his mask. "May I show myself to you?"

"What?!"

"Sure thang," Lee said in his best Texas drawl. The man removed his mask. He was Asian, or at least part Asian; about thirty to forty, with black hair in a ponytail and a small, thin, intricate beard. He was slight, with long fingers like a pianist. For the first time Cole noticed his clothes. He wore gray coveralls under a quilted vest with a gray and rose paisley design.

Under the mask, his smile was thinner. His gray eyes looked dead. "Elizam Hava," he said, bowing again, Japanese style, from the waist. "From the Universidad de Miami. This is my colleague Ruth Lavalle."

The few words of Spanish made Cole realize how learned his English was, how careful, how formal. His partner in the scowling mask bowed, even more stiffly, almost reluctantly. Cole could see now that she was a woman: small breasted, compact; she stood on the balls of her feet as if looking for an opportunity to strike. Sort of like Helen, except that he didn't like her.

Then he remembered that he didn't like Helen either. She was gone anyway; moved away; dead; buried . . . for a hundred, a thousand, how many years?

The woman wore the same gray coveralls and vest the man wore, and carried two extra vests over one arm, like a waiter's towel. Her mask was much more carefully done than his, which was little more than a sketch of a smiling face. Hers was a maniac scowl with narrowed slanted eyes and fierce colors, done in red and white and blue, so that it looked like an American flag—or a baboon's ass, depending on your point of view.

She left her mask on and didn't speak at all. Just bowed stiffly and stepped back.

They both stood silently, watching, one masked and one not. They were waiting for Cole and Lee to do something, but what? Cole wanted to take a picture, but he was afraid. They looked like savages. What if they thought the camera was a weapon? It was Lee who broke the spell. He stood up, pulling Cole with him and before Cole knew what was happening, he was out of the glider, standing on the bunchy grass.

"Whoa!" He had expected to fall through the grass as through a cloud, but here he was. Physically in the future. Not just looking on.

Lee looked dazed as he slipped the Palm PC into one of the pockets of his hideous safari jacket.

Cole stomped; the ground was real. Did that mean the future, this future, was real? Fixed? Unchangeable?

"Here!"

The host, Elizam, took the two vests from the scowling-mask woman and handed them to Cole and Lee. Cole put his on. It was soft, like silk, but thin. It even had a little pocket for the camera.

Lee held his vest over his arm. He apparently didn't want to part with the hideous safari jacket. Welcome to L.L. Bean.

"Bienvenido," Elizam said again. "We were sent here to meet you. We have been waiting almost two days."

"Sent who? What deal?" Lee asked. "¿Tiene ustedes algo por nosotros?"

"Los Viejos." Elizam put his arm over Lee's shoulder, and the two started walking up the hill, toward the ruin. The scowling-mask woman followed them. Cole felt disoriented, unattached, as if he were in a dream—except that he still had to pee.

"Is there a bathroom?" he asked. "Hay baño?"

The woman turned and pointed down the slope. Cole walked toward the water. The grass ended at a short, rocky, ten foot cliff. At the bottom, a few seals were playing with a log rolling in a gentle surf.

He peed down onto the rocks. The seals looked up, and saw him, and started to bark. They were small, gray seals with black, button eyes, long whiskers, and bright teeth.

Cole smiled and barked back.

Then he saw what they were playing with. It wasn't a log. It was a human body, gray and bloodless. Both arms were missing and most of the face was gone. It rolled over and over as the seals nudged it and nipped at it with their little snouts.

Shivering, Cole zipped his pants and hurried up the hill. Halfway up he remembered the camera and stopped. Then he went on.

He didn't want a picture of that.

※

Inside the low, crumbling walls of the ruin, there was an open-sided geodesic tent on two curved poles. Lee and his two hosts sat under it, on the ground, around a small fire. Cole clicked a shot of the cozy little scene, and then joined them. His vest was electric or chemical; it was beginning to warm him.

The low walls blocked the wind: concrete blocks, most of them shattered. It was definitely the Student Center, or what was left of it, a hundred years in the future, or five hundred, or a thousand. So why, Cole wondered, didn't he feel more strange? Why did all this, even the seals, feel so horribly normal?

Perhaps it was the Sill in the distance, that jagged little dino back. Or the silence.

The fog had lifted, and to the south (if they were in fact on Long Island Sound) the ocean and sky met in a soft haze. To the north, beyond the Sill, clouds massed like gray horses.

Elizam carefully placed another stick on the fire. "Please excuse the small fire," he said, in Spanish. "Not much wood." He had taken off his mask but he wouldn't look either Cole or Lee the eye.

"What's with the killer seals?" Cole asked, in English.

"Kill seals!?" Lee looked shocked.

Cole told him what he had seen.

"Vampire seals," the woman said from behind her mask. "Your greatest creation."

"My what?"

"There are many dead," said Elizam, his voice oddly flat, "whom the water uncover. Do you mind if I put my mask on? I can speak more freely."

"Whatever," Cole said. Whatever rings your fucking bell.

Elizam put his mask back on. The idiotic smiling face was an improvement on his own dead look.

"As the seas rise," he said, "they open graves and unlock doors. Unlike many large-mammal species, the vampire seals prosper. Here in New England there are only the dead. The glaciers are still hundreds of miles north, but no one can live here."

"¿Y ustedes?" Lee ventured. His Spanish was a little better than his English.

"We live in Miami, but we were sent to meet you, since we are both experts in late English. We have tapes, movies. The way people talk as well as the spelling is preserved."

"¿Envian por quienes?" Lee asked. "Who sent you?"

"Los Viejos," Elìzam answered. "From the future."

And who are these Old Ones? Lee asked, in Spanish. His Spanish was a little better than his English, but only a little.

"No los sabemos." No one knew who the Old Ones were, or what they wanted. Elizam and his scowling companion had simply been told to meet Lee and Cole here, and send them on.

"Send us on where?" Cole asked, but no one answered him. They pretended not to hear and jabbered on in Spanish. Cole could follow the sense of it. A message had appeared on some kind of academic email server. "Nos da sus nombres," the woman said. "Dr. Lee. Cole."

"It's Doctor Cole," Cole said, interrupting. "Doctor William Wellington Cole."

"Lo siento."

"Yeah, right." Cole was getting pissed. Who were these people? Why were they speaking Spanish which he barely understood? The woman was hunkered down by the fire, across from him. He touched his cheek and pointed at her. "What's with the fucking masks anyway?"

"They express our sorrow," said Elizam, in English.

"And hide our rage," said the woman.

"Rage? Rage at what?"

"At you." She took off her mask. Her eyes were gray and dead, like Elizam's. She was about twenty-five. Though pale, she had tight hair and a broad face, with what Cole's grandmother (who was half half-white) used to call, "a brush of Africa."

"The rage is for what you did. And did not do." Her words were flat and emotionless: What you did and did not do. She stood up.

"May I say it?" she asked nobody in particular.

Lee nodded. Cole shrugged. Whatever. She walked in a circle around the fire as she talked. In English. It had obviously been rehearsed. It was as ceremonial as a dance, and what she said was as measured and as unemotional as a legal deposition, in spite of its content:

"You murdered your own children. You destroyed their home, you pulled the world down around them. You left them crying in the ruins. They were lost and they were our parents. Their lives were all sorrow and their sorrow is all ours."

"Their sorrow is ours," repeated Elizam.

"They died weeping, though they knew not what for, and they knew there would be no one, but us, their children, to hear their cries. If they survived. It is their sorrow we pass on."

"It is their sorrow we pass on," repeated Elizam. "Whoa," Cole said. This was getting like a church service. "You've got the wrong guys! Don't you even know why we are here?" He started to explain that Lee and himself were Green, were activists (each in his own way), opposed to what was happening, sent here to . . .

But after a word or two, in English, he shut up. It didn't matter, did it? They had obviously failed miserably, hadn't they? From here, from the perspective of a few hundred years, there was no difference. They were like the good Germans, or the honest Quaker merchants who had declined to take part in the slave trade, or had even (politely) spoken out against it, while allowing it to prosper.

If Cole had ever had any doubts about Dear Abbey (and he had, though he had never expressed them, even to himself), they were gone. Gone with the wind, now that he saw the world he and his generation had left to their children. Wouldn't any effort to change that, to reverse that, be justified?

"Please continue," said Lee.

Ruth (for that was her name) walked in circles carrying her mask in her hand, as Cole and Lee stared into the fire, along with Elizam, who was masked again. "We watched the animals die," she intoned. "One by one, and then in herds, then one by one again. Even the ones in the zoos. The great mammals are only a memory now: the elephant, the great whale, the rhino, the walrus."

"Only memories," said Elizam.

"Only memories," said Lee, who had apparently decided to join them. He still wore the hideous safari jacket, though he had laid their heating vest across his knees like a lap robe.

"The natural world was trashed, devastated," said Ruth, "and so was the historical, the cultural, the human world. Cities were burned, museums looted. Libraries were flooded and lost under the seas, for global warming wiped out not only cities, but memories, heritages: the Dutch, Singapore, the Polynesian archipelago, entire languages, lost without a trace."

She was giving the speech Cole had always wanted to give, the message he had wanted to convey to his students, and yet he didn't want to hear it. Not from her.

She sat down. Elizam placed another stick on the fire, very carefully.

"What about global warming?" Cole asked, hoping to change the subject. "It is cold as hell!"

"The Gulf Stream is gone," said Elizam, muffled behind his mask. "Europe and New England are uninhabitable. The midwest is hot. Texas is burning. The only temperate zones are in Asia, the Pacific Rim, and along the north of South America, and some on the California Coast."

"What of Africa?"

"Africa?" Ruth raised her mask and turned her blank eyes on Cole. "Africa is gone, sunk, dust. The forests are cinders, the people are dead. The fourth holocaust. First there was slavery, which looted the continent of youth; then colonialism, which despoiled it of riches. Then AIDS which orphaned a generation. . . ."

"Two," said Elizam.

"Ironically, it was the diaspora that saved Africa, at least the people. More than half were gone already. Taking their culture and heritage with them."

"Now can you see why we are surprised to see that you are African?" said Elizam. "It was our understanding that

African people in your century had no education, no rights, no social access. . . ."

"Not strictly true," said Lee.

"Not that far off," Cole corrected. "But you said four. There was a fourth holocaust?"

"The fires," said Elizam. "The drought and then the fires."

"What about China?" Lee asked.

"China leads," she said. "They rebuild. We all rebuild. We do what we can to replace what you destroyed but it takes time, and some of it is not possible. You killed all the big animals, or most of them."

"Not all," said Elizam, getting up to get more wood from a small pile under the wall. "Not completely. There are persistent reports of an elephant seen in West Africa."

"Unreliable," said Ruth. "Like the Loch Ness monster, or flying saucers."

Reports of elephants, like flying saucers. For the first time Cole understood the cliché, "his heart sank," as he actually felt his heart sink. Was it possible that even more than our fellow men we could miss our fellow creatures? He began to feel the same sadness that appeared to depress Elizam and Carmen. He had never seen people so devoid of feeling, of life, of mirth and laughter. And now he was becoming one of them.

"So you still have telephones, computers?" Lee asked, in Spanish.

"Oh, yes," Elizam answered "That's why we are here. Knowledge isn't lost that easily. It's harder to make things, like computers, but the old ones can be repaired, and we are developing the capacity to make them like before."

"Not as cheaply," said Ruth. "Not as thoughtlessly. Not as carelessly. For everything that is made is something unmade, or left unmade. That is what you, our parents, never understood. That is the root of the devastation you bequeathed to us."

Cole looked away; he was tired of her self-righteous bullshit. He discovered to his horror that he identified more with the exuberant, destructive thoughtlessness she attacked than with her. And wasn't it true? When all was said and done (and looking around, it seemed, indeed, that all had been said and all had been done) wasn't he in fact one of them?

The talk died down and they sat, staring into the dying fire. There was nothing more to say. Something besides the world seemed destroyed: innocence and enthusiasm and hope seemed gone as well. Cole wondered what the rest of their world was like. Were he and Lee going to see it?

He hoped not. . . .

He dozed off, and when he awoke, the fire was out. Elizam and Ruth were gone. Lee was down the hill, sitting on the glider with his Palm PC on his lap. Cole hurried down, afraid the Chinaman might leave without him.

He needn't have worried. Lee was shaking his head. "All fuck figures. No home. You get pictures?"

"Yes, yes," Cole said patting the pocket of his vest, where he had put the camera. "Pictures of what? Masks? Fires? It's cold here. Just get us the hell out of here!"

"The hell," said Lee; now he was shaking his Palm PC as well as his head.

Cole looked up the hill and saw Elizam and Ruth approaching, carrying their masks in their hands. "What is this shit?" he demanded. "Did you mess up our time machine?"

"Infrared," said Elizam in English. He held up a small device, like a flashlight. "I entered the figures Los Viejos gave us."

Cole turned to Lee. "Who? What? Do you understand any of this?"

"Hold horses," Lee muttered, in English, punching in numbers.

It was almost dark. Cole didn't know whether to be pissed off or scared. He had to pee again but he had no desire to see what the seals were dining on, let alone photograph it. He walked back up to the ruin and pissed on the fire.

Ruth and Elizam followed and watched from behind the wall, unreproachfully. It was as if they expected it of him.

"You can both go to hell," Cole said, as he zipped up his pants. "Okay? Capiche? Comprende?"

They followed him back down the hill. "Gracias para venir," Elizam said to Lee. "We are honored to meet you."

"Fuck you and the world you spun in on," Cole said. Then he stopped, hearing a small insistent sound:

beep beep

Lee's Palm PC.

"Hold horses," Lee said. "Have cursor. All aboard." He patted the seat beside him.

Cole didn't need to be told twice. He sat down, and Lee covered his big hand with his own small one.

Elizam and Ruth stood silently with their masks on, their hands raised in farewell, or so it seemed. Then Cole realized what it was they wanted—their vests back. Lee's was across his knees; Cole took his off and tossed them both to Ruth.

Lee hit RETURN, and there they were, the army of mice. Coler kicked to even up the swing.

"Damn!" said Lee, as the mists of light closed around them. Cole felt it too. Something was different, different in the same way as before.

They weren't heading home. They were falling. Falling farther and farther, into the future. . . .

❋

+1000

Spinning.

Cole was about to throw up. He wondered if it was the whiskey, which he could still feel, when, suddenly, the spinning stopped. Blue striations flickered through the air, and he found himself on a seashore—again.

But this time it was warmer and the sky was bright blue. And he didn't like it. Not at all.

Lee let go of Cole's hand; Cole grabbed Lee's back. "Long Island?" he asked. Even though he knew it wasn't.

In the near distance, there was a cone-shaped, steeply pointed island, with what appeared to be trees growing toward the top in a spiral. The whole thing looked artificial.

"Pitcher?" said Lee.

Cole let go of Lee's hand and reached into his pocket for the camera. But there was no pocket; no camera.

"Shit," he said. "It was in the vest."

Lee shrugged. "Only for formula, just in case."

"Still, stupid," Cole said. "My fault." Photos of the future, and he had lost them. "Can we go back and get them?"

"Don't think so," Lee said. "Just pitchers."

"True, but sorry," Cole said. He was beginning to talk like Lee. It was time to change the subject. He leaned back in the glider and looked around. "Where are we? I mean, I wonder where we are."

"Figuring," said Lee, bending over his Palm PC.

"Capps Island," said a voice from behind them. Cole sat up and looked around, alarmed. A man was standing behind the glider. Had he been there all along? It was as if the world were being drawn in, slowly; it was like visiting a website in the old days on a slow line.

He was a tall white man, unmasked (Cole noticed that right away), in a soft brushed velveteen suit. At least it looked to Cole like velveteen. There was something about it that was proudly, flamboyantly artificial.

"Welcome, Dr. Lee," he said. "So pleased, Dr. Cole. As you can see, we have a crossing to make. That is, if you want to see the island. There is not much time. Do you need to rest?"

"See island? No problem," Lee said. He stood up, and Cole stood up with him.

"I am Hallam," the man said in his odd, unaccented English. He pronounced every word carefully, as if he were trying it for the first time. He stuck out his hand and Lee took it. "I am pleased to meet you on your journey."

He dropped Lee's hand and took Cole's. "I am Hallam," he said again. "I am pleased to . . ."

"What journey?!" Cole asked. "Lee, where are we? Do you even know?"

Lee didn't answer, but the man, Hallam, did. He pointed toward the peaky island. "Capps Island," he said again.

A plane, or some sort of craft, was taking off near the top of the island. It was too far away to tell what it was, or how big.

"There are one hundred and twelve of these Earthwatch stations around the world," Hallam said. "They are all connected on a network of . . ."

"Whoa! Slow down," Cole said. "What year is this? Please."

"Year? Oh, yes, of course," said Hallam. "Well, 724. Your year, the Jesus time, is . . ." He pulled up his sleeve and checked a wristwatch. "I am sorry . . . is 3124. I should have thought. Of course you would want to know."

"Jesus!" Cole said, sitting back down.

"We don't use the Jesus calendar," Hallam said, tapping his wristwatch. "But I have it here."

The glider didn't move; it had that strange inertia Cole had felt before, as if it had the mass of a car.

313

Lee was tapping at his Palm PC, looking worried. Cole was beyond worry. A thousand years. What could happen to him? He was already dead, he could feel it in his bones. His bones which were already rotting somewhere under the earth on which he stood. If they had not been exhumed by seals.

The glider felt creepy. Cole stood up again. The ground felt solid under his feet; too solid. Was this real, then, this future now?

It was. Real. He shivered in the bright sunlight.

"We have the Hong Kong calendar," Hallam was explaining. "We measure from Hong Kong Colloquium, 724 years ago. That's for politics. For spirit, we measure from the Crossing. That makes this year 114,844. But come." He started down a path toward the water.

Lee and Cole followed, both of them. What else were they to do? "The Crossing?" Cole asked. "What Crossing?"

"Long ago there was a war," Hallam said, "with much fire, for fire was a weapon of war in those early days, and then a plague of some kind. For the first time, but not the only time, our kind had all but murdered themselves. There were only thousands then, but thousands died. A few women gathered what was left of the First People, all three bands that had warred, mostly children, and led them North, out of the Valley of Bones, and across the Great Basin that would become the Mediterranean, though it was dry then, from the Ice."

"A hundred thousand years ago? How do you know?" Cole asked.

"One hundred fourteen," said Hallan. "The eight forty four is an agreed on approximation. We dated it with DNA and carbon tests; we reconstructed it from legends and rock paintings; we knew it all along in our bones, it was our beginning."

314

A small airplane was landing on the water below. Cole hadn't heard it approach. He wondered if it was the same one he had seen taking off from the island.

Meanwhile Lee had his own questions. "Hong Kong?"

"The coming together," said Hallam. "The meeting where we began to develop the systems that led to Earthwatch. That ended the Sixth, finally."

"The Sixth?" Cole asked. "The Sixth Extinction? You call it that?"

Hallam shrugged. "We call it what it was. It was the sixth for the planet. Thousands of species died, wiped out, forever, without even a farewell. It lasted for over five hundred years, and it was in many ways worse that the wars that led to the Crossing, for we killed so many others. It led to the Mourning and the Restoration. Even though it was not nearly so close as the Crossing close, for us. There we were reduced to less than two hundred souls. In the Sixth Extinction to just over two hundred million."

"Now how many?" Lee asked.

"That, you are about to see," Hallam answered. They were at the water's edge. The little plane was taxiing toward them across the water.

It had short, thick wings like a cartoon plane, with deep leading edge slots that apparently added to their lift. There was a big propeller powered, they were told, by a remote magnetic field. There was no engine, and no noise.

There was no one in the pilot's seat. There was no pilot's seat.

They clambered in and took off with a whistling noise that diminished as they gained speed and altitude. There were no seat belts. For some reason, Cole thought of Helen. The last time he had looked at the clock it had been 9:11, and that seemed days ago. She would be halfway to London by now. And dead a thousand years as well.

Lee's inscrutable little smile was back. Cole smiled too. There was something very peaceful and reassuring about this little plane, the sunlight, the blue water below and the island ahead, rapidly getting closer—the steep coast receding behind.

"A hundred thousand years. From that perspective," Cole said to Hallam, "we are almost contemporaries."

"We are contemporaries," their host replied. "A thousand years is only a moment in the life span of a species. Less than a moment for rock and water and the Earth. A hundred thousand years is itself only a few moments. We mark our spiritual history from the beginning of that scattering, that diaspora, which ended only a thousand years ago, in your time."

Spiritual. Cole had never liked the word before. They flew very slowly. No one here seemed in a hurry. As the plane gently touched down on the water, Hallam explained what they were about to see. "We have been rebuilding the earth since the Sixth . . ."

Which had happened. In spite of all our efforts, Cole thought gloomily.

". . . and we have linked all the climatic regions, the populations of animals and plants, the meteorological and tectonic information. The result is a self-monitoring global system that looks after the environment, letting us know us know about long range trends, etc."

They taxied to a rocky shore, where they were met by a woman who introduced herself as Dana. She was dressed in the same velveteen, only orange—and considerably more shapely, Cole noticed.

"You're African!" she said, taking both Cole's hands in her own. So was she; not just a little, like the masked woman (or Cole himself), but a lot.

"Afraid so," Cole said. She looked puzzled and he

immediately regretted his tone. While he had beaucoup problems with being African-American, he had always given thanks for the fact that he was, at least, not white. But how explain all that, a thousand years in the future?

"Just a joke," he said. She smiled politely.

They were riding a kind of escalator (without steps) up the hillside to a tunnel.

The tunnel led inside the mountain, to a large egg-shaped room with LCD monitors built into the walls. Data was flowing down the screens like water.

Except for the screens and themselves, the room was empty. "Who watch?" Lee asked.

"It watches itself," Dana said, who didn't seem surprised or bothered in the least by Lee's cowboy pidgin English. "This is one of a network of fifty-five Earthwatch stations, all over the earth, including one under the Arctic Sea. The Arctic ice cap, which was gone in your day, is back, you know."

It wasn't gone in his day, Cole wanted to say. But what did she mean by "your day"?

"The screens are just for show. The system monitors itself. Maintains itself, too."

"It's intelligent?" Cole asked.

"Of course," Dana said, giving him a look. "Why would anyone build a system that was not intelligent?"

"Earth balance," said Lee, nodding. "What to do. Cool."

"Actually," said Hallam, "instead of telling us what to do, it tells us what it is doing. Earthwatch has taken over most of the work itself, using bacterial nanobots to intervene in out-of-synch natural systems. The system has only been on line for a hundred and forty years, and it's still changing."

So the Earth does have a chance, Cole thought. It can be restored, at least partially. Even without Dear Abbey, even though he and Lee had obviously failed. . . .

Or had they?

"Is this why you brought us here?" Cole asked. "To show us this? To warn us of what would happen if we failed—or if we succeeded?"

Dana looked puzzled. "It wasn't us. The Old Ones brought you here."

"You're not the Old Ones?"

"Oh, no. They are the ones who told us you were coming," said Hallam. "That's how we learned your language. We are the only two who speak it."

"The Old Ones will send you home, I suppose, when the time comes," said Dana, leading them back out the tunnel. "Meanwhile, there are, or will be, five stops I think. But we must get you back to the rendezvous."

"Pronto," said Lee, holding up his Palm PC.

The cursor was blinking.

※

Cole felt a strange, deep sadness as they rode the stepless escalator back down the mountainside. It was peaceful here in the future—but look at the price.

"From eight billion, in our time, to less than two hundred million," he said to Dana, as they climbed into the little plane. "Was there a particular, uh, problem, that set it off? A sort of slow-motion catastrophe?"

"Catastrophe?" asked Hallan. "There were hundreds. Famines, floods, wars, diseases, murdered so many."

"And murdered the soul," said Dana. "The Restoration went on for hundreds of years."

"The masks," Cole said.

"They couldn't face themselves, or each other, directly. There had been so much violence and destruction. Protocol was everything."

"During the Restoration, they thought the Mourning was

over," said Hallam. "We look back now and see that they were still in the middle of it."

"Just as some say we are still in the Restoration," said Dana.

The take off was silent, except for the rush of air. As they climbed, Cole asked Hallan where they were.

Africa, he was told. "On your maps this would be the coast of Mozambique, and that city in the distance—"

Hallan spoke gently to the airplane in a strange language that sounded a little like Chinese, and it rose higher. Between two hills, they could see a scattering of pastel buildings, like wild flowers in a clump.

"—would be Aruba, and there—"

And there, floating on the horizon like a cloud or the dream of a cloud, was the white robed summit of Kilimanjaro. The snowcap it had lost was back. Even though Cole had never seen it nor, indeed, ever been to Africa, it was familiar from a thousand pictures, its vast hump unchanged and undiminished. A thousand years is nothing to the world of rock and ice.

They descended, and Kilimanjaro slipped under the horizon, still there, but invisible, like the past—or the future.

Hallam and Dana kissed them both, Cole and Lee, French style, at the foot of the hill. What an eerie kiss they share, Cole thought, they who live a thousand years apart. It was for him like kissing a dream or a hope; for them, he imagined, a ghost.

"Farewell."

"Farewell."

"So long," said Lee.

"When you hit RETURN you will go on another stage," said Hallam. "There will be five more. That's what we were told by the Old Ones. Told to tell you."

Lee nodded gravely and headed up the path. Cole caught up with him at the top. "Five more?" he asked. "I thought we were supposed to be picking up Dear Abbey. What happened with that? And who are these Old Ones?"

"Beats me," Lee said. "Time ride!"

He showed Cole his Palm PC. The cursor was blinking, surrounded by numbers, all scrolling upward in a slow flood. "I swear to God, Lee, I think you're just pretending you don't speak English! That means nothing to me. How do we get back to our own time? And what are we doing here in the first place?"

But Lee just smiled his inscrutable Oriental smile. Arguing with him was pointless. They were at the glider, and the wind was suddenly sharp. Cole wished he still had his vest. Lee buttoned up his hideous safari jacket. If he imagined that Kilimanjaro, unseen but still present, lent it a certain appropriateness, he was dead wrong, thought Cole. It looked as stupid, and he as nerdy, as ever.

"Let's go, then." Cole was pissed without knowing why. He pulled Lee down beside him on the glider and covered his little pale hand with his own big brown mitt. "You're the big shot."

"Huh?"

"Just hit RETURN."

※

+10,000

They didn't return. Not right away.

They went on.

On, forward in Time, or so it seemed to them at the "time," although as they were to learn, Time Travel is only possible once, at the End of Time, when there is no forward left. Then and only then is a loop back possible, for there is only one End of Time.

They knew nothing of that, then. "Then"—how strange that word seems, now. "Now". . . .

On they fell through Time. The small death sea-smell was gone, though Cole still felt the "football injury" pain in his leg. Lights flashed, striated: hot, cold. Lee's hand gripped his, tighter and tighter, until the glider slowed and stopped, at the front end of its arc-less swing, and suddenly it was warm, almost hot. The world was white, like fog, fading. And they were in a grove of small trees with silvery-striped trunks.

Music was playing. Cole looked all around; he was surrounded by people, most of them young, mostly dressed in black and white. They were all applauding. Lee was applauding too; applauding himself, it seemed. He and Cole looked at each other, laughed, and stood up and took a bow. Their hosts all laughed merrily and led them to a table under a tree, where a laughing waiter was pouring wine.

They all spoke French, which Cole could understand only with difficulty, until one of the group laid a small thick cloth the size of a long sock across his right shoulder.

"*Pardonnez-moi*," she said. "OK?"

It clung to his shoulder, heavy yet flexible, like one of the lead robes they used to give you in X-ray.

"Okay," he said.

"Excellent," said Lee, who had just gotten his own. "This is some kind of instantaneous translator, no? And you are still speaking French?"

"Yes, yes," said another of the group.

Whoa! "Hey, Lee are you speaking English or French?" Cole asked.

"Neither," Lee replied. "Mandarin. And now Cantonese. And now Russian. . . ."

"Okay, okay," Cole said. "I get it." It was amazing. Lee's voice sounded slightly processed, like someone on long distance; but the Texas accent was, mercifully, gone.

They were in Paris. The Old Ones, whomever they were, had landed them in a small park in the Marais in the year 12879 HK (their year, "Jesus" year, 15242 JC) Their hosts were students of history who assembled once a year to study and discuss the Modern World (which is what they called the ancient world, our world), and ultimately to meet them.

"The message from the Old Ones was that you would arrive today, June 23, for only a few hours. A crowd gathered to watch the materialization, which was quite a show."

"I'm sure it was!" said Lee.

"But we asked them to leave us alone so we could talk. Would you like some more wine? It's a very nice Alsatian." A fortyish white woman named Kate explained all this to Lee and Cole. She wore a short black skirt and a black and white striped top. Her legs were long and thin and, Cole thought, beautiful. They were sitting at a table outdoors under a plane tree, with her and her three friends. Two were men, one of them African, though much much darker than Cole. The other woman was younger, about Helen's age. Cole didn't like her thin, polite smile.

What the Modernists, as they called themselves, didn't know was more interesting to Cole than what they did know. They knew Mozart, Ellington, Liszt, but had never heard a live orchestra. They understood what capitalism was, but not what it was like. "Can you live anywhere you like?" they asked, and when Lee answered no and Cole answered yes, they all laughed and had another glass of wine. A very nice Alsatian.

Once Lee had discovered he could talk, there was no shutting him up. Not that the Modernists wanted to. They were fascinated by the pre-HK era (which they saw as lasting from about 1500 to 2500 AD, or Jesus Time). They had questions about China, about the USA, about the "nuclear war that never happened" (was Cole ever relieved to hear that phrase!) and so on, and Lee had answers to them all.

"It was like an explosion," he said. "Technologically and culturally. It was exciting and terrible at the same time. It was . . ."

Lengthy, wordy answers. Cole wasn't so sure he didn't prefer the old laconic cowboy Lee. Besides, he had a few questions for Lee himself. Questions like, who were these Old Ones? and what had happened to their original mission, Dear Abbey? And most important, how would they ever get back to their own time?

Oddly, he was in no hurry to ask these questions. He felt curiously relaxed, almost numb. Perhaps, he thought, it was a time travel version of jet lag. They were in the garden of a restaurant, and people came and went, some staring, but Cole didn't mind. The wine was "very nice," the cheese was tart, the bread was thick and chewy. He wondered how long he had been hungry.

He looked around for a clock. Kate showed him her watch. It was analog, and the date was in French—1100 h, Juin 11, Juedi. Cole asked if they had Time Travel, and Kate looked shocked. There was no such thing. It was an impossibility.

"What about us, then?"

"You are an anomaly," said the African man. "Every impossibility comes complete with an anomaly." They all laughed, though Cole didn't get it.

"You are a special project of the Old Ones," said the younger woman, whose name Cole didn't catch. She sat next to Lee and stared at him worshipfully. She even seemed to think his safari jacket was cool. In fact they all seemed to find Lee fascinating: pouring his wine, cutting his cheese, hanging on his every processed word.

Cole found all this annoying, and must have showed it, for Kate pulled his sleeve and whispered: "Let's you and me take a walk."

＊

Paris looked as Cole remembered it (from pictures, and one brief trip, not with Helen but an earlier Helen) except that there were fewer cars. They were still tiny and they all still honked their horns.

The Paris in which they found themselves was both a living city and a replica, continually being rebuilt but always more or less on the old 18-20th century (JT) plan. There were lots of people on the streets but most of them seemed like tourists. Everyone strolled, no one hurried.

About a fourth of the people on the street were African, more or less, like Cole. People in the shops and stores were polite, but disinterested. There didn't seem to be much to buy. One or two brands of cigarettes; one or two brands of gum. The newspapers were one page only but the print changed when you touched a square at the top of the page. The language, the print, the stories all seemed to change. The only languages Cole identified were French and Chinese; English seemed forgotten. Katie bought Cole a paperback book that doubled in size when he opened it. He wanted it because of the author's picture on the back. She paid for it by blinking twice into the newsdealer's little mirror. Cole wasn't the only one wearing a translator on his shoulder. Most of the men wore baggy pants and long shirts, but some wore khakis and sport coats, and others jumpsuits. He saw two men urinating on the street, into a hole. This was apparently common.

"I thought you might want to see a little of your world," said Kate. "I will be able to see a vid of your friend's presentation, later."

"My world?"

"The world you made," she said. "You are our ancestors; you brought us here."

Cole asked about travel. Those who were in a hurry to get

from Europe to Asia or America did it in two to three hours, but most commerce and trade was conducted by sail. People worked four to six hours a day and had half the year off. The countryside around Paris was filled with small farms, Katie assured him (he never saw them), though much of Europe was wild. They walked down the Seine toward the Eiffel Tower, which was replaced (duplicated) every 1200 years, by contract. Cole was afraid to get too far from the garden restaurant in the Marais where the glider had "landed." He had accepted the fact that they had gone from observing the future to walking around in it. He trusted Lee not to leave without him (and he assumed Kate had some kind of cell phone or communicator, in case Lee's cursor started blinking). But still, he was still a little nervous . . . .

Paris had cinemas and cafes amazingly like those of our own time. Cole was told that this was deliberate. Other cities had other diversions. London, for example was devoted to clubs and plays, while Mexico City specialized in pottery and auto racing.

They stopped at a vid kiosk and Kate showed him maps of North America and Africa, with large swaths of wilderness. Industry was mostly recycling, and it was against the law to take minerals or oil out of the ground.

Cole wasn't sure of the protocol. Was he allowed to ask about the part of the past that was still his own future, and therefore, at least to him, still uncertain? He risked it. "Was there some bio-catastrophe, in Modern Times? Some man-made catastrophe, causing a lot of chaos?"

"It was all catastrophe," Kate said. "And all man-made, wasn't it. But we survived, didn't we?"

Cole decided to be more direct. "Did you ever hear of an—event, a strategy—called Dear Abbey?"

She gave him a blank look and he realized he didn't even know how the translator had rendered the phrase, much less his halting attempts to define it. Did she think Dear Abbey was a monastery like Mont St.-Michel? What was French after a thousand years?

"I'm sorry," she said. "Many of our studies are incomplete. We did explore a gold mine last year. I know you loved gold."

"Not me personally," Cole said (remembering the ring Helen had wanted; that Helen). "But yes, gold was very popular in what you call 'modern' times."

"I found the mine strangely beautiful, in a dark sort of way. People wanted to close them up, years ago, but I'm glad some were left. They are like scars, like tattoos, showing the marks of humankind on the world. A kind of love. A memento of the time when our relationship with the mother planet was more intimate."

"And more destructive," Cole said.

"Motherhood is always destructive, to the mother," she said. "Today, heavy metals like iron and nickel that can't be recovered from recycling are mined from asteroids."

"So you do have space travel, then?"

"It's not exactly travel, is it? Oh, people have been to all the planets, and even to a few nearby systems. There are people who live on Mars and Venus and the Moon, for research. But most of the mining, and the shuttling from orbit, is done by robots."

There was another research station on Titan, according to Kate, and a more or less permanent colony had set out for a planet of a "nearby" star. But there was less and less interest in space exploration once it became clear that life was rare in the universe—and multicellular life even rarer.

"No first contact, then," Cole said. "Contact was our dream. That was the whole point of exploration, space travel, science fiction—the stories we told. The dream of encountering the Other."

"Oh, I guess we encountered the Other," Kate said. "Only it was here. It was her. ARD."

"Ard? "

"ARD is earth's name for itself. After the Sixth, and the Restoration, a monitoring system was put into place that linked every ecosystem, geological system, and weather system on the Earth. The idea was that never again would we be unaware of the condition of our fellow species on the planet, or of the planet itself."

"I know of this," Cole said. "Earthwatch."

"It was self-maintaining, and installing. And, we discovered several thousand years ago, self-conscious. After the network had been installed for almost half a millennium, ARD contacted the various governments (social, political, economic, all interlinked and elected) and for the first time humankind contacted a consciousness other than itself."

"But one that we had created," Cole pointed out.

"Yes and no. ARD is in a sense, I supppose, our child, but she is also our mother. According to her, she had been conscious all along, and we had merely given her the desire and the means to communicate. But then, every consciousness thinks it has always been. These were questions that led to much strife. We had a renaissance of religion, and then of war, for the two are closely linked. But there was a kind of joy in it, too. The universe can be a very lonely place."

"Yes," Cole said, as they climbed the hill of Montmarte. Paris was spread out below, looking neither old nor new but eternal. "So what is ARD like?"

"We don't know much about her," said Kate. "She established contact with us, but never had any interest in us. She will only speak with groups or organizations, never individuals. She is still there, maintaining the systems, as indeed she says she always had—wordlessly—since the emergence of life on the planet and even before. This is her claim. She changed certain things; she has let us know that there are closed areas on the planet where humans must not go. This seems appropriate to us. But she almost never speaks to us, or we to her."

They walked down the hill, making a great circle. Back at the restaurant, they found Lee and his three Modernist companions sitting under the trees, drinking absinthe. Kate and Cole ordered a bottle of Bordeaux to catch up.

Cole had several questions he wanted to ask Lee, now that they could communicate. But Lee was still holding forth on the terrors of the Sixth Extinction. As amazing as it was to hear him speaking eloquently, thanks to the translator, Cole had heard it all before. So he amused himself opening and closing his book, making it large, then small again.

"Chester Himes," whispered one of the two men, the white one. "A favorite. Well known in your age?"

"Our age has hardly heard of him," Cole said.

"This visit with you, to your world, is an unexpected gift," Lee was saying. "We thought the earth would be a cinder by now. Or a trash midden."

"We live more simply now," Kate said. "In the cities or in the villages, people are more modest in their needs. Everything doesn't have to get bigger and bigger all the time."

"Nonsense!" said one of the men, the African. "Everyone is tired of having to get permission to travel to Paris, or to Lagos. I want to be able to go where I want, when I want."

"When you are fifty-five," said the other woman, whose name was Michelle. She explained that there were two periods in everyone's life—between the ages of eighteen and twenty, and between fifty and fifty-five—when they are free to travel anywhere on the planet (anywhere not restricted by ARD, of course) and not required to work. She was twenty-four.

"What about children?" Lee asked.

"There is no restriction on the number of children you can have," said Kate. "Although in fact mortality rates are adjusted for the population limits of the planet."

"And what might those limits be?" Lee asked.

"Approximately six to seven billion. ARD adjusts it, according to some formula that is not revealed to us, and ARD lets us know how many children must be cancelled. If you live to be fifteen, you can generally count on living to be seventy-five or eighty, barring accidents."

"What do you mean, cancelled?" Cole asked.

"You don't want to know," Michelle said, looking down into her absinthe as if into a green crystal ball (and giving them another view of her perfect little breasts). Then she looked up with a laugh, tossed her hair back, and ordered another round of the *fee vert*.

Cole was relieved when Lee covered his glass with his hand.

"Our cursor is flashing," Lee said. "I believe the time has come when we must bid farewell to you all." He got up from the table, and so did Cole, and everybody kissed them on both cheeks. Kate was last.

"Where are we going?" Cole asked in a whisper.

"Onward," said Lee. "We are being sent on, forward, by these Old Ones."

"What about Dear Abbey, and the formula we were sent to get?"

"Perhaps that's why," said Lee. "Perhaps that's what Los Viejos have for us."

The Modernists were all waving goodbye. Or so Cole thought at first. They were actually pointing and reaching for the translators.

They were tossed—Michelle caught both, one in each hand.

Cole suddenly realized he had left his Himes on the table, under the trees. But Lee had already hit RETURN, and there they were, the army of mice. . . .

☀

1+

The booming sound told Cole they were back at the Student Union. He heard the rap music from upstairs (Busta Cap, calling his posse to order) even before the room drew itself in—floor, walls, door, clock. . . . 9:17

They had only been gone ten minutes? It seemed like days! Cole felt odd, like something was wrong. Then he saw the sleeve of Lee's safari jacket, and Lee sitting beside him, and he knew, or rather remembered, what it was.

"Lee, what are we doing back here? I thought we were going forward."

Lee looked at Cole. "Home . . ." Before he could say more, the door opened and Parker's big head poked through. He looked displeased, like Elmer Fudd in a Bugs Bunny cartoon. "Dr. Lee!—Mr. Cole? I thought I heard something. What in the world are you doing here this time of night? I mean, are you. . . ?"

"No problem," said Lee.

"I have to start clearing the place out in half an hour!"

"No problem," said Lee.

The door closed with a disapproving click.

"Why is he always surprised to see us?" Cole asked. "Is this some kind of Groundhog Day thing?"

"No problem."

"No problem? It seems like a problem to me." Cole yanked his hand free of Lee's and stood up. "What's going on here? Who are these Old Ones? Where's the Dear Abbey formula we were supposed to get?"

"Hold horses!" Lee's Texas accent was back. He studied his Palm PC; he started punching in numbers.

"Lee, talk to me, damn it! What I'm wondering is, maybe we need to reconsider this whole idea. I mean Dear Abbey."

"Not for us," Lee said. "Hold horses!"

Beep beep. The Palm PC was beeping. The screen was empty except for a blinking cursor, in the exact center. "New time slice open now," Lee said, patting the seat beside him. "Not finish somehow."

"You may not be finished," Cole said, "but I sure as hell am." He meant to walk away but he didn't. He just stood there until Lee grabbed his hand and pulled him down onto the glider beside him.

"Don't," Cole said, but Lee did. He hit RETURN, and there they were again:

The army of mice.

※

+100,000

Falling—

Spinning—

Cole was a veteran time traveler, one of the two most experienced (as far as he knew) in all human history; he knew enough by now to keep his eyes closed. At least he thought they were closed. The colors continued to spin, and when they faded to white, he thought (he hoped) that they were back in Paris. He opened his eyes—or had they been open all along? They were in a bare, wood-floored room lit from outside through French doors. He could hear music in the distance, a strange soft business of strings and drums and bells. The alarm, the panic, all was gone. He was in no hurry to get up from the glider. He seemed to remember that there had been a problem, but what? So what? The air smelled soft and sleepy. He closed his eyes and leaned back and listened to someone muttering in Chinese.

It was Lee. He was tapping at his Palm PC, his lips in a twist, like a kid trying to get a knot out of a shoelace. "Awaken yourself, Cole," he said without looking up. "We have completed another slice."

"I know," Cole said. Then he noticed that there was no translator draped across Lee's shoulder; or his own. "You're speaking English again!"

"No, it is you who are understanding Mandarin."

It was true. A small, translucent fold appeared in the air next to Lee's right ear when he spoke. Lee spoke in his own voice (not a simulation, like in Paris) and if Cole watched the fold out of the corner of his eye, he understood Lee's words, even though Lee was speaking Chinese.

"Where are we?" Cole asked. "Or I guess the question is, when?"

"I am trying to puzzle that through. This is a entirely different set of algorithms. In the meanwhile . . ."

"Meanwhile, we're alone," Cole said, "and you're speaking English, or I'm understanding Mandarin, or you're understanding English, or . . ."

"I have always understood English," Lee said with a smile.

"Whatever. Anyway. So let's talk. Why don't you tell me what the hell is going on, for real. Where are we? Where are we going? What about Dear Abbey?"

Lee nodded. "All that is what I do not know," Lee said, standing up and replacing his Palm PC in his pocket. "Someone has added to our algorithm, by infrared. A subroutine. But come. First we will see where we are."

"You mean when." Cole followed Lee through the French doors, onto a narrow balcony. The city spread out before them was no Paris. It was a quiet, sprawling, low-rise town where the scratching of palm leaves on window glass was louder than the traffic.

The second floor (first, in French) balcony on which they were standing overlooked a wide, busy street. Most of the traffic below was on foot. A few machines like golf carts weaved through idling walkers dressed in loose, bright clothing. The faces, hands and arms that Cole could see ranged from pale to dark brown. The air was tropical, muggy but pleasant. He could smell fish, and smoke, and new wood, and something unrecognizable.

The future? It looked to Cole rather as if they had slipped into the past—a peaceful, easy past. But he was immune, for the moment, to its charms. "Why are we here?" he asked again. "And more to the point, where is the DNA patch or whatever we were sent to get?"

"Perhaps we will learn that from the Old Ones," Lee said. "I am as much in the dark as you."

"You are? I thought all this was your idea."

"Only the beginnings of it," said Lee. "Let me tell you a story. It begins in the distant past."

He smiled to show that he was joking. Cole smiled back to be polite, even though he wasn't feeling polite.

"I was at MIT," Lee said, "investigating certain mathematical anomalies that I had begun to explore in China: cross-dimensional quantum congruencies, which give mathematics the power to unravel the fabric of space-time, even if 'only' temporarily, which is of course the point. In spite of my fugitive status, I was in touch with colleagues in China, who were also what you Europeans so curiously call 'environmentalists' . . ."

You Europeans!? But Cole decided to let it go.

". . . clandestine, of course, with links to others around the world. Things in The Realm are both looser and tighter than you Europeans might think. The idea of Dear Abbey appealed to them, to us, as much as to you. We even liked the name—*The Monkey Wrench Gang* is a favorite in China, though we didn't perhaps get all the other associations."

"And you had no—hesitations?"

"Of course we did. But the chaos and suffering Dear Abbey would cause didn't bother us as much as it did you. We had gone through the Cultural Revolution, after all. So we were as disappointed as you when it became clear that the last gene sequence required to engineer the event was, itself, dependent on a cellular inventory that would take at the very least a century to complete and compile. It was frustrating. We knew exactly what was needed, we even knew where it was—a hundred years in our own future. It was as if it were on a shelf, just out of our reach."

"And so—this is where you came in."

Lee smiled. "It was while I was at MIT working on the quantum anomalies logarithm that I got a message, an e-mail. A most unusual message."

"From the future."

"More unusual than that. From myself in the future. It was from Paris, although I didn't find that out until later, when I got there, and the Modernists gave it to me in the garden. I sent it to myself while you were on your tour of *les arrondissements*. I knew to send it because I knew I had gotten it. What a strange feeling, Cole! Can you imagine the experience of being, briefly, to be sure, the very temporal anomaly your calculations predict: cause and effect coexisting in the same Heisenbergian orbital trajectory!"

"It was weird, I'm sure," Cole said. "So if it was Les Modernistes who gave you the time travel math, why didn't they just give you the Dear Abbey patch while they were at it?"

"They did not have it; they had never heard of it. What they gave me was the algorithms and the coordinates I needed to travel into the future and get it; of course, in quantum anomaly math the coordinates and the algorithms are the same. That is why when I saw the email from myself I knew immediately what it was, and what it was for."

"You got it before you sent it."

"Ten thousand years before, Cole. Think of it. I contacted my colleagues, and yours as well, and began to prepare for this journey. I had to leave MIT. That was the most difficult part, professionally."

"I can imagine," said Cole. "You left for privacy?"

"No. It is easier to work at Swick, for certain, since no one knows or cares what you are doing. But actually I moved for location. Time is not site specific, but the loops in which it is accessed are. Anyway, you know the rest, as much as I do. The purpose of our little trip was to enter the loop and get the sequence patch. I assumed we would not be able to actually enter the future, which is why I took the camera. And everything went according to plan, until . . . well, you saw what happened."

"I saw," said Cole. "So who was he, the guy who got shot before he could give us the patch?"

"I don't know. One of the Old Ones, perhaps. Someone who wanted us to have the patch. Someone who wanted to make sure Dear Abbey happens."

"Who was shot by someone who *doesn't* want Dear Abbey to happen?"

"I don't know," said Lee. "All I know is that we don't have what we came for. And that we are in the future, not just observing it. We are being brought forward, in stages. At every stage my numbers are changed, some times by infrared, some times by other means. These Old Ones, whoever they are, are pulling us deeper and deeper into the future. Perhaps, I hope, to give us the patch."

"Maybe they want to warn us," said Cole. "Maybe they want us to see what Dear Abbey will do before they give it to us. Maybe they . . ."

Knock! Knock!

It came from behind them, the rap of knuckles on glass.

They turned to see a very tall, very black man in a bright blue robe in the doorway. He rapped on the open door again, politely.

"Welcome—" The same small translucent fold in the air appeared beside his ear. "—Dr. Cole, Dr. Lee. I hope your journey was a pleasant one."

He spoke a kind of sing-song Chinese, or at least so it sounded to Cole, who watched the fold and understood every run-together word.

"It has its delights," Lee said, in his own Mandarin. "You have the advantage of us, for you know our names. You are one of the Old Ones we seek?"

"No, no." The man smiled apologetically. "I am Amadou Pessoa, your guide, instructed by the Old Ones to meet you, and send you on."

"On?" Cole asked. He didn't like the sound of it. "Can you tell us what year is this?"

Just hearing it made Cole feel dizzy. He wanted to sit down but he was afraid that might seem rude, so he leaned back against the rail of the balcony and closed his eyes until his head stopped spinning; then he followed Lee and their host down the stairs, into the street. The year was 116157 (HK), 118520 (JC). They were a hundred thousand years in their own future.

Their guide, Amadou, took them around the city, Bahia, somewhere on the eastern coast of South America, which was now a separate continent. They rode around the bumpy streets on a little open car with three fat wheels. The car seemed to drive itself, or maybe Amadou controlled it in some way that Cole couldn't see. Many of the people on the street wore makeup so bright that they looked like clowns escaped from a circus, though some wore no makeup at all.

Cole's fears of the African race disappearing from the human genome were put to rest on the streets of Bahia, where people were all colors from ebony to pale (though mostly dark) and varied in height and hair as well.

No one seemed to be working, and Lee asked if they were in a holiday center, but Amadou's "fold" either didn't translate this or he didn't want to answer. Lee didn't press the point. "Maybe we are so far in the future," Cole whispered to Lee, "that the entire human race has retired."

"I think you are joking," Lee said. He was more interested in the Old Ones. Who were they? What did they want with them?

Amadou had no answers. "They don't speak with us directly. The time and place of your arrival all came through RVR, a forwarded message, from the far future. A one-time thing. I was chosen to wait and meet and guide you. It's a great honor."

"The honor is entirely ours," said Lee. "But tell us about this RVR."

And so he did. Lee's formal speech, as well as Cole's ability to understand it, were all due to RVR, which was the "folds" in the air, and much else as well—a worldwide database for communication, translation, archiving, accounting and keeping track of almost every aspect of human intercourse in this far future world. It was almost like a personal genie for everyone on Earth, reminding Cole of Arthur C. Clarke's dictum that any sufficiently advanced technology would appear to be magic.

"RVR tries to anticipate our needs as well as fulfill them," Amadou said. "He even tries to cheer us up when we are sad."

"You are some times sad, then," said Lee, "even in this seeming so perfect world?"

"Of course," said Amadou. "Neither the world nor the creatures that make it up are perfect—or perfectible."

"Just as I always suspected," said Lee. While he and Amadou discussed this interesting-only-to-them concept,

Cole learned from RVR himself (who whispered into his ear, in English!) that he had been designed and built—self constructed from neo-biological nanos—19376 years before. "Official name, RVR, or—" and he pronounced the full acronym in some dialect that was totally incomprehensible to Cole, since the fold itself had no fold to watch.

※

Amadou picked up his daughter and a friend from school, which was a low building set into a clay cliff beside an arm of the sea. Two little girls of about seven ran out in bright dresses, and shoes that changed colors with every step.

In case you are wondering what these little girls thought of time travelers from the distant past—they thought nothing at all. Cole and Lee were just two more grown ups, looming in the background of their lives like trees. The girls twirled and chirped and ran and skipped with each other, ignoring the adults (including their father) altogether.

Cole was interested in the global communicator/net, RVR.

"RVR keeps track of things," Amadou said. "Suppose you want to get in touch with that flautist you met four years ago at that Music Festival in Norway. . ."

"You still have nations, then," Cole said.

"Oh, yes, of course," said Amadou. "They are language groups and culture matrices. Without nations where would music or art come from? After the family there is the tribe, and then the nation. These are the things we are careful not to change. We are social beings, and society requires both a One and an Other. It's simply that we have grown beyond the conflict between the tribes and the nations. We had to outgrow that or die."

"So the guy in Norway . . ."

"Who said it was a guy?" Amadou laughed. "But yes, RVR keeps track of such things. RVR knows his name, knows where he lives and knows if he wants to hear from you."

"What if I just want to be left alone?" Cole asked.

"RVR takes care of that too," said Amadou. "RVR is not always so great with ideas, but good with feelings. That's because RVR has feelings. Touch him, like this." Amadou put his hand up beside his ear, like a listener, and inserted two fingers into the cone.

Cole did the same.

"See?"

See? Cole felt. It was a warm—indeed, wonderful—feeling that flowed up from his fingertips through his arm, to his heart and head and down to his toes. It was like a first hit of tobacco after long abstinence; he blushed and felt it in the backs of his knees.

"That's RVR," said Amadou.

"RVR doesn't even know me!" Cole said.

"Oh, yes he does. RVR knows us. Humans. People. Our whole million year history. It's us he loves. All of us." In fact, as RVR (and Amadou, who joined in) explained, RVR had responded to humanity's need for companionship. RVR even shared the disappointment that ARD, the only other intelligence in the universe, was totally uninterested in humans, who were at the same time both her creations and her creator.

"RVR loves us," said Amadou. "What hurts us, hurts him too. ARD is cold. We love ARD but she doesn't love us, not really. And that hurts."

"And this RVR does?" Lee asked. "Love you? Love us?"

"Try it, Lee," Cole said. "You'll see."

Lee tried it and Lee "saw." He closed his eyes and raised his hand, and all he said was, "Oh, my goodness!"

✳

As that long, slow, sweet afternoon dragged on, it became apparent that Amadou was only killing time, entertaining his guests until it was time for them to leave. Unlike the Modernists in Paris, almost a hundred thousand years ago (were they really that gone, that dead? *Ou sont les nieges?*), Amadou had little interest in Cole or Lee or in their time. Perhaps, Cole thought, humankind had finally left the past behind altogether and moved entirely into the future.

Which worried him, more than a little. "We have to be getting back," he said to Lee. "We shouldn't be getting so far from the glider. We have to get back before ten."

"We can do no thing until the cursor begins to blink," said Lee, showing him his Palm PC. "Until then, there is nothing we can do. In the mean time, let us enjoy tomorrow today."

Enjoy tomorrow today. Lee should write fortune cookies, Cole thought. And yet it was true: the future was theirs to enjoy. Time seemed loose there, like comfortable clothing. Humankind had apparently abandoned (outgrown, perhaps) the obsessive slicing of the day and the hour and the minute into ever smaller slices; the day was just morning, early and late, and afternoon, early and late; although the days and months were still, of course, intact, being ruled by the Sun and Moon.

Lee was interested to learn that the day was longer than it had been in his time by almost a minute. RVR did the math for him. Perhaps, Cole suggested, this contributed to the sense of unhurried leisure that seemed to prevail in Bahia.

"And what about disease?" asked Lee. "Or have bacteria ceased to evolve?"

"Nano-docs," said RVR. "Everyone dies of either accident or old age."

"Which is what?"

"Ninety, a hundred. After that the nano-docs are whelmed."

"You mean, overwhelmed."

"No, whelmed."

They were at the seawall, having abandoned the car, which someone else took up as soon as they dropped it. Cole let Lee and Amadou and the two girls walk (skip, run) ahead, while he stopped and shared a cigarette with an old couple sitting on a flat stone, looking out to sea.

Smoking, they told him, was allowed and even encouraged after age sixty-five. "Before that you can bum them but you can't buy more than a pack a week. Gives you something to look forward to." They were seventy-three and seventy-seven and had just come from a funeral of his ex, who was seventy, killed in a fire.

"Died too soon," said the woman, whose name was Pearl (the same as her little dog). "But not too soon for me," said the man, whose name was Rob. He started to tell a long involved story of love and madness, but Cole excused myself and left. Except for his grandparents he had never liked old people. And now he was, in a sense, the oldest of all.

Second oldest. He caught up with Lee and Amadou and the girls at a break in the seawall. The sea seemed unchanged in a hundred thousand years, as in (Cole assumed) the millions or hundreds of millions before. There was that same small death smell. Sailboats skimmed over the waves. Far in the distance, on the horizon, he saw a larger ship, with white sails; and when he looked again it was gone.

He checked nervously with Lee. Still no beep, still no cursor.

The sky was a high, bright blue. Behind them the city was more trees than buildings. Cole asked about the other cities in the world. Cairo and Paris and Peking were Amadou's favorites. He and his wife had been to them all.

His ex-wife lived in Hong Kong, which he didn't like. Too steep, too crowded.

Amadou asked about New York, where his aunt and mother lived. Cole told him he knew it well . . . rough, hard, loud, old-fashioned, even in his own time. "But magnificent," he said. "A magnificent city."

Amadou was clearly not convinced.

And wars? "There are conflicts," Amadou said. "And even killings, but before they go too far they are settled in The Hall, our once-a-month government. The day-to-day details of administration are handled by RVR, and by ARD when they involve the earth, which most decisions do."

ARD and RVR got along fine, Amadou assured them, even though ARD didn't share RVR's love for humanity. Cole wondered if it had to do with humankind's behavior in the past, his present—the Sixth Extinction—but Amadou said that ARD's feelings were more disinterest than dislike.

"That is even worse," said Lee, sailing a stone off toward the sea where it skipped eight times. That feat surprised Cole, who realized how little he knew about his companion. Even Amadou's daughters applauded. While they waded barefoot into the green, shallow waves, Cole held their shoes—little blue shoes that curled up in his hand like kittens.

Lee was interested in farming, most of which was done in the sea. Cole was bored and tuned out. A group of children passed by, riding on an elephant.

"They're back?" Cole exclaimed.

"They were gone?" For the first time Amadou seemed interested in the distant past. "You didn't have elephants?"

"We did," Lee said. "But we did not take care of them."

Amadou looked puzzled. "Don't they take care of themselves?"

"They tried," said Cole.

"Not all were killed in the Sixth," said RVR. He was better

with information than with ideas. "There were a few left in the jungles of Africa. The Indian elephant, however, was truly lost. Is sadly gone forever."

Sadly gone forever. Instead of cheering him up, as expected, the elephant made Cole melancholy. As the shadows grew longer, they started back toward the glider in the house overlooking Grand Street. Lee's Palm PC still wasn't beeping, but the day was clearly drawing to a close.

"There's so much more I would like to ask before we go," Cole said. "What about Africa? What about the USA? What about sea level."

Africa had been repopulated, RVR said, now that the Sahara was gone. Sea level was about what it had always been and always would be, he hoped. The USA was split into language and ethnic communities. Hadn't that happened in Cole's own time? The dismantling of the mega-states . . .

Not exactly, Cole said.

There were some six billion people (5,987,097, 543, RVR whispered) on the planet and most of them lived in cities. A few people lived in the "wilds" but ARD preserved most of the wilderness for other species. Humans used it only for hunting.

"Hunting is allowed?" Lee asked. Cole was surprised; he hadn't realized Lee was listening, or that RVR was talking to anyone but him. It seemed such an intimate, one-on-one experience.

"That's the part of us that ARD relates to best," said Amadou, who had also been listening. "I'm a fisherman myself, but some people like to hunt. I guess it's part of our genetic makeup."

"I don't have a genetic makeup," said RVR. "But I like to go with you when you hunt. It's the only time ARD is pleased with you."

"What about the animals that are killed?" Lee asked. "Do they like to be killed?"

"Nothing that is living likes to be killed," said RVR. "Though everything that lives has to die."

"Including yourself?" Cole asked.

"I don't think about that," said RVR. "I don't think about things I don't think about. But hunting, I like to think about. The chase, the kill. It's the only time we are all together as one: ARD, myself and you."

Cole suddenly realized that as far as RVR was concerned, they were all one person. All humankind. He was hurt, but only a little.

✳

The Sun was setting over the blue hills in back of the town, which was not noisy enough (for Cole) to be called a city. The girls were gone, having peeled off at a little open air community center where a party was in progress. The sleepy city seemed much given to parties, elaborate dress, good food—the finer things in life.

"And why in excellence not?" Lee said to Cole as they strolled along behind Amadou. "Why not, after surviving the explosion of technology which began in 1500, which I must admit I did not think we would survive, why not then relax to enjoy the life span of any species, which might be any where from a million to ten million years?"

"It just seems to good to be true," Cole said.

"Ah, but I am Chinese," said Lee. "We understand patience, time, the slow march of change. Do not forget we have a stable society that lasted two or three times as long as your Roman Empire. You Europeans know only change. Instability."

"*Our* Roman Empire?" Cole said. "I'm not European!"

"Yes you are."

They passed a stall selling seafood and ate oysters on the half shell, which Amadou paid for with a blink (literally) of his eye. Accounts were retinal, and all went into the economic database kept by RVR. Lee and Cole shared a plate and washed them down with a kind of icy beer in bottles that got cold as soon as they were popped open. Cole was just thinking of ordering another beer when he heard the sound he had been waiting for.

Beep beep.

Lee showed him the cursor: blink-blink.

They commandeered another car and headed back across town for the glider. The car remembered where to go even though they had come in another car entirely.

Amadou rode on the back, stifling a yawn. Gracious but bored, he seemed glad to see them go. "Tell the kids good-bye," Cole said. He sat down on the glider and felt Lee's hand, still cold from the beer, cover his own.

Lee pressed RETURN, and there they were, the army of mice—and Cole knew from the silence that followed them that they were still far, far, far from home.

※

+1,000,000

It's an indication of the relative importance to consciousness of the mind and of the body, that on this "slice" Cole felt disoriented for the first time—not because he was living a million years after his own death, but because he was one-sixth his usual weight. The pounds were more important than the years.

For the first time he felt truly strange, even though he knew immediately where they were. He was looking up through a clear dome toward a blue planet hanging over an ash-colored horizon that was so close he that could almost touch it.

He was on the Moon.

"Whoa," he said quietly. "I didn't exactly bargain for this."

"Nor did I," said Lee. "But here in fact we are." Cole was relieved to see (and hear) that they still had their translator, RVR. There he was, hovering by Lee's ear and his own.

He and Lee stood up together, still holding hands. They were so light it felt like someone was helping them. They were in a sort of greenhouse, lighted by luminous strips along the floor—and by the blue and white Earth.

"Hello?" Lee called out. "Anyone home?"

"Yes, of course," said RVR. His gruff whisper in Lee's ear was reassuring. "She is coming. Look around."

The room was long and narrow, filled with big-leafed plants. They heard a high singing sound. Cole looked down a long aisle between two rows of plants and saw a white-haired woman in a wheelchair coming toward them. The wheels had some kind of invisible spokes that sang.

"Dr. Lee, Dr. Cole, so here you are," she said. "Would you like coffee? We grow the best here."

The "we" turned out to be a bit of an exaggeration, since she was the only human on the Moon. Her name was Zoe Zoesdottir and her hair was not really white but pale yellow. She wore a soft buttery jumpsuit with footlets, like a child's pajamas. She looked about sixty. The coffee was excellent, almost as good as the wine in Paris or the beer in Bahia. The moon base, Laurens, was three hundred and seventeen thousand years old. It had been abandoned for over half that time, but the Old Ones had asked that it be repaired and reoccupied since it was on Lee and Cole's trajectory.

"You know, then—you can tell us—who these Old Ones are?" It was Lee who asked.

No. Zoe and her collective had only gotten a message, like all the others before. This moon base was only a way station on Lee and Cole's journey to wherever it was that the Old Ones wished to send them.

Zoe had been there for almost a year, waiting for them. "I like living alone," she said. "And at my age the lower gravity helps." She told them her age: ninety-one. She had lost the use of her legs in an accident back on Earth, eleven years before. Her companion/husband had been killed in the same accident. Spinal injuries could be healed but the nanotechnology was expensive and time consuming. "I don't have that many years left," she said. "I like spending them here, with Rover and my plants. I'm weary of people."

People lived in 100-150 person collectives, based on work and language and family. But they were loose, and Zoe had untangled herself from her own.

She took Lee and Cole on a tour of her greenhouse. Lee wanted to know where the air and water came from. Zoe pointed to a range of jagged mountains streaked with white. A comet had been diverted there some two hundred thousand years before.

"A big mistake," said Zoe. The Moon was lighter than they had known, and the collision had put a wobble into its orbit. The tides on the earth were now erratic. The comet's ice was still providing water and oxygen for the Moon colony, but the colony hadn't lasted.

"None of them lasted," she said. "There were colonies on Ganymede also, and Mars. But eventually they all shut down. The only space travel is by mining ships, and there's not much of that. There was a colony sent to a planet in another star system, but they haven't been heard from in a hundred thousand years."

She spoke through RVR, which she called Rover. They all spoke through him—Lee to Cole, Cole to Zoe, her to them both. Without RVR Cole was as distant, linguistically, from Lee as from Zoe. RVR linked them all, like words holding hands. Cole couldn't imagine how they had gotten along without him.

Cole was even getting used to Lee's L.L. Bean safari jacket, which somehow didn't look so silly on the moon. Perhaps the 1/6 gravity made it drape better.

Zoe had never heard of Hong Kong time, so Lee plotted them on the stars. They were somewhere (anywhere) between one and 1.3 million years in the future. For some reason, this knowledge was as liberating to Cole as the one-sixth gravity. He felt like a ghost. Zoe took them for a walk outside. No space suits were needed; they wore a sheath of "sticky air" that was good, she said, for six or seven hours. Cole got cold after two, and there was nothing to see outside but gray ash and dull stones, unpolished by air or water. The Moon had an unfinished air, like an abandoned construction site.

Zoe brought them back in and they all undressed, quite unselfconsciously, and slipped into the hot tub and had more coffee. Cole was usually rather shy, or perhaps reserved is the word, but somehow nakedness felt natural in the lower gravity of the Moon; perhaps, he thought, our bodies remember a simpler time, when we were smaller—hominids, or children. They sat in the warm water under the dome looking down on the sea blue Earth, the Pacific, streaked with white, like a boy's favorite marble; his taw. A million years! Our planet looked like a single bright idea in a dead universe.

Lee sat on the edge of the tub with his feet in the water. He re-checked his numbers. He seemed exhilarated.

"A million years is only the beginning, in the life of a successful species," he said. "The dinosaurs lasted hundreds of millions. We also could live that long. We are infants still."

Infants? Cole's hand found Zoe's under the water. She was old and he was even older. "We at least survive our own madness," he said. "Does that mean we don't need Dear Abbey?"

"I don't know," said Lee. "Maybe we survived because of Dear Abbey. Because it was used."

"Maybe from here it doesn't matter," Cole said.

"What is Dear Abbey?" Zoe asked.

After a million years, they could tell her. So they did.

"That's pretty harsh. Were things really that bad?"

"They looked that bad," said Cole, and Lee nodded gravely, in agreement.

"So Dear Abbey was designed to save the earth, not humanity."

"You might say that," Cole said.

"The one depends on the other," said Lee.

"Well, don't expect ARD to thank you," Zoe said. She pointed down—or was it up?—at the blue planet spinning slowly in space. "ARD is so cold, so uncaring. Rover is different." She touched the air beside her ear. "I think the Moon would be very lonely without him. Wouldn't the universe be very lonely without you, Rover?"

❄

Unlike Amadou, Zoe loved to talk. Cole wondered if she talked to RVR when she was alone; and RVR told him, without his asking, that she did. Lee kept his own counsel, while Zoe and Cole drank a sort of sweet Moon grappa, and she told him her story. She had been born in Iceland almost a hundred years before. "That's not our normal life span," she said. "In low gravity, perhaps. Plus, sorrow has made me—enduring." She had buried three children and three husbands. The barren plains, the gray ash overlooked by blue: it was the bleakness of it all that appealed to her. It reminded her of home.

Lee left them for the plants. He wandered through the aisles, touching the leaves and smelling the big flowers on their narrow low-grav stalks. Many of the plants were new species, brought forth on the Moon. Although Zoe cared for them, in a way, she had little interest in them. It was RVR who talked of the plants with Lee, while Zoe and Cole listened in, laying back in the slow moving water that seemed, in that thin gravity, as thick and silvery as mercury.

The Moon base didn't (as Cole realized he had hoped) mark a revival of interest in space travel. "There was never a call to space," Zoe said. "Space is just a hole. The earth is just a stone falling through a universe of hole. Once we knew we were alone, that there was just us, there was no reason to go exploring."

No shining alien cities, she explained; no galactic empires to enslave, or befriend, or even notice us. No towering intellects or evil hive-beings. No fairies, no angels, no gods: for wasn't it all the same childish dream? "And no surprise," she said, pointing up. "Look at the Earth. Old Home. It literally teems with life. Nothing we could do even slowed it down. Life grows in every nook and cranny. It is the ideal environment, warm, wet, nurturing, and yet . . ."

And yet?

"And yet life arose only once, even there. Only once. All that fecund tangle of beasts and plants and molds and bugs and ponies and birds and germs and slimes—all of it is variations of one life form. One only, a peculiar replicating carbon twist of DNA. Even on the sweet Earth, Old Home, it happened only once. How could we have ever expected to find it all over the universe?"

They were holding hands. Zoe held their hands up out of the water and they looked at them and at each other tenderly, with astonishment, as one might look at a miracle even as it is happening. Or winding down.

The blue Earth beyond was turned to Africa. Poor Africa, thought Cole. Its outlines were almost unchanged. A million years is only a moment, after all.

He told Zoe what it was like to be African in our day, a million years ago. "Partly it was prejudice, and part truth. Africa was the last to develop."

Lee, back from his plant safari, sitting with his tiny, bone-white feet in the water, shook his head ruefully. "That is a foolish equation," he said. "Particularly from a million years in the future. It is only in the tiny window of our own small era that Africa appears backward."

"I beg your pardon," Cole said. "It was Europe that developed science. It was Europe, in the form of America, that first crossed space. It was Europe that first crossed the Atlantic. Perhaps China could have, but China didn't. Africa wasn't even close."

"Do not be so sure," Lee said. "There are signs that Africans may have crossed the Atlantic five hundred years before Columbus. The Europeans themselves did but did not notice. It did not count because the world was not ready. When it was ready human culture burst into the flame of science everywhere. That five hundred years from 1500 to our year 2000 was only a moment in the history of our species. Less than a moment it was really an instant. Science was certain to flare up somewhere in the tangled overheated pile of human culture. It was ready to happen and it happened to happen in Europe and not China or India or Africa. So what? When you throw a stick on a fire one end will burn first. Which end little matters because it is the same stick."

"A fire," Zoe said, changing the subject. "That's the only thing I miss, here on the Moon. Fire. I wouldn't be lonely at all, if I had a fire that I could sit by and stare into."

"Me too," said RVR.

Zoe reached up and rubbed him. Cole saw and did the same. It was as if they were touching each other. Lee had set the Palm PC upright so they could all see when the cursor started flashing.

"I think you had better call it off," said Zoe. "This Dear

Abbey. There's enough grief and catastrophe in every person's life without adding to it on purpose."

"I wonder," Cole said. "Lee, what do you think?"

"I think," said Lee, "that the history of humanity's first one hundred and fifty thousand years is so filled with catastrophe and strife and disaster that one more or one less makes little difference. And might make all the difference."

Cole shivered, even though the water was warm. "What do you think, RVR?"

"I don't know." He sounded confused. "Do you want me to know?"

"It is not up to us anyway, Cole," said Lee. "We are not tourists here, Cole. We are part of an organization."

"Speak for yourself, Lee. As I told you before . . ."

As if deliberately, to end the discussion, the Palm PC went beep beep.

Lee was already dressed; he was on the glider in an instant, patting the seat beside him. His hand was like the cursor, a rhythmic signal.

"Okay, okay!" Cole said. He hated to say good-bye to Zoe—it was forever. But it didn't seem to bother her; she was one of those people who likes good-byes, and good-bye/forevers best of all.

Lee hit RETURN and you know the rest.

※

+ 100,000,000

No matter how far ahead in Time they traveled, the trip always was the same. A light that wasn't light, a noise that wasn't noise—it was like the controlled terror of an airliner's take off, and like an airline passenger, Cole was getting used to it.

It no longer seemed strange to be traveling through Time. Hadn't he been doing it all his life? It was a gift, to see humanity's future. Was that long and peaceful future the result of the gene sequence that they were chasing? Or was that future in spite of it; or even a result of their failure? Surely the Old Ones, Los Viejos, would be able to tell him. Why else would they have sent for them across a million years?

A million years! And so it was that, with his companion, he rode the endlessly cresting, white-capped wave of Time . . .

He opened his eyes when he felt the glider stop. Lee was pulling his hand away.

Not home. That was Cole's first thought: not home.

They were outside, on a wooden deck, overlooking a wide plain that rose to mountains in the distance. Their outlines were unfamiliar. They were covered with golden or amber grass to a certain height, and above that snow. No rock, no ice, no trees. There seemed to be as little life or diversity here as on the Moon.

"Where the hell are we now, Dr. Lee?"

"You see that I am doing the numbers, Dr. Cole. We have all new numbers now."

The glider faced a round table big enough for four. One man sat across the table, smiling at them. Cole was becoming used to this gradual fade-in of a world, and knew that the man had probably been there all along, watching them as one might watch a child awaken.

"Hello there," Cole said.

"Hello," the man answered. "Welcome. Would you like a cup of tea?"

"Perhaps you have coffee?" Lee asked.

"Of course."

"We both prefer coffee if it is not too much trouble, thank you."

"No trouble at all."

Cole had stopped thinking of black and white. The man who had watched them arrive was golden-skinned and Asian in the face, like Lee. He had dark gray hair pulled back into a pony tail. He wore embroidered slippers and his feet made whispering sounds as he brought coffee from inside the house. His name was Hilary and he was about sixty. Cole was no longer shy about asking, but people had stopped keeping exact count.

And he was not one of the Old Ones. Cole knew better, by now, than to ask. But he asked anyway.

It was getting dark outside, first the mountains, then the sky, but it was bright inside the house behind them. Cole could feel the warmth from the door that opened and shut behind Hilary. He could hear music, faint but oddly familiar.

"Perhaps you can tell us who these Old Ones are?" Lee asked. "And where we will find them—or when."

"Aha!" Hilary said as he set the cups down. "We hoped perhaps you knew!" He explained that the Old Ones had communicated only once, to announce that Cole and Lee would arrive. Hilary and his wife Brin had been selected and sent to this place, which had no name, to welcome them and send them on their way. Brin was in Edminidine for the day, visiting their oldest daughter, Plenty. She would be back for the evening meal.

The door had stayed open behind Hilary, and now Cole recognized the music that was coming from inside the house. He had heard it in Paris as well. It was Miles Davis, the long, slow, sad modalities of "Kind of Blue."

He asked about Paris. Hilary had never heard of it. Europe is all forest, RVR said in a voice that was lower even than a whisper. The largest cities are around the South Atlantic and the pacific Rim. Lagos, Bonaire, Goral.

Had RVR acquired a new power? He seemed to be answering Cole's questions before they were asked. "Are you reading my mind?" he asked, uneasily.

"No, no," RVR said. "You must be subvocalizing. But if it bothers you . . ."

No, no. Cole felt comfortable with RVR, and a little bit of nosiness didn't bother him. He took it as a sort of compliment.

Out on the darkening plain he could see shapes— antelope? Deer? Horses? They would run and then stop, run and then stop, gliding like a shadow across the grass.

While Lee was still calculating the size of their last slice, RVR whispered it into Cole's ear. They were ten million (10,521,022) years in the future from our "present," from dreary little Swick; and 10,518,123 from the Crossing, the beginning of human history.

Why didn't you just give Lee the figures? Cole asked silently. Because Dr. Lee likes to work it out for himself, RVR answered.

The coffee was thick and sweet, served in tiny porcelain cups. Cole's cup had a design of a dragon emerging from a cloud. To make the coffee hotter, you ran your finger around the rim of the cup, clockwise, and a red flame appeared from the dragon's mouth. Or you could cool it down.

"Ten million years!" Lee said, closing his Palm PC and pursing his lips to indicate a whistle. Hilary nodded gravely; it was indeed a very long long time. Cole realized that he and Lee were, to Hilary, First Men. Exotics, primitives. Cave men.

He stopped playing with the dragon on his cup. "Ten million years," he said. "And we are still here, on the earth!"

"But of course!" said Hilary. Cole's amazement was that humans still existed, but Hilary thought he was talking about space travel. There was nowhere else to go, Hilary explained. People still occasionally went to the Moon, but hardly ever to

Mars, and the colonies on the moons of Saturn and Jupiter had long been abandoned. Asteroid mining had declined long ago; with recycling there was no need for new supplies of heavy metals.

The universe was mostly emptiness. There was little to see and nothing to do. And even after ten million years, we were still alone. . . .

There had been a gradual increase in life span (still less than 100) and a corresponding decrease in the birth rate, and now there were some four billion humans on the planet. (ARD kept exact numbers, RVR told Cole: 3,978,098,356.)

"Here comes one of them now," Hilary said, his voice brightening. He pointed toward the mountains, where a small flyer was coming over the crest, descending. But Cole and Lee couldn't keep their eyes on the plane. Instead they watched, astonished, as Hilary's hair arranged itself on his head into long gray cornrows.

Minutes later the little plane landed and Hilary's wife Brin got out, slipping gracefully through a sort of liquid door, her face all creased with smiles.

The plane's stubby wings were transparent, and disappeared, like the door, as soon as the big propeller stopped turning. Cole thought of Wonder Woman—and Brin was almost as good-looking. Better, really; better outfit, anyway. She wore an Amelia Earhardt-style leather jacket over flowing silk pants.

"Dr. Cole, Dr. Lee!" She was younger than Hilary (so that had not changed!) and appeared to be of Indian ancestry, though who knew what ancestry meant anymore? Was there still an India? Cole wondered. (No, RVR told him; though there were several languages of Indian origin.) Brin's skin was the color of warm ashes. Her hair was coiled on her head in an intricate "do," and Cole wondered if it had done itself as she landed, like Hilary's.

"Hilary and I can't leave together," she said, as she invited them into the house. "It's the only problem with this assignment."

Cole realized that they had been outside on the deck only to wait on her. She was a lot more talkative than Hilary, and he became more talkative when she was around. Cole and Lee's arrival had been pinned down to plus or minus four months, Brin said as she and Hilary prepared dinner, working together. The wait had been a welcome vacation, an opportunity to spend a few months alone together here in a remote and beautiful area that was closed by ARD to human habitation. That was why it had no name; names were seen as an encroachment, a mark on the land.

"We just call it 'house,'" said Brin. Houses grew themselves in a few months, according to a multiplicity of plans; this one would decompose swiftly after Brin and Hilary left, like grass.

※

There is a curious phenomenon in the life of couples, Cole noticed. The fires of young love are sometimes matched by a later fire, after the children are gone, and the body's beauty has fled, or at least softened. This glow, which he had seen between his Gramma and Grampa in Tennessee (certainly not between his mother and any man), he now saw between Hilary and Brin. Oh, they paid attention to Lee and him; they cooked them a fabulous meal. But they could hardly keep their eyes or their hands off each other as they chopped and stirred. Cole found it touching, but it made him lonely, too.

They had drinks, a peaty single-malt. Like Miles Davis, scotch persisted in its original form. Ten million years! There was no stove but a pot that heated itself as Hilary threw in slices of meat (horse, Cole was told) and potatoes and leeks. A Mongolian dish, RVR said, "showing" Cole a map in some limbic area of his brain. It was a new trick, both impressive and disturbing. The continents still had their customary shape, although North and South America were no longer connected. Scotland was an island to itself, and Europe smaller. The Great Lakes were gone. Africa was almost split in two by a large bay where the Congo used to be. The plain they now overlooked was not too far from the old highlands of Tibet, though lower and wetter according to the map.

Cole wanted to "look" at the cities but realized he was being rude, so he returned to the dinner table conversation.

"How was it that your hair done?" Lee was asking.

"RVR," Hilary said, reaching up beside his ear to pet him. "He senses my excitement and pleasure that Brin is coming home. He wants me to look good."

"I mean how, physically," Lee said.

"Physical? You mean the movement? Some kind of electrical plasma thing. You'll have to ask RVR. It's all electrical or something."

Cole reached up and touched RVR. "Hair is easy," he whispered in his ear, as if that explained everything. "I copied the design from ancient Africa."

"Before my time," Cole said.

"No, after."

Dinner was served: little pointed breads and horse and a yeasty beer that grew cold in the mouth. While they had coffee, Hilary showed Cole and Lee pictures of their children which floated in the air, in three dimensions. Cole could direct them with his eyes, here and there. Peace was in medicine, which had mostly to do with trauma, since the details of diagnosis and treatment were handled by nanobots in the blood. Plenty lived in Edminidine, near the sea, where she helped administer a sea farm and "dabbled in literature."

"A writer?"

"No, no," said Hilary. "There is quite enough already written, don't you think? We have enough to do to read and understand it all, without adding to it."

Hilary and Brin showed Cole and Lee their library. The books opened backward, and the print was a strange cross between Cyrillic and Chinese, but it was ink (or something very like it) on paper, or something very like it.

The print turned into English when Cole ran his thumb down the page. But he closed the book; he didn't feel like reading.

"Hands like books," Lee said approvingly. "Hands and eyes." The authors were familiar, some of them: Tasso, Cicero, King, Bruno, Shakespeare, Lafferty, Dryden, Huilvet, Gourg, Yi-Lun.

Cole looked for his favorites—Dick, Himes, Abbey, Sandoz. But they were either forgotten or absent from this particular library.

Like literature, music was finished, according to Brin, though no one actually used the word finished. She played guitar, "but not fancy," and only for herself. Cole thought she was being modest until she played for him. Back outside, they passed a pipe around the table while they watched the sun set. Cole had hoped for marijuana or some new, unheard-of drug, but it was that jealous old queen, tobacco. It seemed rude to turn it down. It was his first hit in almost eleven years, since an earlier Helen had made him quit, and it warmed me all the way down to his toes.

The setting Sun seemed larger than it should, and Hilary explained that there had been an increase in stellar radiation in the past million and a half years, the first change in over three billion. It had been compensated for by atmospheric adjustments, a joint project between humanity and ARD.

"Another drink?" asked Brin.

"That is a quite fine whiskey," said Lee. "There is one thing that you Europeans got right." He winked to show that he was teasing Cole, who didn't really mind. One would have thought that Cole had had enough whiskey earlier in the evening; but since that was ten million years ago, he allowed Hilary to pour him two fingers; okay, three.

The sun had set and only the snowy tops of the mountains still glowed. Cole saw the glint of a plane, high up, but no vapor trail. These people left no mark on Earth or sky. And what an Earth! What a sky! "What a gift," he said to RVR. But it was Lee who answered. "Gift?"

"What you said before, in Paris." Cole passed Lee the pipe. "That humanity gets to live, amidst all this beauty, for millions of years. It didn't have to be."

"The gift is the ability to change," said Lee. "Man is a reed, but a thinking reed. To evolve, to make a choice."

Choice? Cole wasn't so sure. It seemed to him that humankind, given a choice, always chose the worst option.

"It was you who did it," said Hilary. "You went from surviving the world, to dominating it, to cooperating with it. You went from prey to predator to caretaker, and you did it in less than a hundred generations."

"It seemed impossibly slow to me at the time," Cole said. "Still does."

"A hundred generations is nothing," said Brin. "We are an exceptional species, the only one with such control—for good or ill—over our environment. But we are also part of the environment. We are a species, still, and what we want is in our bones as well as in our minds."

"What we want is—" Cole stopped. They were all looking at him. "This," he said, with a wave of his hand that was meant to encompass it all: sky, sunset, whiskey, company, tobacco, the darkling plain . . .

"All this is ours, it will be ours, if we can learn to coexist and not destroy," said Lee. How can he speak of the future here, in the future? Cole wondered. But according to Lee, humankind's journey had only just begun. "Then we can, we will, settle down to enjoy the life span of a successful species, which is anywhere from ten to a hundred million years."

Cole had heard Lee's rap before but he didn't mind hearing it again. Ten million years. They were ten years old, into a life span of a hundred. They had only just begun. It felt like immortality. Or maybe what it felt like was good whiskey, tobacco, the sunset.

"The explosion started in your your time," said Brin, "with agriculture and cities. Surplus. We ceased the wandering that had taken us all over the world. Your generation, those who lived in the tiny sliver of time between 1500 and 2500, merely saw its end. And began the mopping up. It must have been a scary business."

"I think that is true," said Lee. "Five thousand years, five hundred. There is little difference from here."

"The main thing is, you did it," said Brin, relighting the pipe and passing it to Cole. "There are those who would have been happier if humankind had lived and died in a brief blaze of glory, like Jimi Hendrix."

Cole grinned. "You've heard of Hendrix?"

"Of course," she said. "The Age of Empire. Hil and I studied it, for this assignment, which I assure you is a labor of love. I even know a little English. Don't translate, RVR. Let me go it alone."

She said something unintelligible. Cole and Lee smiled politely. Cole recognized Lee's smile; it was the inscrutable one, the one he had always shown to him before RVR.

✳

It was an evening Cole would always keep with him, in dreams if not in memory, for the beauty of the place as well as for the sweet contentment of Hilary and Brin, who were thankful for the opportunity to live closer to unspoiled nature, if only for a while.

"ARD usually only allows brief forays into what she calls the 'Open Areas' (which are closed to us)," said Brin. "We were thrown out of the Garden of Eden ten million years ago. We should be used to it by now. We live in the cities, and only come into the Open Areas as hunters or hikers or herders.

"Hunters?" Lee asked. "Still that old thing?"

"Nature red in tooth and claw," said Hilary. "It is often said that ARD doesn't love us but I don't agree. The man ARD loves is ancient man, one of her killer species. Man, the bloodletter. ARD loves killing. We learned that during the ARD wars."

The ARD wars had started with an anti-RVR cult some two hundred and sixty thousand years before. A group from what had once been India, south of the Great Plateau, becoming convinced through a series of dreams and prophetic utterances that RVR was a malevolent entity, had moved into the wilderness. It was a great pilgrimage, of hundreds of thousands. Colonies were set up in remote locations with the permission of ARD and the cooperation of the rest of humanity, which was living with numbers of about seven billion (6.756) in the major cities and in smaller locations around the world. Over two hundred thousand years passed and the "pilgrims" were forgotten, except by historians (and of course ARD and RVR) until a series of earthquakes and floods sent refugees streaming. The colonies and ARD had come into conflict, and ARD had destroyed them. It was Sodom and Gomorrah all over again. A few humans filtered into the cities, but their language was untranslatable and they were no longer truly human. In fact they had regressed to the hominid stage (which explained, Cole thought, some of our "junk" DNA) and could no longer intermarry with humans. They died off through disease and heartbreak. This was the last speciation of the human race, and it was a repeat, a reversal.

"And no other life-forms?" Cole knew but he had to ask again. The stars were beginning to appear, one by one. He couldn't find any familiar constellations; he had never been very good at picking them out, but now even the Big Dipper was gone. Flung apart by Time.

"None to speak of," said Hilary. "Or to speak with. Molds and slimes, mostly. Not good company."

"Speaking of company . . ." Cole saw that the ponies were grazing right up next to the house.

"They like people," said Brin.

"Like dogs," Lee said. It turned out that Hilary and Brin had never seen or touched a dog. They had long been extinct.

"Tell us about dogs," said Hilary, and Cole did, as much as he knew, from the days they had first seen man's fires and crept closer, fascinated and comforted by our talk and our singing. Hilary and Brin listened with what seemed to Cole a polite but diminishing interest. The long partnership, the love affair, had long been over. Humankind had forgotten the dog.

"That's a beautiful story," said RVR.

The ponies gathered around the deck, compact, silent and shapeless in the darkness, while the people smoked and talked. Man the destroyer is loved by the other animals as much (or more) than man loves them, Cole thought. Even though we kill them and eat them, they love us, and shouldn't it be so? Life kills us and eats us, yet we worship it in our way. We fall all over it.

The wine was perfect. No surprise, thought Cole. After ten million years, would there be a place in the world for bad wine? Ditto the clothes, which fit perfectly. Cole wondered how he and Lee looked to Hilary and Brin, particularly Lee in his hideous L.L. Bean safari jacket (which Cole had gotten used to). There was of course no way to know. If there was one thing this couple of the far future had, in addition to their love for each other, it was manners. Not that there was any coldness about them—no, only a perfection of warmth and *gravitas* and style, with just enough bite, like a perfect whiskey.

Crime, sorrow, even catastrophe were still part of the human condition, Cole and Lee were assured. Not war, though; war was crime sanctioned, even sanctified, which was unimaginable. Cole looked up at the stars and they looked even colder, even more distant than usual, now that he knew that they were empty. They had looked to him, to us, to Early Man, so much like a great city in the distance. We had wanted so much to go there, to be welcomed in. And now he knew that what we had thought, had hoped, was a beacon, was in fact just dumb fires, sparks, not even ruins. This tiny house of Earth was all there was. We were more alone than any of us had ever imagined possible.

So melancholy came with the gift. Even the dog, man's companion, had slipped under the dark waters of Time.

"Nothing at all," Cole said, looking up. "No one. It is hard to believe that in all that immensity . . ."

"It's getting late," said Brin. "Shall we go for a ride?"

The ponies liked to be ridden; it gave them an excuse to strut about. They were bone-shaking little trotters, with one liquid smooth canter, like the Icelandic ponies Cole and his second Helen had ridden on their honeymoon, when a black face in Iceland was rare. The Icelanders had thought Cole must be a jazz musician. They had asked him about Miles Davis, and he had pretended to have known him, in his old age. It was even partly true: he had met him once, as a child, with his uncle Will, who had sold dreams in the form of drugs to the rich and famous.

Were those clouds on the Moon? They were. Brin explained that they were the result of a long ago comet, deflected to the moon for its ice, gradually sublimating into mist that wrapped the poles like a sheer scarf. I know all about that, Lee said. He told of seeing the white streaks on the lunar mountains, and Brin and Hilary wanted to hear about Zoe, almost ten million years ago. Zoe and Cole and Lee were all contemporaries, to them. Brin and Hilary slowed their ponies to a walk, so that they could hold hands. Cole and Lee would soon be gone, and they would return to Edminidine, the long littoral city along the China coast. They were ready to resume their life among their friends and their children. But they would miss the ponies, the stars, the sea of grass.

So would Cole. He was riding bareback across the grass-smelling plain, like an Indian. The stars bore down like a burning blanket. Even though he was not familiar with the constellations, he knew they were all changed, changed utterly, irretrievably. The hundred thousand years behind his long-ago birth, the short trail from Africa to America, was nothing compared with the ten million since, which had carried the galaxy and the solar system into new immensities. He looked up, into the hole that is the heavens, and understood for the first time, in his very bones, the awesome enormity of the journey on which humankind had embarked when we first looked up from our small fire and saw the stars.

What if, Cole wondered, we had known then what he knew now—that it was all empty? That we were like a child, alone in a great empty house? Forgotten . . . worse than forgotten. Worse than abandoned. Alone forever from the beginning unto the end, from dust to dust, all, all alone. Would we have, could we have, still survived?

"Cole. Duty calls."

Beep beep. Lee showed Cole his Palm PC. The cursor was blinking; it was time to go.

Hilary and Brin led the way. They rode side by side with their arms around each other, an awkward but lovely sight. The house was a beacon, a far-off ship across the sea of grass, a nearest star.

"What would happen," Cole wondered out loud, as they rode back slowly across the plain, toward the frail ship of House, "What would happen, if we didn't hit RETURN. If we stayed here."

"ARD would not allow it," Lee said.

"I don't mean *here* here. I mean here, on this late afternoon Earth, with these good people."

"And forget what we were sent to do?"

"You mean Dear Abbey. I wonder now if we should be doing it at all, even if we find it and return with it."

"I think that is not for us to decide, Cole, you and I," Lee answered, kicking his pony and trotting ahead.

Cole looked up at the still-, always-, ever-to-remain-unfamiliar stars, and shivered, and kicked his little pony too.

※

1+

There they were, the army of mice. Soon Cole knew, without opening his eyes, that they were back in the Student Union. He could hear the thumping from upstairs, and there was a smell of cinder blocks and Coca-Cola.

The door opened and Parker's big head stuck through. "Dr. Lee!—Mr. Cole? I thought I heard something. What are you doing here this time of night? I mean, are you. . . ?"

"It's okay," Lee said, opening his eyes and letting go of Cole's hand.

"I have to lock up at ten," said Parker, sounding annoyed. He looked meaningfully toward the analog clock on the wall. It was 9:46.

"No problem," said Lee.

The door closed with loud click.

"Why is he always surprised to see us?" Cole asked.

"Time loop, till ten." RVR had been left behind, or rather ahead, ten million years in the future, and Lee was speaking English again. Pidgin English.

"I hope this isn't some kind of Groundhog Day," Cole said.

"Ground what?"

"Nothing. I thought you said we weren't done. So why are we back here?"

"Beats me," Lee said, pulling a cell phone from his safari jacket and punching in a number.

"Wait! Who are you calling?"

"You know. Beeper."

"Wait, Lee!" Cole said, reaching for the phone. "What about Los Viejos? What about Dear Abbey? You and I need to talk first."

"All come around," Lee said, handing Cole the phone. Cole heard it ring once, then click.

"Damn!" he said. "So what now, Lee? We wait for Pell and Flo, or whatever her name is, so they can decide what we saw and what we think? But who am I talking to? There's no talking to you!"

Cole punched in his own number; might as well check his messages. While it rang, he watched the clock make one jump, to 9:48. Time moved so slowly here, in the present. That tiny isle. He was beginning to feel like an islander: slightly homesick away, hugely restless at home.

"You have reached . . ." Cole couldn't believe the sound of his own voice on the machine. Was he really that dark, that gloomy? "Leave a message if you insist."

Cole punched in a code. The machine's computer-generated voice was so much more pleasant, more human than his own. "You have ONE message."

A last piece of nastiness from Helen? Cole was just punching in the retrieval code when he heard a beep beep beep.

Lee's Palm PC was blinking.

"I thought we were done! I thought it was over."

"More slice," Lee said, smiling inscrutably. "Old Ones? Los Viejos? Let's ride."

Cole folded the phone. He didn't have to be asked twice. He was more at home off the island than on. Besides, in the future he and Lee could talk. He put one hand on Lee's and the other up beside his own ear, for reassurance, but of course, RVR wasn't there. Not yet—

"One more slice," Lee said again, and there they were, the mice. And the centuries, streaming down, covering the two of them over like drifting sand. . . .

※

+225,000,000

It was dark.

It was cold.

Something was wrong with the air. Cole smelled smoke and ash and ozone mixed with fear; an ugly smell. He knew it well. It was the smell of downtown New York City after the World Trade Center attack. He had helped a friend (not a Helen) sneak in and loot her own apartment, how many years—how many centuries—ago?

The glider was squeaking to a stop. They were on a terrace overlooking a dark valley, all in shadow. Cole could see a few lights moving far below. The Sun, huge and dark red, hung over a range of hills on the other side. It was setting, or so Cole thought. It looked squashed and impossibly near; but surely that was illusion, a trick of the air. Behind them was a stone building. A light came on, spilling through a long window.

Someone opened a door. "Contact!"

Three people came outside, all dressed in the same gray and blue uniform with hoods, like homeboy sweatshirts. Their apparent leader, a woman, carried a coil of glowing rope that looked like soft neon. "They're out here!" she barked in a harsh, unfamiliar tongue. Cole could see the fold in the air beside her ear that told him RVR was back, and back at work.

He reached up and touched him. *Hello old pal.*

"Dr. Cole, Dr. Lee!" the woman said. "Come inside. It's cold out here." It was cold. The sun was too big and too orange; too easy to look at. The wind had a wrong, raw, wrung-out feel.

They gladly followed her inside. "This has to be them, the Old Ones," Cole whispered. "Ask them if they have something for us. Ask them why they brought us here."

Lee didn't respond. He was studying his Palm PC and shaking his head.

"If you don't ask them, I will!"

The woman with the glowing rope turned to Cole and smiled. He smiled back, and started to ask her . . . but she and the other two "hosts" had already turned their backs.

They were busy over a small console with a plasma screen that changed size and colors, and seemed to be taking pictures of the Sun, or of lots of different suns.

"This is the end of everything," Lee said mournfully, to himself as much as to Cole. "We can look at the Sun."

"What are you saying?"

"I am saying, we can look at the Sun. It is old and dim."

"This must be them, then," Cole said, shaking Lee's arm. "The Old Ones. What year is it, can you tell?"

Lee nodded and showed him on the Palm PC. +231,789,098. Cole felt dizzy. They were two hundred fifty million years in the future. A quarter of a billion turns of rock and air around the Sun, and now the Sun itself was going cold.

The Sun. There it was, through the window. Cole couldn't bear looking at it but he couldn't look away.

"So did they bring us here to give us Dear Abbey? Or to tell us that it doesn't fucking matter anymore?"

Lee didn't answer; he just looked from his Palm PC to the dying Sun, and back, again and again.

Finally a door opened (in a wall, where there hadn't been a door) and a man in uniform brought them both a cup of hot chocolate. Cole would have preferred a drink, but it was hot, and it was chocolate.

"Are you the Old Ones? Do you have something for us?" Cole asked the man, who seemed to find the question amusing. He told Cole his own name was Cole; he had been named after him. "The Old Ones sent for you," he said, "and we take that as a sign of our certain success. Of our survival. Therefore we honor you."

He excused himself and left the way he had come. Through the open door (before it turned back into a wall) Cole could see children, all standing in rows, dancing or exercising to . . . it was almost Mozart, but a little off, with too many strings.

Not like the Miles Davis he had heard earlier. Two hundred million years earlier.

Through the window he saw needle-shaped ships rising out of the valley, silently, like a volley of arrows. "Is there a war on?" he asked RVR, reaching up to touch him again. "Is that what's wrong?"

"No, no war. It's the Sun," RVR said. Their hosts were trying to keep the Sun from going nova, he explained. It had already exploded in a flare called the Helium Flash, which had killed over two billion people directly, and three billion more in the natural fires and famine that followed. That was almost a thousand years ago. The nuclear fires had since been stabilized with an ongoing "innoculation series" (the ships Cole had seen) but only temporarily. It was a holding action. The Sun's hydrogen was almost all consumed and our mother star was in the process of converting herself into a helium giant, unless prevented. It was still touch and go. All humanity was down to about a billion and a half people, living on a narrow habitable band. The atmosphere had been altered, which accounted for the smell. Oxygen had been down to less than fourteen percent, but was now back up to eighteen. Cities? They were only memories. People lived underground in long warrens. Several hundred thousand had left on a starship, but they hadn't been heard of since.

ARD had died. Not even RVR knew exactly how, or why, or when. Her communications, increasingly erratic and peevish, had finally ceased altogether. No one had marked the date; people had long since ceased to notice, and RVR's attention was mostly, if not entirely, on people and their concerns.

"So where are the Old Ones who sent for us?" Cole asked. "These people hardly notice us."

"Maybe these Old Ones are the starship people," Lee suggested. "Maybe they are no longer on Earth."

"They died," said RVR. "There are no starship people. I have told them here, but they keep 'forgetting.' They don't want to know."

"What happened?"

"They just died. There is nothing between the stars. Too much nothing. It is no place. No place for man, no place for RVR."

It all seemed a sad end to a long adventure. Humankind was a quarter of a billion years old. We had been on the earth longer than the dinosaurs, as long as the hermit crab or the cockroach; we were the new champs. There wouldn't be any champs after us. The day was now forty-four hours long—old hours, that is, original hours; though what indeed was an hour but a portion of a day? What indeed was a day, or a year: all were just spinnings.

The stars no longer looked strange or frightening or promising or mysterious to Cole. They looked as random and as temporary and as unimportant as the glint of light on waves.

"What about Dear Abbey," Cole asked. "If these guys don't have it, who does?"

"I believe we missed it," said Lee. "Perhaps you are right and it is just as well. From here, what does it matter?"

Cole had to agree. Still, they had come so far . . . "It was our decision to make. And we never got the chance."

"Was it ours? Yours and mine? I don't think so."

"It was sure supposed to be somebody's," said Cole. "But maybe you're right and it doesn't matter." After all, all was lost. And yet—weren't these people staying busy, saving the world? Maybe the world had to be saved over and over.

Their hosts were consumed in their task of shooting rockets at the Sun, and had little interest in them. Lee and Cole watched, waiting for the cursor to start blinking. There was food but neither of them had an appetite; the chocolate was enough. Cole paced; Lee sat silently staring at the dying Sun. Even RVR was quiet. But when Cole put his fingertips up beside his head, there he was. "Is this it?" he asked. "For us, I mean. Is this the last slice?"

He hoped so. He might have loved Paris, or Bahia, or even the no name plains of no place, but not this, not here: not this barren rock that wasn't even Earth any more, with ARD gone.

"Not yet," said Lee. "According to the Palm PC there's another slice."

"How can that be? And what about Justine, I mean Flo. Didn't you already beep her?"

"Pell. He knows we have returned. But he couldn't be there yet. Only minutes have passed." Lee held up the Palm PC. The cursor was blinking. "Plus, you do understand that we have no choice. Not if we desire to get home. We must follow the logarithm, the path the Old Ones have laid down for us."

"Whatever." Cole didn't want to see what lay ahead. But he didn't want to stay here either, waiting for the Sun to go out. He sat down on the glider and watched as Lee hit RETURN for what they both hoped would be the last slice of time.

And there they were, faithful, diligent, mindless as ever . . . the army of mice.

✳

+2.4 billion

Cole had learned to keep his eyes shut until the spinning stopped.

When he opened them, he saw stars. Then stones. Then his own hands, feet, knees. Lee was sitting beside him; they were on a rocky ledge overloooking a wide valley all in shadow. The same valley? It was hard to tell. *Yea, though I walk through the valley of the shadow of death. . . .* It wasn't the same Sun. It was redder and smaller, back to less than its "normal" size (the size Cole remembered). It hung low over rolling hills as soft and as round as waves. A few towers stuck up from a fold in the hills. Lights flickered across them. There was what appeared to be a road but nothing moved on it.

Cole smelled smoke. He stood up, pulling Lee with him. "Let's go and meet the Old Ones," he said.

"Yes," Lee said, agreeing finally. "This must be the End of Time."

It wasn't, not quite, but who knew? There was a fire, a few feet below. A path led down to the fire. Cole followed it down. His legs felt funny. His feet hardly worked, and no wonder. They were 2.4 billion years in the future, on the steep, narrow, stony path to the End of Time.

Lee had shown him the numbers on his Palm PC.

A man sat by the fire, poking it with a stick. He nodded as Cole and Lee came up. He pointed with the stick where they were to sit; they sat.

"Welcome back, Lee, Cole," he said.

"Back?" Lee asked. "Who are you? Are you the one who summoned us?"

"You were here before, or will be," the man said. "It all overlaps, or will, you see. Or will see."

He passed Cole a bottle. It was whiskey, smoky, but not scotch. Cole took a drink and passed it to Lee, who took a drink and passed it on around the fire to their host. He was a black man, not quite as dark as Cole, with thin, lank white hair, tied back in a ponytail, and a short white beard. He was old: seventy, eighty, maybe a hundred, who could say? He wore dark coveralls and boots dirty with ashes.

"Are you one of the Old Ones?" Cole asked.

The old man chuckled and poked the fire with his stick. There was no wood on the fire but stones, like gray coal. They barely burned. They gave off little heat.

"There are no Old Ones. There is only me. And RVR of course. It was he who brought you here. He did it for me. I wanted to see you, to say farewell, to thank you. This last thing is hard. I did not want to die alone."

"It was you?" Cole reached up beside his ear.

"Not exactly," RVR said. "Others found a way to travel in time, long ago, before I was born, or rather, made. They are the ones who opened the loop. All I did was use the loop they made."

"What about Dear Abbey?"

"That was the paper they had for you," said RVR. "I brought it here, to bring you on."

"So it was you," Lee said.

"There is your Old One," said the old man, patting the fold beside his ear. "Not so old as us, but old."

"But how?" Cole couldn't imagine RVR with a physical form.

"He sent me," said the old man. "From here, you can go everywhere, with the right math, but only once. I brought the paper back. I have it here." He patted the breast pocket of his coveralls

"You killed that man," Lee said.

"Actually, I didn't. They were killing each other without me. All I did was pick up after them. But, you know, from here, everyone is already dead. Including you."

"Where is it?" Cole asked. "Do we get it?"

"Of course." The old man patted his pocket again, but didn't reach into it. "You get everything." He stirred the fire and took another drink, then passed the bottle back around. He coughed—a sound more human than a word or a laugh—and Cole realized they were talking to the last man. There would be, there could be, no more. Some had gone to try and settle the stars but they were dead, according to RVR. They had made it less than halfway across the emptiness that separates every tiny star from every other. The universe was not really a place for them. For us.

Cole shivered. He was cold, colder then he had ever been. It was a cold he knew no fire could warm, but he moved closer to the tiny fire anyway, turned out his hands in a gesture as ancient as . . . as himself. He didn't know what to say, so he nodded toward the Sun. "Setting?"

"It no longer rises or sets," the last man said.

"The Earth is locked in a synchronous orbit," RVR added, in Cole's ear. "Like the Moon used to be, when there was a Moon."

So it wouldn't set; it would just go out. Was it Cole's imagination or was it growing dimmer as they spoke? He looked at the stars. They seemed the same as ever.

"They were trying to stabilize the Sun," said Lee. "It didn't work?"

"Oh, it worked very well," the last man said. "That was a very very long time ago. We survived that crisis just as we survived the others. The first close call was the one they call the Crossing, when a few hundred of us left Africa and went on to settle the entire planet. Then not much later, there was what they called the Sixth Extinction, when in our arrogance we destroyed many species and almost destroyed our home and everything that made life worth living. That was the closest call of all, for without it we would have been just an experiment that failed, like a five-legged frog. But we survived, just barely. Thanks to you."

"To us?" Cole hunkered down beside him. He sat the way Cole had seen his grandad sit, in Tennessee, a few hundred million years ago.

"Yes, you," said the last man. "You are the ones who had to make the change. Who lived through the hope and the horror without going mad. Once the change was made we could live to enjoy the life span of any successful species. There were scares, close calls, new diseases, disappointments . . ."

"One great disapppointment," Cole said. He was thinking of the universe and how empty it was. But that was nothing to how empty it was going to be, from now on. Forever.

"The last crisis was the Sun itself, the helium flash, but you lived through that one," said RVR. "You monitored the Sun and slowed its burning down. The Earth was reinhabited from pole to pole. Repopulated, but the population was kept down to three and a half billion."

The last man pointed up toward the sky with his stick. "Mars was briefly resettled, but only for a few million years. It was the afternoon of our time. Now it is going out, like the fire, and so am I. There must be an end to everything, even to us. Do you see?"

"I think so," Cole said.

"I see," said Lee. "I think I understand." And he did.

beep beep

The last man stood up. "Your cursor is blinking," he said. He walked them back up the path. The Sun felt cold on their faces and the backs of their hands. Behind them a luminous pearl-colored ring was rising, like a knife, to halve the sky. There was no Moon.

In front of them was the glider.

"One other thing," said Cole.

"Oh, yes," said the last man. He reached into the pocket of his coveralls and pulled out a folded piece of paper. "This is what you came for."

"And do we use it?" Lee asked.

"I don't know. From here it doesn't matter," said the last man, handing it to Lee. "It's your decision, your world. Whatever you do, we know it leads here. To this farewell."

"Farewell, then," said Cole, embracing the last man.

"Farewell and thank you, for everything. It is not every man who gets to say farewell to his most distant ancestors. Thanks you for coming here."

It's not like we had a choice, Cole wanted to say; but didn't, of course. He reached up and stroked RVR. *So long, old friend . . .*

"Farewell, and thank you," said Lee. He too embraced the last man; then he took Cole's hand and pulled him down beside him, onto the glider and pressed RETURN, and the last man disappeared as if he had never been.

There were no lights, no army of mice, no sound at all. Only a weird wrong-way lurch, like a car getting tapped from the side. "Whoa . . ."

And they were still there, on the stony hillside. They hadn't gone anywhere. "What happened?" Cole asked, but Lee was already up, out of the glider.

Cole followed him down the path. The knife-like ring had either set, or hadn't yet risen.

There was the fire, but the ashes were cold. And there was the last man. Cole realized he had never asked his name. He had been dead for quite some time. Wordlessly, straining in the thin air, they buried him in the rocks. There was very little dirt there, on the last rocky hill, overlooking the dying sun.

"Okay," Lee said, dusting off his hands. "Let's go."

"Wait," said Cole. "What about Dear Abbey?"

"What about?"

"That was the point of the trip, remember? We wanted to shape the future, but the future shapes itself. Now we know that we have a future. Dear Abbey doesn't seem like such a great idea."

"Maybe future because of Dear Abbey." Lee patted his left patch pocket. "Takes guts, go for it."

"Takes guts to stop it, too." But something was wrong; something else. "How come you're talking that stupid fucking cowboy talk again? Where's RVR?"

Lee shrugged. Cole reached up beside his ear.

Nothing.

"Trail's end," said Lee, pulling Cole down the path toward the glider. "Last round-up."

"Meaning?"

"Let's ride. Head home." The cursor was blinking. Lee took Cole's hand and pulled him down onto the glider beside him.

"We can't leave RVR here alone," Cole said.

"Done deal," said Lee. "Listen up, careful."

And then, for the first time, Cole heard it. Distant, faint at first, like the background radiation that fills the universe: a long, slow, mournful wail, almost a howl, rising and falling, filling the emptiness between the stars. It was all desolation, all longing, all loss. It was RVR mourning for us, for all of us; for you and for me, and all those still to come, and yet to die.

"Farewell, old friend," Cole whispered, reaching up again; but of course there was no one there. On a sudden impulse he reached down just as Lee hit RETURN, and pulled the paper out of Lee's pocket, and stuck it into his own.

"Hey," said Lee.

But Cole didn't answer and Lee didn't pursue it. They both were listening to the saddest sound either of them had ever heard: the lonely howl, the lamentation that drowned out even the army of mice: RVR, inconsolable, mourning for Man.

※

1+

"Whoa!" I pointed at the clock. It said 9:55. "How did you do that?"

Lee was smiling. That inscrutable, enigmatic . . .

"What happened!?" I asked, pulling my hand from Lee's. The pain in my knee was gone. The smell was still there, but fading fast, like a dream. It was familiar, almost identifiable, then gone.

"Beats me, " Lee said. "Figures all gone." He was shaking his Palm PC.

"It's over," I said. But what? What was over?

`I looked at the clock. 9:56. I heard a booming. There was Parker, sticking his big ugly head through the open door. "Have to close up, Dr. Lee," he said.

Behind him was Pell. Parker left; Pell came in and closed the door. "What happened?" he asked in a loud whisper. "Did you get it?"

Lee shrugged. "Guess not," he said.

"What do you mean 'guess not?'"

"Excuse me, Dr. Lee," said Parker, opening the door again. "Gotta close up."

"Outa here," said Lee, standing up. I stood up beside him. I was still dizzy. My knees felt funny.

"No luck? Damn," said Pell. "I thought this was a done deal. All checked out."

"Not such critter," said Lee, gathering up his stuff. "Algorithm not work, always possible. Probably most probable. Or see-tomorrow algorithm too good, pull too far, all way to End of Time. Or work right, which pull through multiverse, then larger slice, eck-cetera."

"The End of Time," Pell said. "I guess if you'd been to the End of Time you would know it, right?"

"Guess so," said Lee, dropping his Palm PC into his cowhide briefcase. I was surprised to see that the pattern I had thought was formulas was actually cattle brands.

"So much for Dear Abbey," said Pell. "And too bad, too. I thought it was a neat idea, even though I never really thought it would work. So what was it like? Did you just sit there and swing?"

"It wasn't like anything," I said. *A neat idea?*

"Then why are you guys both looking so sad, like you just lost your best friend?"

"You don't want to know," I said. "Where's Flo?"

"Don't ask." Pell looked smug. I wanted to slug him, but no, I didn't. Instead I helped him and Lee shove the glider into the corner behind the piano, one side at a time. It was heavy and of course it had no wheels.

"Thanks!" said Lee as Parker locked the door behind us. In the parking lot, I borrowed Lee's phone. I winced when I heard my voice on my machine. I had never before realized how cold my own voice sounded.

"You have reached . . . leave a message if you insist."

I dialed in the access code.

"You have TWO messages."

Two? The first was from Helen. "Surprise. You will find the dog still there. At the last minute the new home crapped out. Sorry but I have a plane to catch and you two deserve each other." No good-bye, no farewell, no adieu.

The second was from Helen as well. "Oh, and fuck you."

I had to smile. Helen would be disappointed to know that I was, actually, glad to have somebody waiting for me at home. Lee's phone was a throwaway and I had apparently used the last call, because when I handed it back to him, he tossed it into the trash.

There was a piece of paper in my pocket. I unfolded it. Somebody's math homework, spattered with . . . was that blood? Had to be. I folded it back up.

I felt sad but I didn't know why. Dear Abbey? Helen? It was something less tangible but more personal than either.

All I knew was, I felt like being alone.

Pell was astride his BMW, warming it up. Lee was waiting in his car but I declined a ride. A Prius glides off as silently as a ghost. My feet in the leaves were pleasantly loud, all the way home.

I felt apprehensive as I opened the door; Helen is known for her unpleasant surprises. But what greeted me was neither a surprise nor unpleasant

"Rover! Hello boy! Glad to see me? Yes, you are!"

I went into the bathroom and peed, thinking, for some reason, of seals. Then I unfolded the blood-spattered paper and burned it, carefully, holding first one corner and then another, and flushed the ashes down the toilet. Good security habits die hard.

AUTHOR'S AFTERWORD

"I Saw the Light" is a dog story, a genre second only to science fiction in appeal. Ellen Datlow, a cat person, bought it anyway for *SciFiction*. The title is from a gospel song written by Hank Williams. The idea of a "sentinel" on the moon is swiped from Arthur C. Clarke, of course. It's the second story I have swiped from him. I'm not ashamed. We have all been looting his mansion for years.

I managed to slip "Death's Door" into Al Sarrantonio's fantasy anthology, *Flights*, even though it's clearly SF (note the mention of *Discover* magazine). I was naïve enough to think "death takes a holiday" was a new idea. I still think it's a cool one. Make that chilling.

"Openclose" is a thinly-disguised political diatribe. It is being adapted as a radio play for the Knee-Jerk Theater ("We don't tell you what to think. We just tell your knee what to do"). Gordon Van Gelder, a knee-jerk liberal, bought it for *The Magazine of Fantasy & Science Fiction*.

"Scout's Honor" (*SciFiction*) is about one of my favorite

subjects, and indeed a favorite of many SF writers, a close encounter between ourselves and a cousin hominid species. It was, in part, inspired by (not based on) Paul Park's brilliant autistic sister, Jesse.

"The Old Rugged Cross" is another gospel title. The fit on this one is, I hope, tight enough to be uncomfortable. Patrick Nielsen Hayden bought it for one of his *Starlight* anthologies.

"Come Dance with Me" started with an email from a rock star, who was kind enough to want a story from me for her *Stars* collection. There may be those who say no to Janis Ian, but I am not one of them. Nor do I wish to be.

Ellen Datlow published "Super 8" (*SciFiction*), my first attempt to draw on the experience of the hippie communes, which are now aged enough (in borrowed oak) to be tapped, at least to sample. I swiped the hive-mind narrator from Karen Joy Fowler. Or was it Jane Austen?

"Almost Home," which was an *F&SF* cover story, was written for my first cousin, and first best friend, Elizabeth Johnson Lightfoot, known as Toot, as she lay dying. We all fight and lose the same battle, but some of us with more courage, dignity, and style than others.

"Greetings" (Datlow again, *SciFiction*) is about getting old. There are no stories about getting young. I swiped the Oregon coast from Ursula Le Guin.

Every once in a while, I write a traditional SF tale, just to show that I can. "Dear Abbey" is about a trip to the End of Time, complete with TimeTravel Paradox. It was published in England by PS, and short-listed for the British Science Award. I lost to Neil Gaiman. The film version will be shortlisted for the Spirit Award in 2011. I will lose to Sofia Coppola.

This is my third collection of short stories, and my first for Tachyon. I hope you will find something new in it, gentle reader, and something familiar as well.

Thanks.